PRIDE AND PASSION

CHANTAL—She was the daughter of the most powerful family in Louisiana and lived like a princess on a vast plantation. Yet she was slave to her father's plans for her future, and shadowed by a shameful secret from a past that would not die.

RAFE—He came to New Orleans from Ireland with nothing but the memory of a family fortune that had been lost. His fierce determination was to make stiff-necked society bow to his success and the most ravishing woman in its tightly closed ranks yield to his burning love.

LAZARE—He had never met a man he could not best on the field of honor or a woman he could not possess with the power of his birth and wealth. And he would use all his savage strength and ruthless cunning to annihilate the upstart who tried to win Chantal—*his* promised bride and ultimate prize.

One coveted woman and two strong men—locked together in a struggle that shocked even

NEW ORLEANS

COMING IN MAY

"An important and revolutionary book."
—Barbara Ehrenreich, *Mirabella*
"Neither women nor marriage will ever be the same."—Gloria Steinem

THE EROTIC SILENCE OF THE AMERICAN WIFE

Dalma Heyn

This riveting book shatters the silence about married women and extramarital sex today. Based on hundreds of intimate, in-depth interviews with married women who have had affairs, this insightful book may startle you. The stories these women tell challenge every myth about women's sexuality. "Another silence broken—it's about time women gave voice to all their dimensions, including the erotic, without shrinking in guilt."

—Gail Sheehy

NEW
ORLEANS

by

Sara Orwig

AN ONYX BOOK

ONYX
Published by the Penguin Group
Penguin Books USA Inc., 375 Hudson Street,
New York, New York 10014, U.S.A.
Penguin Books Ltd, 27 Wrights Lane,
London W8 5TZ, England
Penguin Books Australia Ltd, Ringwood,
Victoria, Australia
Penguin Books Canada Ltd, 10 Alcorn Avenue,
Toronto, Ontario, Canada M4V 3B2
Penguin Books (N.Z.) Ltd, 182-190 Wairau Road,
Auckland 10, New Zealand

Penguin Books Ltd, Registered Offices:
Harmondsworth, Middlesex, England

First published by Onyx,
an imprint of New American Library,
a division of Penguin Books USA Inc.

First Printing, April, 1993
10 9 8 7 6 5 4 3 2 1

With many thanks to: Leon Hooker, Stan Ritchey, Curatorial Division, The Historic New Orleans Collection; Jude Solemon, Louisiana Historical Library; Chester Cromwell II, the Meredith Collection; Michaela Hamilton; and my editor, Jennifer Enderlin.

Chapter 1

December 14, 1857

"I don't want to be tied!"

"Darcy, you don't want to bounce around the cabin like a ball," Rafferty Michael O'Brien said, holding his youngest brother's wiggling body as he lashed him to the bulkhead. Rafe heard the creaking of wood as the ship rose on another wave. Standing beside the bunk, Rafe looped a line around his waist and tied it, looking down at his mother huddled beneath blankets.

"Listen to the wind!" Caleb said, and Rafe wished he *couldn't* hear the keening whine that accompanied the roar of water smashing against the ship. Caleb was tied to the bulkhead, his brown curls knotted by the all-pervading dampness belowdecks.

"I want to be home!" Fortune O'Brien snapped, his fifteen-year-old voice cracking.

"Rafferty, give me your hand," Annora O'Brien said, her blue eyes filled with determination.

At the touch of her cold fingers Rafe felt panic. Framed by black hair, her pale face was beaded in sweat, yet she was ice to the touch. He wanted to shout in frustration. This was the land that was supposed to be warm and sunny and would heal her. The Great American Desert. Hope for a new life, a warm climate where she would grow strong again. Instead they were still miles from shore, caught in a raging gale, sailing on a dank ship that had crossed the ocean at a terrapin's pace.

She pulled off the emerald ring that had been in the O'Brien family for generations. "Take this." She slipped it on his smallest finger. "Use it, because it's all you have to take care of the boys except for a few sovereigns.''

"You keep it," he insisted, pressing it into her hand, a knot coming in his throat, because he knew how dear she held the ring. It was a tie to his father and their home.

The boat listed, followed by a sweeping drop, and he braced for the roll to starboard, the smash of the curling wave. Instead the ship crashed against something solid, a jarring crunch that threw Rafe against his bonds. He flung himself back to hold Annora.

Wood splintered and the ship shuddered, and in spite of the howl of the storm, Rafe heard the snap of timber.

"We've struck something! Unloosen the lines! We may be going down!" he cried.

Bells clanged. Someone pounded on the hatch and was gone.

"Take the sovereigns!" Rafe snapped, jerking his head at seventeen-year-old Caleb, who was already reaching for the small metal box that held all their money.

"What'll I do with it?"

"Put the sovereigns in your boots and in Fortune's. Caleb, you hold on to Darcy. Don't let go of him on your life!" Rafe ordered, trying to think of everything they should do. How could he protect Mother? He untied Darcy, who gazed at him with wide blue eyes that mirrored his own. As if a miniature of himself, Darcy's thick black hair was a tangle, his face pale with fear. "You hold on to Caleb; do what he tells you!" Rafe yanked a slicker from a hook and pulled it on his brother. Darcy was so small, so young; pray God, Caleb and Fortune could take care of him.

He handed Darcy to Caleb and reached for another slicker, tugging free the knots that held his mother bound to the bunk. The deck tilted, the ship listing at a sharp angle, rolling with the pounding waves.

"What's happening, Rafferty?"

"I think we've struck something! We have to get out!"

"You go! Take the boys! I can't go with you!" She caught his hand and slipped the ring on his finger. "You take care of your brothers. Leave me here, Rafferty. I'll join your father."

He felt a knot of fear that kept him from answering. He wanted to beat his fists against the bulkhead in fear for her safety. He wasn't going to lose her. They had come this far. Unfastening the lines holding her to the bunk, he pushed away the covers. "Mother, either you come with us or we all stay."

"Please, save the boys! All of you know how to swim. I don't," she said, her eyes filling with tears.

Leaning forward to balance against the slow tilt of the deck, he helped her into the slicker and scooped her up. She was a featherweight in his arms. Eighty pounds at most. How could she last if they had to go into the water? Blinking back tears, he clamped his jaw shut.

Caleb held Darcy's right hand, and Fortune gripped Darcy's left. Caleb's green eyes were solemn.

"When we reach shore, we go to New Orleans." *How could anyone reach shore in this storm?* "Stay there until we're together again. Understand?" Rafe asked Caleb, who nodded. He looked at each brother and into Darcy's frightened gaze.

"Boys, give me a kiss," Annora said, and Rafe held her while she kissed each one and touched them, running her hands over Caleb's cheek, across Fortune's head, hugging Darcy to her while tears spilled down her cheeks. Rafe hurt as if a knife were twisting in his chest.

He wanted to curse and he wanted to hold her close, to protect her from what lay ahead. The ship groaned and the deck slanted, causing Rafe to struggle to maintain his balance. "Get going!" he snapped.

Caleb yanked open the door and water gushed into the cabin, sweeping him back against the bulkhead. Regaining his balance, he moved forward. With black icy water swirling around his legs, Rafe held his mother against him, feeling her lock her arms around his neck as he climbed the ladder. The wind buffeted him, and the cold rain blinded him.

A wave smashed against the ship and knocked him back. He caught a line and inched toward the rail. Men shouted; the ship listed to starboard. The masts were broken, the spars were jagged stubs, and the sails trailed over decks and into the water. The ship's steam engine was silent.

Rafe caught a sailor's arm. "A boat?" he shouted, desperate to keep his mother from the sea.

"Two are in the water loaded with men! Ship's going down! Get off, or you'll go with her!"

The man was gone, and his brothers had vanished. Two men went over the side. The deck slanted, and Rafe slipped. With a grab for the rail he felt cold metal slide beneath his fingers, and then he was falling.

Icy water closed over him. He went down, and then burst to the surface, gasping for breath. Feeling panic for his mother, he caught a floating chunk of wood and wrapped his arm around it.

"Rafe, the boys . . ." she said. He felt the sag of her weight.

"Mother! *Mother!*" Wind caught his words as he struggled to keep their heads above the turbulent sea. Feeling terror, he placed his hand on her throat. There was no pulse. "Mother!" Knowing she was gone, he clung to her while hot tears were washed away by seawater and rain. "Dear God . . ."

He was caught on a giant wave, then dropped into the trough as water smashed over him. He swallowed water, gagging, fighting to hold Annora, refusing to give her up to the sea. Another swell caught them, and he felt her slip from his arms. Clutching at her, he cried out, water swamping him. As she slid out of his grasp, his hands groped but found nothing. He went down, flailing, gagging.

"Mother!" Bursting to the surface, he yelled. A wave hit him. "Mo—" Salt water filled his mouth and he choked. Where was she? Water swallowed him, taking him down into a dark, wet world. *Can't find her,* he thought. *Give up. Can't survive. Have to breathe.*

"The boys . . ." His mother's last words came. His brothers. *Get to the surface,* an instinct commanded him. But he felt as if he had to take a breath. The same instinct told him he would drown. *Caleb, Darcy, can't let go. . . .*

Rafe burst up through the surface and coughed. Something struck his shoulder. A piece of the hull bumped him. Struggling, Rafe pulled himself up onto the piece of hull and held fast as it was lifted by another wave. His head spun as he locked his fingers over the jagged edges of timber.

"Mother . . ." he gave a faint cry.

The bitter taste of salt was in his mouth. *Mother is dead. The boys . . . where are they? Have to find them.*

"Caleb!" How could anyone hear him over the storm? How could anyone see him for all the water? The world was a blur of sea and rain.

How many times was the bit of wood lifted and dropped over the next hours, as the water poured over him? When did the storm abate?

Now stillness pervaded, and a soft pink suffused the surface as dawn came. A bit of wood floated nearby. There was no sign of the shipwreck, no bodies, no survivors, nothing except him and his raft.

He was thirsty; his head throbbed, and his shoulder ached. Too much effort to do anything. Mother was lost. *The boys . . .* They had to be all right. He had made it. Caleb and Fortune would take care of Darcy.

The calm surface belied the violence of the night. How could he have drifted so far from the wreck? So far from any survivors? Too tired to move, he fell back, closing his eyes.

Time lost meaning; when night came, he was chilled. Was he drifting out to sea? The emerald ring was a dark blur on his finger. He unfastened his black trousers, finding lose threads in a seam and tying the ring where it would lie against the inside of his thigh. Exhausted, he lay back and closed his eyes.

Want water. . . . Don't drink sea water. Can't last

without water. He sat up and gazed around, noticing a dot on the horizon. He stared at it wondering if it was his imagination, but it grew steadily. "Help!" His voice was a croak, and the ship was still too far for anyone to notice him. He could only wait, but it came steadily on until he waved his arms wildly, using the last bit of his strength. Voices rose over the steady putter of an engine as the ship loomed within yards of him, men pointing toward him.

"Please . . . help!" A whisper. He waved his arms. "Help . . ." Dizziness struck, and he crumpled on the raft. As the world spun, unconsciousness came.

The next time Rafferty stirred, he felt cold water trickle past his lips. "Where am I?" A stench made him gag.

"Here's water," came a deep voice, and a chain rattled. A cup was raised to his lips. As he drank, his eyes adjusted to the darkness. Surrounded by men, he was in the hold of a ship that was filled with a seething mass of humanity, men talking and moaning in low voices. Chained men. Rafe's head throbbed and he felt faint. Jammed against the ladder, he was beneath an open hatch, where a breath of air stirred.

Bodies crammed every available inch. Row after row of men on their sides, fitted together like spoons.

"Where are we headed?" His head spun, and he ached all over.

"The States. Louisiana. They tossed you here because they expect you to die," the man said in a melodic, slightly British accent. "The man who had your space died two nights ago. You want another drink?"

How the hell did the man know English? Rafe lifted a shaky hand to the cup held out to him.

"Thank you," he said. "I'm Rafferty O'Brien. You speak English."

"I'm Tobiah Barr. Haitian, but my father is British. I'm to be sold with the others. My white father in Haiti wanted to be rid of me." He jerked his head toward the hatch. "Captain Boyden doesn't expect you to live."

Rafe looked around again. Bodies glistened with sweat. The smell made his stomach churn, sour odors of fear and sweat. Tobiah Barr from Haiti. Exhausted, Rafe sank down on the hard planks. "No one else helped me," Rafe said, looking at Tobiah, unable to see his expression in the darkness.

Rafe fell asleep, to wake with a hand beneath his head and the cup of water again at his lips. He drank, feeling better than he had since the shipwreck. He sank down and closed his eyes. When he opened them again, he was alone. Slim shafts of sunlight streamed through portholes. He stood up and walked around, looking at the vacant hold and empty chains.

Stumbling, he moved on weak legs to the ladder. A breeze swept over him and he inhaled, stepping on deck and looking around. Fresh air and freedom. He felt a loathing for the system that enslaved men; Tobiah Barr's water had probably saved his life. While sailors worked on the ship, the Africans walked unrestrained. Rafe crossed the deck to a sailor. "Where's the captain?"

The man turned to look at him. "We've taken bets whether you'd make it or not."

Rafe himself wouldn't bet that he would, if he had to stand in the blazing sun much longer. "The captain?"

"Over there, mate, but you won't get much from him. You won't bring a price when we land. These devils will."

Rafe clutched the rail. "Can I get food?"

The sailor shrugged. "If you're some nabob who was lost at sea, or a ship's captain, or a man of wealth, Cap'n Boyden will come around. Eh?" He squinted at Rafe. "If your pockets aren't lined with gold—too bad, mate."

"Do the Africans get food?"

"Course they do. They're worth more than good horses."

Rafe couldn't continue the conversation. "When will we land?" he said, changing the subject.

"Tomorrow we put into Paques' plantation and sell

our smuggled cargo. It's illegal trade, but still big business. Then we go upriver to New Orleans.''

Rafe's knees buckled, and he staggered to the shade of a sail and sat down on a cask.

"Morning, Mr. O'Brien.''

He looked up at a giant of a man whose tawny skin covered hard muscle. "Tobiah?''

"Yes, sir.'' The man nodded.

Rafe felt his stomach knot. He needed food. "Captain,'' he said, pointing and standing up, catching Tobiah's arm. Tobiah helped him across the deck, but just before Rafe reached the captain's quarters he pushed Tobiah's arm away. "I'm grateful to you.''

He knocked, and when the captain called out, Rafe entered. The cabin was sparse, littered with papers and tobacco stains.

"Sir, may I talk to you?''

"It'll have to be brief,'' he answered. His red beard was thick; one long braid hung down his back. His bright blue shirt and white pants were dotted with yellow stains. The smell of the cigar in the corner of his mouth made Rafe's stomach heave.

"Thank you for coming to my rescue. I'm Rafferty O'Brien.'' It was an effort to stand and talk. "I need food. I don't have money.''

"Irish,'' the captain said with contempt. "You can work. Scrub the deck. You work and you can eat.''

Feeling dismayed by the man's callousness, Rafe stared at him. "I haven't eaten since the ship went down. I'll work, but I need to eat. I can't walk ten feet without feeling faint.''

The captain picked up an apple from a small crate. He pulled out a knife to peel it. Rafe's mouth watered, and he wanted to snatch the fruit from the man's thick fingers.

"You work, you'll eat. Find Rienzi. He'll put you to work. You can go.''

Anger flared. Rafe opened his mouth to protest, looked at the narrowed black eyes staring at him, and closed his mouth. How could he get out of the cabin without falling down? He closed the door behind him, took two steps, and felt the deck spin up to meet him as he slammed against it.

When he came to, he was back in the hold. Tobiah shook him. "Eat, while no one is watching," he whispered.

Tobiah held out a biscuit. Grabbing it, Rafe bit into it.

"Careful. I'll go above again before I'm missed. I stole this from the mess."

Too hungry to talk, Rafe nodded, chewing the tough biscuit. It was the grandest food he had ever tasted. In front of him was a battered tin cup half-filled with water, a bit of dried beef, and an apple. A banquet. Tobiah went up the hatch and left Rafe alone to eat.

Shouts came from above. A sailor thrust his head through the hatch. Rafe tried to shift his body in order to hide the cups of food and water, but he was too late.

"He's got food!" the man yelled.

Defenseless, Rafe gobbled his meager rations. The noise on board was raucous, and then a bell clanged.

A sailor thrust his head through the open hatch. "Cap'n says to get your arse up here. The slave gets a beating for slipping you food."

"Dammit!" Rafe was horrified. Tobiah had saved his life with the food and water. When Rafe stepped on deck, men were lashing Tobiah's wrists to a grating in the deck. The captain stood watching, his features impassive. Rafe unfastened his pants, reached inside, and yanked free the ring.

He buttoned the front flap of his trousers and moved forward, pushing through the crowd. Sailors lined up to watch the flogging. A mate stood with a whip, raising it high. It came down with a crack and Tobiah bucked beneath the blow.

"Captain!" Rafe yelled, lengthening his stride as he heard the second blow fall.

"You're fortunate I don't have you strung up beside him!" the captain snapped.

"Stop the beating! Let me buy him right now!"

Captain Boyden's eyes narrowed. "I don't trade work for a slave. Cash only."

"Stop the damned flogging! I'll give you this for him." Rafe held out the ring. The emerald caught the sunlight in its depths. Rafe stared at the glittering stone, its bright color conjuring up the green meadows of home and the rugged cliffs above the shore. Five generations of O'Briens had passed down this ring. Now the O'Brien emerald would go to a greedy slave-trader. But if Tobiah had not fed him and given him water, the ring would have gone to the bottom of the sea along with his body.

Captain Boyden took the ring from Rafe and held it up. A blow fell. He turned toward Tobiah and watched another lash cut across his back. "Release him!" he ordered. He pocketed the ring. "You have your man." He looked at the men on deck. "Back to work," he told his first mate, who called out the order.

"Sir, I want to free Tobiah," Rafe said.

Boyden shook his head. "Not on my ship. You bought him."

"Then I want a bill of sale. I can't take a slave into Louisiana without one."

"Very well. Come to my cabin. Crawford, tell the man that Mr. O'Brien is his new master."

"Aye, Captain."

Rafe followed, then watched while the captain wrote out the necessary paper and handed it to him. "Keep him out of trouble. You bought a troublemaker."

"I want him with me, not below with the others."

"You're making a mistake if you don't chain him at night."

"Where can he go?"

The captain shrugged. "He fought like a crazed animal before we brought him on board. Man is strong as an ox. If he causes trouble, he goes into chains."

"Fair enough."

"And I expect you to work unless you have something else to buy your passage." Boyden added in a sly tone, "Where was the ring hidden?"

Rafe gave him a level stare. "I'll work for my passage." He folded the paper and left the cabin.

Three hours later, a shadow fell as he scrubbed the deck. Tobiah squatted in front of him. "Thank you, Mr. O'Brien."

"I saved you a beating. You saved my life. When we get to a town, we'll have papers drawn to set you free. Boyden won't do it. I asked him."

Something flickered in the depths of Tobiah's dark eyes. "We may not reach town. They forget I understand English. They plan to murder you before we reach land tomorrow. With you out of the way, they can sell me again." He glanced up and moved away. In seconds a sailor passed Rafe.

"You bought yourself a passel of trouble, mate. Watch he doesn't jump you," the sailor said.

"Thanks. I'll remember," Rafe answered.

When the slaves had been put in the hold for the night, Rafe motioned Tobiah to his side. "You're to stay with me. We'll sleep on deck."

They stretched out to starboard on coils of hemp. Rafe turned on his side, his voice a whisper. "We're in sight of Louisiana. They say at dawn we'll land at a plantation where they'll sell the cargo. Can you swim?"

"Yes, sir."

"In the middle of the night, we go over the side. It'll be a long swim, but the water is calm."

Tobiah nodded. Had he already planned to escape? Was he the troublemaker they had described?

Rafe stared at the stars. Where were his brothers? He was convinced they had survived. Had they been picked up by a ship headed to the United States? Or were they returning to Ireland, or sailing the world? He closed his eyes. He had eaten two regular meals with the crew, and his strength was returning.

The moon had risen high overhead. It was bright on the water, making it more dangerous to try to swim away. Nonetheless they climbed over the rail and slid into the sea. As water closed over his head, panic seized Rafe. Remembering his mother slipping from his grasp, he felt a cold fear that made him sink.

He struck out, but he checked himself and avoided making a noisy splash. Swimming without a sound, Tobiah was yards ahead. Rafe began steady strokes, gliding through the water behind him.

In the daylight as they neared the mouth of the Mississippi, they were picked up by a steam packet loaded with spices from the West Indies. The whistle shrieked as the packet rounded a bend of the muddy Mississippi. Rafe knotted a line, and his breath caught as he looked past tall trees draped with lacy tendrils of Spanish moss. Beyond twin live oaks that stood like sentinels was a house two stories tall, with white Doric columns along the galleries. A gazebo with trailing vines and another small house stood in front of the big one.

"Lord, look up there!"

"They don't have houses that grand in Ireland?"

"I didn't expect to see anything like that here," Rafe answered, staring at the house. Suddenly he felt a strange, fierce determination. "I'll have a house like that someday."

"We're as far removed from that house, Mr. O'Brien, as a mud turtle is from the sun."

Rafe shook his head. "No," he said. "I'll have a fine house and I'll have a family."

Tobiah laughed. "Sir, you gave the last valuable you owned to buy me. I'm all you have, and you've said you're going to set me free. You're penniless."

The river curved, and the tall moss-draped cypresses along the bank obscured the view, but Rafe couldn't stop looking until the house was gone from sight.

"Ever been here, Tobiah?" Rafe asked, as he returned to knotting the line.

"No, sir. I was educated in England."

"Your father sent you to England, and then gave you to a slaver?"

As Tobiah's head lifted, a muscle worked in his jaw. "My mother fell out of his favor." He stared at Rafe. "I hear men talk who are from Louisiana. You're Irish. Your life may not be easy here either, Mr. O'Brien."

"Rafe. It might as well be Rafe."

"I'll call you Mr. O'Brien. I know my place. I was taught that as soon as I could walk."

"Help me lift this canvas," Rafe said. They folded the large canvas and stowed it. An hour later they rounded a wide bend and Rafe moved to the rail. New Orleans. Buildings and houses were spread out along the crescent in the river. Wharves held ocean-going ships. Ahead he could see luggers being unloaded of their silvery catches; other boats carried mounds of green bananas. Steam packets bobbed beside the long wharves, and down the quay were keelboats.

The wharf teamed with stevedores and peddlers. There were grain wharves, molasses sheds, and cotton sheds. Stacks of sugar hogsheads and bales of cotton were piled high. Rafe felt a knot of excitement as he looked at the city. Three tall spires of a church thrust into the sky. Mule-drawn drays moved through the throng on the dock.

He inhaled deeply. "Smell. It's like springtime and water and delicious food, all at the same time."

"I smell fish and molasses."

"That too," Rafe said, close enough now to see a beautiful woman emerge from a carriage and cross to a vendor, while a servant held a dainty blue parasol over her head.

"New Orleans," he said, feeling an eagerness grip him. "My brothers may be waiting."

"You have brothers in New Orleans?"

"I have three brothers, and they sailed with me. When the ship went down, I lost my mother. My brothers and I agreed that we would meet in New Orleans."

"You can't believe they survived! You were only half-alive."

"They survived," Rafe said, and Tobiah closed his mouth.

Work was not difficult to find, and the two of them spent a few days unloading spices and barrels of rum, loading skins and kegs of pork. Quitting one afternoon before Tobiah, Rafe stepped off the plank onto the wharf, coins jingling in his pocket. He spent the next hours until sundown roaming the wharf to ask about his brothers. He met Tobiah at the ship as he came ashore.

"Any luck in finding them?"

Refusing to think they might not have survived, Rafe shook his head. "Not yet. Let's find lodging, Tobiah."

In steaming midday sunshine they crossed the levee and passed the open stalls of a market, where bins of green melons and bunches of yellow bananas made Rafe's mouth water. Red crawfish were piled high on chunks of ice.

"*Calas! Nous avons du bon calas! Ells sont délicieuses!*" called a black woman vendor selling sweet cakes. Her head was wrapped in a Madras tignon; a white apron covered her linsey-woolsey dress. Odors of rum drifted from grog shops. Following a sign that read DUMAINE, Rafe and Tobiah headed farther into town. On houses of brick or pale plaster, ornate wrought-iron balconies overhung walks; through shadowed passages doors opened into sunny courtyards. Tempting smells of black coffee assailed him, while shiny carriages passed and ladies strolled with rustling silk skirts.

"It's not Ireland," Rafe said, captivated by the strange new sights and sounds of houses that reminded him of Paris. "But it's not France either."

"You've lived in France?"

"I was sent to England to school, and I traveled in France," he answered perfunctorily.

"Your family must have been well-fixed." Hearing the solemn tone of Tobiah's voice, Rafe glanced at his companion, who was six inches over six feet tall—two inches taller than he.

"My father farmed, but he also gambled away all we had. He was killed one night when his carriage careened off a cliff into the sea. My mother's health failed, and we were bringing her to the warmth of this country."

Rafe's attention shifted to two ladies who passed in an open carriage. In dresses of pink silk and a soft blue organza, they were breathtaking. His pulse raced with eagerness for this city that held exotic houses, beautiful women, and tempting sights and smells. He laughed, and Tobiah glanced at him.

"What makes you laugh?"

"This New Orleans. I like it!"

"Look around you. Men are armed. The ladies cost a fortune to dress. The houses are elegant, and you have nothing."

"We'll see. First I set you free—and we'll have it done by an official, so you'll have the proper papers. Second, I find lodgings and a job."

"None of which will be easy."

Three weeks later, on the eighteenth of January, Rafe recalled the conversation with Tobiah as he jabbed a shovel into a wagonload of white shells and tossed them down to repair the road along Bayou St. John, from Lake Pontchartrain to the Vieux Carré, the French quarter in New Orleans. Shells clattered as he worked. On the opposite side of the road was a stone fence, the boundary of a plantation. Beyond a meadow dotted with sweet gum was a field of sugarcane.

Tobiah had been right. Things weren't easy. New Orleans had passed a law that slaves could not be set free, so Tobiah still belonged to him. Since Tobiah was not allowed to share a place with Rafe, they each had separate homes. Rafe had seen an advertisement posted outside city hall for laborers to work on roads, so he had applied. Work was hard, and his muscles ached, but with every scoop of the shovel his determination to succeed grew.

As Rafe shoveled, he noticed riders beyond the stone fence. A party of ten rode into view, five women in riding apparel, five men in suits and tall hats. A wagon followed, and when it stopped beneath an oak, servants climbed down and spread a picnic.

Glancing occasionally at the party, Rafe felt mild envy, thinking it would be marvelous to enjoy the morning in such a manner.

As the sun climbed, he became hot and stripped off his shirt, pausing to wipe his brow. He walked to the wagon and picked up the bottle of water to take a long drink. As he lowered the bottle and capped it, he saw a man help one of the women to mount her horse. The man then mounted his bay, holding the prancing horse in check. When the two horses bounded forward, Rafe watched them race. The woman could ride, and she had a sleek, long-legged sorrel beneath her. Giving her horse rein, she drew up to only a length behind the man.

As they galloped across the meadow they parted at a grove of sweet gums, the man riding to the southeast, the woman galloping around the trees toward the southwest. Both raced for the low stone wall that marked the southern boundary of the land.

Frank Moriarty, a nearby worker, paused. "Look at them! I've never seen a woman ride like that!"

Rafe narrowed his eyes.

"Damn!"

Both riders hurtled on at breakneck speed, the woman heading toward the southwestern part of the stone wall, and danger. On the other side was land owned by the parish, and there road builders had dug away earth that had been a few feet below the top of the wall. Now it was far below, and this low-lying area was filled with water. Rafe had thought the riders would stop or turn long before they reached the wall, but now he saw they both intended to jump it. The man's mount galloped toward solid ground beyond the stone wall. He could vault the boundary without harm, but the woman could not.

"God in heaven, she's going over where we removed the land! Hey!" he yelled.

Calling and waving his arms, Rafe threw down his shovel and ran. She didn't appear to hear him. He ran with all his strength, his long legs stretched out. She didn't turn around, so intent was she on the wall. There was only one way to stop her.

Rafe sprinted toward them to head them off, running into the horse's path. His heart pounded with the effort. Then he was in front of them, and they were on him.

Her eyes flew wide and she yanked the reins, the horse missing stride as it turned. The sorrel loomed over him, its dark eyes rolling, nostrils flaring.

The horse raked against him. Rafe spun away, flung to the earth and knocked unconscious.

Chapter 2

"Please, please be all right!"

Rafe inhaled the sweetest scent . . . like a field of clover after rain. Something soft moved over him. He opened his eyes to look through blue dotted tulle. A lock of golden hair curled on his cheek, and an angel pressed her cheek against his chest. He wrapped his arm around her waist.

"The horse killed me," he said.

Her head rose, the blue veil lifted, and wide, velvety-brown eyes gazed at him. "*Dieu merci!* You're alive!"

"Oh, no. I know the horse killed me. I'm in heaven, and you're an angel."

"I'm no angel." She smiled, a smile that curved rosy lips and brought a twinkle to worried eyes. "Thank heavens you're all right!"

"If you're not an angel, who are you?"

"Chantal Therrie," she said, looking relieved and satisfied.

He tightened his arm, inhaling her sweet scent, feeling her soft skin, looking into eyes that made his pulse race. She gazed back, her smile vanishing, brows arching, studying him in a curious, solemn manner. The moment crystallized and became unique as time was suspended.

"Dammit! Chantal!" Hoofbeats sounded; the spell was broken. And then Chantal was gone, yanked to her feet by a tall, brown-haired man who caught her around the waist and set her on her feet. The man leaned over him. A fist slammed into Rafe's jaw.

As his head reeled, Rafe lurched to his feet.

"I should put a ball through your filthy heart!"

Standing and doubling his fists, Rafe found himself gazing into the muzzle of a pistol. He wanted to smash his fist into the arrogant jaw of the man brandishing it, but he stopped short as he stared at the weapon. The bastard should come out from behind his pistol. The man's face was florid; his heavy features and thick lips twisted into a scowl.

"No!" Chantal Therrie stepped between them.

"Get out of the way, Chantal!" the man snapped.

Rafe's temper boiled over, and he stepped out from behind her. She glanced over her shoulder, and with a swirl of her blue faille riding skirt stepped in front of him again.

"Chantal! Step aside, dammit!"

"You mustn't hurt him! He saved my life!"

"He had his filthy hands on you! He's trash! I should have him horsewhipped, and then put a ball through his heart."

Rafe stepped to one side and raised his fists.

"Lazare, he saved my life!" She moved in front of Rafe. "Can't you hear what I'm saying? Look!" She swung her hand toward the fence.

"The coward keeps hiding behind you!"

"Dammit! Pardon me, ma'am," Rafe said, stepping away.

She moved in front of him again. "Lazare, look!" She tugged on the man's arm. "Look at the other side of the wall! For a few yards they've dug away the earth! If I had let Caesar jump, I could have been killed, Caesar could have been killed!" Her voice was soft and lilting, and Rafe wanted to go on listening to her. He stepped aside.

"When the devil did that happen?" the man said, peering beyond the rock wall. He turned back to face Rafe, and Rafe looked into pale gray eyes that held rage. Rafe felt a dislike boil in him that he had never before felt for a man. It was as hot and intense as the sun on his shoulders. How grand it would be to smash that arrogant jaw! As they stared at each other, Rafe saw that the hatred was mutual.

"Get back to work!" the man ordered, and Rafe felt his control slipping away from him.

"Lazare!" She sounded impatient. Her cheeks were flushed, and she looked at Rafe. "Thank you, sir, for your warning."

"Come along, Chantal. I won't have you talking to the likes of him." Lazare pulled out two coins and tossed them at Rafe. "Here's for your trouble. Now go."

Rafe let the coins fall at his feet, his gaze never leaving Lazare. He turned and walked away, returning to pick up his shovel.

"Are you all right?" Moriarty asked, pausing as he shoveled.

"I'm okay," Rafe answered, feeling his shoulder throb where the horse had struck him. He gazed back at them. Chantal Therrie and Lazare rode side-by-side back to the party. Lazare reached over to touch her hair, and Rafe felt something twist inside him. He drew a deep breath as he watched them.

The servants loaded the wagon and soon the meadow was empty. While Rafe shoveled, his thoughts turned toward Chantal Therrie. *She's certainly a cool one,* he decided, turning the sorrel the moment she saw him, bending over him after he had been knocked flat. She was lively as well, defending him to her angry companion. And she was beautiful. He remembered the full, soft breasts that had pressed against him, and he sighed.

That night, as they came out of The Green Tree Tavern on Gallatin, he tried to tell Tobiah about her. "She is the most beautiful woman I've ever seen. And she wasn't wearing a wedding ring; I looked at her hand."

"It wouldn't matter, even if she never meets another man. You can't socialize with a woman like the one you're describing. My world is more narrow than yours, Mr. O'Brien, but you're bound by limits too."

"Only the financial kind."

"Bah! I've seen the society in Haiti. It is even more

inbred here in New Orleans. I hear talk at the store. I see the people come into the shop. The Creoles are a closed society. The Spanish are hot-blooded. The Americans keep to their section and their own parties, while some of the Irish are ostracized.''

''There are ways to win acceptance.''

''You're from a different world.''

''If you were educated in England, then you're from a different world also. What do you want, Tobiah?''

''My freedom. This city has free men of color. You've given me a chance to earn my way, and sometime I want what you want—my own home. I want to bring my mother here.''

Rafe looked away, feeling a pang at the thought of his mother.

''Any word today about your brothers?'' Tobiah inquired.

''No. My notice in the paper will run for one more day. I've made my rounds at the docks again. Now some of the men remember me, and answer me even before I've asked about my brothers. When they do arrive, there are several men who will tell them I've been looking.''

''Still certain they'll arrive?'' Tobiah asked, his voice soft with sympathy.

Rafe didn't want to yield to the fears that plagued him all too often. ''Mother always said to expect a rainbow.''

Tobiah laughed softly. ''I wish I could view the world with such optimism.''

Rafe glanced at Tobiah. ''You like your carpentry work?''

''I'm fortunate to be hired. And now I work two hours a day with a *forgeron*. I'm learning to do the fancy iron work. As my owner, you're supposed to get my wages.''

''We've been over that. You keep what you earn.''

''You won't have an easy time here, if you associate with me.''

''To hell with that. I have to change my fortune,'' Rafe said as they walked along Gallatin Street. ''The

O'Briens have always owned land. I want to own property. I want a house. I promised my mother I wouldn't gamble, but I don't want to shovel dirt and shells all my life."

Tobiah laughed. "You talk as if all you can do is win."

"When I gamble, I expect to win."

A commotion sounded a short distance way. A man ran around the corner into their sight, his yellow coattails flapping, a cane in his hand.

"Get him!" a man yelled. Another man jumped him. Four others carrying cudgels came after these, two men swinging their stout weapons, five against one. Rafe and Tobiah saw the man in yellow draw a sword that had been hidden in the cane, but it was no match against the clubs. He went down again.

"It isn't a fair fight," Rafe observed.

"It isn't *our* fight," Tobiah said.

"No, but he's outnumbered. He needs our help." Rafe watched, hating bullies. "C'mon."

They ran, and Rafe caught a man's shoulder and spun him around. Rafe ducked the club, feeling a cool rush of air as it swung past his head. He slugged the man, feeling bone crunch against bone.

Tobiah lifted a burly man high and tossed him over a fence, while Rafe ducked a blow and lashed out with his fists. It was over in minutes—two bodies on the ground, two men running away, one thrown over the fence. Rafe extended his hand, and the man on the ground took it, standing and shaking his head, wiping blood off his face. A long scar crossed his face from temple to jaw.

"*Merci*. I was set upon by the Live Oaks."

"Who?"

"Bill Wilson's gang of ruffians, the Live Oak gang. They sleep at the foot of the Elysian Fields at the river, and beat any man who gets in their way. Get their name from the oak clubs they wield. It's what I get for being on Gallatin. Touzet Lacquement," he said, offering his hand to Rafe.

"Rafferty O'Brien. This is Tobiah Barr."

"M'sieus. Thank you both. I buy you drinks now."

"You can walk?"

"Of course," he said, but with the first step, he stumbled. Rafe caught an arm and Tobiah another arm. But within a block, he was standing on his own.

"Mr. O'Brien, I'll leave you now," Tobiah said, moving off, leaving Rafe as he always did when they were in public, heading for a gambling hall where he was allowed.

"I'll buy you a drink, but we'll leave Gallatin and go where it's safer," Touzet announced. As they walked along Levee and crossed St. Phillips, two carriages rounded the corner and stopped in front of a house. A couple left the first carriage and entered the house.

From the second carriage a man emerged and turned to offer his hand. Rafe paused in the shadows, catching Touzet by the arm. "Look at the lady."

A deep green cape swirled around her skirts as she stepped down from the carriage. She tilted her face up, and Rafe felt a skip in his pulse as he studied it. The street light illuminated the features Rafe already had memorized: the straight nose and high, pink cheeks, her slender neck. In an instant she was gone, and the door closed behind them.

"Did you see her?"

"Yes, my friend. Why do you ask if I saw Mademoiselle Therrie?"

"I'm in love with her. I intend to know her well."

"*Mon dieu*! I was rescued by a madman! Impossible!"

"Chantal Therrie," Rafe mused. He glanced again at the house. "Whose home did she enter?"

"The Brouillettes', my crazy friend."

"Tell me about her, and why you protest," Rafe said as they continued their stroll down the street.

"First, sir, and do not take offense . . ."

"I won't."

"You saved me from a vile beating, perhaps worse. I wouldn't offend you were it not necessary."

"Go ahead," Rafe said, still lost in thoughts of

Chantal and only half hearing the Frenchman. Rafe could remember down to the smallest detail the moment she had pressed against him, soft, warm, and deliciously sweet.

"I would never insult you. . . ."

"Damn you, get on with it. Say it!"

Touzet stopped and Rafe paused, turning to look at him as the Frenchman gazed from Rafe's head to his toes and waved his hand. "Sir, Mademoiselle Therrie is New Orleans' royalty. Old family. French blood. Do you know the Irish Channel?"

"Below St. Charles, near the wharf, where Irish immigrants live," Rafe said, getting the drift of the conversation and feeling impatient. "I don't live there, but if I did, I'd belong. I'm Irish. I'm an immigrant."

"And . . ." Touzet paused. "No offense is intended. I would never insult a man who has saved my life. . . ."

"Sure, and I'm damned well more offended by your going all around the rear of the cow to get to the nose! Tell me what you're trying to say, or I'll finish what those brigands started!"

To Rafe's surprise, the Frenchman laughed. "My impatient Irishman! You have no idea to whom you talk, do you?"

"No. Should I?" He gave up the conversation. "I need that drink."

"You will come with me," Touzet said in a merry tone, heading toward Exchange Alley. "You're in desperate circumstances. You cannot look at Mademoiselle, because you're Irish. You're poor. You're beneath her station in life."

"So far you haven't come up with a good reason. I can get beyond Irish. Look back there," he said, pointing to red-brick buildings with black ironwork. "The fine Pontalba apartments were designed by James Gallier; the Irishman and his son are adored by society. Timothy Joyce is an excellent carpenter. Look at the Kenners—I'm told they're of Scotch-Irish descent. I don't intend to stay poor. I'm looking around for opportunity, and I'm learning. I don't intend to stay at this station in life forever.''

"Ah, my foolish friend. How can you get out of it? As much as I like you, you do not look on the verge of inheriting riches, eh, *mon ami*?''

"I won't inherit, but I can acquire.''

"Robbery, perhaps. She cannot consort with a criminal. She is up there''—he gestured toward the sky—''while you . . .'' He waved his hand toward the ground, and Rafe laughed.

"She didn't look as if she belonged on a cloud.''

"Her father is powerful, strong, and wants the very best for her,'' he said as they passed the crowded Coffee House Exchange.

"I don't blame him.''

"You are a madman. I have not given the biggest reason you never will have so much as a dance with her.''

"Still going around the tail for the nose!''

"She is out of your reach as much as a star. She belongs to another man.''

For the first time Rafe felt a cold chill of worry, and stopped walking to turn and stare at Touzet. "She's married?''

"No, but she's promised.''

"Is *that* all!'' Rafe let out his breath. "It has to be that bastard Lazare.''

"You know M'sieu Galliard?''

"We've crossed paths. She was in a race with Galliard, and her horse was about to jump a stone wall. The land was dug away on the other side of the wall and she could have been hurt. I stopped her horse and was knocked flat. And in the process I got a whopping blow from Galliard, for touching her when she knelt down to see if the horse had killed me.''

"*Mon dieu!* You are good at saving people! And if you touched Mam'selle, you've made an enemy of Lazare Galliard.'' Touzet shook his head. "We're here not a moment too soon. Come inside.''

Rafe followed him upstairs and waited as he lighted

oil lamps in a large, empty room with mirrors placed along one wall.

"Now, my ignorant Irish friend, I'll teach you to fight in the gentleman's way," Touzet said, pulling off his coat, picking up two rapiers from the floor, and flinging one to Rafe. "Here is the weapon of choice, the colichemarde, a small sword."

Rafe caught the rapier and slid his hand over the wire-wound grip, rubbing his thumb on the ball-shaped pommel. He gripped the handle and lifted the sword, slashed the air with it, seemingly amused by Touzet.

"Ahh, the man knows how to fence after all! You didn't learn *that* in Ireland."

"My father sent me to school in London for two years."

Touzet frowned. "We have something new here. Most of the Irish immigrants have fled from famine."

"We fled from my father's debts. My father was landed gentry, until he gambled away everything," Rafe said, moving to his left, circling, watching for Touzet's first move. "He died, and my mother's health failed. We were bringing her to a sunnier climate. She died at sea. I was separated from my brothers, and I'm still searching for them."

"I regret your loss. Now let us see what you have learned."

"You're a *maître d'armes*," Rafe said. He had heard about them when drinking, and knew they taught fencing and fought duels with great success.

"Correct. These few blocks are lined with *salles d'êscrimes* taught by other *maîtres d'armes*. 'Titi' Rosiere and Pepe Llulla are the best." Touzet thrust, Rafe countered, and in seconds he knew it would be only a matter of minutes before Touzet had disarmed him.

Touzet feinted, Rafe thrust, and with lightning speed the Frenchman's rapier sliced across Rafe's forearm, cutting through his sleeve and drawing blood. Rafe inhaled and frowned, allowing his concentration to lapse. The rapier was flicked from his hand and flew

through the air, to clatter and slide across the floor.
The point of Touzet's blade now touched Rafe's chest.

"I could run you through."

"What the hell . . . ? I just saved your life. I'm
bleeding. . . ."

Touzet stared at him. "You are serious about Mademoiselle Therrie?"

"Yes, dammit!"

"Then you shall have to fence as well as I do, or
Lazare will do more than slice your arm. He'll cut you
to ribbons and run you through. He has buried eight
men after duels, three by fencing, five by pistols."
Touzet lowered the rapier and offered his hand. "Now,
my friend, I offer to become your teacher, although I
would prefer that you give up such a foolhardy notion
of the heart. There are many beautiful women in the
city. I'll introduce you to some. Beautiful and willing.
Not proper misses who have to be courted under the
watchful eyes of a powerful father and a stepmother.
No, my friend. Beautiful women who will melt in your
arms and comply with your wishes. Pick up your rapier and we'll commence the first lesson. Feet farther
apart, hands higher. Very good.

"Now, M'sieu Irish, move to your right. Right!
Blade higher. Thrust now! Counter, raise your wrist."

Later, as they walked to a tavern, Rafe thought about
Chantal Therrie. "Tell me about her family. Who are
they?"

"M'sieu O'Brien, *forget* Mademoiselle Therrie. If
you pursue such folly, you will have nothing but sorrow. As I would be happy to show you, there are others equally beautiful."

"There isn't another woman as beautiful as Chantal
Therrie," Rafe insisted, lost in thoughts of her, paying
little attention to Touzet's promise to introduce him to
someone beautiful.

As they entered a tavern, Rafe saw men playing faro.
"I can't get wealthy shoveling shells for a roadbed,
but I promised my mother I'd never gamble."

"Foolish promise. You didn't gamble in her life-time. Now you're free of your promise."

"No I'm not, but this is one promise I may have to break," he said. He was impatient to move up in the world, and right before him was a means to do so, something he knew well.

"You can play faro here, gamble all you like in this place. If I stay at your side, you should be safe."

Rafe grinned. "Seems I recall five men who didn't hesitate to take after you."

Touzet arched his black brows. "They didn't know they attacked a *maître d'armes.*"

"I'm not sure they would have cared." Rafe watched the games, noting that the wagers were small. It was late when he told Touzet good night and went to the small room that held a bed and table and washstand. He yanked off his boots, pausing to run his hand on the leather. The clothes on his back were the only pos-sessions left from Ireland. For an instant he felt a tight pain in his chest. *Where are Caleb and Fortune and Darcy?* It hurt, and he tried to cling to the idea that they were somewhere, on a ship or traveling on land, trying to get to New Orleans. He clamped his jaw shut. They would make it.

As he stretched out on the sagging mattress of corn husks, his last thoughts were of Chantal Therrie.

He spent the weekend along the docks, asking on ships and in grog shops, talking to sailors about his brothers, but still there was no word. Every night for the next week he had a fencing lesson, and afterwards Touzet accompanied him to a gambling house. At night Rafe counted his winnings, hoarding the money, spending only what he had to on food, running a no-tice in the paper each week about his brothers. In the following week, Touzet told Rafe he wanted him to meet someone.

"I don't need to meet beautiful women," Rafe an-swered dryly. "I want to find a gambling house where the stakes are higher than Pierre's, where they have vingt-et-un and écarté and faro."

"You will move into a dangerous circle. When the

stakes are higher, the men are more in earnest. Next week we will go to McGrath's. Not tonight. Come with me, my stubborn friend.''

"Only if we're going where I can play faro.''

Touzet nodded, and they walked down Custom House. They reached a block on Hercules where carriages lined the street in front of gambling houses. Touzet turned into one and motioned to Rafe to follow. As they walked through a narrow hallway, rooms opened on both sides and Rafe saw men at faro, vingt-et-un, and craps tables.

"They shoot craps?''

"Ah, you know this game? We have a leading citizen, one of the Marignys, who made craps popular here. It was he who named the Rue de Craps.''

Rafe and Touzet crossed a courtyard filled with blooming yellow bougainvillaea and green banana trees. A fountain splashed in the center, lanterns flickered. The wall had been removed between the house and its neighbor, their courtyards joined, and next door soft piano music came from a corner behind leafy green plants. People milled around. There were iron tables and chairs, and Rafe noticed beautiful women dressed in nothing more than scanty, frilly chemises, or clinging silk.

Touzet paused. "Next door there are women as beautiful as Mademoiselle Therrie.''

"Touzet, not tonight. This isn't what I want,'' Rafe said.

"Very well. But if you still wish to gamble for higher stakes, you have come to the place. This is the highest in town, with the exception of the Elkins and other exclusive men's clubs.''

"Who's allowed at the Elkins?''

"*Crème de la crème.* Plantation owners, bankers, brokers, politicians.'' As they crossed the courtyard, Rafe glanced over his shoulder, looking at lovely bare flesh. How long had it been since he had held Molly in his arms? Molly Dwyer, his childhood sweetheart from Brandon Point. He felt a twinge of sadness, remembering their parting and how she had cried. Now those moments seemed far in the past; Ireland, but a childhood memory.

Touzet spoke briefly to a servant, and in seconds they were being ushered through another hallway into a large, empty sitting room. A thick Persian carpet covered the floor, and the carved rosewood furniture was tasteful and comfortable. Rafe, who had expected something gaudy, was pleasantly surprised.

They waited a moment, Rafe's patience thinning when a woman entered the room. He came to his feet along with Touzet.

"Jolie, ma chèrie. Comment allez-vous?" Touzet said, taking her hands.

"Ca va bien, merci." She smiled. She was beautiful, with a translucent clarity to her skin, a long, slender neck, and golden hair piled on her head. Rafe had never known a woman to own a gambling hall. This woman would be at home on the elegant plantation he had viewed coming upriver to New Orleans. She was slender, her bones delicate, her coloring fair. Her wide blue eyes gazed at Rafe with curiosity and she reminded him of someone, but he couldn't think who. Lord knows it wasn't Molly, with her full-blown voluptuousness. How did a woman become the owner of a gambling place? And a fancy one at that?

"Permettez-moi de vous presenter Rafferty O'Brien. Rafferty, je te présente Jolie Fouquet."

"Enchanté, Madame Fouquet," Rafe said, trying not to stare.

She motioned them to be seated, and Touzet lapsed into English. "Jolie, M'sieu O'Brien is new to town. He has seen a beautiful woman who is promised to another."

Rafe felt uncomfortable with Touzet's speaking for him as if he were a child. He treasured his brief memory of Chantal Therrie, and he wasn't ready to tarnish it yet with a tumble in the hay with another woman.

"I hope he will go next door to Madam Crystal's. Perhaps you can persuade him, and put his night on my account. I want him to find a woman to make him forget. If you don't, my friend here, who saved me from brigands, will be called out and run through by an expert.''

''I do know how to speak for myself,'' Rafe said to her, exasperated with Touzet's plans for him.

She smiled, her blue eyes twinkling as Touzet stood up. ''I leave it up to you,'' he said to her. *''Bonsoir.''*

And he was gone, leaving Rafe alone with her. ''Touzet has his ideas,'' Rafe said, studying her. ''Actually, I prefer your place and a game of faro or the craps table. I have money, but perhaps Touzet will learn a lesson if I use his payment as a stake.''

She laughed. ''Very well. You don't need to rush. I've been alone all evening.'' She turned to the table beside her. ''Would you prefer cognac, whiskey, claret, or coffee?''

''Whiskey, please.''

''She filled a wine-glass with claret and a tumbler with whiskey, and handed his drink to him. ''You're new to this country?''

''Yes. I'm from Ireland.''

''I was born in a small town north of here, along the Mississippi,'' she said in a quiet voice he found soothing. ''My father rode the riverboats, and sometimes I was taken along with him. He was a gambling man.''

''We have something in common there. My father followed the same call. My parents are no longer alive.''

''Nor are mine. My mother died from yellow jack—yellow fever. We have epidemics every few years. The last terrible one was five years ago. Eleven thousand died.''

''Eleven thousand!'' he cried, stunned by the high number. ''And your father?''

''My father was shot by another man on a riverboat. He was what they called a 'sure-thing player.' He used every trick. He had 'strippers,' which are shaved cards, and 'readers,' the planted, marked cards. I was fourteen then, and three months before my father was shot he wagered *me* and lost, so I belonged to someone when my father was killed.'' She said all of this in a matter-of-fact tone, as if she had long ago become accustomed to her fate.

Rafe stared at her, trying to imagine his own father wagering his children. "You were given to a man to satisfy a gambling debt?" he asked, then realized it might not be the correct thing to say. "I mean . . ."

"I was fourteen. I had no choice. The man who won me sold me to another man on the river. I've seen most of the towns along the Mississippi. When I came to New Orleans, I knew this was where I wanted to stay. And I knew a great deal about gambling and gambling establishments. Do you like it here?"

"Yes. I expect to stay." *Where the hell does she get these polite manners, if she's been handed on from one man to another?* "New Orleans is different from Ireland."

"Very different, I imagine! I hope you like it. Are you familiar with our political parties? The Democrats, and the Native American or Know-Nothings."

"That's a damned strange name."

She laughed. "Ask one of them about his party, and you'll see where the name originated."

"They know nothing about it," he guessed, and she nodded.

"The Know-Nothings have a strong platform opposed to foreigners, and want to tighten the naturalization laws. They've given particular trouble to the Irish in town—or have you already found that out?"

"No. I've just learned to be careful on Gallatin. Who're the leaders of these parties? Tell me about your government."

"The city had a tripartite government, but now all three municipalities are united in one. In 1852 we consolidated under a mayor and a common council. The council is made up of a board of aldermen and a board of assistant aldermen," she said, and went on to explain other aspects of local and state government. Talk switched to Ireland, and he told her about the farm. She gave him her undivided attention, and an hour later Rafe realized he had been doing most of the talking.

"You're a good listener," he said, wondering about her life.

"I hope you find your brothers soon." She smiled. "I can take you next door to Madam Crystal's and introduce you to a beautiful woman."

"Madam Fouquet, Touzet wanted to be helpful. But all I can think about is the beautiful lady. I'm not afraid of a duel, although it's unlikely I'll get close enough to provoke one. I don't move in her circle."

"It won't hurt you to talk to someone else for a few minutes. The time has been well paid for."

"Thanks, but tonight, I'd rather you introduced me to your craps table."

She laughed. "Very well. Follow me."

He watched the soft sway of her hips as he followed her out of the room. She was an enigma to him: She was polished and polite, yet she ran a tough male business.

As soon as Rafe was at the craps table, he forgot Jolie Fouquet. He played with a vengeance, and in the early hours of the morning in his room from beneath a table, he withdrew the metal box that held his hoard of money. He stared at it with a swift surge of satisfaction—he had enough to go to a bank and open an account, and he knew he had to get the cash out of this room, where it could be stolen at any time.

Three nights passed before Rafe again saw Touzet, whose eyes glittered with smug satisfaction. While Rafe pulled off his coat and selected a rapier, Touzet watched him.

"We go to toast Madam Crystal tonight after the fencing lesson. Eh? I get you out of trouble. Lazare won't have to call you out. There are other beautiful women in New Orleans, yes?"

"Yes, Touzet, there are other beautiful women, but no one as beautiful as Chantal Therrie."

"Aagh!" Touzet reeled against the wall. "You cannot mean that!"

Rafe grinned and tossed a rapier to Touzet. "I never went to Madam Crystal's, but Madam Fouquet's craps

and faro tables are marvels. I will give you back your
money; I used it as a stake.''

"Craps! Faro! Ayee, you are a crazy one!''

"As to dueling, see if I'm improving.'' He sliced
the air and moved back, never trusting Touzet when
he got behind steel.

Touzet came at him. "You still dream of Chantal
Therrie? Then you'll fight Lazare Galliard. And he
will do *this*.'' He feinted and thrust. Rafe matched
him. In minutes he was fighting in earnest, suspecting
that if he slipped Touzet would again cut him. Yet
Touzet was right. Someday Rafe intended to take Lazare Galliard's woman away from him. Although she
wasn't truly Galliard's yet. Their marriage had been
arranged when they were children. That had little to
do with what was in Chantal's heart. Rafe envisioned
her beautiful brown eyes. Touzet's blade sliced across
Rafe's arm, drawing blood.

"Dammit!'' He wanted to throw down the rapier
and slam his fist into the little Frenchman's jaw. Instead he forced himself to calm his temper and concentrate, moving with care. All he had ever been able
to do was defend himself, but tonight he inched forward and gave a little back to Touzet.

Sweat rolled down Touzet's cheeks as the blades rang
and slid apart. Seeing an opening, Rafe thrust and
yanked his wrist up. Touzet's blade flew from his grip
and hit the mirror, dropping to the bare floor with a
clatter.

Touzet's eyes were round as Rafe moved forward
and thrust the tip of his rapier against his friend's chest.
Touzet stared at Rafe over the long slim blade, and
they both laughed.

"*Magnifique!* I buy the drinks!'' Rafe picked up the
fallen rapier and tossed it to Touzet.

Later, as they went out the door, Touzet's expression
became solemn. "You're good, but make no mistake,
Galliard is a champion.''

"He isn't better than you,'' Rafe replied.

"He is larger, so perhaps stronger. He'll have anger

and passion giving him more power. When you and I battle, I think only of the drinks we'll have later."

"Liar!" Rafe laughed. "You're as earnest when we fence as Galliard will ever be! When you have a blade in your hand, you turn into a bloodthirsty fiend."

"I should take back my offer to buy the drinks."

They went from one tavern to another, spotting Tobiah and stopping to talk to him before going to Madam Fouquet's to gamble.

As they stood at the bar, Touzet raised his glass of rum. "Where does Tobiah go at night?"

"There are taverns for free men of color. He's with them."

"But he's a slave."

"Everyone knows I've given him a letter to set him free, and that the recent law here prevents his freedom." Leaning against the bar, Rafe watched a game of faro. He picked up his drink. "I'll be back, Touzet."

Rafe joined the game at the craps table. He played until two in the morning, and when he left with Touzet his pockets were heavy with money.

For once Touzet was quiet, and Rafe glanced at him. "You won too. Why so quiet? Is something wrong?"

"Now I worry. When your mother made you promise not to gamble, did she know how easily you can win?"

"Probably. But she also knew how badly my father lost in the last year of his life. My brothers and I grew up gambling with my father. If I didn't want to have an extra task on Saturday night, I had to wager over it."

"*Mon dieu!* Your mother allowed this?"

"Hell, no. She didn't know it, but Pa did it with the three older boys. Darcy was too young."

"I thought Chantal Therrie was beyond you, that you would moon over her and perhaps get in Galliard's way sometime and earn a beating, but now I worry. You are a *maître de craps*. If you win at faro and craps just once a week the way you won tonight, you won't be shoveling dirt for long."

"Before another month is up I expect to own some piece of property in this town, even if it is only a patch of swamp."

"My earnest friend, we'll continue fencing. And you had better buy a pistol and practice your shooting."

"I stole a pistol from the slaver, and I practice."

"You're carrying a pistol?"

"No. But I practice."

Music came from the open doors of a saloon, and they could hear raucous laughter. They angled across the street and turned along Bacchus, where the street was darker and quieter. As they reached the next block, Rafe heard horses and glanced over his shoulder. Six men on horseback approached.

"There he is," a deep voice said. "The tall one."

Rafe looked to see which man had spoken. One rider was taller than the others, broad-shouldered and thick through the chest. His hat was pulled low. Rafe felt a rush of anger. Lazare Galliard—and trouble. Rafe wasn't armed, and it wasn't Touzet's fight. He would face them, but Touzet should be out of it. Doubling his fists, Rafe turned toward the horsemen.

"Touzet, run!" he ordered. "This isn't your battle."

Chapter 3

"Go!" Rafe yelled again, as he watched men jump off their horses. Damn Galliard! His pistol was at home.

As four men closed in, Rafe swung his fists. Something slammed against the back of his head and pain exploded. When he pitched forward, someone hit him again.

A man stood on his arms while another lashed a rope around his wrists. Pulling him to his feet, they mounted their horses.

Burning with rage, Rafe yanked against ropes looped around his wrists. The men led him behind their horses until there were no houses or people anywhere around. One eye was puffed shut. His jaw and head ached, and blood ran from his lip along his jaw.

He glanced around. *Where is Touzet?* To his relief the Frenchman wasn't with them. Someone hit Rafe's shoulder, pushing him forward.

"Tie him to the tree. Over there."

Shaking with anger, Rafe ground his teeth together. He recognized Galliard's voice as easily as if he had known him for years, although he couldn't see his features beneath the broad brim of his hat. Galliard rode in front of Rafe, reining his horse and staring down at him, moving his hand to his waist.

Moonlight glinted on a silver blade. With only a flash of silver as a warning, Rafe jerked his head as a knife sliced across his ear down to his jaw.

Gasping, he felt the sharp pain. Enraged, he ran at Galliard, but was jerked back.

"Remember this night when you look at the scar," Galliard said, backing his horse away. Standing in the stirrups, a man tied Rafe's wrists to an overhead branch while Galliard watched.

"You shouldn't touch a lady. You're an ignorant, filthy bastard who doesn't know what courtesy is, so you'll learn tonight."

"Go to hell, Galliard!" He knew it was a stupid thing to say and would only make Galliard more angry, but he didn't care. If only he could pull Galliard off the horse and get to him!

"Don't ever touch her or speak to her again," he continued in a low voice that sounded like a hiss. He nodded to someone behind Rafe, and a whip whistled through the air.

The blow fell, and Rafe clenched his jaw shut to keep from yelling. Another lash came, and another. The pain was white-hot, each blow feeling as if it cut to the bone. Yet each one was also a dry log heaped on a burning pyre of rage. Blood ran over his neck from the knife cut.

"I'll get you, Galliard," he said, grinding out the words in a deep voice. He gasped with the next blow. His hands unclenched and then wrapped around the slender branch.

His head lolled back and he looked up at the branch. In a blur of agony, he locked his fingers tightly around the limb. Rafe bit his lips as waves of pain washed over him. He jumped, leaping up and coming down with all his weight on the branch.

"Hit him! Dammit! Hit him!" Galliard bellowed.

The blows came faster, and spots danced in front of Rafe's eyes. Galliard rode forward with a pistol in his hand, the butt raised as he stood and swung it to smash Rafe's hand.

Before the pistol hit, the branch snapped. Wrists still lashed to the branch, Rafe yanked it up, hitting Galliard's arm and sending the pistol flying.

"Dammit, get him!" With a jerk on the reins, Galliard backed up his horse.

Rafe spun around and saw two men coming at him. Lowering his head, Rafe ran at one, butting him in the

stomach. The other jumped on him and they went
down.

They rolled, and Rafe jammed his elbow into the
man's stomach as another came at him. He lashed out
and kicked the attacker, hearing a grunt from the one
beneath him. He rolled away and came to his feet,
splashing through the swampy ground.

Two men closed in on him and he ran at one, holding up the branch and catching the man across the
throat. As he fell, two men jumped Rafe from behind.

They all went down, and Rafe felt blows pound him.

A shot shattered the night, its blast heard above the
roaring in his ears. A horse whinnied, and men yelled.

"Let's go! Get out!"

Hooves pounded while waves of pain enveloped
Rafe. He groaned as someone pulled him to his feet.
Muddy water was in his eyes, one almost puffed
closed. Hands steadied him.

"Quick, mount up," Touzet said.

Rafe felt the cold blade of a knife as the ropes were
cut. Tobiah boosted Rafe to a saddle and swung up
behind him.

"We have to return the horses. I took them from the
livery stable," Touzet said. "I couldn't believe my
eyes, but I should have known, my tough Irish friend,
you would not stay tied to a tree."

"That damned son of a bitch. I'll get Galliard,"
Rafe said through clenched teeth.

"*Mon dieu!* Next time you won't get a chance to
fight back. He will shoot you, and I will find you at
Our Lady of Guadeloupe, the mortuary. You must
carry your pistol."

"Thank you both," Rafe said. His head reeled, and
waves of nausea rolled over him. He hurt everywhere,
but the pain seemed a little more than a blur beneath
the hot fires of rage. "I'll get Galliard."

"Men are in St. Louis Cemetery who have said the
same thing! *Tu danses sur un volcan!*"

Rafe felt the earth spin and leaned forward, slumping over the horse's neck.

He stirred as hands jostled him. Tobiah pulled him

down and carried him inside. He heard them moving
around. Better to lie still and close his eyes. If only
he might pass out again . . . Damn Galliard! Damn
him!

"This is necessary," Touzet said, pouring liquid
over Rafe's back.

"Damnation!" Rafe yelled. He felt Tobiah press him
down on the bed.

"You'll get well sooner," Touzet said. "Hold him.
I don't want to feel one of those fists in my face." The
liquid came again, and again Rafe wished he would
pass out. He clenched his jaw. Someday he would take
Galliard's woman. Someday he would get Galliard
down off his horse and fight him, man to man.

Tobiah and Touzet moved away, and then Touzet
came close to the bed. "I leave now, but Tobiah stays.
I doubt if Galliard is finished with you. You must watch
where you walk, Irish, and you must carry your pistol.
I warned you about crossing him. This is just the
beginning."

"To hell with him."

"If you persist, it'll earn you worse than this beating. You don't have the social standing yet to be challenged. He will shoot you next time. I'll go to St.
Louis Cemetery, *compère*, and I'll place a bottle of
brandy on your grave."

Rafe stirred, trying to rise up. "My money . . ."

"Be still. Galliard has no interest in your money.
He wants your hide. *Bonsoir*, stubborn Irish."

It was too much effort to answer. He closed his eyes,
remembering Galliard. He touched his stinging jaw.
*Lazare Galliard, we have another settlement between
us. Bastard royal . . . Someday . . . someday.*

It was another week, the first of February, before
Rafe felt normal. A red scar now crossed his ear and
ran down to his jaw. If he had not turned his head, he
would have lost an eye. He renewed the fencing "lessons" which were now practice sessions. After one
session, he and Touzet went to Madam Fouquet's.

At one in the morning Rafe held his breath, watching the dice roll across the table and stop. The spots seemed to jump at him. *Two and three*. His gaze shifted to the mound of money riding on the bet. As he scooped it up, a note for a small parcel of land fluttered on top. He had watched Elbert Drumgoole scribble out the note and toss it on the heap. Now Rafe stuffed his winnings into his pockets, gathered up the rest, and went to find Touzet, who was engaged in faro. Touzet glanced his way and nodded. Minutes later play had finished, and he moved away from the table.

"So what have you won?" Touzet inquired. "The house?"

"Something just about as good." Rafe waved the paper at him. "I now own land," he said, feeling ridiculous pleasure. He could imagine what it might look like, thinking of the green, snake-filled swamps.

"I'm not surprised. Not any longer. When I met you, I didn't know what kind of man you were. If we gathered up all the stubbornness and determination in this room tonight, it would not equal yours."

Rafe grinned at him. "Let's have a drink. We'll hire a carriage and ride out and look at my property."

"Don't get your hopes too high."

"I don't give a damn if it's ankle-deep in gators and mud—I own land."

They moved toward the bar, and half an hour later strode into the night.

"Another night of winning for both of us!" Touzet pronounced with satisfaction as they left. "It's early. We'll go to the livery stable and ride out and look at your land, and then perhaps try our hands again. When we leave Jolie's, we're leaving the place with the most fun. Everyone goes to Jolie's, including your precious Chantal's father, Ormonde."

"Jolie knows Lazare."

"Of course she knows Lazare. Every beautiful woman in New Orleans knows Lazare, and every man in town gambles at Jolie's place. Galliard, our *bon vivant*, is at gambling houses; he is at the races; he is always at the quadroon balls."

"Quadroon balls?"

"My ignorant Irish friend! I forgot you know nothing of this city. The balls are held every week, and with the winnings you're accumulating you can have the proper clothes made and you'll be allowed to attend. I'll take you to my tailor." He looked up at Rafe. "When can I take you? You work from sunup until dark. With your winnings, I don't know why you persist with such a job. I'll make an appointment for tomorrow night and we will burn your Irish pants and shirt."

"Fine," Rafe answered with a smile, glancing down at his double-breasted shirt, the pantaloons with their front flap, the legs tucked into his Wellingtons. "What is a quadroon ball?" he asked, glancing down the street. They would be at Pierre's tavern, six blocks away, before he got his answer.

"A quadroon is a *femme de couleur,* woman of color. A quadroon is a mixture of a mulatto and a white. A mulatto is a mixture of colored and white. These *placées* are beautiful women, groomed by their mothers to please a man, and they are presented at the quadroon balls. If you can afford one and you want one, you make arrangements with the mother to set the daughter up in a house along the ramparts and pay for her keep. She will remain faithful to you so long as you have the arrangement; some, forever."

"You know men with these mistresses?"

"Of course," Touzet replied. "I myself had one, but she died during an epidemic of yellow jack. *Ma chèrie* Nicolette. She was very beautiful, and could please a man more than any other woman I've known. They are beautiful, these girls. Many men keep two families."

"Doesn't the wife mind?" Rafe asked. He couldn't imagine his mother in such a situation.

"The ladies look the other way. They know it's custom, and they can't stop it, so they ignore it. In all other ways their husbands are good to them."

"I want to go to the ball. I've never known of such balls. We'll see the tailor tomorrow night."

"Society balls are staid, polite affairs. At the quadroon balls the dresses are festive and fancy; the music is livelier. You'll enjoy yourself."

"Does Lazare go?"

"Of course he goes. Right now he has an octoroon mistress."

"What's an oc—"

"Part quadroon, part white. Her name is Delia, and she's as beautiful as Mam'selle Therrie. The quadroons are like wives in some ways, like slaves in others. Chantal can have Delia publicly whipped if she displeases Chantal or is insubordinate."

Rafe felt a chill. "Has Chantal ever done this?"

"No! I doubt if Chantal knows Delia exists. Chantal is seldom at the Therrie house in the Vieux Carré. Usually she stays at Belle Destin."

They turned the corner onto Custom House. A sound overhead captured Rafe's attention. He peered up through the darkness and caught his breath.

On the rooftop, a woman was edging toward the flat roof of the next house, her silhouette outlined against the sky. At the space between buildings she halted, as if to gauge the distance. Rafe clutched Touzet's arm.

"Will you look up there?" Rafe whispered.

"*Sacrebleu!* What is she doing?"

As they watched, she gathered her skirts and jumped from one rooftop to another.

A door burst open around the corner behind them, and men's voices rose. "Which way shall we go?" one yelled.

"Split up. He can't be far."

Rafe pushed Touzet. "Someone's after her! Lead them away from her."

"Why me? *Mon dieu! You* lead them!"

"Go, dammit! Here they come!" Rafe stepped back into an archway and placed his hand on the pistol tucked into his waistband.

"*Scelerat! Sacrebleu!*" Touzet ran and the men gave chase, disappearing around a corner.

"There he goes! After him."

As the men raced past, Rafe squeezed back against

the rough plastered wall. He listened until their footsteps had faded, then stepped out to look at the empty rooftops. Where the devil was she? She couldn't have gone far. He walked around the corner.

She was climbing down a wrought-iron railing, and he was curious and amused. A black cape hid all but her pale arms and hands.

Footsteps sounded coming back. "Here they come again," he said quietly.

She gasped and paused to look down at him, the dark hood hiding her features in shadow.

"Jump, or they'll see you! I'll catch you. Jump!"

She started climbing to the rooftop again, but the long swirling cape caught in the wrought iron. She jerked at it.

The footsteps grew louder. Rafe scaled the iron and yanked free the cape. He dropped to the ground, landing on his feet. "Now, jump!"

She released the railing and he reached out, scooping her into his arms and running around the corner. He set her on her feet and took her hand, pulling her into a doorway and crushing her against him. She wasn't wearing hoops or crinoline, and he could press her close. Feet pounded as men ran past.

"Where is he?" a man asked.

"I think he went the other way!" another answered.

"Over here!" someone called.

She was taking deep breaths. She smelled like the pink Irish roses that had grown along the hedgerow at home. The hood of the black cape covered her hair. Voices and footsteps faded.

"Come with me," Rafe whispered. "I'll get you out of here."

"I don't know you. I can't go with you!" As she turned to run from him, he caught her wrist.

"Don't be ridiculous! They'll find you." Footsteps approached, and he tugged on her wrist. They rushed across the street and along an alley. Two more turns and they had reached the door to his small room. "In here." He opened the door and stepped back.

She tried to run, but he reached out and seized her

around the waist and pulled her inside, closing and
bolting the door.

"I won't hurt you. I promise."

She put down her head, led with her shoulder, and
tried to push him over. Laughing, he fell against the
wall and caught her as she pulled at the bolt.

"I won't hurt you!" He picked her up, carried her
across the room, and dumped her on his bed.

He turned away to light an oil lamp. The soft glow
left dark shadows in the corners of the room as she
jumped up to run to the door.

He grabbed her, his hands closing on her tiny waist
as he spun her around. "When a safe amount of time
passes, I'll take you home," he said.

Her hood had fallen away, and he felt his heart contract in his chest.

"Miss Therrie!"

Chapter 4

She gasped and stopped struggling. "You!" She blinked, and her face was suffused in pink. "This is the *second* time you've saved me! And I don't even know your name."

"Rafferty O'Brien." He felt as if she had been conjured up by his imagination. How many times had he lain on his narrow bed, fantasizing that she lay there with him?

There was a silence while they studied each other. She looked as stunned by his presence as he was by hers. "You were on a rooftop? Men were after you?"

"Yes," she said, wringing her hands and turning away. As he moved close behind her to take her cape, he inhaled the scent of roses in her hair. He wanted to lean forward and kiss a pale place beneath her ear. Reaching around her to unfasten the cape, his fingers brushed her throat. Her flesh was warm and smooth, and he felt his heartbeat quicken.

She turned to look up at him. "You mustn't tell that you found me on the roof."

"I'll reserve judgment on whether I should tell or not until I've heard why you were there," he said, teasing her. He couldn't believe he had her all to himself, and he had no intention of taking her home right away.

"Please! If Papa found out, or Lazare . . ." Her hand flew to her cheek. "If Lazare discovers I'm with you, he'll challenge you. I never meant this to happen!"

"I'll worry about Lazare. He isn't going to discover

you're with me. He doesn't know where I live," he said, hoping Lazare hadn't had men following him.

"I must go."

"They're searching for you out there. Do you want them to find you?"

"No!" Her eyes were enormous, and filled with uncertainty. "But all this would compromise me if anyone found out."

"No one will ever know except the two of us," he said softly. He placed her cape over a chair and poured two glasses of brandy. Then he motioned to her as he pulled out a straight-backed wooden chair.

She blinked and crossed the room to sit down. He took the chair facing hers, then set a glass of brandy on the narrow table. She glanced down at the amber liquid.

"I'm not allowed to drink anything strong," she said, her eyes wide and fathomless, large amber pools that had a pinpoint of golden lamplight reflected in their depths.

He wanted to touch her. "You're allowed to clamber about on rooftops?"

She smiled, seeming to relax a little. "No, not that either."

"Take a sip of brandy. It might be the thing tonight."

He held out his glass. "Here's to a grand escape." *Here's to us, my love,* was Rafe's secret toast. He touched his glass to hers and drank, watching her over the rim all the time. He couldn't stop looking at her. Chantal Therrie was in his room! He had her all to himself! And what kind of woman was this, who scampered about on rooftops?

She drank, but then coughed and blinked. "It's strong! Why do men like brandy?"

Her golden hair had come partially unpinned and fell to her shoulders in disarray. He saw it would reach far below her shoulders when it was completely unpinned, and he imagined it tumbling free. "They like it," he said softly, "because it's intoxicating and it becomes a habit. It's irresistible."

Her eyes widened as she realized he was talking about her rather than the brandy. Her cheeks once again became pink, and she took another drink. "Will I become intoxicated? How much may I drink before that happens?"

"Your glass holds only a small amount. I won't let anything happen to you," he said, thinking that he would protect her with his life. "Won't your father look for you?"

"No." She swirled the brandy. Her fingers were long and slender, and he wanted to kiss each one. Her dress was deep blue organza, with a white lace trim. He let his gaze wander lower. The material was gathered and covered in lace, but his imagination peeled it away to envision the golden body beneath. Her breasts were high, her waist tiny. He felt his body responding to his reverie, and he wiped his brow.

He had forgotten his question when she looked up. "Papa has another plantation upriver from Belle Destin, north of Baton Rouge. Once a month he goes for a few days to take care of it, and he's gone now."

"And your mother goes with him?"

She frowned. Something in his question displeased her. Her lips were full and rosy. Very full, and they looked soft. He wanted to touch them, to kiss them, to feel their softness beneath his mouth.

"No, my stepmother is at our house here in the Vieux Carré."

"Where is that?"

"On Royal Street."

And a million miles above Rafe's tiny room, given the layered social strata of the city. He poured more brandy into Chantal's glass.

"No, thank you!" she exclaimed as it splashed. But he poured her glass less than half-full.

"I won't give you too much. I promise."

"You've saved me twice now," she said, studying the scar across his cheek. *Does she find it offensive?* he wondered self-consciously.

"Do you do these things often?"

She laughed, and he was dazzled. She had dimples,

and her eyes twinkled and seemed full of merriment. No fainting miss this one!

"Perhaps too often!" she replied, looking sure of herself now, and he realized she was accustomed to flirting with men. "You weren't hurt when my horse struck you, were you?"

"No, it was nothing," he lied, remembering how his shoulder had turned black. "So your father won't know, and your stepmother won't know what you've done. Do you enjoy rooftops?"

She laughed, and he wanted to spend forever making her laugh. "No! Of course not!" Her mirth vanished, and she frowned. "No. I'm very worried about my brother." As they both sipped their brandies, Rafe waited for her to explain. "Are you involved in politics?" she asked.

"No. I just arrived from Ireland."

She looked relieved. "Do you know our political parties?"

"I've heard about them. The Democrats and the ones with the strange name, the Know-Nothings."

"Sometimes they're called the Native American party. My brother and Lazare are Know-Nothings."

It certainly fits Galliard, Rafe thought wryly.

"The Know-Nothings say they know nothing in their rules that is contrary to the Constitution. My father is a Democrat. Election time in the city is . . . Papa says it's a time of turmoil. Men sometimes have to defend themselves in order to vote." She threw him a teasing glance. "Papa says politics were dignified and honest as long as the Creoles were in power. It's the Americans and Irish who have changed things."

Rafe smiled at her. "So how are you involved in all this?"

"Sometimes men vote who shouldn't. They all talk about reform, but Papa says it doesn't change. Now a group has formed called the Vigilance Committee. Many are from the Whigs, a party that's almost gone." She finished her brandy, and he poured more. "Diantha—she's married to my brother—came to me. She's frightened, because my brother has joined this group. She wants me to beg him to get out of it.''

There was one white button at the throat of Chantal Therrie's dress that was unfastened. Her collar was open a fraction, but he couldn't take his eyes away from the neckline and the row of tiny buttons that ran down the front of her dress. He gazed at the slight gap in her collar and felt his desire for her burn like a flame. He wanted to lean over the table and kiss her there, to reach out and unfasten the next button and the next. He tried to listen to what she said.

''Did you talk to your brother?''

''No. He's five years older than I am, and when it comes to politics he thinks women don't know anything. He won't listen to me, but he might listen to Papa.''

''How will you explain your learning of these plans to your father?''

''I can just tell him that I overheard Alain. He won't inquire where I was when I heard.'' Rafe nodded when she explained. ''You live here?'' she asked, looking around.

''Yes,'' he said, seeing it for the first time as a woman of quality might. His clothes were on hooks on the walls; a shirt was tossed on the bed, which was still rumpled from last night's sleep. A washstand stood in the corner, and two books were on the floor beside the bed. The room was tiny and unkempt, but his delight that she was a part of the scene was stronger than his sense of shame.

''I've never been alone in a man's home before.'' She looked at his bed, and her cheeks turned pink again.

Her eyes were wide, and he guessed she was aware of him as a man. He couldn't resist leaning forward to brush a curl of hair behind her ear, letting his fingers linger over the curve of her ear.

''I shouldn't be here now,'' she said breathlessly.

''And I can't tell you how happy I am that you *are* here,'' he replied. ''You're beautiful, Chantal Therrie,'' he said, relishing the saying of her name. Her face flushed, and he had to fight to keep from leaning across the short space that separated them and kissing her.

"Thank you," she said, staring into his eyes. "I've never been alone with a man like this," she repeated.

"Then I'm glad you're with *me* for the first time," he said, thinking that he wanted her to say the same thing when she was in bed with a man for the first time. "We will have some more firsts, Chantal."

Calling her "Miss Therrie" had gone with the removal of the cape. He could never be so formal with her again. Only a few yards away was a bed, but it might as well have been in the next parish for all the good it would do him. *Be thankful she is sitting only inches away,* he thought, *looking like she's never been told that she is beautiful.*

"Sir, you are very bold!"

"No," he replied in a solemn tone. "I'm not bold. I'm truthful."

She looked at his mouth, and he felt his manhood throb against the tight confines of his trousers. Sitting there with her wide eyes and her blushes, her pink tongue running over her lips each time she tasted brandy, her dark eyes changing with her emotions, she was astonishingly sensual, and he was certain she was unaware of it. As sensual as she was beautiful. She blushed again and lowered her eyes, and he wondered if she had any idea of the effect she was having. Organza stretched over her breasts as she inhaled.

"Why were you on the roof?" he asked, his voice thickening.

"My father would call you out if he knew I had been here. I should leave," she said, looking away.

"You've already said yourself that your father won't know," he said. *She feels something too.* "It's too soon for you to leave. With men wandering the street looking for you, you're safer here. Suppose your brother found you alone on the streets at this hour?"

She blinked and looked up in surprise, as if she hadn't thought of that possibility.

"You know I won't hurt you. Now, why were you on the roof?"

"I followed my brother. They met first in the University Building at Common and Bacchus; then he met with others in the Vieux Carré on Burgundy. I went up the stairs to listen through the door, to hear what the meeting was about and what they were planning. If Papa is going to stop Alain, Papa needs to know what the Vigilance Committee intends to do." All the time she was answering his question, she never raised her eyes from her brandy glass. He reached across the table, placed his finger beneath her chin, and raised her face.

"Something's wrong?"

She caught her lower lip with small white teeth. He was in agony. "You disturb me," she said softly.

I disturb her! He almost groaned. "Why?" he asked, knowing full well why.

She drew a breath, then changed the subject. "While I was listening in the hallway," she said, speaking with deliberation, "I bumped a table, and one of the men heard me. I had to run, so I took the stairs to the roof." She drew her fingers across her brow. "My, it's warm in here. I think brandy doesn't set well with me. I feel . . . swoozy."

" 'Swoozy'? Here, lassie, you're buttoned to your chin, as if a cold northern gale might begin to blow." He reached out and unfastened another button at her throat.

"Sir!" She caught his fingers and looked into his eyes. He leaned forward.

"I'm only unfastening two more buttons. Your dress still will be fastened to your chin," he said softly. "So proper, so chaste, and yet . . ."

Her eyes widened, her lips parted, and she lowered her hand while he unfastened one button and then another and pushed the neck of the dress open.

"Yet? Yet what?" she whispered.

He smiled at her. "You respond like a rose to sunshine," he said softly. Even though he had unfastened several buttons, her dress was still buttoned within inches of her collarbone. He reached for the next button, letting his hand rest against the soft rise of her bosom.

"That's enough!" she said, but the words were breathless, and he could feel her pulse racing beneath his hand.

"You were saying you took the stairs to the roof." He unfastened one more button and pushed open the organza. She was buttoned high enough to be chaste, but now her delicate collarbone showed. He let his fingers drift to her ear. Perspiration dotted her brow, causing tiny tendrils of golden hair to curl against her temple. He reached up to pull a pin from her hair and release another silken lock.

"They went through the hallways and in rooms to look for me, but they didn't go to the roof."

"Chantal, why do I disturb you?"

She blinked and shrugged. "I shouldn't be here, you know. If you hadn't rescued me before, I would get up and run."

"I won't hurt you, I promise."

She was the most beautiful woman he had ever seen. He was in love. He wanted her. Never at any time had he thought he wanted to marry Molly, or Kathleen before Molly, but he knew with certainty how he felt about Chantal.

"I'm glad that I disturb you; I'm glad that you're here. So you went out on the roof, and then I found you. Did you hear their plans?"

"Yes, and I'm afraid for Alain."

"Will you talk to him?"

"Yes. And probably to Papa. He'll listen to Papa."

He couldn't picture Molly or Kathleen or Maeve or any other female he'd ever known spying on a group of men and climbing over rooftops.

"You just came from Ireland, so you don't vote," she said, risking a quick look at him.

"Not yet. I have to become a citizen. I have become a landowner, though," he said, thinking of the small plot of ground he had won earlier at the craps table.

"Did you come alone?" Chantal asked, wiping her brow again. Her words had slowed.

"No. My mother and brothers were with me, but before we reached New Orleans, there was a gale and the ship sank."

"Oh, no!"

"My mother died, and I was separated from my brothers," he said stiffly. It still hurt to talk about his loss.

"I'm so sorry," she said, sounding as if she meant it. "My real mother died when I was a year old. We had a fire; Belle Destin, the plantation house, burned, and my mother and three-year-old sister, Honoria, died. I've always missed my mother and wished I had known her. Even a slight memory would be such a treasure. My father met my stepmother in Paris and brought her home. I have a younger sister, Amity."

"I'm twenty-two."

"I was seventeen last week."

Seventeen was so young, as young as Caleb! "And Amity is . . . ?"

"Fourteen. A baby. Where are your brothers?"

"We were separated when the ship sank. We agreed to meet in New Orleans. They may have been picked up by a ship sailing away from here. I have notices posted at the docks, so that if any sailors should hear they'll know where to contact me."

"I hope you find them soon. How many brothers do you have?"

"Three. Caleb is seventeen, Fortune is fifteen, and Darcy is eight. My father died almost eight months ago."

"I'm sorry. How did you get here after your ship sank?" she asked, studying him.

"I found a piece of wood from the ship and clung to it. A slave ship picked me up, and a man from Haiti befriended me."

"I should go home now," she said in quiet tones.

"You shouldn't take the risks you did tonight, Chantal. Suppose I hadn't known you, and my intentions weren't honorable?"

"No one would harm me. They would be afraid of Papa and Lazare."

"There are sailors in this town who could truss you up and haul you away on a ship, and your father and Lazare would never know what had happened to you."

She looked startled. He reached out to touch her cheek, to let his finger slide along a lower lip that was as soft as velvet.

She blinked and moved back. "I have to go home." She stood up, swayed, and caught the table. "Oh, Mr. O'Brien! I shouldn't have had any brandy!"

Amused, he moved to her side, lifting a lock of hair off her neck. "Chantal," he whispered.

"Sir . . ." She stepped away, picking up her cape and reaching for the door. He put his hand up against the door as she tugged at the bolt.

She spun around. Her eyes were enormous, and her face pale. "You won't hold me here! You said you wouldn't harm me!"

"I won't harm you." His voice was deep and husky, and he gazed down into eyes that seemed as black as a raven's wing. "I'm going to know you much better someday."

"Sir, I am promised to Lazare Galliard. My father will never let you call on me."

"Do you love Lazare Galliard?"

She blinked. "Of course I love him! I have to go home. Sir, you are very bold and improper!"

"Wait, please. Propriety is often a waste of time. Give me your cape." Watching her, he took her cape and tossed it on the chair.

"Sir?" She seemed to be torn with indecision.

"It's Rafferty," he said, his voice becoming husky. "We're going to know each other. Say my name, Chantal. Rafferty."

As he moved closer, she leaned against the door. "You promised you wouldn't hurt me."

"Do you really think I'm going to hurt you now?" he whispered, and tilted her face up to his.

"No," she answered softly. Chantal Therrie looked up into determined blue eyes. Seldom had any man looked at her with the blatant intent that was so obvious in Rafferty O'Brien's expression. He looked at her as if he had never seen a woman until now, and as if he intended to kiss her.

Her heart thudded against her ribs, and she knew she should protest, but the words wouldn't come. Her head spun. *Never again drink brandy! He will kiss me, and Papa or Lazare will kill him for it. They don't have to know! Scream, or run, or struggle. Do something besides staring up at him. Something . . .*

He slid his arm around her waist and bent his head to brush his lips over hers.

"Sir, I must protest," she whispered. "I am promised to Lazare . . ."

"And Lazare is probably far too selfish to kiss you as you should be kissed," Rafferty O'Brien whispered in return, yet again brushing her lips slowly with his, and this time touching the corner of her mouth with his tongue.

Her pulse danced, while a roaring commenced in her ears. Her lips tingled, and she felt a delicious torment that made her knees seem as sturdy as sunshine.

"Put your arms around me," he commanded, his gaze holding the warmth of a smoldering fire.

Knowing she shouldn't, unable to resist, she wrapped her arms around his muscled shoulders and drew a deep breath, her breasts straining against his solid chest. Where was her will? Watching her, he leaned forward to play his lips over hers again until she moaned softly, a sound caught in her throat. Then the real kisses began. They were hot and wild and teasing. She wanted more. She felt his fingers in her hair. His tongue touched the corner of her mouth, tracing her lips until she placed her tongue against his.

How can I let him kiss me? How can I resist? Sweet merciful angels, what is he doing to me?

He seemed to shift, to press her more closely against him, and she was startled, feeling his manhood against her. His body was lean and hard, shape and textures so different from Lazare's. She tried to draw away, but she was held fast. Again Rafferty's lips settled over hers, parting them, his tongue thrusting into the warmth of her mouth, touching everywhere inside her mouth.

She moaned again, feeling his soft hair in her fingers, yielding to him. Never had she been kissed like this. Never . . .

Between kisses he raised his head to look down at her; his crystal-blue eyes were thickly fringed with black lashes. Her gaze lowered to his full underlip, which now appeared tantalizingly sensual. "I want you to say my name. Rafferty. Say it, Chantal."

"Rafferty," she whispered without thought, her mouth tingling, her head spinning. *Confounded brandy. Don't stop, please don't stop. Rafferty . . . Rafferty . . .*

He lowered his head and kissed her long and hard, until she felt giddy. She thought of shooting stars streaking across the sky, and felt as if she were caught on one of the swiftest of them. His kisses were taking her on a spinning journey.

He released her slightly. "I will call on you someday, Chantal."

"I'm promised. . . ."

"To hell with that," he whispered, and she felt as if her heart missed a beat. He sounded so certain. Yet it was impossible. Forever impossible. She felt sad and at the same time, on fire. A terrible longing washed over her for something that could never be. Rafferty O'Brien was impossible. She was promised to Lazare, and she loved Lazare. Even if she had been free to decide her own fate, she would have told Rafferty O'Brien good-bye and rushed home to Lazare.

She pushed Rafferty away. Her breathing was ragged, and the scalding look he gave her made her forget what she had intended to say. Unbidden, her gaze ran down the length of him, seeing the tight strain against his trousers, feeling the response of her own body heat.

"I have to go home now," she whispered.

He nodded and picked up her cape and held it for her. "Where's your horse?"

"At the livery stable. Instead of the stable Papa uses on Barracks, I went to the one on Perdido."

"I'll take you home on my horse. Can you tell someone you rode home with a friend or neighbor, and have the horse brought to you tomorrow? At this time of night your appearance at the livery stable would get back to your father."

She nodded. "Yes, that's fine," she agreed, wondering how long it would be before she could draw an even breath and her voice would sound normal.

"I don't want to let you go, but I promised. We'll have another time together, Chantal," he said in a husky voice, tracing his finger along her cheek.

She shook her head, feeling her heart pound again. "No, we won't. I'm promised, and I love Lazare."

One corner of Rafferty O'Brien's mouth rose in a crooked smile. He picked up one of her curls to let it slide through his fingers. "When I kissed you, I don't think you remembered Lazare Galliard. I rushed you tonight. Next time I won't rush you."

She yanked back the bolt. His hand slammed shut the door before she had opened it two inches. Furious, she spun around. "You're impossibly brash! You said I could go!"

He gave her a lazy smile that melted her anger. "It'll be safer to go out the back. This way."

Feeling foolish, she followed him, noticing the width of his shoulders. He was leaner than Lazare, and perhaps an inch or two shorter. She glanced around the room once more, knowing she would never forget this night. Betrothed to Lazare since childhood, she had never been kissed by another man. None would dare to stir Lazare's anger. Men talked to her and asked her to dance, but they didn't call on her and they certainly didn't try to kiss her. Or at least, not until tonight.

Rafferty O'Brien opened a door and motioned to her to wait. His head was well shaped, his black hair thick with curly sideburns; his dark hair was longer on his neck than Lazare's. She gazed at the back of Rafferty O'Brien's neck and remembered how his hair had felt beneath her fingers. Her cheeks grew hot at the memory.

He motioned her to follow, and crossed an alleyway. They went to the livery stable. Half a block away, Rafferty stopped her. "Wait here, and I'll fetch my horse."

She nodded, and in minutes he was back on a big bay stallion. He leaned down and scooped her up onto the horse, pulling her close against him and keeping his arm around her. She was aware of his breath against her temple, his arm around her waist, his long hard body against hers.

"Take St. Charles, Nyades; I'll direct you to the river road," she said, pointing. He turned his horse.

"We'll be safer if we avoid the main streets. Keep your hood pulled up, so your face isn't revealed if we meet anyone."

"Lazare is in town. I haven't seen him this week. We're going to a cotillion Saturday night," she added.

Aware of every jog of the horse that created friction between their bodies, she was acutely conscious of him, constantly aware of the strength in the arm holding her waist. They rode in silence along quiet streets, passing Tivoli Circle and elegant homes. "I've never been beyond Louisiana Avenue," Rafferty said.

"This is the American sector. On one side of Canal are the French and on the other are the Americans, with the neutral ground between them down the center of Canal."

"This is as elegant as the French."

Trying to think about houses instead of the Irishman breathing on her nape, she gazed on large mansions with well-tended beds of plants in yards beyond iron gates. "Their homes are newer; the Americans put yards in front of their houses."

As she talked, wheels rumbled and a harness jingled up ahead.

"Dammit, here comes a carriage. Keep your head covered."

She reached up to adjust the hood. Her heart skipped

a beat when she saw the brass leaping lion on the side of the approaching carriage.

"Please, turn around! It's the Galliard carriage!" she whispered frantically. If Lazare discovered them, he would kill Rafferty O'Brien on the spot. "*Please, go back!*"

Chapter 5

"Keep your head covered. There's no reason for him to recognize us, and I'll keep my face turned away."

"Oh, please! You run a terrible risk! If he—" Having twisted around to look up at Rafferty, she caught her breath when she found that his face was only inches from hers.

"Yes, Chantal?" he asked with amusement in his voice.

His mouth was too close. Memory was vivid of his kisses. She blinked, watching him study her with a sardonic gaze as he pulled the hood closer.

"The only danger we have here is of that hood slipping away and your hair showing. Then we would draw his attention. Few women in town have hair the color of spun gold. As it is, he wouldn't guess you could be on this horse."

With each word Rafferty's voice lowered to a still huskier depth. She forgot her argument, but it was impossible to forget the danger. Her heart pounded, for she knew Lazare.

She heard the wagon draw abreast. Her forehead touched Rafferty's chest and she held her breath, not daring to glance toward the Galliard carriage. She could feel the warmth of Rafferty, catch the scent of his cambric shirt. The carriage moved past, the sound of the horses and wheels diminishing. She sighed with relief and peeked over Rafe's shoulder to peer at the carriage. It had reached the end of the street, and now swung in a wide circle.

"They're turning around!"

He glanced over his shoulder. "There's no way he could have recognized you."

"But could he have recognized *you*?"

The carriage picked up speed. "I don't think so, but we won't wait to find out. Hold on." He tightened his arm around her waist and flicked the reins. In minutes they were streaking past houses. Feeling she would be unseated from her precarious perch, Chantal slid her arms around Rafferty and clung to him. She burned with embarrassment at holding him thus, but more than half her attention was on the hard, lean body she held.

When Rafferty finally slowed, she rose up to look over his shoulder. She turned around, shifting her voluminous skirts. Thankful she hadn't worn hoops and crinoline, she slid her leg across the horse to ride astride. She couldn't continue to cling to this man, as if she were a trollop. She shook away the hood and inhaled. "We're in what was Lafayette, and we'll go through Jefferson."

"And south of here is the Irish Channel." Slowing the horse to a walk, Rafferty turned to look behind them. With their bodies still pressed together, she was aware of every moment he made.

"The city is changing. When I was a child, Jackson Square was known as the Place D'Armes. Now city hall has moved to Lafayette Square. Papa says the Americans take over more every day, and someday the Creoles will be forgotten."

"Never. Not in this corner of the world. Which came first," he asked, speaking close to her ear, "the French or the Spanish?"

"Spanish explored here, but the French were the first to settle. Pierre le Moyne, Sieur d'Iberville, and his brother, Jean Baptiste, Sieur de Bienville established a settlement named after the Duc d'Orleans, the French regent," she said, repeating what she knew by rote while all her awareness was on his warm breath against her nape. "My family came almost one hundred years ago. Maurice Therrie was the first; he was murdered on the Trace. Grand-père fought with Andrew Jackson in the Battle of New Orleans."

They rode to the outskirts and angled north. He smoothed a stray lock of hair behind her ear. Every movement of the horse shifted their bodies against each other, and her awareness of him was growing intense.

"We pass Étienne Boré's plantation," she said, feeling fluttery as Rafe's breath tickled her nape. "He's the one who found a way to granulate sugar, and the sugar industry grew."

"We're safe now," Rafe said, keeping his arm around her waist. The night was cool and pleasant, with the only sounds the deep chant of frogs and the steady clop of the horse's hooves. Fireflies winked against the dark woods lining the river road, while silvery moonbeams danced across the ebony ribbon of water.

"Lazare is not a man to cross. I know what he would do if he discovered us."

"What?" Rafferty asked, sounding amused.

"He would kill you. You don't worry sufficiently, sir." She twisted to look at him. "I have heard rumors that he had you beaten for saving me that day at Louvierre plantation."

"Have you asked him about the rumors?"

"He changed the subject."

With a flash of white teeth, Rafferty laughed. "Good idea. Now you'll have to tell me where you live."

It surprised her to find someone who didn't know the location of the Therrie home. "Stay on the river road until I tell you to turn. My great-grandfather built the original house, and then Grand-père enlarged it."

"Is your grandfather still alive?"

"Yes. Grand-père Therrie is. He has a house in the Vieux Carré, because from there he can walk to the Merchants' Exchange and the Gem, the bar across the street from the Exchange, and the Absinthe House. He can sit with his cronies in the lobby of the St. Louis Hotel or go to the cockfights on Dumaine, and sometimes he goes to the races with Papa. Sometimes he stays at Belle Destin, but it's seldom."

"So finish telling me about the house."

"When I was a baby, Belle Destin burned. I had an older sister, Honoria, who died in the fire."

"Were you too young to remember her?"

"I was only a year old. I don't remember anything about it, and Alain seldom talks about it. I wish I had known her, and I wish I'd known my real mother. Papa rebuilt the house and made it larger. Now he's added improvements, and we have water piped to the house. When my brother, Alain, married Diantha, Papa bought land north of us, and Alain lives there. Papa and M'sieu Galliard bought land for a wedding gift for Lazare and me. They're building a house— Soleil Plantation."

"Sunshine."

"I named it, because it is sunshine to me. I want it more than I've ever wanted anything. I want my own family."

"You talk as if you haven't come from a happy home, yet from all you've said yours is a happy family."

"Not always. Papa keeps things to himself, but there are tensions. And my stepmother. . ." Chantal shrugged. "It isn't what I want for *my* family and *my* home." After a moment of silence she added, "I've heard other rumors about you."

"How's that?"

"I've heard you own one slave, but you treat him as a free man."

"Tobiah Barr. I told you about him. He's the man from Haiti who saved me on the ship. And you heard correctly. Louisiana law won't allow me to free him now. When he helped me on board ship, I bought him."

"I've never known anyone who freed his slaves. But the people I know are men like Papa, with fields of cotton or sugar to care for, and slaves are needed."

"I wouldn't want to be owned," Rafferty said. "And you wouldn't either."

She laughed. "I *am* owned! Women have little more freedom than slaves!" She glanced over her shoulder at him. The corner of his mouth was raised in a half-smile, giving him a rakish air. She turned away at once. It was safer to look down the darkened road ahead than to gaze into his startling blue eyes.

"You can do as you please," he argued. "Follow your brother to town and spy on him; you can—"

"Merciful angels, if anyone other than you had discovered me tonight, I would have scandalized the family and brought down my father and stepmother's wrath! I must do what Papa says!"

"Why do I doubt that?"

"You know I have to, and when I marry I'll have to obey my husband."

"Were I your husband, I know how I would want you to obey me," he said in that deeper voice that made her feel as if something warm had moved deep inside her. He leaned close and his breath tickled her nape.

"Sir! You must stop!"

"Stop what, Chantal?" he drawled.

"You know you're doing brazen things you shouldn't!"

He chuckled. "Propriety and protests can vanish in the blink of an eye!"

"You're the most exasperating man!"

"And you're the most intriguing woman," he said, sounding merry.

She laughed. "You don't know me well enough to find me intriguing!"

"Yes, I do, Chantal. No other woman roams over rooftops. No other woman would react as you did that afternoon we met. You turned your horse in time in a very collected manner. And when I opened my eyes . . . I shall never forget you."

Her face was hot. She wrapped her fingers in the coarse mane of the horse and hoped Rafferty couldn't hear her pounding heart.

"There's our road," she said.

He turned the horse. "The ride is far too short. I'll think about you all the way home now," he whispered, close enough for his breath to fan over her ear.

"I can imagine the number of ladies you say such things to. We won't see each other again."

She turned to look at him and he caught her chin, his finger warm and his touch so light, compelling her to look into his eyes. As they rode out from beneath branches of oak, moonlight splashed his features, and his solemn expression made her heart lurch.

"I told you, Chantal, we will know each other. We'll see each other again."

"Sir, you are bold and brash and stubborn. And you are also wrong," she retorted, but the words held a hollow ring, and were belied by the prickling across her skin as she stared up at him. "Rafferty O'Brien," she whispered, feeling a strangeness, a momentary fear that what he said might indeed prove true. "Don't upset my life," she whispered.

"I told you, I won't ever hurt you," he said, running his finger along her cheek.

She had seen Auntie Bella draw circles in the dirt and chant. Whenever she asked what she was doing, her broad face would break into a patient smile. "Protecting against ha'nts," she would answer. Papa had said it was all foolishness, that there were no ghosts at Belle Destin or anywhere else, but at this moment Chantal felt she should draw a circle, and wished she knew a chant to protect her from Rafferty O'Brien. He wasn't a ghost, but he frightened her in a way she had never been frightened before. Her life was orderly, planned, while Rafferty O'Brien was as wild as a windstorm.

She turned around. "You should leave the road and circle to the north. There's an oak outside my room, and I'd rather climb in there than risk one of the servants seeing me slip in the door."

"Does anything frighten you?"

"Of course! Papa frightens me, and the bayous and the river." She couldn't tell Rafferty that *he* frightened her.

"Can you swim?"

She shook her head. "No, and I'm careful to stay back from the river's edge. Water terrifies me. Now go this way. There's Belle Destin," she said, seeing the white columns through the trees up the slope of lawn, two hundred yards from the river.

"Your home is grand," he said, and she detected a strange tone in his voice. She wondered if he was comparing it with his own small room. She looked at the familiar two-tiered, pedimented portico that surrounded the house, with its thirty-two massive Doric columns. The Greek Revival house was made of brick that had been fired on the property. Rectangular lights surrounded the door, and jib windows opened onto the front. There was a *pigeonnier,* the pigeon house, and a *garçonnière,* the bachelor sons' house, in front of the big house, and a statue hewn from Carraran marble in the center of a round flowerbed.

Chantal loved Belle Destin, but it was as much a part of her life as her dresses. She gave little thought to its grandeur, feeling comfortable and satisfied within its sheltering walls. Rafferty O'Brien owned no home. It must be dreadful, Chantal thought, to be uprooted from one's native land, to lose one's family and possessions at sea, to have only one tiny room. She would have been in tears every day. "I'm sorry you lost everything at sea," she said, twisting around to look up at him.

Each time an emotion prompted her to face him, she became lost in the captivating gaze that made her forget all else, except her intense awareness that he was male and she was female.

"I'll have a home and a family again, and my brothers will get here someday. We'll be reunited."

"Don't you have doubts?"

"Not about things I feel with all my heart."

She felt shaken again by the quiet determination underlying his words. How could he be so certain? He was a strange man, undaunted and entirely positive. She hadn't known anyone like him. She wondered about the beating. Lazare wouldn't discuss it and neither would Rafferty O'Brien. If Lazare had had Rafferty beaten, he would have told her of it in scathing terms, saying that the rascal deserved it. He hadn't done so, which made her wonder. What had happened to stir such a rumor? What really had transpired between the two? And how had Rafferty O'Brien acquired the scar across his cheek and ear and jaw? She knew it hadn't been there at their first encounter.

"Stop where it's dark. There's the oak, and see, it leads to my window," she said, pointing to a curved oak that looked as if someone had trained it to grow toward the house.

"How many times have you used this path out of your room?"

"Too many!" She laughed.

"And how many times have you been caught?" he asked, dropping to the ground and reaching up to put his hands to her waist and lift her down. His hands remained there, and they stood in the darkness beneath the drooping limbs of the oak. His face was in shadows and she couldn't see his expression.

"I haven't been caught. Thank you, Mr. O'Brien, for coming to my rescue."

He placed his finger on her lips in a touch that, while light as a feather, tingled every nerve. "Chantal, call me Rafferty."

"It isn't proper, and I barely know you, sir. I think of you as Mr. O'Brien."

"Do you now?" he asked, his voice changing like quicksilver from solemnity to a dancing amusement. "Do you think of 'Mr. O'Brien' when I do this?" he asked, as he leaned down and covered her mouth with his, pulling her against him.

Thoughts spun away out of control, and she placed her hands against his solid chest as his kiss scalded and stirred a hot longing in her. She couldn't resist such kisses, kisses that made her heart pound and thought cease. *But he shouldn't . . .*

She pushed against him. "Sir! I must go inside. Thank you for saving me." She felt hot with embarrassment, and with emotions she didn't want to acknowledge. Get away from him. He was more wizard than man, turning her world topsy-turvy. She ran off and crawled up the wide trunk of the oak, which bent as if designed as a passage from the upper story to the ground. Rafe stood with his arms akimbo, watching her. As she swung her leg over the sill her skirt fell back, revealing her leg from her knee to her ankle.

When she had stepped into her room, he swung up into the saddle and waved at her. She felt a strange mixture of emotions. Longing, confusion, and beneath it all, fear. This strange man sounded so certain that he would see her again. As if there couldn't be a doubt in anyone's mind.

As she dropped her cape on the floor she felt sadness envelop her, for as surely as Rafferty O'Brien was riding away from Belle Destin, Lazare would sooner or later call him out and kill him.

"No, it's ridiculous!" she protested to the empty room. "I *won't* see him again! Mr. O'Brien is a man filled with dreams!" But it wouldn't do. Chantal knew in her heart that no mere dreamer would step in front of a galloping horse and try to alter its path. Or scramble up an iron railing after someone in trouble.

As for Alain and the Vigilantes—there was *real* trouble! He would be enraged when he discovered she had spied on him. The Vigilance Committee thought the Know-Nothings wanted to overthrow the whole existing political system. With election day four months away, the Vigilance Committee was determined to stop them.

Chantal tossed aside her garments and pulled on a high-necked white batiste gown, before climbing into her canopied bed. She realized that, as the committee's leader, Alain was in terrible danger. Their candidate for mayor, Major Beauregard, the supervising architect for the Custom House, had been at the meeting, and he was a friend of her father's, a man who had been entertained in Belle Destin's parlor. He was well liked and respected. Lazare was urging his friends to vote for Gerard Stith, the Know-Nothing candidate. But slowly politics faded from Chantal's thoughts; she stared into darkness, as a vision danced before her of Rafferty O'Brien leaning forward to kiss her.

Rafferty O'Brien was a dangerous intrusion into her orderly life. Dangerous and exciting. She tingled with memories. Tomorrow she would shut away all thoughts of him, but tonight she wanted to remember his hot kisses, his compelling blue eyes.

She groaned and rolled over, her body heated and aching.

It' was the first of the next week when Alain appeared at Belle Destin. The moment Chantal managed to get him alone, she closed the library doors. She dreaded confronting him, but she had to change his mind about his politics.

With black hair and brown eyes identical to her father's, Alain strode across the room and flopped down on a leather wingback chair. He looked amused as he withdrew a cheroot to light it. "What now, Chantal? What have I done this time?"

Keeping a chair between herself and her brother, she turned to face him. "You're involved in a dangerous matter, and I'm going to tell Papa if you continue." The words spilled out too fast. "I know about the Vigilance Committee, and I know what you plan to do."

His mouth dropped open, and he stared at her until the flame from the match burned his fingers. "Dammit!" He shook out the match and tossed the cheroot into the fireplace. Chantal's heartbeat quickened as he stood up and frowned. "How do you know what we plan? Not even Diantha knows that. How do you even know I've joined the Vigilance Committee?"

"I hear things. I know the Vigilantes are going to interfere in the next election. They want to stop the Democrats and the Know-Nothings."

"Dammit to hell!" He crossed the room, and she danced away behind the desk. He came after her.

"Alain, let me alone, or I'll run to Papa!"

"Damn you!" He vaulted a settee and caught her wrist, spinning her around. "You had one of the servants follow me to a meeting! We wondered who the spy was!"

"No! Let me go, Alain!"

"You little baggage!" he exclaimed, scowling and releasing her. "Which servant did you send?"

"I didn't send anyone!" She struggled, and his brown eyes blazed with fury.

"I'll have his hide flayed off his back. You tell me now!"

"No!" She felt a rising panic. "Alain, you could get killed if you join men who want to overthrow our city government!"

"Tell me *now,* dammit!" He pursued her around the desk again until he caught his toe on the foot of the desk and stumbled, whacking his shin on the desk.

"Dammit to hell!"

The door burst open, and Amity rushed into the room. "What—Alain! Alain, did you hurt Chantal?"

"Does it look as if I hurt her?" he ground out beneath clenched teeth, rubbing his shin. "Ask about *my* welfare, dammit!"

"Amity, I'm all right," Chantal said.

The door was pushed open wider, and Maman entered. "What in heaven's name is all this fracas? It sounds as if a common street fight is occurring in our library." She closed the door behind her. "Alain, what's going on here?"

"This is between Chantal and me! It's not for children to hear," Alain said in a tight voice. He appeared angrier than ever. Not since they were children had he chased her. And now Maman was into it. The worst that could happen would be the meddling of their stepmother.

"Amity, leave the room!" Maman ordered.

Amity blinked and looked at Chantal, as if to assure herself she was all right. When Chantal nodded, Amity left the room and closed the door. Maman crossed the room. "What's going on here?"

"My little sister sent one of the servants to town to spy on me at a political meeting. It caused all kinds of trouble, and now she's protecting the slave and won't tell me which one."

Step-Maman stood in front of Chantal; all Chantal

could feel was dislike, and she could see it mirrored in her stepmother's eyes. Chantal felt the tension; Papa had taught her years ago to address her stepmother as Maman, but she was Step-Maman in Chantal's heart and she would always be.

Maman slapped her. The blow made a smack in the quiet room. Her stepmother leaned forward. "Whom did you send?"

"I can't tell you," Chantal said, feeling tears threaten and hating to cry. "I'll discuss it with Papa."

"And he'll side with you, as he always does," Maman snapped, and Chantal knew that was just part of the constant clash with her stepmother. There had always been friction between them. With a rustle of her lavender silk dress, her stepmother moved away. "You may as well give up, Alain. The little chit knows she can twist her father as she pleases."

"Papa will listen to reason, and Alain's life may be in danger," Chantal said.

Maman arched her auburn brows, her painted red lips pursing. "You're risking your life, Alain? What have we here? What's underfoot?"

"It's politics. Mayor Waterman refuses to run again," Alain replied. "So far, the Democrats have no candidate. That leaves Gerard Stith, the Know-Nothing candidate, with an unchallenged victory, making the Know-Nothing party stronger than ever. A group has developed to try to reform our system. Chantal is full of foolishness, and I'm damned angry that she sent someone to spy on me. It could have caused me embarrassment if one of Belle Destin's slaves had been discoverèd. And he almost *was* caught. We chased him for blocks. He had long skinny legs and could run like the devil, but that describes half the men at Belle Destin."

"You might as well yield, Alain, unless you intend to beat it out of her and then face your father's wrath. Unfortunately, he doesn't believe we females should receive beatings." She looked at Chantal with a malevolent gleam. "But once you marry, little Chantal, you'll find your husband has no such qualms."

"Lazare would never hurt me!"

Maman laughed and left the room, closing the door behind her.

"Tell me, dammit! Who was it?" Alain caught Chantal's shoulders. "Tell me!"

"I can't tell you! And you let go of me!"

He released her and stomped away. "I don't suppose it will help to ask you to keep what you've learned to yourself?"

"I don't want you killed!" she said, wiping her eyes.

His face flushed and he bit his lip. "Confound it, Chantal, I'm sorry I lost my temper. Damn, if you just knew how embarrassing it could have been if one of Belle Destin's slaves had been caught eavesdropping. You know what his punishment would have been."

"Alain, please reconsider joining the Vigilantes. There's bound to be bloodshed."

"You're a woman, and ignorant when it comes to elections. Issues are growing more important. There are anti-slavery agitators, and this state can't exist without slavery. Whoever listened to us probably didn't understand what he heard. I have half a notion to have old William whipped just to set an example."

"You know it wasn't him! William is as old as Grand-père! You couldn't be so cruel!"

Alain rubbed his forehead and frowned. "No, I couldn't. But you're meddling in something you shouldn't. You know Papa's a staunch Democrat and he'll never change. There have to be reforms in our system. We had 'King John' Slidell's men floating down the bayous, voting over and over again. Judah Benjamin's aides gave cash to buy carriage licenses so men would be considered property owners and could vote. Men have to go to the polls armed, and some come away cut to ribbons and still not having cast their vote. Do you think that's right?"

"No! But from what I've heard about the Vigilantes, you intend to take over by force. Is that the answer to force?"

"Sometimes it has to be," he said bitterly.

"You *know* that isn't a good solution. Please be careful, Alain!"

He inhaled deeply, making his chest expand. She thought about Rafferty O'Brien, who probably was half a foot taller than her stocky brother. A lock of Alain's straight black hair fell across his forehead, tanned from days of riding over his fields in the sun. He crossed the room to stand in front of her.

"You've really angered me, Chantal. Do you have to tell Papa?"

"I'm frightened for you," she said, wary of his volatile temper, but frightened for her brother.

"Look, I'll urge the Vigilantes to a more prudent course. Before you go to Papa with this, give me time to see if I can persuade my friends. Major Beauregard is our candidate, and you know he has an impressive record. He's a fine man." Alain pushed open his coat and placed his hands on his hips. "Dammit, you mother me, Chantal, even though you're younger than I am!"

"I wonder what would have happened if our mother had lived. Of course, then we wouldn't have had Amity."

"We have a mother—the only one you've ever really known. I barely remember Celine—just as a pretty woman who sang to me. Anyway, once my mind is made up about my politics, Papa won't be able to stop me."

"Diantha must be near a collapse."

"Don't you worry her! She knows nothing about my politics, and I intend to keep it that way!" He glared at Chantal and then, his square jaw thrust out, he left the room. His temper had grown shorter with the years. When they were children he would turn on her, exploding in fury, chasing her and yelling at her, but it was always over soon and he seldom hurt her. Now he was in danger, and she was frightened for him. Would he urge his friends to change their plans? She doubted it, but she would wait and see.

She rubbed her arm and looked outside. A servant was spading a front bed where azaleas and camellias would soon bloom. Where was Rafferty O'Brien at this moment? Who were the women in his life? With his manner and looks, there had to be women. Would she ever see him again?

Two weeks later, on a Tuesday evening the twenty-third of February, as Chantal played the piano in the parlor on the second floor of the house in the Vieux Carré, the butler crossed to her father to lean down and speak to him.

Ormonde Therrie nodded to the man, then rose from his seat cursing. "Dammit! Summon my carriage."

As Chantal lifted her fingers from the keys, Maman looked around. "What is it, Ormonde?"

"I need to go," he answered, in his accustomed cryptic manner.

"Why do you need to leave?" her stepmother persisted. How many hundreds of times had the two of them traded these same questions and answers? Her taciturn father invariably kept his problems to himself, unless someone managed to pry some answers from him.

"The mare I bought this morning," he replied, pulling on his coat. "She's having difficulty, and Saxton says he's losing them both."

"What did she cost you?"

"Too damned much if she dies! I'm going to the stable."

"My foal may die," Chantal said, standing up. Her father had promised her the first foal. "I want to go with you."

"It isn't proper for you to be in a stable with men and the mare trying to deliver," Maman said.

"I'm there at Belle Destin when the mares foal. Amity helps."

"That's different. The public is allowed in the livery stable," Maman replied.

"I've been there before," Chantal said. "Please, Maman? Please, Papa, let me come along! It's my horse, too, Maman!"

"Blaise?" he asked.

"Ormonde, you spoil the girl silly!"

"It'll be all right. Come along, Chantal." He clamped his jaw shut and strode to the hall.

"It's all right, Maman!" Chantal flung over her shoulder, as she rushed to keep up with her father's long stride.

"Damn that Saxton! He's lost three foals and one mare of mine."

Chantal scrambled into the carriage and as they rode through the Vieux Carré, she kept quiet, knowing her father preferred silence. Did he ever share his innermost thoughts and worries with Maman? He never did in front of the family, and he shared little of himself with his children. Now he gazed out the window, and the moment they had reached the livery stable he bounded out of the carriage and strode toward the wide door.

Yellow light spilled out, and men stepped aside for him. Men always moved out of his way, unless they were close friends, in which case they acknowledged him with hearty greetings. Women turned to look at him. Chantal hurried beside him. His straight nose, deep brown eyes, and square jaw gave him a handsome face, but sometimes when she studied him she felt it was more his manner than his looks that made people turn to stare.

"Sir, Mr. Therrie," Thomas Cregan, the stable owner said, rushing to meet them and yanking off his cap. "Sir, the foal's about dead. Mr. Saxton gave up, and a man who was watching said he could save the foal. He said the mare may die, and Mr. Saxton said she would."

"Confound it all! Saxton stopped caring for my horse? Is another man delivering the foal?"

"He's trying, sir. He said he knows horses. Sir, we did the best we could for her. She's been in trouble from the start."

"All right, all right." A circle of men were gathered around the stall and lanterns hung on hooks, lighting it. Smells of hay and horses assailed Chantal as she crossed the hard-packed floor beside her father.

The crowd melted away and she moved forward with her father, until they were standing at the open door of the stall looking down at a man bent over the prone mare. His arm was inside the mare as he worked. Perspiration beaded his face and his sleeves were rolled high; his black hair curled damply over his forehead.

Chantal gasped for breath. Rafferty O'Brien struggled to help the mare deliver the foal. Many times over, Chantal had wondered if and when she would see him again. Now he was only a few feet away, working to save a colt that would be hers if it survived.

Suddenly the foal's legs appeared, and then the small body came out, and Rafe stripped away the afterbirth. The baby unfolded its long, spindly legs and, after several unsuccessful attempts, managed to stand, its stubby tail switching while Rafferty cared for the mare.

"Tobiah, let's get cold water in here," he ordered, and a tall black man moved away. Drenched in sweat, Rafferty O'Brien's shirt clung to his body. As he knelt, his denim pants molded themselves to his long legs. Men rushed to do as he asked, and finally he stood up and wiped his brow. "I'll stay with her tonight."

"It's my horse, and *I'll* stay!" Saxton said, coming out of a corner. Both men had their backs to Chantal and Ormonde.

"You almost killed that foal!" Rafferty snapped. "I'll sit with her."

"She's not your horse! I've been hired to tend to her care!"

"Hell of a lot of care you gave!"

"Damn you Irish trash!" Saxton said, yanking on Rafe's shoulder. He slammed his fist into his jaw, and Rafe fell back. He lurched and twisted to avoid falling on the colt, crashing against the side of the stable.

"Saxton! Stop this this instant!" Ormonde Therrie's cold voice stung the air like a lash.

Both men turned, and Chantal once again looked into Rafferty O'Brien's blue eyes.

Chapter 6

"Mr. Therrie!" Saxton exclaimed. "Sir, you have a new foal. I had assistance here."

"Begging your pardon, sir," a man said at Ormonde's elbow, "but the wee one was in a bad way. One leg came out, and he couldn't be birthed until Mr. O'Brien worked on the mare."

"Sir, I—"

"That's enough, Saxton. You're dismissed. Come to my office tomorrow to collect your wages."

The man opened his mouth to speak, snapped it shut, and pushed through the crowd. Ormonde faced Rafferty O'Brien.

"What's your name?"

"Rafferty O'Brien," he answered clearly, without glancing Chantal's way. She felt her cheeks grow hot, just remembering her moments with him.

"Where did you learn about horses?"

"I grew up on a farm in Ireland, sir. My father bred and raced horses."

"What kind of farming?"

"We grew barley and raised hogs and horses. We were on the sea, so we fished as well," Rafferty answered, still keeping his eyes on Ormonde. He withdrew a handkerchief to mop his brow while a man handed him a tin cup of water.

"Thanks, Tobiah." Rafe glanced down at the mare. "We need to get her cooled down," he said to the stableboy. Another man knelt beside the mare and began to sponge her off.

"How long have you lived here?"

"I arrived last December from Ireland."

"You're married?"

"No, sir. I came with my mother and brothers, but the ship went down. My mother died, and I was separated from my brothers."

"Do you miss the farming?" Ormonde persisted. Chantal glanced up at him. Why this unaccustomed interest in a mere farm hand?

"Yes, sir. We grew up on the farm, and have never been away from it until now. This is a fine horse, sir."

"She's supposed to be. Did you come because your crops failed?"

"No, sir. We had ill fortune, and my mother's health failed. We hoped to bring her to a warmer climate." For the first time in the conversation he glanced at Chantal. It was momentary, so brief, yet it stopped her breathing and made her more self-conscious.

"What type horses did your father own?"

"Arabian. The stallions could be traced back to Matchem. We had two fine brood mare sires."

"What sort of work do you do?"

"I've hired out to do roadwork, but that's temporary."

What was Papa doing? Why all the questions? Since it involved Rafferty O'Brien, Chantal found the questioning to be unnerving. Papa chatted only with close friends, unless it was a political discussion or business. So why did he want to know more about Rafferty?

She felt afraid. Could he have heard about her night of spying and the long ride home with Rafferty O'Brien? Papa's brow was dotted with perspiration. In his fancy coat and shirt, he had to be on fire.

"Where were you educated?"

"My father sent me to England for two years."

"That accounts for your speech. I'm losing my overseer. Would you be interested in coming to Belle Destin and talking to me about the job?"

Chantal felt as if the earth beneath her feet had just shifted. Stunned by the thought that Rafferty O'Brien soon might be living at Belle Destin, she felt a prickling across her nape. He had been so positive he would see her again, and now Papa was offering a job that would move him to the plantation. If he felt surprise, it didn't show. Something flickered in his blue eyes, and a corner of his mouth lifted in a faint smile.

"Yes, sir, Mr. Therrie, I would be very interested."

"Good. Thursday morning at nine o'clock I'll be back at Belle Destin. It's along the river road. Just ask. Anyone can tell you how to get to Belle Destin."

Blue eyes shifted to her. "Someone has already told me how to get there," he said. "I couldn't possibly forget."

Her heart missed what seemed like several beats. Merciful angel, the man was bold! And he was going to live at Belle Destin! She felt hot and dizzy, and didn't hear anymore of the conversation between her father and Rafferty until her father took her by the arm. "Chantal, this is Mr. O'Brien, who may be our new overseer. Mr. O'Brien, this is Miss Therrie, my daughter."

"Actually, we've met," Rafferty replied politely, but amusement danced in his eyes. "Although Miss Therrie may not remember me. Her horse was about to take a jump over a wall."

"Oh, my!" She felt confused, embarrassed, and foolish. *What is it that he does to me?* She had been so busy worrying about their last meeting she hadn't thought about the first, which could easily have gotten back to Papa.

"I'm sorry, Mr. O'Brien. I was in shock." Her father was giving her a keen-eyed gaze that she didn't relish. "Lazare and I were racing on the day of the picnic, and I was going to jump a wall," she explained to him. "I didn't know the ground had been dug away on the other side. Mr. O'Brien stepped into Caesar's path and was knocked down for his efforts."

"I owe you twice, then," Ormonde said.

"It was merely a matter of turning her horse. I look forward to our meeting, sir," he said.

"I'll compensate you for all you've done for me tonight. We'll discuss it Thursday."

"Yes, sir."

"I'd appreciate it if you'd look after the mare and foal until I can get them moved to Belle Destin. I just purchased her, and it was too late to move her."

"Yes, sir."

"Till Thursday morning, Mr. O'Brien," Ormonde said and turned to go, taking Chantal's arm. She glanced at Rafferty, who gave her a mocking smile.

Her cheeks on fire, she turned away. Rafferty O'Brien would live at Belle Destin. She might well see him daily. What a threat that would be to her peaceful world!

She glanced back to where he stood outside the stall, his hands on his hips as he watched her. At the door to the carriage she couldn't resist one last look. Rafe was out of sight, and she guessed he must be with the mare.

"Papa, you barely know the man!" Chantal protested once the carriage was under way.

"True, Chantal, but I know men. There are indications of a man's ability. He saved the foal and the mare. He didn't know he would get a penny for his efforts, yet he was willing to fight Saxton to protect my horse. That's a good man. He's educated, intelligent, and knows how to use his wits. And he knows farming."

"I doubt if he's ever even seen a cotton plant!"

Ormonde's features relaxed into a smile. Papa was a handsome man, and she knew why all her friends' mothers paid so much attention to him. When he smiled, he looked particularly debonair.

"It won't take a smart man long to learn. Chantal, how could you forget him if he saved you from a terrible fall?"

"I only saw him for a few minutes," she said stiffly, feeling a flush in her cheeks. "Lazare and I rode away. I didn't remember."

"It makes you sound ungrateful. The man may have saved your horse from destruction, and God only knows what would have happened to you."

"Yes, Papa," she said with a sigh.

"You sound as if you don't approve of my hiring him."

"Oh, no! It's just that he's a stranger."

The words rang hollow and her father's gaze narrowed, causing her to look out the window. Rafferty O'Brien at Belle Destin. Living only yards from the house. The mere prospect made her fluttery.

"I suspect Mr. O'Brien can move in at once, from what he said. The poor fellow lost all his family at sea," Ormonde said.

"He thinks his brothers survived."

"He didn't say that. He just said they were separated."

"Oh, I thought he meant they survived as well."

"Perhaps," he replied, giving her another curious look.

"What shall we name the foal?"

"He's yours, Chantal. So you may name him." Ormonde settled back on the seat. "Now I can relax. I have a new overseer."

And I have a multitude of new problems. Several blocks later, her thoughts shifted to Alain. Now that she had Papa alone it would be a good chance to discuss the Vigilantes, but she had promised to give Alain time, so she would wait.

"How were things up north?"

"The same as always," he answered, and they passed the remainder of the journey in silence.

At nine o'clock Thursday morning, Chantal sat on a rocker on the upstairs gallery and watched the oak-lined drive. *He'll see you waiting. Go inside,* she told herself. *There's time to go inside when he first appears.* The mental argument continued until she saw him approach on the big bay. *Go inside, so he won't see you!*

"Is that the new overseer?"

Stepping outside, Maman wore white organza, with her auburn hair caught in a full bun on the back of her head. She moved to the rail and leaned against a column to watch him.

"We should go in and stop staring at him, as if he were a curiosity on display," Chantal said, glancing at her stepmother.

Maman laughed. "*You* were staring at him until I joined you. And he *is* a curiosity on display. My, is he a curiosity! Ormonde has told me about him, but he left out how handsome the man is."

Chantal felt the twinge of anger that always came where her stepmother and other men were concerned. "He's older."

"Perhaps to a green miss who's only seventeen he's old, but not to a woman. No, he looks young and strong and handsome. And Ormonde said he's educated. I can't believe it, an overseer educated in England? And handsome! What luck. Ormonde said Mr. O'Brien saved you from a fall." She twisted to look at Chantal.

"Yes, I was racing Lazare."

"Mr. O'Brien stepped into the path of your horse, and you didn't remember him?"

"I saw him very briefly."

"I heard Lazare had him whipped for saving you."

Merciful angel, Maman knew! Did Papa know? "Knowing that, I'm surprised Papa still wants to hire him."

"Your father doesn't know it. He was away. And I won't tell, because I want Mr. O'Brien to become overseer of Belle Destin," she drawled in her husky voice. "He should liven up the long hot days."

"He'll be out in the fields," Chantal said, hating the irritation Maman could arouse in her almost without effort. Maman gave her a mocking smile.

Rafferty approached the house. It would be unkind to go inside now without acknowledging seeing him. Chantal stood up and waved, and he waved in return. Out of the corner of her eye, she could see Maman wave. There were moments when she hated Maman. Then guilt came as always, because Papa loved Maman but Chantal didn't. The fact that Maman fawned over Papa annoyed Chantal, for when Papa wasn't present she flirted outrageously with other men. And she never cared if it was in front of Chantal or Amity. She knew she was safe. They would never tell Papa, because it would only hurt him.

Maman was beautiful with her alabaster skin and wide, green eyes, the thick auburn hair, but when she was angry her lips thinned, her skin flushed, and she looked like a witch. Once Amity asked Chantal if Maman had the biggest bosoms in Orleans Parish, and Chantal decided that perhaps she did.

Chantal entered the cool hall that ran from front to back to allow breezes to blow through the house. Rafferty O'Brien was downstairs talking to Papa. All she had to do to see him was walk downstairs.

"I'm going to meet him," Maman announced. "I might as well meet him now. Are you coming along?"

Torn between wanting to see him and feeling reluctant to watch her stepmother with Rafferty, Chantal hesitated. "No, you go ahead," she said, even though she wanted to see him.

Maman left with a swirl of skirts. Chantal waited a moment, then moved to the stairs. Maman entered the library. Chantal heard Rafferty O'Brien's deep voice. Her heart beat faster, and she felt as if disaster loomed over her. She was promised to Lazare, and another man shouldn't make her heart race and her breathing alter. He shouldn't invade her dreams. *He shouldn't live only yards away!*

She hurried out to the stable and asked Remi to saddle Caesar. In minutes she was riding away, turning down the lane away from the house toward the tangled, oak-filled land that was yet uncultivated. She wanted to be with Lazare, to have him flirt with her and kiss her and wipe out all the jarring images of a laughing, blue-eyed Irishman. Saturday night couldn't come too soon. "Lazare," she said aloud. "Lazare . . ."

In the Vieux Carré Lazare Galliard sprawled on the pale yellow satin settee. He had tossed his coat aside, and squinted slightly as smoke from his cheroot rose in front of his face. Two oil lamps burned, and the corners of the spacious bedroom were in shadows.

"It was so urgent I see you tonight?" he asked, feeling annoyed. "You ran a risk sending a message to me. Although you don't run the risk I do in coming here to see you. And why are you in town?" He felt the brandy heat his stomach. When he had been summoned by a sealed note, he had left a successful game of faro. It was two in the morning, yet risk hovered at the edge of thought and gave an added dollop of excitement. And guilt.

He had sworn to himself he wouldn't see her again. It was dangerous beyond words, for he would lose everything if discovered. How many months now since he had been with her? Five months and two weeks. And he had sworn never again would he be alone with her, yet here he was. She swirled her brandy and reached up to unfasten the row of pearl buttons at her throat.

He felt his temperature rise as he watched. She licked her red lips and unfastened another button and another, finally pushing them open. He drew a deep breath, downing his brandy and tossing his cheroot into the fireplace. He crossed the room to her. He pushed open the dress, freeing her heavy, lush breasts and cupping them in his hands, their dusky tips hard beneath his thumbs. He bent his head to take a nipple in his mouth and bite gently, teasing her with his tongue.

"Damn you, I shouldn't be here. If we're caught I—"

"You will kill him. And I will be widowed."

He raised his head and wound his hand in her auburn hair and yanked her head back. "You'd like that, you vixen!"

Blaise Therrie smiled at him, unbuttoning his trousers and freeing him from their constraint. "You won't get caught. Ormonde is at Belle Destin, and he thinks I had to see my dressmaker."

"You're a lying bitch," Lazare murmured, burying his face against her breasts. He pushed the dress and chemise away, and she wore nothing else beneath them. He picked her up to carry her to the bed, then dropped her and rolled her over. He bent down to kiss behind her knees and work his way up her pale thighs. Moaning softly, she turned over.

"This is why you summoned me, isn't it?" he asked gruffly, placing his hand between her legs. "This is the secret, urgent news, isn't it?"

She laughed deep in her throat and then gasped as he kissed the moist softness between her thighs. He groaned and lay down to pull her on top of him and crush her in his arms, kissing her hard. She moved over him and he thrust into her, moving with her until she cried out and he gasped with pleasure.

Drenched in sweat, he rolled her beside him and lay still while their breathing returned to normal.

She trailed her fingers along his thigh. "Chantal doesn't deserve you, my love."

He felt a twinge of annoyance. He didn't like it when she talked about Chantal. His conscience nagged him. Nor did he like to hear Blaise call him "my love." There was something too proprietary about it.

He swung his long legs over the side of the bed and moved across the room to pour brandy into his glass. He took a sip and sat down on the settee, stretching out his legs. He still wore his shirt. He had tossed away his silk cravat and his collar, and unbuttoned the shirt. He watched Blaise stand up and move to the chifforobe. She brushed her long hair, as casual about walking around in front of him as if she were dressed instead of naked.

She refilled her glass with brandy. She was a damned beautiful woman. He couldn't think of anyone else who had the full breasts and tiny waist Blaise did. And the long legs to go with them. He thought of Jolie Fouquet and wondered for the thousandth time about her. He had offered her a princely sum and she had turned him down, the only woman who had ever turned him down. She had to be a whore to run a gambling house. Her rejection had stung at first, but then he had asked around and learned there were no men in her life. Rumor had it there had been one who was important. Still, Lazare was unaccustomed to rejection, and it was a goal to succeed in getting between her legs.

"How's your pretty little mistress?" Blaise asked.

"She's fine. Leave her alone. She's done nothing to bother you."

"You keep her shut away in that house, and the only times she goes out is occasional closed carriage rides in the country. You have a selfish streak, Lazare."

He laughed. "Listen to the grass call the tree green! There is only one person you love."

She laughed. "Perhaps it's better that way." She crossed the room to the bed and stretched out on the pillows in a provocative pose. He knew she was trying to tantalize and arouse him again. He sipped the brandy and stood up to pull on his trousers and boots.

"I'm going now. I don't want dawn to come and anyone to see me leave." He picked up the silk cravat and struggled to tie it.

"Dawn is hours away, and you know it."

"Damn, I can never tie these things. I need Benjamin."

"I'll do it." Sauntering to him, she stood in front of him.

He couldn't resist looking at her and caressing her. She slanted him a sultry look. "Shall I tie it or take it off again?"

"Tie it. You're a seductive temptress, and you do this to see how much power you have over me."

When she was finished she said, "There. That's as good as Benjamin does. But does he stand this close, without any clothes on, when he ties them for you?"

Lazare laughed and caressed her breast, leaning down to kiss her. Her hands slid up his legs, and he drew a deep breath and moved away. "Sometimes I wonder if you *want* me to get caught. If you want me to kill him for you. You'd like to own Belle Destin and not have to answer to Ormonde." Her amusement disappeared, and she pulled on a blue silk wrapper. He turned toward the door and picked up his hat.

"You're leaving without learning why I sent you the note."

He paused to turn around. She was seated on the

settee, her legs crossed, the wrapper falling open over her knees.

"There was more reason than this?"

"Yes. I know something I thought you might like to know. Of course sooner or later, you'll know it."

"What's that, Blaise? Did Ormonde tell you the Democrats don't have a candidate for mayor, or that there are rumors of a secret new group, the Vigilance Committee, with Pierre Beauregard as their candidate?"

She laughed. "Come give me one more kiss, Lazare, and I'll tell you."

His patience snapped. He didn't like to be toyed with, and he didn't like to be ordered around by anyone, save his father. He flung down the hat and crossed the room in long strides to yank her up. "Damn you, I'll kiss you when I want to!"

"And I'll tell you my news when I want to!" she snapped, breathing hard.

"You like it when you anger me, don't you?" he said, his temper shredding as he wound his fingers in her hair and pulled her head back. "Tell me!"

"You don't want to kiss me?" she asked, untying her sash and letting the gown fall open while she watched him with cat-green eyes.

He drew a deep breath and pulled her head to his, grinding his mouth on hers until her lip bled, wrapping his arms around her and bending over her until she clung to him and moaned. He released her and let her fall to the settee. She lay sprawled below him, and he wanted her again. He unbuttoned his trousers and pushed her to the floor to move between her legs and thrust into her, pounding her, feeling her hips move against him until he gasped with release and heard her cry out, feeling her fingers dig into his buttocks.

He stood up and straightened his clothes, buttoning his trousers. She pulled on the dressing gown and turned toward him, looking as lovely as ever, a satisfied smile on her face.

"I thought you would like to know," she said in her

husky voice, "that Ormonde just hired a new over-seer."

"What the hell do I care if he hired a damned over-seer? I knew all you wanted was to get me in your bed. Either that, or I'll walk out and find Ormonde riding up because you've summoned him. Ormonde is an excellent shot, and I don't want to tangle with my future father-in-law."

She laughed. "Sometimes, Lazare, you sound as if you hate me. Yet you don't act like you hate me."

"I don't hate you, that should be obvious. Good night, Blaise." He strode toward the door. Women were impossible to understand. Women and their games. Chantal was too innocent yet, and thank God, Delia was too well trained in pleasing a man to play games with him.

"Lazare," Blaise's voice floated after him as he stepped through the doorway. "Belle Destin's new overseer is a man named Rafferty O'Brien."

Chapter 7

Lazare felt shock, and then a slow-kindling anger. He stepped back into the bedroom and closed the door. Her smug smile fueled his temper.

"You're lying!" he said. She wasn't. She looked as if she had just imbibed champagne. "How did they meet?"

"Mr. O'Brien saved a foal and mare Ormonde had at the livery stable. Saxton had almost killed them."

"Why didn't you tell me sooner, dammit? If I had known and talked to Ormonde about that blasted Irishman, Ormonde wouldn't have hired him!"

"By the time I knew, he had already talked to the man about the job. He likes him."

"O'Brien will live at Belle Destin!" Lazare exclaimed in disbelief, feeling anger grow. Whereas he was chaperoned every moment with Chantal, the brash scum would be where he could see her almost daily.

"Yes, he lives at Belle Destin, yards from the main house. He sees Chantal, he can talk to Chantal. If he's clever, he can ride with her. You know how she loves to ride alone." Blaise's voice was soft, taunting. "And he's so handsome."

"Dammit to hell! I'm going to talk to Ormonde about the man! He can release him as swiftly as he hired him!"

"Only he won't. He thinks O'Brien is a marvel. He went to school in England, you know."

"How in blue blazes did an Irish peasant go to school in England?"

"He wasn't a peasant. Landed gentry."

"Then why is he here without anything?" Lazare

wanted to shake Blaise; she enjoyed tormenting him, and worming answers out of her was exasperating.

"He lost everything on the ship on the way over. He lost his family and money and possessions."

"Why would he leave Ireland if he had such a home?"

"His father gambled away the family home."

"You know a hell of a lot about him. Does he know a hell of a lot about you, like how you are in bed?"

She spun around and threw her brandy glass at him. He ducked and it smashed against the door.

"Temper, temper, love!" he said mockingly, feeling better to see someone angered along with him. He wanted to smash things himself, to break everything in the room. "O'Brien will be found dead on the river road some night."

"Oh no, Lazare! I don't want him killed. If that happens, I'll go straight to Ormonde and tell him what you threatened."

"If I denied it, Ormonde would believe me," Lazare replied, curiosity rising. "Why do you care so much? You want him for a lover?"

"He's a handsome man, and unusual. I haven't decided if I want him or not, but I want to be able to make the decision and not have you put a ball through his back on some dark road." She smiled. "Besides, his presence makes life interesting."

"Slut." Lazare threw open the door, slammed it behind him, and strode away. She raced to the door and flung it wide as he took the stairs two at a time. A vase crashed just above him, and he lengthened his stride. The only way out was past the slave quarters, but they knew everything that happened anyway. He ran across the courtyard, past the row of quarters, and through the back gate to mount his horse.

He rode a circuitous route away from Royal, to the narrow house on Rampart. When he entered the bedroom Delia came awake, looking sleepy, tousled, and tempting.

"M'sieu Galliard! I'm glad you're home," she said as she swung her feet to the floor. A demure chambray

gown covered her from throat to ankles. After leaving
Blaise, there was a refreshing quality to Delia.

"I'm tired, Delia, and I want a hot bath. You heat
some water, and I'll fetch the tub."

"Yes, sir," she answered, pulling on a blue organza
wrapper and scurrying past him. He heard the clatter
of a kettle and in minutes she was back to help him
undress. As she helped him unfasten and remove his
clothing, she threw her arms around his waist to hug
him. "I'm glad you're here," she whispered.

Stroking her back, he felt enveloped by a warm,
tender fondness for her that was almost as strong as
the feelings he had for Chantal.

Chantal and Rafferty O'Brien at Belle Destin . . .
Anger returned, and Lazare pushed Delia away. "I
need to soak in hot water, and pour me a dollop of
brandy."

"Yes, sir," she said, and left him alone.

As he soaked in the tub, his anger simmered at the
thought of the Irishman's being so close to Chantal.
Chantal was unpredictable, strong-willed, and Ormonde spoiled her. While Delia sponged him, Lazare
closed his eyes. When he married Chantal, he would
sap that strength of hers before she became as impossible to manage as Blaise.

Blaise relished manipulating men. Lazare knew that
Chantal would never use power the way Blaise did.
Chantal didn't hunger after men, but he didn't want to
marry a woman who had any self-will whatever. He
wanted a woman like Delia. He opened his eyes. Delia
leaned over him. Her sleeves were rolled above her
elbows and she sponged his chest, her eyes on her
task.

"Delia, take off your gown."

She paused, her gaze rising to meet his. She dropped
the sponge and stood up, drying her hands and unbuttoning the gown. Letting it fall around her feet, she
stepped out of it. He knew she was still embarrassed
to parade nude before him, but he liked to watch her
and he liked her to obey his orders without a whimper.
That's what he wanted from Chantal, and as soon as

they were married he intended to see that she understood and learned to obey him.

Delia knelt to continue sponging him off. He let his hand stray over her. She was slender, with much smaller breasts than Blaise or Chantal. If only Delia were the woman who held society's approval—and would inherit thousands of acres of prime cotton land. But not all the Galliard power or wealth would ever allow her to be accepted. Pity, because she was perfect in every other way. Everything she did she did to please him. Feeling a surge of fondness, he stroked her back, and her limpid dark eyes filled with warmth.

"Get in the tub," he commanded, feeling desire stir, reaching to help settle her with him. For tonight, he would forget Rafferty O'Brien and the problems he posed.

It was Saturday night, and Rafe and Touzet sat in the parlor at Jolie's while she opened a bottle of champagne.

"I've saved this bottle for a special occasion. I insist we drink this toast to our new landowner." She smiled, carrying two glasses of the pale bubbly liquid across the room to Rafe and Touzet. Her pale blue skirt swirled gently, the hoop swaying as she returned to fill her own glass. She faced them and Touzet stood, both raising their glasses as Rafe came to his feet. He couldn't resist a grin.

"Congratulations, Mr. O'Brien! This is a special moment in your rising career. May you acquire the house you want, and the business you want," Jolie said, her eyes sparkling.

They clinked their glasses, and Rafe drank the bubbling froth and leaned forward to kiss Jolie lightly on the cheek. "Thank you. It's probably covered in water, but I'm delighted, as both of you know. You know what I want, and this is a step in that direction and it makes me feel good."

They all sat down, and within minutes Jolie had poured another round. Rafe lifted his glass. "Here's to you, two of my closest friends. I hope you have good fortune this year.''

They raised glasses in the toast and drank, Touzet lowering his. ''And good fortune, for me, isn't a bit of swampland! Now if Jolie would accept a proposal of marriage—*Chèrie, veux-tu m'épouser?*''

She laughed. ''You tease, my darling Touzet! You have never been tied in matrimony, and I know you're not about to be so now.''

''*Ma chèrie! Au contraire!* You break men's hearts, and you break mine!''

''I don't break men's hearts,'' she said, looking down at her glass, and Rafe wondered about her. No one knew anything about her past. There were rumors that she had loved one man deeply, but no one knew what had happened, and no man's name had ever been linked with hers. She was a beautiful, charming woman, and he wondered about her solitary life.

''You break mine now, *amour de ma vie!* Such a waste of a beautiful woman. Well, if not marriage, perhaps a private game of cards?''

She laughed. ''If we set a limit on the hands, for I know our friend here is going out to take a look at his new property,'' she said.

Rafe grinned, thinking that her solitary life was a waste. And he guessed she had a continual stream of proposals, because she was as successful in her business as she was appealing. Who was the man who had hurt her so badly?

From an adjoining room, a small child with blond curls and blue eyes thrust her head into the room. ''Mrs. Fouquet?''

''Come in, Sharon. Sharon, this is Mr. O'Brien and M'sieu Lacquement. Gentlemen, Sharon is staying with me for a time, until we can locate her aunt who lives in Texas.''

The child bobbed her head and clung shyly to Jolie's knees.

''Sharon, if you'd like to watch us play cards, you may.''

"Yes, ma'am," she said softly, following Jolie to a table in one corner of the room.

"Jolie, I'd like you to join us when we look at my property," Rafe said as he crossed the room. "Tobiah is going to meet us here in an hour from now, and accompany us."

"Of course, Jolie. Ride with us. I'll hire a carriage if you'll come along."

She shook her head, as Rafe had suspected she would do. Always the cool one, she stayed slightly removed from people, yet he had heard about the little girl who had lost her mother recently. The mother worked next door and Rafe didn't know where the child had lived, but now she was staying temporarily with Jolie. And he knew this wasn't the first time Jolie had given help and shelter to others.

She moved to a table, and they joined her as she reached for a deck of cards. Rafe settled into a chair. She had taught him a new game, poker. One his father hadn't known, but one Rafe liked. It was seldom played in the gambling halls. And Jolie was as good a gambler as any O'Brien. They had something in common there.

An hour later, after losing to Jolie half the time and winning it all back the other half, Rafe mounted up and rode between Tobiah and Touzet, the three leaving town as the sun slanted in the sky. They headed north, and shadows grew long as they rode past swamps on both sides of the road. The moss-draped cypress trees were tall, their shade bringing night earlier, while the flat green water hid creatures swimming below. The steady croak of frogs added a bass chorus to the scene. Gradually the water disappeared and the land was weed-filled, water standing only in the low places.

Rafe held papers in his hand, and in the next mile they began to slow while he studied directions. He finally drew rein. "It's here. There's supposed to be a road." They rode back and forth searching for it.

"Rafe!" Tobiah shouted. A narrow path led from the road and disappeared under water and weeds.

"My property!" Rafe exclaimed, thinking of the

payment he had slipped across the desk to make certain he could register the deed in his name, even though he wasn't yet a United States citizen. He dismounted, splashing in the water and sending a black snake wriggling away. Rafe ignored it and held out his arms. "I'm a landowner!"

Touzet and Tobiah gave a whoop of merriment, and then Touzet pulled a bottle of brandy from his saddlebag and waved it in the air. "To our landowner, and the smallest plantation in the South, a kingdom of snakes and gators! Congratulations!"

Rafe strode across the ground, splashing with each step. Suddenly he sank to his knees and caught his balance quickly, stepping up out of a hole while Touzet doubled over and Tobiah tried to contain his laughter. Rafe grinned sheepishly and moved back to higher ground. He looked at Tobiah.

"It isn't much, but I own it."

"It's a start," Tobiah said. "I'd feel the same, and sometime soon I'm going to buy me a place. I want roots."

"Le début," Touzet said grandly, waving his arms. "The beginning." He opened the brandy and retrieved three glasses from his bag.

"Good enough," Rafe said, accepting a glass. He raised his high. "May you each have the same good fortune!" Touzet laughed and they all drank.

"So, now what will you do with this? Raise snakes?" Tobiah asked.

Rafe laughed. "Nothing. Just keep it until I know what I want to do with it. I'm satisfied just to know I own it, and I hope I can add to it. I want to look it over." He strode off, brandy in hand, and Tobiah and Touzet followed, wandering to higher ground to the northeast and then back to soggy mud.

By the time they had mounted to return to town, the second brandy bottle was empty. Touzet smashed one against a tree. "I crown thee, 'Le début'!"

"Well said and done," Rafe said. "Now let's go to town and see if we can add to our coffers."

Tobiah thrust out his hand. "Congratulations, sir.

This is a milestone, one of the things you wanted to accomplish.''

Rafe shook and gazed into solemn dark eyes. ''This is nothing, Tobiah. May we both have one hundred, no, one thousand times this.''

Tobiah grinned. ''I'm beginning to think some things are possible after all.''

''Indeed, my giant!'' Touzet said, looking up at Tobiah. ''Look at this land—grass, trees, water, snakes, and turtles. What more could you want?''

Rafe laughed and mounted, turning for home but glancing back once more over his shoulder. ''It's a sorry bit of swamp, but I like it. And I quit the road job.''

''To the man who saved my life!'' Tobiah added. ''Already you are far removed from the man who swam toward New Orleans with nothing in his pockets.''

Rafe grinned. His friends' teasing only added to his exhilaration. He surveyed his domain. It was a weed-filled, snake-infested semi-swamp, but he loved it.

''I have eleven thousand acres. Ninety-four hundred here, and the remainder up north,'' Ormonde Therrie said, riding beside Rafe along the edge of a field where wagonloads of cottonseed were being hauled from the ginhouse. Rafe watched workers moving along the plowed rows, starting to sow the seeds by hand. ''The original tract of land was ten arpents fronting the river by forty arpents in depth, bounded upstream by Canouet Bayou and bounded downstream by land held by Luc Gaudin, but my father bought more land and I've acquired more. In the early days we planted indigo and now our primary crop is cotton. Last season cotton brought nine cents a pound for medium varieties. I hope for a better price this season.''

''This is fine topsoil,'' Rafe remarked, gazing at the black clay. Less than a mile to the west was the wide Mississippi, and all the land he had seen at Belle Destin was rich and fertile.

''This is upland cotton. Sea island cotton brings better prices. Ours seldom gets above twelve cents. I hear you own a slave," Ormonde said. "You can put him to work in the field, unless you think he would be more suited to the house."

"Tobiah builds furniture and he's good at it, so I'll leave him where he is."

"He might be helpful to you out in the field."

"I'll give it some thought."

"I heard you tried to free him," Ormonde said, his dark eyes studying Rafe. "Look at all this." Ormonde waved his hand and Rafe gazed at the field full of people. "The South has to have slavery or its economy will fail. I take good care of my people."

"Yes, sir," Rafe said. No need to argue with his new employer, but he couldn't erase his memory of the moments on the ship when he had been with men in chains. He could never view slavery with the same equanimity as Ormonde Therrie did.

The first week in New Orleans, he had seen an auction. A prime field hand brought a thousand dollars, sometimes over a thousand. A man like Tobiah would bring over a thousand. Rafe's gaze swept the fields around him. Ormonde Therrie must have a million dollars tied up in slaves, and a million dollars would make a man favor the system.

"I read in the *Daily Picayune* about the Dred Scott case. Last year the United States Supreme Court ruled slavery extends into the other states and territories; it isn't limited to the South," Rafe said.

Ormonde surveyed his land. "I don't think the North will fight over slavery, but if they do France and England will come to the South's aid, because they rely on us for cotton. If we get into war, cotton prices will go to the sky. My factor suggests turning all available acreage to cotton. My hands can pick a hundred pounds a day. Fourteen hundred field pounds will make a three-hundred-and-fifty-pound bale. By May these seeds will be up and need scraping—weeding out the weak plants. All summer we'll have to fight the bugs. It'll be ready to pick in late fall. You'll learn the process—whipping, ginning, and packing. We'll send it by flatboat from our landing downriver to the docks in town, where it'll be unloaded at the warehouse of my factor.''

He turned in the saddle. ''You've met the drivers. Each driver will be in charge of a gang of ten workers. You give the drivers daily orders, and they'll pass them to the workers. My workers can each tend from six to nine acres. They get a noon break, and the rest periods are up to you.'' His gaze drifted beyond Rafe to his land.

''Last year Belle Destin produced two thousand, two hundred and fifty-nine bales of cotton.''

Rafe looked across the field of thriving plants. At nine cents per pound, he quickly figured, that was over seventy thousand dollars from cotton.

''Good morning, Papa. Mr. O'Brien,'' Chantal said, riding up behind them. Rafferty turned in the saddle.

Chantal was wearing the blue faille riding dress she had worn when he'd first met her. A flat straw bonnet was perched atop her hair. He felt his pulse skip as he looked into her dark eyes. Her gaze slid away and her cheeks grew pink. A younger girl rode beside her, her black hair fashioned like Chantal's—parted in the center, with braids looped and pinned over her ears. Her eyes were large and dark brown and gazed at him with a frank openness as she smiled. Her full mouth seemed too wide for her dainty face and pointed chin, but warmth radiated from her smile and he returned it with a nod.

''Amity, this is Mr. O'Brien, our new overseer. Mr. O'Brien, my youngest daughter, Miss Amity.''

''How do you do,'' Rafe said.

''Papa, they say a steamboat is coming.''

''That's right, Chantal. And we have goods on this one. You and Amity go ahead. I'll be along soon.''

With one more flash of dark eyes at him, Chantal turned her horse. Rafe tore his attention from her and tried to listen to Ormonde Therrie.

''I'm fortunate in my children. Chantal cares for my people, and Amity cares for my horses,'' Ormonde said, as if to himself. He looked at Rafe. ''I know you're riding over Belle Destin at dawn and you've worked until dark. I don't expect you to keep long hours all the time.''

"I'm trying to learn my way. Belle Destin is enormous, compared to what I've known at home."

"The mare's doing fine now, my groomsman said."

"She'll be all right, and the foal is a dandy. Giraud showed me your unmanageable stallion."

"That damned horse—I should sell him. At first I had some good offers, but word got around about his disposition."

"We raised horses. May I work with him?"

"You can try, but no one has been able to stay on his back more than ten minutes before all hell breaks loose. I don't allow the women near him. He's a prime stud. Has one colt that's going to win a lot of races for me. Giraud is a good trainer, but he can't gentle the monster. I don't want anyone hurt; I don't want the horse hurt."

"Yes, sir," Rafe said.

"I'll get down to the landing," Ormonde said, turning his gray horse as Rafe went back to work. Rafe was trying to learn workers' names and get acquainted with a plantation that was a small town unto itself with its stables, hospital, smokehouse, kitchen, springhouse, slave cabins, tool house, gin and cotton houses. The west boundary of Belle Destin was the Mississippi River; to the north was Bayou Canouet, which emptied into the river, and Spider Creek, which cut across the northern part of the plantation.

As he learned the land, Rafe also assessed his future. He had moved up in the world. His winnings from gambling were now in the Louisiana State Bank. He could have lived on them alone, but he wanted to learn about cotton and, for now, to live at Belle Destin, near Chantal. He had seen the hunts and one ball at Belle Destin; he had seen her leave for soirees and balls elsewhere, and when she was with Galliard, she was chaperoned. As far as Rafe could tell, Galliard made no effort to get her off to himself. As long as he lived at Belle Destin, Rafe would have constant opportunities to see her away from the watchful eyes of her parents.

He now owned the small parcel of land that he had won at faro. He would earn twelve hundred dollars a year as overseer, beyond bed and board. Yet there was still a bottomless chasm separating his place in life from Chantal's, and he had to make that leap before he could court her. He felt a sudden pang of longing to see his brothers. But Caleb was tough, and so was Fortune, and they would have fought to their last breaths for Darcy. They had to be all right.

Rafe glanced over his shoulder and thought about Chantal. In his dawn rides he had seen her, but always at a distance. He had found the winding paths she took on her rides. Once he had seen the younger sister with her, but most mornings Chantal rode alone, and he longed to talk to her again.

Each evening he stopped work an hour before sundown and went to the stables to work with Daedalus, the unruly black stallion. Rafe slipped on the bridle, talking to the stallion, walking him, touching him, but he avoided trying to ride him. He would curry the horse, rub him down, feed him, and each night the stallion's ears would lay back and he would go into a frenzy, trying to kick or bite to get Rafe away from his side.

"He's just a damned mean horse," Giraud said. The tall horse trainer shook his head, the silver earring in his dark ear winking in the dusky light of the stable. "A dozen men have tried to ride him. Mr. Therrie tried to ride him, too. That horse hates mankind. He's crazy. Just loon crazy."

Rafe gave it two weeks before he finally swung up into the saddle. He had worked the horse for three nights with an empty saddle on his back, and no one had been around, but that evening, as if he had blown a trumpet, observers appeared—the groomsmen and stableboys sitting on the fence, Giraud holding a rope and smelling salts, Amity Therrie, and then Mrs. Therrie joining her. Rafe was on the Belle Destin racetrack, and the moment he settled into the saddle he

flicked the reins, determined he would wear the stallion down.

Daedalus burst into a gallop and Rafe leaned over
him, racing him around the track once and then a second time, forgetting the audience. The damned horse
was a runner. The power in the long stride was in-
credible, and with a smaller rider the horse would do
better. When the stallion began to lather, Rafe let him
slow to a canter. As he came around the turn, he saw
the entire Therrie family watching. Pinned in Chantal's hair was a gardenia. Watching him with a solemn,
wide-eyed expression, she looked lovely and exotic,
with her golden hair and dark eyes. He shouldn't
stare, but it was an effort to pull his gaze away. He
reached the area near the gate and drew the reins,
swinging his leg over the horse's withers and dropping
to the ground.

"Good ride. Damned good horse," he said, running his hand over the stallion's wet neck. The horse
shuddered, and then let Rafe lead him. Giraud was the
first to reach him.

"That was a sight to see, but don't let him fool you.
Nobody's tried to run him. They've always tried to get
on and just walk him around, and no one can stay on
him at a walk, including you. No, sir. You can't ride
him any other way except in a dead run. That probably
suits him, too. Until he sees a filly and takes off with
you on his back!" Giraud laughed.

"I didn't know he could run like that," Ormonde
Therrie said, falling into step beside Rafe. "I'd like
to put one of my riders on him and see if he can race
him, but the horse is too unpredictable, and you're not
small enough to race him."

"Mr. Therrie, you put little Remi on him," Giraud
said, still chuckling to himself, "and that cussed stallion will toss him to Plaquemines Parish."

"It was an amazing ride," Ormonde said. "But it
doesn't mean he's gentle. Damn shame. What a powerful horse! How I'd like to let him go at Metarie track,
but he has a wicked streak in him that's part of his
nature. I won't allow anyone to beat it out of him."

"You don't mind if I try to ride it out of him, do you?"

"No. But the day you slow down to a walk, he'll pitch you into the oleanders. Good night, boys." Ormonde Therrie walked away. Rafe glanced over his shoulder and saw the women in a cluster waiting for Ormonde to join them. Chantal faced him, breezes teasing her hair. She lifted her chin and turned her head.

He caught Giraud's curious dark eyes on him, but Giraud remained silent.

"Now we'll see how much energy he has left." Rafe led the stallion through the gates to the stable yard and swung into the saddle. The horse pawed the ground, but began a sedate walk as Giraud moved to the other side of the fence to watch.

The stallion's ears were laid back. One second later, the horse's muscles bunched and uncoiled like released springs. He leaped into the air and came down with a jolt that almost shook Rafe from the saddle. The stallion bucked and twisted, and in seconds Rafe was flying through the air. As he hit the ground, air burst from his lungs, but he got up and walked to the horse, who watched him with rolling eyes. Now eight field hands and the stable crew had joined Giraud to watch.

Rafe got on again. This time he lasted less than a minute. He felt a hot determination to ride the stallion. The O'Briens' had never owned a horse they couldn't ride, and while this wasn't his horse, he felt a challenge.

The next two throws landed him on his stomach, and he got a mouthful of dirt. The throw after that ripped not only his sleeve, but some skin from his right arm. By now there was a crowd, men laughing and yelling encouragement.

The next ride Rafe lasted longer than before. One minute or four? It seemed an eternity bouncing on the horse's back. Again he sailed through the air and slammed to earth. In dogged determination he climbed back on and was tossed over and over again, until he lost count of the times.

After each fall, red and blue stars danced in his vision while the earth spun beneath him as he tried to stand. Two Girauds appeared at his side. "Let's get you out of here. You're as stubborn as the damned horse."

"No. You haven't . . . seen stubborn," Rafe said, pushing Giraud away.

"Mr. O'Brien, condition you're in, you can't stay on his back ten seconds."

"We'll see. Does he look tired?"

"Hell, no! He'll kill you if you keep this up."

Up in the saddle, two jarring bucks, and he was off again. Rafe shook his head and tried to get up on his hands and knees.

"Mr. O'Brien, that's enough." Ormonde Therrie's quiet voice carried through the night. Lanterns hung from posts, and a white moon peeped over the roof of the stable.

Trying to focus on his employer, Rafe swayed. Feeling a deep-running determination and frustration, he crossed to the fence and fell on it. "Sir, begging your pardon, but I'm not hurting your horse."

"No, Mr. O'Brien, you're killing my overseer."

"I'm a little groggy, but I've been in fights with my brothers worse than this. I'm not hurting him, and I'll survive. He hasn't had anyone get back on him like this. I'm going to outlast him."

"Dammit, man, the stallion has enough energy to throw you into next week! I don't want you to get a broken back or neck."

"No, sir. I don't want that either." He wiped a smear of blood from his temple. Everything hurt, and he wondered if he had broken ribs. He turned to look at the stallion, who stood with lather on his black coat. The horse now faced Rafe, and he was no longer pawing the ground, snorting, or rolling his eyes.

"Mr. O'Brien, you won't be fit for work tomorrow."

"Tomorrow is Saturday, sir. Just the morning is all the hands work. I'll work. I'll stop trying to ride if it interferes with my ability to work."

Rafe suddenly noticed that another man stood beside Ormonde Therrie. He was shorter and stocky, yet he had the same jaw, the same dark eyes and hair. As Rafe studied him Ormonde said, "My son, Alain Therrie. Alain, meet my overseer, Mr. O'Brien."

He nodded to Rafe, who nodded in return. "How do you do?" The words were an effort. Rafe shifted his attention back to Ormonde Therrie.

"Sir, if I can gentle that stallion, you'll have one of the finest racehorses in the state."

While Ormonde Therrie thought it over, Rafe felt as if he would slide to the ground and pass out. With effort he drew himself up, wincing at the pain in his side. "He's a magnificent horse."

The Therrie women had returned to watch him. Rafe stood a little straighter. *Not going to pass out in front of Chantal. Will ride the son of a bitch.*

"Very well," Ormonde Therrie replied. "But do try to avoid letting him kill you."

"Yes, sir." Rafe returned to the horse, who stood still while Rafe ran his hand along his neck and over the sleek hide and the hard muscles beneath. Rafe gathered the reins and swung up into the saddle, almost sliding off on the opposite side. The world spun. He flicked the reins, and they began a sedate walk. He had made five turns around the yard when the stallion's ears went flat, giving Rafe one second's warning. The stallion reared, pawing the air. He came down, and all four hooves left the ground. He bucked, and Rafe clung to him.

The horse shuddered, and Rafe urged him to a walk again. Rafe locked his hand on the saddle. The world spun, every breath was a pain, and he had to fight to maintain consciousness. Mumbling an old ballad to himself, he tried to concentrate and remain conscious. One eye was puffed closed. He remembered his first big fight with the Derrynane boys. He and Caleb had come home bloody and bruised, and carrying Fortune. For three days their mother had cried and scolded them about the evils of fighting. As soon as they'd recovered, their father had taken them behind the barn and

lined them up, gazing at them with blazing blue eyes.
Rafe had expected a beating for getting into the fight.
Instead, Hanlan O'Brien told them that if they were
going to fight, they were going to learn how. As he
raised his fists to teach them, he warned them that if
they came home so whipped again, he would beat
them. They still got beaten in fights, but never again
so badly as they had in the first battle with the Der-
rynanes.

*Hang on. Don't fall now. Go around again. Keep
the bastard moving.*

At some point Rafe noticed that his audience was
gone, except for Giraud, Tommy, Remi, and Ormonde
Therrie. Then only Giraud was left, perched on the
fence in silence. Rafe drifted into and out of awareness
of surroundings. Twice he caught himself slumping
over the neck and sliding down, and he would struggle
upright again. The pain was a constant throb.

He felt the breath go out of him when he hit the
ground. He groaned and tried to get up, but couldn't
move. Hands lifted him.

"Giraud?"

"You can't get back on that horse, sir."

"I don't plan to."

Giraud carried him to his house. Rafe collapsed on
his bed, and felt Giraud sponging off his face.

Three weeks later, in the morning hush when pink
rays were sparkling the dew before the plantation
stirred, Chantal turned Caesar along a riding trail. Rafferty O'Brien had gentled Daedalus, the impossible
stallion. She had stood and watched him that night,
until Papa had ordered Amity and her to the house.
After she had dressed in her gown for bed, she stepped
out on the gallery to look at the stable. Rafferty still
rode, a dark shadow in the lantern's yellow glow.
Moving like a wraith in the darkness, Amity joined
her.

"Is he riding Daedalus?"

"Yes! Look, Amity, the stallion is as gentle as a
lamb."

"My gracious! Three years Papa has tried to break that horse. Mr. O'Brien is the stubbornest man!"

"He's very brave."

"Maman said he was stupid to take such risks over a horse."

"Maman doesn't like to ride, and she doesn't like horses."

"No," Amity said. "He's still riding. Papa said every bone in his body should be broken."

They sat in silence until Amity yawned. "I'm going inside. He's handsome, isn't he?"

"Who?" Chantal asked, feeling her cheeks grow warm.

"Who do you think?" Amity said, laughing. "You know Mr. O'Brien is handsome, and I don't know why you won't admit it!"

"I suppose he is, but not as much as Lazare."

"Lazare is handsome. But Mr. O'Brien is the most handsome overseer we've had!"

"I'll agree with that! Mr. Buchane didn't have front teeth, and Mr. Cantrell looked like a ghost with spectacles. And—Amity, look! Mr. O'Brien's fallen off the horse!" Feeling afraid, Chantal stood up.

"He isn't moving."

Giraud picked him up like a child and strode through the gate, carrying Rafferty to the overseer's house.

"Do you think he's alive?" Amity asked.

"Yes," Chantal answered. "He's alive, or Giraud would be running to get Papa. Mr. O'Brien must have fainted."

"He rode Daedalus," Amity said. "Papa has bet men no one could ride Daedalus for five minutes. Papa won two hundred dollars when Lazare's papa brought a Galliard slave over here to ride him and the fathers wagered on it."

The two sisters went to bed but Chantal lay awake, haunted by memories of fiery kisses, disturbed by a man who was so undaunted by every challenge.

Chantal dismounted to let her horse drink at the river. As she smoothed her blue riding dress, she heard hoofbeats.

"Good morning," Rafferty O'Brien said in his deep voice, swinging down out of the saddle and leading his horse next to hers. He wore a white cotton shirt and black trousers, with high black boots. In the simple work clothes, he was extraordinarily handsome.

"You don't have to work this early. It'll be over an hour before they ring the bell for the field hands."

"I ride at dawn for the same reason you do."

"Papa is delighted about Daedalus. You got over your hurts," she said, her gaze going over his features. Amity was right; he was quite handsome. It was his clear blue eyes that were unforgettable and unique. And the determination in them. She thought about his ship sinking, and knew there must have been a fierce struggle to save his mother.

"Any more rooftop running?" he asked, touching her collar. She drew a deep breath as she looked up at him. The brush of his fingers had been nothing, yet she tingled as if it had been an intimate caress. He stood too close; she was too aware of him.

"No," she replied. "I've spoken to Alain about the Vigilante's plans, and he said he would try to talk his friends into a moderate course, but he may have said that just to appease me." She cocked her head at him. "Papa says he told you to bring Tobiah Barr to Belle Destin, and you refused."

"Tobiah's good with his hands and works for a furniture maker. I can't free him, but I can let him work where he pleases," Rafferty said, still touching her collar, her shoulder.

"That's a strange course to follow. Allowing him to choose where he works." She should move back, so Rafferty couldn't touch her, but she stood where she was. A lock of black hair curled on his forehead, and his broad-brimmed slouch hat was pushed to the back of his head.

"Tobiah's where he belongs. He's a good carpenter. He's making a desk and a sofa for me."

"You don't need furniture! Your house is furnished. Are you discarding Papa's furniture?" she asked in amusement, remembering Rafferty's threadbare abode in town compared to the comfortable overseer's house.

"No. But I won't work here forever."

Startled that he was already planning to quit, she studied him. "I've never known anyone like you."

"I hope not. How am I so different?" he asked, taking her arm and leading her around the horses to a log where they could sit. She was aware of his hand holding her, aware of every brush of his fingers, of his proximity when they sat down. He tossed aside his hat and raked his fingers through his thick hair.

"You don't doubt things. You say 'I'll do this,' or 'I'll do that,' as if there's no question. Everything in life is questionable. Well, some things aren't, I suppose. I'll marry Lazare and Amity will marry Talmadge Dalier, and Papa will raise cotton and support the Democrats."

Rafe shrugged. "When it's something important, I prefer to think I can accomplish what I want."

"Do you always get what you want?"

"No. I wanted to save my mother. I want my brothers with me. I wanted to save our farm."

"I'm sorry," she said, feeling contrite, "because I know you wanted those things."

He leaned closer to her and spoke in a low voice, reaching out to unfasten her bonnet. "And you won't marry Lazare."

"There you go again—so positive about something neither you nor I nor Lazare can change! We're pledged. What *are* you doing?"

"I want to see you without the hat." He pulled it off and tilted her chin up to study her. She drew a deep breath and her lips parted. His gaze trailed over her, down to her hands in her lap and back up, a leisurely perusal that made her pulse skitter.

"Papa says he still can't trust Daedalus," she said in a rush, feeling compelled to talk although she knew she sounded breathless. "He'll have to see you ride him again and again before he'll let anyone else near him."

"I've been riding him nearly every night."

"Papa's quite impressed by you. He says you're a natural farmer."

"I should be. It's all I've known since I could toddle."

"He says you have more feel for it than Alain. Are you going to buy your own farm?"

"I haven't decided what I want to do," he said, a husky rasp coming to his voice. He looked as if he intended to kiss her, and she felt as if she couldn't get her breath.

"Farming here, if it's to be successful, involves owning other men. That gives me pause. And at home, nearly every farm failed. We've had terrible famines. My folks survived by raising pigs and barley and horses, and by fishing."

"What else would you do?" she asked, studying him. He leaned closer to her.

"Chantal," he whispered, and leaned the last few inches to brush her mouth with his.

For an instant she yielded, feeling his mouth on hers, feeling an ache start inside.

"No!" In a seething turmoil, knowing he shouldn't touch her, that she shouldn't want him to touch her, she flung away from him and strode toward the horses. In seconds, he caught her.

"Chantal . . ."

"Don't you touch me!" She pulled away and rushed in front of his horse. The earth crumbled, clods tumbling into the river, and she slipped, screaming as she flailed the air.

Rafe caught her, pulling her to him and laughing. "Do you always get into trouble?"

Throwing her arms around him and barely hearing his question, she clung to his solid shoulders. "Don't let me fall!"

He stepped back from the water. "You're safe."

"I *hate* water!" She glanced over her shoulder. They were yards from the rushing muddy water, and she relaxed.

"You don't know how to swim," he said. She became aware of his arms around her. His gaze held a smoldering hunger as he looked into her eyes. He leaned forward, placing his mouth firmly on hers and opening her lips. A deep twist of longing ignited like a flame low within her. His tongue touched hers. *I shouldn't let him kiss me!* She pushed against his chest.

He tightened his arms. "You'll fall in the damned water if you push away," he whispered, kissing her ear and then turning his head to kiss her hard on the mouth again.

His kiss became an aching torment. She couldn't resist; she pressed against him, returning his kiss, letting her tongue play over his. He was irresistible. His hand drifted around her waist and up across her breast, making her tremble with longing. He was bold, touching her where he shouldn't, yet she didn't want to stop him, didn't want to pull away from kisses that tantalized and made her burn with longing.

Finally she twisted free, and her breathing was as erratic as his. Looking as if he wanted to pull her back into his arms, he placed his hand on her saddle and blocked her from mounting.

"You *know* I'm pledged to Lazare! You *know* you'll lose your job, and worse, if Papa catches you!" Her heartbeat deafened her, and she felt torn between wanting to run from Rafferty O'Brien and wanting to throw herself back in his arms.

"You're not worried about my job," Rafferty drawled, touching her cheek. She jerked her head away. She loved Lazare, and Rafferty O'Brien could ruin all her plans. For years she had dreamed about her future and her own home, her babies.

"I won't let you interfere in my life! I love Lazare! He would kill you if he knew you had kissed me!" She felt anger grow, because Rafferty O'Brien was too bold, too much the scoundrel to observe decorum and society's rules.

"I'm not afraid of Lazare Galliard."

She tried to settle her bonnet and tie it. Rafferty reached out to straighten it and took the bows from her fingers, tying it slowly, letting his hands brush her throat.

"I'll do that!" she said, yanking the hat off and reaching for the pommel. He blocked her way and she glared at him, her anger increasing. "Get out of my way! And *stay* out of it! I don't want to see you again!"

"No? You're so in love with Galliard that you can't see another man? So in love that your every thought is of Galliard?" he said in dry tones. "Even when you return my kisses?"

"I'll marry Lazare, and I love him!" She pushed against Rafe's chest and slipped her foot into the stirrup to mount. His long slender fingers, which could be so strong, caught her around her waist and yanked her back against him, turning her swiftly.

Her heart slammed against her ribs as his mouth slanted over hers. His kiss scalded her, made thoughts spin away. She struggled briefly but then she was lost, sliding her arms around his neck to cling to him, relishing his kisses, returning them.

He released her with an abruptness that was startling. "You don't love him," he said in a quiet voice, in that deep tone that was a caress in itself. "You couldn't kiss me like that if—"

"One word to Papa and he'll have you whipped or shot!" she snapped in fury, angry with herself for responding to him. *What does he do to me, that I lose all reason and control?*

Yanking the reins, she started to mount. Hands closed on her waist and Rafferty lifted her into the saddle. She gazed down at him. "I'll tell Lazare if you try to kiss me again."

"Afraid?" he asked in a sardonic tone that only heaped more kindling on her smoldering anger.

"You're stronger than I am, but you can do nothing to stop my marriage to Lazare, nothing! And I *do* love him! I barely know you, and you're too bold, too . . ." She closed her mouth and glared at him.

"Too *what*?" he asked in amusement. "You're doing what your father wants, not what your heart wants."

"Do you think *you* are what my heart wants?"

With a straightforward expression he gazed into her eyes, and she realized his answer. "You're as conceited as you are bold, sir!"

"It's not conceit, Chantal," he said solemnly, stepping back. "If it puts you at ease, next time I won't kiss you."

"There won't *be* a next time!"

"Frightened to talk to me?"

She wheeled her horse around and rode away. Standing with his hands on his hips, arms akimbo, he laughed.

Feeling a swirl of emotions, like a leaf caught in a gale-force wind, Chantal rode home. "I love Lazare!" she declared aloud. "I do! And I won't ride in the morning again!" But Rafferty O'Brien's laughter haunted her thoughts. He was impossible! So bold, looking at her as if she weren't wearing a stitch of clothing, pulling her into his arms . . .

That night sleep eluded her. Memories of Rafferty's kisses were a torment that made her toss and turn. She sat up in the dark. "I love Lazare!" she whispered.

She lay back down and watched the white lace curtains blow in the breeze. She was promised to Lazare and nothing would interfere with that, *nothing*. And even if Lazare hadn't existed, Rafferty O'Brien was the Belle Destin overseer, as far removed from a chance to court her as if he still lived in Ireland instead of only a few hundred yards away. He could *not* interfere in her life, in her future with Lazare. An image floated to mind of Rafferty O'Brien being tossed to the ground, sliding on the hard earth, standing up while bleeding, climbing back onto Daedalus's back. She shivered and pulled the covers high, even though moments earlier she had been damp with perspiration and had tossed away the sheet. Rafferty O'Brien had done what everyone had said couldn't be done—broken the wildest horse at Belle Destin. But just because he rode a horse, that didn't mean anything where Lazare was concerned. Yet, oh yet, how persistent and bold this Rafferty was!

Stubborn, stubborn man . . . He had come to New Orleans with nothing, and now he was the Belle Destin overseer. His blue eyes again danced into her mind, devil's eyes that teased and tormented and promised— or was it threatened?—the impossible. She wouldn't ride in the morning, it was as simple as that.

For four mornings she somehow managed to keep her vow, and then on Wednesday she dressed in her new green riding habit and had her horse saddled.

Chapter 8

In the cool, hushed woods, a dove's gentle coo was the only sound except Caesar's hooves and the creak of her saddle. Mist hovered over the green finger of a bayou, and dew was silvery in the shadows. She inhaled fresh air and was glad she had decided to ride. It was spring, April, with azaleas and camellias in bloom.

Four minutes later she turned a bend to see Rafferty O'Brien on his bay in her path. Rafferty's black hat was pushed to the back of his head, a lock of his black hair curling over his forehead as it often did.

Her pulse jumped and raced. "You startled me!" she exclaimed, knowing that he hadn't startled her at all. She had been thinking about him from the moment she'd left her room.

"Good morning."

"Get out of my way!" she snapped, feeling fluttery and angry at the same time. Another feeling ran deeper, one she wanted to bury and ignore. "I won't talk to you."

Amusement softened his features, and he wheeled his horse to ride beside her. "Very well. Don't talk. We'll just enjoy the dawn."

She bit back a protest. *Don't say a word to him, and he'll go away. Don't stop riding; don't kiss him.* He looked fit and handsome, with his sun-kissed thick raven's hair and his blue eyes. She glanced at his hand holding the reins and remembered watching him run his hands over the stallion.

They rode in silence, yet she couldn't recall a time when she had been more aware of her companion.

"Papa is so pleased over Daedalus," she said finally, slanting Rafferty a look. He was keeping to himself, having ridden without a word for what must have been half an hour now. With a lazy grace he turned his head to look at her.

"He knows you ride him every night," she added, feeling compelled to talk.

"So I can talk now?" Rafferty inquired, his voice laced with amusement.

"As long as you just talk, and don't—" She was aghast at what she had said. The words had leapt out without thought. Her face flooded with heat, and his soft chuckle did nothing to help. She raised her chin.

"And don't *what*? Would that you'd say the rest of your thoughts, but that's too much to hope."

"You enjoy other's discomforts, sir!"

His eyes danced with merriment. "Only when I'm plagued with curiosity about what has been left unsaid. What is it you don't want me to do?"

She laughed. "You scoundrel, you know perfectly well what is being left unsaid and undone! And it shall stay that way!"

He leaned over to yank her reins, and both horses halted. Rafferty caught her chin in his hands, turning her face to his. Her heart thudded. Dappled shade played over his features, and she felt captured by his hand and his gaze. "I can't remain impersonal when you laugh, when your eyes sparkle and your words are breathless."

Her heart pounded until she thought she would faint. They were in a shaded lane, but she felt as if the sun were blazing on her. He turned and flicked his reins and they commenced riding again as if nothing had transpired. She gulped for air and felt a twinge of disappointment and *loss*. Impossible. It should be relief. The silence pressed on her, and her thoughts spun with images and memories of his kisses.

"You've done the impossible in gentling Daedalus."

"Not impossible. I just outlasted him. The real test will come when Giraud rides him. It won't be much of a victory if I'm the only one who can ride him. I didn't know your father watched me later."

"Yes, and he always hears from Moss or William or Bertram, his valet, about everything that happens at Belle Destin."

The trees stopped and the trail forked, the left lane running several yards to a wide, hard-packed road leading to the river, the other continuing in a narrow winding trail. Rafferty halted to turn to her.

"Want to race?"

The proper thing would be to say no. He was waiting, a challenge dancing in his eyes that she couldn't resist. "Yes," she answered, glancing at his horse and knowing she would be in for a tough race.

"To the grove of trees around the bend. I'll give you to the count of twelve for a head start."

"No, Mr. O'Brien. We start at the same place." She lined her horse beside his.

"You may call go."

"Ready?"

"No," he answered softly. "No race is worth running without a wager."

"I can't wager!"

"I didn't mean money," he said, amusement lacing his words. Her pulse jumped at the bold look in his eyes. His gaze slowly trailed down over her.

"You really are a scoundrel!"

"*Now* what have I done?" he asked with great innocence, his dancing blue eyes looking like the devil's very own.

She should have refrained from talking to him at all. Now she was into it, and he was enjoying himself as usual. "I don't want to wager."

"Scared you'll lose?"

"No! You know it's improper for me to wager."

"I know it's improper for you to climb on rooftops," he said in that deep, rich tone that was as tantalizing as music and held only a faint trace of his Irish brogue. "It's improper for you to return my kisses, it's improper for you to race. Why stop now, when it will

make the race interesting? Unless you're scared. I'll
give you a wide lead. While I wait I'll count. . . ."

"You don't need to count!" She felt giddy with the
challenge he'd offered. She rode one of the fastest
horses at Belle Destin, and there was something she
wanted. "I'll wager you, and I'll take your twelve-
count lead," she said, knowing it wasn't necessary,
but wanting to win and afraid to take chances where a
rogue like Rafferty O'Brien was concerned.

"Good! What do you want if you win?"

"I want you to gentle my new foal, Bright Gold,"
she said.

"Done." He moved beside Chantal. "You're riding
sidesaddle. I know you ride astride. Want to unsaddle
the horses and make it more fair for you?"

"You sound as if you want me to win."

"No. I intend to win. I just don't want to take an
unfair advantage of you."

"I asked you if you always get what you want. I
should have asked you if you ever doubt you'll get
what you want!"

He laughed and dismounted. "Get down, and I'll
take the saddle away."

It would be scandalous for her to ride with him like
a man, but at this point everything she had done around
Rafferty O'Brien was scandalous. She dismounted and
stepped away from him at once, receiving a mocking
smile from him. He removed both saddles and motioned to her. "Come here and I'll boost you up."

She drew herself up and moved around. His hands
closed on her waist and he stepped close behind her.
His voice was soft at her ear, sending tingles surging
through her. "You haven't asked what *I* want if *I* win."

If she turned around she would be in his arms. Could
he hear her pounding heart, which was all but deafening her? "What do you want me to wager?" she
asked, staring ahead at the trees. *Why does he have
such an effortless effect on me?* He was going to ask
for a kiss if he won. She would have to kiss him. . . .

"If you lose, I get to teach you to swim."

"No!" She spun around to look at him, and then

wished she hadn't. He was inches from her; the look in his eyes made her words vanish, and scrambled her thoughts like twigs caught in a river eddy.

"I'd like to"—he paused to smooth her collar and her pulse raced—"wager kisses," he said, his voice growing deeper, "but I'm going to wager that you learn to swim."

"No! Papa would call you out and shoot you!"

"We won't invite your papa."

"No! I detest water, and women don't swim!"

"Since when have you ever drawn the line at what women don't do? You live in a city that's almost surrounded by water. Your home is on a river. A stream and Canouet Bayou run through Belle Destin. There are bayous everywhere we travel. You could drown. If I hadn't known how to swim, I wouldn't be here now." His voice lightened, and the corner of his mouth rose in a crooked smile. "Besides, you're going to win this race."

"What makes you so certain I'll win?"

"Because you'll ride like the devil, to avoid learning how to swim."

"I'll ride because the devil will be after me!" she snapped.

He laughed. "You can have all the head start you want. Are you afraid of a challenge? I've done everything to give you an edge, and I know you ride a fast horse. Why so afraid?"

"I'm not afraid of you," she whispered, and turned to the horse. "Help me up."

"Will you wager?"

"Yes!"

He chuckled, a noise that played on her raw nerves. She swung her leg over the horse and arranged her skirt. Her ankles showed, but Rafferty O'Brien was gathering the reins to his horse and not studying her. He vaulted to its back, his hard muscles fluid as he mounted. Chantal knew she would have the lead, knew she had a fast horse, yet still it was risky. To her, water was a murky terror, and she would never learn to swim. The sensible thing to do would be to refuse the challenge, but as she gazed into Rafferty's twinkling eyes she closed her mouth.

"Scared of me? Or do you prefer to change the wager to kisses?"

"No, I don't!" She lifted her chin. "I'll race, and I'll win."

"Whenever you're ready. I'll count to twelve after you call go."

Stop the race. All you have to do is say no. She sat beside him and glanced at his taunting smile.

"Go!" she shouted, feeling ridiculous galloping away and knowing she was leaving him behind. She leaned over Caesar and urged him to his top speed. She couldn't resist a glance over her shoulder. Rafferty O'Brien had started, but there was a wide gap between them. He must have counted with great leisure because he was far back, and she relaxed a fraction. But only a fraction. She couldn't forget the night he'd ridden Daedalus. The man had the most dogged determination.

She glanced over her shoulder again and received a shock. The distance between them was now only yards. He was gaining fast. She leaned down, clinging to Caesar, her knees gripping him. As they rounded the bend in the road, Rafferty drew alongside her. She wouldn't have thought it possible. His horse stretched out its long legs, pulling ahead of hers as they raced into the grove of trees. When they had both reined in, he turned back to her.

"I win, and I'll claim my prize."

"Papa hasn't seen your horse run. He would try to buy him from you," she said, or hoped she had said. She didn't know what to say or do next. Rafferty O'Brien was going to teach her to swim, and she had gotten herself into this willingly. Her horse pranced in circles, and she tried to calm him even though her own thoughts and feelings were in a terrible tangle. She felt suffocated with fear. A man like Rafferty O'Brien wouldn't back down, and he wouldn't allow her to back down. He would hold her to her wager.

No, she thought, *it is absurd! My father is his em-*

ployer. I don't have to do anything with Rafferty O'Brien I don't wish to do. Nothing. Wager or no. It was impossible, absurd. Yet her word was at stake. . . .

"We'll go back and get the saddles soon. Let's ride down to the river," he said with an impossible calm.

"I can't get in the water!" she blurted, knowing he would torment her about it. "I'm frightened of water! It's muddy, and filled with snakes and crawly things. . . ."

"You wagered, and you know you have to honor your wager. And I promise I won't let you get hurt. And we won't do that today."

"I can't do it at all," she said, her voice faint. "I shouldn't have wagered with you." *Why did I? What is there about him that goads and pushes and cajoles and wins me over to things I would never consider under other circumstances?* "Papa would be livid."

Rafferty rode up close beside her, facing her. "Your father will never know. No one will know except the two of us, and we'll wait until a better time. I won't let you get hurt. Now don't worry about it today."

Feeling relieved, she nodded. "Very well," she said. Perhaps she could postpone a swimming lesson forever. She studied the complex man beside her. He could be as hard and stubborn as he had been breaking Daedalus, yet now he had shrugged off her losing wager as nothing.

He caught her reins. "And someday I'll give you another chance to win, so that I may train Bright Gold after all."

"I could just ask Papa, and he would have you do it."

"Yes, you could. On the other hand, wagers make races more interesting."

They veered off the road down a path to the river. He dropped to the ground and lifted her down. She moved away from him, letting her horse drink while she glanced at the wide bend of the river. Moss-draped oaks lined the banks. The water was brown, sticks swirling past in the swift-running current. She shivered.

"You afraid?" Rafferty asked, leaning one shoulder against a tree a few yards from her.

"I don't like water, and the river frightens me."

"It would frighten me too if I couldn't swim," he said. Even when standing loose-limbed and relaxed, he exuded energy.

"I can't imagine you being afraid of anything," she said.

He arched his dark brows. "I am. I'm frightened by things beyond my control. I'm frightened of losing someone I love. I'm frightened when people hurt and I can't help them. I'm frightened by things that frighten other men."

"Why do I doubt that?" *Stop challenging him! Lord, he is handsome, standing there with that mocking smile, looking in command of his corner of the world.*

"I'm frightened of things beyond my control, like wars and cholera."

She felt a scrutiny that made her skin tingle. He was as relaxed as ever, not moving toward her or touching her, with yards between them, yet his gaze held a boldness that made her feel he could see her heart beat, discern her thoughts and reactions before she was aware of them herself.

"I'm not afraid of yellow jack, but Maman said I should be, and it's because I'm young and don't know there's a tomorrow. What do you want, Rafferty? What do you dream about?"

"Besides you?" he asked, with a sardonic lift to one corner of his mouth.

She blushed. "What do you want?" she repeated, trying to keep her voice light and railing.

"I want a family like the one I had. I want a wife and children to love. I want what other men want—a home and land and security. And I want it here in New Orleans. This is a special place, with its misty bayous and big river and lively city. It's cosmopolitan, a mixture of cultures, raw and refined, lazy and bustling, all at the same time."

"Sometimes when I look at Soleil, I get frightened that something will happen and I won't live there," she said, her thoughts shifting to the object of her dreams. "Let me show you the house," she said on impulse, wanting him to see it. Once he had seen Soleil, he would know she was forever pledged to Lazare and would stop flirting with her. "I want you to see it."

He looked as eager to see Soleil as she was to learn to swim. "Please."

He helped her to mount, and she pointed the way. He was quiet while she chattered on, until she realized she was talking too much and most of it sounded foolish. She asked about Ireland, and wondered about the women he had known there.

"There must be someone in Ireland who is in love with you, and didn't want you to go."

He turned his head, and his solemn expression vanished. "Perhaps so."

There was a woman. Or women. From his looks, he probably had many who wanted him. She was sure he made heads turn and female hearts flutter, just as Lazare did. To her surprise and dismay, she found that it annoyed her to think about Rafferty O'Brien and another woman. "What was her name?" she asked, feeling her cheeks grow warm in the sunshine and winding her fingers in Caesar's mane.

"Molly," he answered easily. "My beautiful Molly."

"Are you going home to her?"

"This is my home," he said in quieter tones. "I told Molly good-bye when I left. And Kathleen. And Priscilla. And—"

"You don't need to list them!" she snapped, then knew he'd been teasing when he laughed.

"Do I dare hope the thought of an Irish lass disturbs you?"

"Not in the least!" He laughed, and she realized how ridiculous her protest sounded. Now she was glad she was showing him Soleil, and could curtail this embarrassing chat.

"Turn at the next lane. We ferry the river." The large, flat raft proved sturdy enough for the horses, and soon they were winding down another dirt road. She knew the best approach to the house, and her spirits improved as she neared Soleil. It always gave her a thrill to see it, and to dream of the day she would be mistress of the manor and mother of Lazare's children.

"I love to look at the house. Our fathers hired Mr. Howard as architect. He designed and constructed Belle Grove for John Andrews."

"An American architect?"

"Yes. I come every week and watch them build it. It will have bathrooms in the house with running water; the pipes are being installed. Soleil will have gaslights and thirty-eight rooms and a grand ballroom. It will have closets, because under American rule the closets are no longer taxed. Papa intends it will be a showplace like Nottoway that's being built, or Thomas Pugh's Madewood, or Ashland, but all I want is a home that is mine. Papa said I can move the wisteria and the lilies Grand-père planted at Belle Destin. I want six children. I can't think of anything more wonderful than having my own babies. I love little babies." She turned to find him studying her with a strange, enigmatic expression.

"You're surprised I want a big family?"

"No. You've just told me how much you want all this," he said, with a sweep of his hand. "You talk about babies and home and family, but you don't mention one word about the man in your life."

She felt heat flood her face. "Lazare is the center of that world. I don't have to mention him."

Rafferty caught her chin roughly and turned her to face him, holding it tightly while his gaze probed hers. "That isn't why you didn't mention him. You want babies, but you don't love the man you expect to give them to you. When you make babies, you should love the man."

"Sir, you say things you know no decent woman should hear."

He laughed and released her. "Chantal, you and I both know you cross the lines of propriety with ease. Now where is this wonderful house the papas are building for their children, where so many babies will be made?"

She blushed. "I wish I hadn't brought you here!"

He chuckled and gazed at her with that frank appraisal that made her all the more self-conscious. "You insisted I see this marvel, so show it to me."

"It's around the bend in the road," she said in stiff tones, hating him. He could take her from giddy heights to a maelstrom of anger. As they approached the final turn, her fury vanished. At Soleil, it was impossible for her to stay sad or angry. "Dismount and close your eyes," she said with eagerness. "I want to surprise you."

"All right," he said, pulling on his reins. He dismounted and helped her down. "My eyes are closed. Where do I go?" he asked, facing the woods.

Too late she realized that she should have stayed mounted. Now she had to take his hand, and the moment she touched his fingers she felt a strong-running current, like the river current that runs unseen below the surface. The tension that sprang between them touched a deep part of her that was secret, unknown. She drew her breath and started to pull away, to tell him to open his eyes.

"Where's the house, Chantal?"

"This way," she said, aware of him close beside her. As she looked at the curve in the rutted road she relaxed, and then she glimpsed the construction. The house was less than half-finished, with stacks of lumber and bricks awaiting workmen who would arrive within the hour. Dawn's light bathed the site in pink, and she felt her heart beat with pleasure.

"Now look," she said, turning to see his reaction.

He opened his eyes and gazed without a change in his expression. "It'll be a magnificent house."

"I love it," she said, feeling a surge of pleasure, looking at the grand two-story portico with ten Tuscan columns across the front and single-story wings on each side. "It's what I've always wanted. I get scared I might lose it. Sometimes I dream I'm riding up to it and then the river rises. Water spreads and surrounds me and the house, and the house floats away. When I ride after it, the water comes higher."

She remembered the fear she felt in that recurring dream. "I've dreamed that more than once." She had never told anyone about the dream, not Amity, not Lazare. And she wished she hadn't confided in Rafferty, expecting him to laugh at her, but he remained solemn.

"What happens in your dream when the water rises higher?"

"I wake up and I'm frightened." She looked at the double front doors and fan transom. "But when I look at Soleil I feel loved, and think about the babies I will have."

"I think you're more in love with the house than the man," he said in dry tones.

"No! Of course I'm not! I won't let you spoil this!"

He glanced at Soleil, looking over house and grounds and back at her. "I won't spoil it. Has your engagement been announced?"

"No. Lazare's father insists we wait until Lazare is twenty-four. He says he wants Lazare to be older and settled. I'll be twenty."

"Three more years?" Rafferty asked, with surprise and something else—satisfaction—in his voice.

"Let's go look at the house."

She held back, reluctant to have this stranger traipse through her future home. He moved ahead and looked back at her. "Coming?"

She touched his cheek. "How did you get the scar?"

"A brawl with ruffians. Let's look at the place."

As she walked beside him she talked about the piano her father had promised her, the rosewood furniture Lazare was having made.

"How many acres?"

"This land borders Lazare's home on the south, so when he inherits the Galliard property someday, it will all be one. Papa bought three thousand acres, and Andreas Galliard bought three thousand. They're building the house. Lazare bought the remainder of the nine thousand acres, but he plans to enlarge it to nineteen thousand. His father owns eighteen thousand acres. Lazare wants to be the largest landholder in the South. He also wants to be governor of Louisiana.''

"And you want babies," Rafferty said softly, turning her to face him. "Where have you been around babies?''

"At Belle Destin. Do you want to walk through the house?'' she asked.

"No, I can see it's a grand place. And I can see if I win your hand, Chantal, I shall have to match all this splendor,'' he said in a solemn voice that frightened her.

"You won't win my hand. This is my future home. My heart is here.''

He tilted her chin up, and the blazing, hungry look in his eyes made her breath catch and a flame ignite in her. "Your heart is here,'' he mocked in a husky voice. "So to steal your heart and your love, I have to take it from this—from cypress and mortar and tabby and brick and glass—instead of from another man. I think I shall sleep easier now.''

"No! That's not true!''

"Yes it is,'' Rafferty answered, his gaze going to her mouth. As if she were calmly observing someone else, she stood still as his arms went around her and his head dipped down.

Fiery, tantalizing, breathtaking brushes of his mouth played over hers. His arm tightened around her, crushing her to him, bending over her. His kisses stayed soft and teasing until she felt as if her knees would melt. His body was lean and hard and marvelous. She wound her fingers in his soft hair and parted her lips, while her mind reeled and thoughts vanished. She returned his kisses, her tongue playing against his until he released her.

Dazed, she opened her eyes to find him watching her. "Now when you look at your precious Soleil, you'll always remember how I kissed you here and how you kissed me back.''

Anger flooded her. ''Damn you!'' she said, shocked that the word came. She had never sworn before, but Rafferty O'Brien would tax the patience of a saint. She turned to stomp down the steps. Suddenly arms locked around her and she was scooped up against his chest while he laughed deep in his throat.

Anger exploded in her and she beat against his chest. ''Put me down! I should never have brought you here!''

''You would rather I went back to kissing you?''

''No!'' Her heart raced. His face was inches from hers. Merciful angel, he had thick black lashes. His mouth . . .

''Why are you so angry? I've kissed you before. Scared you can't forget?'' His dancing amusement vanished, and he looked at her with a solemn expression. ''Are you scared you won't forget my kisses, Chantal? Is that why the burst of anger?''

Her rage evaporated. She would not admit what had driven her to anger. She wouldn't tell him that indeed she *couldn't* forget, that she had spent sleepless nights remembering his kisses, that she didn't want to fear moving to Soleil and still thinking about his kisses.

''Set me down, please.''

''What's this?'' he asked in a solemn tone. ''You can't answer my questions?''

''Put me down!''

He swung her to her feet and draped his arm over her shoulder. ''It's a beautiful house,'' he said, as if he had announced it might rain. His voice was matter-of-fact, impersonal.

''I should return home now,'' she said, aware that his arm remained across her shoulders as they walked back to the horses.

He helped her mount and they rode back to get the saddles. When they neared the stables, he halted. ''Good-bye, Chantal. Perhaps tomorrow.''

''Good-bye,'' she said, and turned to ride away, her back tingling, for she felt she was being watched by him.

* * *

Throughout the rest of April they rode together most mornings, until she looked forward to the rides with eagerness. He didn't try to kiss her again, and after the first few mornings she realized she was thinking more and more about his kisses. She was aware of the slightest brush against him, of his fingers on her arm or his strong hands helping her to mount. To her relief, he had never once spoken of teaching her to swim. And when he didn't tease her, she liked his company.

Election day was now only a little over a month away, and as it seemed Alain had no plans to change or to tell Papa about his plans, with reluctance she went to Ormonde. She stood in his office and gazed out the window as she watched Rafferty ride away. She knew she wouldn't see him after she married Lazare. A noise at the door interrupted her thoughts.

"Now what is this 'urgent matter,' Chantal?" Ormonde asked, striding into the room and closing the door.

Chapter 9

Rafe knew which drivers he could depend upon without supervision, which ones he had to keep after to make certain their work was done. The cotton was growing, endless rows of tall, healthy plants, and he wanted to bring in the best crop Belle Destin had ever grown. He was learning about cotton, but also making use of his own expertise from home, urging Ormonde to rotate some of his crops next year. Friday and Saturday nights he went to town, gambling and banking his winnings. He had purchased one piece of property in the Vieux Carré—a small townhouse with one bedroom—but it gave him as much satisfaction as the swampy lot he owned north of town.

There still was no word of any of his brothers, and worries nagged at him because time had passed. It hurt when he thought about them, and he wouldn't admit to himself that he might have lost all three.

He had pushed his hat back, wiped his brow, and mounted to ride to another part of Belle Destin, when he saw one of the house servants approach. In his fancy livery, he looked ridiculous riding a mule in the hot, sunny field.

"Mr. O'Brien? I'm William, sir. Mrs. Therrie sent me to fetch you to fix a broken window."

"Where's Mr. Dune?" A broken window was a job for the carpenter, not the Belle Destin overseer.

"She didn't send me to fetch the carpenter, sir. She sent me to get you," he answered. He had managed to keep his features impassive, but the distaste in his voice was plain, and Rafe felt a prickle across his nape. Mrs. Therrie was a stunning woman. Rafe stared at the gray-haired slave, whose gaze slid away to the horizon.

"Very well. I'll be there as soon as I talk to my driver."

"Sir, I think she wants you to come to the house now."

Rafe nodded and waved his hand. "I'll catch up with you before you get home," Rafe answered, knowing he could overtake the ambling mule.

He joined William as he approached the house. "Where is Mr. Therrie, William?"

"He's gone to town, sir. He won't be home tonight," William answered in the same flat tone.

"I'm not a carpenter. I don't have any tools."

"No, sir. She said to fetch Mr. Dune's tools, and I have. She said you could fix the window."

"Where is Miss Chantal?"

"She and Miss Amity have gone to town with Mr. Therrie, sir. They had dress fittings with the modiste."

He should stop and wash and clean up before entering the big house, but he'd be damned if he would. Blaise Therrie had no cause to summon him for carpentry work, and he didn't care to bathe before seeing her.

In the hallway of the house, he was again conscious of the great gulf of division separating his life from Chantal's. The hall held a great crystal chandelier and tall, gilt-framed mirrors. Egg-and-dart molding bordered the ceiling, and twin cantilevered staircases with mahogany railings spiraled to the second floor. Near the door was a Louis XV ormolu-mounted marquetry folio cabinet, with a marble top. A carved grandfather clock stood across from a mahogany hat stand.

"Here the tools, sir," William said, holding out a box of equipment. Rafe pushed a hammer and pliers into his hip pocket and set the box of tools on the polished cypress floor. For any repair more complicated, she would have to get the carpenter.

"This way, sir," William said, and climbed the

stairs. At an open door he rapped and waited until a
soft voice called out to enter.

"Mrs. Therrie, Mr. O'Brien is here."

"Send him in, William, and close the door."

Rafe entered an upstairs parlor that was elegant, with
sheer curtains tugged by the breeze. The room held
Louis XV beechwood chairs in pale green tapestry up-
holstery, gilt marble-topped tables, and a Louis XV
giltwood green damask settee, but it was the mistress
of Belle Destin who took all his attention. She wore a
forest-green silk dress with a low-cut bodice. Strands
of pearls circled her throat and she looked ready for a
dinner party, not an afternoon of plantation tasks. She
sat at ease, the pale green settee a perfect foil for her
dress and auburn hair.

"Good afternoon, Mr. O'Brien. It's warm today,
isn't it?"

"Yes, ma'am."

"Where are you from?"

"Ireland. I arrived not too long before I met Mr.
Therrie."

She looked amused, and he thought of a cat playing
with a mouse. "Do you have family here?"

"No, ma'am. My parents aren't living."

"So you live alone here at Belle Destin?"

"Yes, ma'am," he replied, aware that she had
known the answer before she'd asked the question.

"I have a broken window, and I thought you should
be able to repair it for me."

"That's out of my line of work," he replied in a
level voice. Waiting, he stood just inside the room,
feeling relaxed. "Mr. Therrie would probably prefer
his carpenter to repair anything, in a house as fine as
Belle Destin."

"He might, but *I'd* prefer *you* repair it. Mr. Dune
is too noisy. Are you noisy, Mr. O'Brien?"

"I expect I am. Probably noisier than Mr. Dune,
because he knows what he's doing."

As the silence lengthened, he wondered if she was
trying to make him ill at ease. She laughed softly.
"You like it here?" she asked him in a seductive voice.

"I appreciate Mr. Therrie giving me a job," he said, determined to keep his employer's name part of the conversation any way he could. She stood up and dropped her handkerchief, bending to retrieve it. He could see the fullness of her breasts, which almost spilled out of the green silk.

"Do you have a wife, Mr. O'Brien?"

"No, ma'am."

"I won't ask if there's a woman. I know the answer to that one just by looking at you. Men like you always have women," she drawled.

"You want a window repaired?"

She laughed and walked over to him. He stood still, looking down at her, and he felt sweat pop out on his forehead. His blood felt hot and thick as he looked into green eyes that were a blatant invitation. She licked her lips. "Are you afraid of me?" she whispered.

"No, ma'am. I haven't seen a woman I fear."

"So what do you feel?"

He laughed. "I think you know damned well what I feel. Ma'am, Mr. Therrie would want me to fix the window and get back to work."

"Mr. Therrie is in New Orleans until tomorrow, and I'm tired of being alone."

"Yes, ma'am, but he's paying me to do a job and I need to do it."

"He's paying you, but you answer to me as well as to him."

"Yes, ma'am." He opened the door and stepped into the hall. "Where's the window that needs repairing?" he asked, hearing his pulse roar in his ears. She smiled at him.

"In my bedroom. In here." She touched his arm and brushed past him, motioning him to follow. Her hips swayed, and he mentally stripped away the green silk. She was a gorgeous woman, and she had issued an invitation that was tempting. Watching her walk away from him, he felt on fire.

She stepped into a bedroom that ran half the length of the front of the house. A canopied rosewood bed was the centerpiece of the room. The pale yellow satin drapes were drawn on all the windows except the one near the bed. The room was dusky, the rustle of her skirt the only sound. "Here's the window, and it isn't actually broken. It's jammed and needs to be loosened."

Any house servant could have loosened the window. He felt a twinge of anger and a flame of desire. It was obvious what she wanted, and she was a damned beautiful woman. His gaze raked over her full breasts and tiny waist. She was one of the most desirable women he had ever seen, with a ripe lushness and a come-hither look that burned into him like a brand.

He crossed the room to the window and tried to raise it. It was jammed because it had been painted over. He pulled out the hammer and removed his handkerchief to place it against the wood, so he wouldn't damage the window frame while he hammered to break loose the wood. He felt a light touch on his arm.

"My, what muscles," she said, beside him. A lavender fragrance reached him, and he was too aware of her nearness.

"I'll have this window free in just a minute, if you'll step back out of the way," he said. His voice sounded deep and strange and far away. He tried to concentrate on the window and forget her red lips, her come-take-me eyes. He struck the wood twice, pulled, and the window came free, rising easily.

"There you are," he said, turning around.

She stood with her bodice unbuttoned, holding it closed with her hands over her breasts. "It's late. You can have your supper with me. I hate to eat alone."

"Mrs. Therrie," he said, unable to take his eyes from the gap at the neckline of her dress. Her fingers slid lower, and his voice dropped also. "Mr. Therrie would want me to have dinner in my cabin. I know he would. He might return tonight instead of tomorrow." He sounded like a blathering fool.

She walked toward him and reached up to run her hands over his shoulders, reaching behind him to pull the drapes. The room was in dusky light, seductive, intimate. She licked her lips and stood on tiptoe, pulling his head down to hers.

He felt her lips hot and sensual on his, and as if of its own accord his arm encircled her waist. He throbbed with desire, his body responding, yet he felt angry with her for what she was doing. The dress was unfastened to her waist, her full breasts pressing against him, and his hand went to their softness.

She ground her hips against him, her fingers caressing him, sliding along his thighs and over his buttocks.

Her hands fluttering over him made him shake. *Blaise Therrie. My employer's wife. Chantal's stepmother.*

"God!" He pushed her away and strode toward the door. "You'll ruin my job!"

"Come here, Rafferty O'Brien," she said softly. Her breasts were exposed and he couldn't tear his gaze from their fullness, their dusky tips that were large and taut. "Come here. You're young and strong, and I want you."

He inhaled and felt the same as he had when he was about to drown. He felt suffocated, enveloped in blackness. The ripe, hot body that was being offered to him was also a woman bent on evil.

She was Chantal's stepmother. *Chantal.* Rafe thought of black eyes and golden hair and a sweetness he would never find in this room. This was a dark flame that would consume him.

"Blaise," he said, the name sounding strange on his tongue, but he knew that "Mrs. Therrie" was beyond him. He was aroused, and she looked below his belt.

"Come here, Rafferty. We have all night. Just you and I."

He stood as if immobilized while he stared at her. *Remember Chantal; think of her kisses.*

"No. My employer gave me a job that includes trust." Never had he sounded such a fool. His voice was thick.

"Trust!" She laughed, and her eyes glittered. With

a swift movement she stripped away the dress, and he felt as if he were standing on a burning pyre.

"God, no," he said, knowing what it would mean to touch her.

"You walk out now, and I'll tell him you tried to force yourself."

He blinked, and realized what she could do to him. But he had to face Chantal. And he had to be able to tell Chantal the truth, no matter what Blaise said.

"You're the most beautiful woman I've ever seen," he said. "You know the effect you have on men." He looked into her eyes and saw her frown and blink. "And you know what you're doing to me."

He turned and fled, racing down the stairs, her screams ringing in his ears as he left the house. He heard something smash behind him and looked back to see sparkling crystal, like teardrops sprinkled over the floor. He ran outside and slammed the door behind him, mounting to ride to the stable, where he dropped off the horse. Giraud turned to look at him, his gaze going from Rafe's groin back to his face.

"It doesn't look as if she succeeded," he said, both amusement and surprise sounding in his voice as he straightened up and studied Rafe.

"You know about her?"

He shrugged. "Half of Louisiana knows about her, but Mr. Therrie's in the half that doesn't know. If you did what I think you just did, you made an enemy who'll ruin you."

"What are you talking about?"

"You refused what she offered?"

"Maybe I did," Rafe said, reluctant to talk about her.

"Sir, you better pack your belongings and move to New Jersey or New York or somewhere out of her reach. I can't say I've ever known anyone who refused that woman anything without regretting it. Not *anything*. You've made an enemy."

"How do you know that?"

"She had a slave girl who didn't like her and ran away. Missus had her found and killed."

"I don't believe you. Mr. Therrie is good to his people."

"Yes, he is. He didn't know what happened. She had a reward posted, and when they brought that child back here she just disappeared."

"Maybe she ran away again."

He shook his head. "We'd have heard. All we heard were stories how she drowned in a bayou when she was running away again."

"That's just a tale," Rafe said.

"Wait and see if you think it's a tale. She'll do something you'll regret."

Rafe sat down on a bale of hay and leaned back against the post, closing his eyes.

"I'd oblige the lady," Giraud said. "Mr. Therrie will never know, and she can ruin you. Oh, yes sir, I'd oblige the lady. Or I'd pack and move a hundred miles away from her."

"Instead, I'm going to ride Daedalus. I feel ready for a fight."

Within minutes he had swung into the saddle on the stallion and begun a trot. As he made a wide circle he glanced at the house, and saw the figure in deep green standing on the upper gallery gazing down at him. Remembering her full, lush body pressing against his, he felt desire stir again.

He didn't see Chantal for the next few days, and he didn't feel like taking morning rides. Wednesday afternoon, as he worked in the barn with five slaves, he heard a loud cry.

Chapter 10

One of the men fell back against a post and dropped to the ground, while another yanked away the pitchfork. Willow had run two of the tines of the pitchfork through his foot.

Rafe bent over the bloody foot. "Let's get you to the hospital. Dr. Baines isn't here today, but I can bandage you up." Rafe helped him from the barn to the small building that served as Belle Destin's hospital, where Rafe cleaned and bound Willow's foot. "Take a dose of laudanum, and stay off your foot for a few days until the swelling goes down."

"Yes, sir."

"I'll help you back to your quarters." Tall and thin, Willow couldn't have weighed one hundred and forty pounds. As Rafe supported him Willow felt all bones, yet Rafe had seen him lift logs that had to be twice his weight.

"Willow, is your woman in the field?"

"No, sir. Zena's with child. Any day now."

"Can she cook for you?"

"Yes, sir. My quarters are where the pink flowers are."

"You'll get a holiday now," Rafe said, heading for the small cabin with a pot of pink flowers on the porch.

"Yes, sir. Wasn't worth getting stabbed in the foot."

Rafe laughed. "If you need more laudanum, you send someone to me and I'll get it. No need to be sitting there hurting."

"Yes, sir. Thank you, Mr. O'Brien."

In the hot afternoon, with cicadas thrumming and bees buzzing around shafts of purple vitex, a baby's wail pierced the air. Rafe paused, aware of Willow's head jerking up.

"Lordy, Zena's time's come!" He broke away from Rafe, then yelped with pain as he hobbled up onto the porch.

Rafe followed him onto the shaded porch, smells of collards assailing him. He heard voices, and then a thin, young black girl appeared carrying a pan of water. She stepped back in surprise when she saw Rafe.

"Pearlie, where's Zena?"

"Afternoon, Mr. O'Brien," Pearlie said, the words spilling out and a smile breaking through. "Willow has a baby boy."

As he turned to the bed, Rafe's eyes adjusted to the darkened cabin. He stared in shock, feeling as if an apparition had materialized before him. As the midwife worked over the new mother, Chantal sat beside the bed. Her hair was tied in a kerchief and she held a small bundle in her arms. She glanced over her shoulder at Rafe, and then looked up at Willow.

"You have a son," she said, holding the baby for Willow to see.

"A boy!" He looked down and bent over the bed. "Zena?"

"I'm fine, Willow," came a soft voice.

Chantal turned to Rafe. "Want to see the baby?" she asked, holding him out.

Startled beyond words to find Chantal there, Rafe barely heard her question. As he stared at her, heat pressed in on him, and smells of sweat and powder assailed him. Chantal of silks and perfume and dainty dresses, of sweetness and innocence and soft kisses, that very same Chantal was now sitting beside a mother in labor and offering support in a sweltering slave cabin. More startling, she was completely at ease. She smiled and held the baby out to him.

"Look at their baby."

He stared at a round head, eyes squinted closed, and tiny fists. "That's a fine baby," he said, glancing at Willow, who was unaware anyone existed except Zena.

"I'll be outside," Rafe said, stepping onto the porch

and wiping the sweat off his brow. He could still hear
Chantal talking in a low voice. He waited, feeling as
if he were caught in a dream, but he knew that the
heat was real, and the smells were real, and—strangest
of all—that Chantal's voice was real.

Finally she emerged, carrying a folded bandanna.
A damp sheen of perspiration had caused tiny tendrils
to curl against her temple, and she lifted her hair off
her neck and smiled up at him.

"What are you doing?" he asked. He sounded like
a simpleton.

"I'm just here to give some comfort, and to help
the midwife in any way I can."

He took her arm. "Come here," he said. "You don't
have to go home this minute." He led her far from the
rows of cabins, down to the winding creek. As soon
as they had reached the stream, he knelt and dipped
the bandanna in the cold water. He wrung it out to
wipe her brow and dab at his own.

"Your father allows this? He allows you to attend
birthings?"

"I've been around mamas and babies all my life,
and early on I would follow Dr. Baines."

"Does Lazare Galliard know this?"

"Merciful angels, no! And no one here will tell him.
Maman wants the marriage as much as Papa, and once
I'm mistress of Soleil it will be quite seemly for me
to tend our people."

"It isn't quite seemly now—in fact, it's damned unusual. And far from proper. . . ."

She laughed. "We had a good midwife, Auntie
Bella, until she died of yellow jack. She and Dr. Baines
knew I liked babies, and Auntie Bella would let me
watch and offer comfort to the mother. At first Dr.
Baines wouldn't allow me to attend, but he knew that
she let me. And then we got Fenella, and she's happy
for me to come sit with her patients."

"You must have been a child when you started."

"How old do you think these mothers are? Zena is
fourteen. The mistress of the plantation is supposed to
tend the sick, but my stepmother isn't going to care

for anyone except my father and herself. She doesn't want to go near the slave quarters, and she won't think about offering them comfort if she has to sit with them. So I do it. She won't complain to Papa, because then *she* might have to care for someone.''

''Do you sit with them in epidemics?''

''I have,'' she answered calmly, ''until Papa gets word of it, and then he won't allow me to go near the cabins. But I like the births best. I love little babies more than anything.''

He stared at her, and his feelings for her underwent a change, like sands shifting and blowing into new hills and patterns. That first afternoon he had fallen in love with Chantal because she was beautiful, exciting, with a dancing sparkle in her eyes and a lack of shyness that intrigued him. His feelings for her had grown stronger when he'd discovered her clambering around on rooftops, doing what no other woman he knew would do. But now he was seeing another side to her. Admiration and respect were becoming the bedrock foundation for the fiery attraction.

This was a woman who met life head-on, a woman in the fullest sense, sweet, innocent, sensual, capable. Her lips curved in a faint smile, dimples showing, curiosity lighting her eyes. Perspiration still shone on her brow and her dress held wrinkles, and in that moment he wanted to pull her down in the grass and possess her, bury himself in her softness. Desire ignited in him, burning like a raging fire. And passion must have shone in his face, because her smile faded and she drew her breath. The vein pulsed faster in her regal neck.

''Chantal,'' he whispered, and bent his head to kiss her, crushing her in his arms. He was dusty and hot, but he forgot everything except her. He leaned over her and slid one hand to her breast, feeling her nipple through the thin material, sliding his hand down over her, wanting to kiss her and to peel away her dress. He had just glimpsed an earthiness to her he hadn't known before, and he suspected that when a man possessed her she would be an eager partner. He ran his hands over her hips and fought for self-control.

It wasn't the time or place, and when she pushed against him he released her. His manhood strained against his tight trousers, and he ached with a need that could be satisfied in only one way.

"You shouldn't do that, Rafferty."

"I hav ta," he answered in a rough voice, lapsing into a thick Irish brogue. "And you like me ta kiss you."

She shook her head. "I shouldn't like it."

He stepped to her and tilted her face up, with his arm around her waist. "You like it, and you should. All that stands between us is a social order and a fortune. If I acquire the fortune, I can overcome the social order."

"No!" She flung away from him, putting distance between them. "There's far more standing between us. I'm promised to Lazare, a pledge that is binding and forever. We have Soleil, our home."

"Oh no! Soleil isn't a home. And it isn't yours and Lazare's yet. You haven't lived in it. It's unfinished brick and wood, a shell."

"It's my *home*! It's all I've dreamed about, and I'll have Lazare's babies!"

Hot, bursting with desire for her, her words goaded him. He reached her in one long stride and swept her into his arms, crushed her to him. "You can't marry a man you don't love! And you don't love him when you can do this!" Rafe said softly and kissed her, his mouth teasing her full soft lips.

She pushed against his chest, but her tongue thrust over his. Then she sagged against him, her hips moving as her arms twined around his neck.

He was on fire, shaking with need, while trying to maintain an iron control. He bent his head to kiss her breast through the material, heard her moan, felt the hard bud of her nipple.

She gasped and pushed away from him. Tears streaked her cheeks as she hurried away. He let her go, but he felt a tiny flame of exultant hope. And absolute determination to do all in his power to win her. But first, he would have to win her father.

Feeling as if she were being chased by a demon, alarmed and fighting emotions that tugged at her, Chantal closed the door to her room and leaned against it. She gasped for breath and crossed the room to the mirror, to stare at her wild-eyed reflection. Her mouth was red from his kisses, her dress a mass of wrinkles from being crushed in his arms. As she stared at herself her own image faded from sight, replaced by that of smoldering blue eyes that made her heart pound and her breathing slow.

"Rafferty," she whispered, and closed her eyes. He stirred within her something deep and wild and terrifying, something she didn't want to know. It was a pull of fleshly wants, a pull of tantalizing kisses that spun webs of magic around her. And yet . . .

Stop! Don't think about him! Don't remember! Think of Soleil, and Lazare, and Lazare's arms! But Lazare's kisses faded in comparison. They were tame and—

No! Her eyes flew open and she shivered in fright. "I will forget you, M'sieu Rafferty O'Brien. You're wicked and stubborn and, if I let you, you'll take everything from me."

Stop riding in the morning! Stop walking in the woods with him! Stop talking to him! Yet she could tell him anything. She hid her escapades from Lazare. She didn't tell him about her visiting the quarters to comfort the ill and be present at births. Papa and Maman hid that from him, too. Lazare would be enraged if he knew, yet Rafferty O'Brien had looked at her as if she had done something miraculous and praiseworthy. His voice had held awe, and his eyes . . .

She tugged on the bell pull and when Loretta, her servant girl, appeared, Chantal motioned to her. "Loretta, prepare a bath and lay out clean clothes."

"Yes, Miss Chantal." Her face broke into a grin. "Did Zena have her baby?"

Chantal's tension eased, and she smiled. "Yes. A baby boy. A fine baby boy."

"Did she now! I have to tell Addie and Theodore."
She rushed out of the room and Chantal felt better.

That night Alain and Diantha joined them for supper. As they sat around the long table and Theodore
passed out silver dishes of crawfish gumbo, hot biscuits, candied yams, and thick slices of pink ham,
Chantal's feeling of joy over the new baby was replaced by a growing foreboding.

Always pale and quiet, that night Diantha was even
more subdued, eating little and speaking only when
spoken to, while Alain seemed tense and talked too
much. Alain was hiding something. It had to be the
Vigilantes.

The moment the ladies were in the drawing room
and the men shut in the library to smoke their cigars,
Chantal turned to Diantha.

"I want to show Diantha my dress for the Vacheries'
ball," she said, catching Diantha's hand and leading
her from the room before Amity or Maman could protest or join them.

When they were upstairs, and the door closed behind her, Chantal turned to Diantha. "Something is
making you afraid, isn't it?"

"Yes," she said, closing her eyes, sitting down on
the edge of the cedar chest, and putting her face in her
hands.

"Diantha, what is it?" Chantal rushed to her side
and patted her round shoulders.

"I'm not supposed to tell you, but I know Alain is
going to get hurt! Next Friday night men are going to
the Irish Channel. They're going to fight the Irishmen,
and try to drive them from town."

"No!" Chantal exclaimed, her mind racing to Rafferty. At Belle Destin he was safe, but she knew that
most weekends he went into town to Irish saloons.
"Rafferty O'Brien is Irish," she said.

Diantha blinked. "Who?"

"Our overseer."

"He's safe. He's here at Belle Destin. But I'm so
scared Alain will get hurt."

"Lazare will be with Alain. Lazare is a Know-Nothing, and this sounds like their doings."

Diantha burst into tears. "Alain warned me not to tell you, because you'll go to Lazare, but I want you to try to stop Alain."

"I can talk to Papa."

"No! Please don't do that. Alain would be enraged. Just talk to Alain."

"I've tried, and it was useless."

"Please, Chantal!" she pleaded. Her pale brown eyes were red from tears, and wisps of her black hair had come loose from pins and hung on her temple. "Sometimes he'll listen to you. You're brave and you stand up to him. When I try he gets so angry, I can't bear it. You mustn't tell Ormonde."

"Alain will listen to Maman."

"She knows," Diantha said with bitterness. "You know how she loves violence and excitement. She thinks it's grand, and is urging him to do these wild things. He discusses it all with her."

Shocked, Chantal sat down and stared at Diantha. "He discusses that with Maman and not with you?"

"Yes," Diantha said, her shoulders shaking as the tears came yet again. "Sometimes I think she weaves a voodoo spell over him."

"Of course she doesn't!" Chantal exclaimed, knowing Maman did indeed favor Alain. Chantal rubbed her wrist ruefully. All of them fighting: Lazare, Alain, Rafferty.

"You don't know the two of them. He sees her in town more than he does here."

A knock startled them into silence, and Amity entered. "Maman said to fetch you both."

Diantha dried her eyes, rose from off the chest, and glided to Chantal's side. "Please talk to him," she whispered in her ear, while Amity stared with wide-eyed curiosity. They returned to the parlor, where Blaise waited alone. She studied Diantha's red nose and eyes.

"Why have you been crying, Diantha?"

"I worry about things."

"You're frightened of shadows. Alain should get you with child, and then you'd have something to occupy your time."

Diantha's cheeks grew as red as the rest of her face, and Chantal searched for another topic of conversation. Diantha wanted children, and had been unable to conceive. Blaise's constant jibes certainly did nothing to help her.

"Do you know how many will be at the Vacheries' ball Saturday night?" Chantal asked.

Blaise shrugged. "It will be the usual crowd."

The doors to the adjoining parlor opened, and the men entered the room, Alain frowning as he noted Diantha's condition. The couple left early, and as Chantal sat by her window looking down at the darkened overseer's house, she worried about the weekend.

On Monday afternoon, after rehearsing what she would say, Chantal waited in the lane for Rafferty to ride home from the fields.

Wearing the emerald-green goutil riding dress with a green bonnet, she had dressed with care.

"Chantal! This is a pleasure," he said as he approached, flashing her a smile that made her tingle. His teeth were even, white against his copper skin. His shirtsleeves were rolled high, and his boots were dust-covered.

"I want to talk to you," she said, seeing the pleasure and curiosity in his gaze.

"Of course. And it's a good time to talk to you about a matter we've avoided."

"Oh?" They turned off the lane and she rode beside him, knowing he would lead her somewhere private and shaded.

"Now what's this urgent matter?" he asked.

She had rehearsed a dozen ways to lead up to asking him about the weekend. Now they all seemed ridiculous. "I haven't seen you for a while. Do you like working here?" she asked, feeling foolish now and at a loss.

"Of course. Your father is a good man. I've learned about cotton."

"Enough to want to grow it yourself?"

"I still have reservations there," he answered.

"Are you staying at Belle Destin this weekend?" The question just popped out, when she had intended to lead up to it in a subtle manner.

"Now why this great curiosity about my where-abouts on the weekend? If you want me to stay, or if you'll see me, of course I'll stay."

"No! I was just asking."

"I can't tell you how disappointed I am," he said, in a teasing voice that made her annoyed she had bothered to try to warn him.

"I think we should go back now."

"Oh, no! Not until I know what's behind this. You didn't ride out to meet me to ask about the weather or cotton. What's on your mind?"

"I was out anyway, and I was being courteous."

He laughed. "Courteous, hell! C'mon, Chantal. Why the sudden interest in my weekend?"

"You can be the most exasperating person!"

He laughed and drew her reins and dismounted. "Get down."

Her pulse pounded as she stared at him. "I'm going home."

"I said get down." He reached up and swung her down to the ground. They had ridden to Spider Creek, which fed into the river. A cool breeze blew, and oaks shaded them. She glared at him as he leaned one arm against his horse and faced her. He pulled down a handful of curling Spanish moss and looked at it. "They say this isn't really moss. It feeds on air."

"There's an Indian legend that during a flood a mother and her two children climbed a tree. In the cold night the mother prayed to the moon to shine on them for warmth. The moon shredded clouds and tossed them to the tree to make a blanket, and Spanish moss has grown in the trees ever since."

Dropping the moss, he reached out to untie her bonnet. "You lost a wager to me. It's time you learned to swim."

"No!" She stepped back.

"Yes. You'll never learn with soggy skirts wrapped around you," he said, yanking his shirt over his head and tossing it down. Her heart lurched and her breath caught.

"Sir! Don't take off anything else!" she exclaimed, shocked, her pulse racing.

He yanked off his boots and laughed, his eyes sparkling. "I'll keep on my pants if you prefer, but you're going to learn to swim before you fall into the river and drown. Do you know how many boats go down around here? Several people drown every few months, and you get into far too much trouble to—" He broke off to pull off his other boot and unfasten his belt.

Her pulse was erratic and she burned with embarrassment—she felt as if the afternoon had heated another hundred degrees. Still she couldn't resist looking at his broad, tanned chest with its dark curls, its muscles rippling when he moved.

"Sir, my father will have you horsewhipped!" She felt on fire. She had never been with a man in such circumstances.

"He's in the city, and you know it. Your sister is at the house, and your stepmother wouldn't venture out in this heat for anything. There's not a hand around here, or anyone else for that matter. No one can hear you yell; no one will come to your aid."

Shocked, she stared at him. "You would have the audacity . . ."

"Yes, I would. I don't want the woman I love to drown."

Stunned, her shock was transformed to anger, but beneath it the words swirled in a dance that played through her thoughts over and over: *the woman I love.* . . . She backed up a step. "Don't you touch me!" She saw the look of determination on his face. Yards behind him the creek was brown, opaque, hiding heaven knew what. All emotions coalesced in a fear that made her feel as if she were suffocating.

"I can't go in the water. It—"

"Isn't proper," he said in unison with her and he laughed, but she felt only chilling fright.

"You can go in your dress, and its weight will pull you under and you'll hate it, or you can take off the dress and go in your shift."

"Sir! Papa will beat you senseless! I'd be compromised! That's scandalous!" she snapped, outrage refueling her anger.

"Your papa won't know. I've seen women in their shifts before, Chantal," he said in a dry voice, "and I'll turn my back until you're neck-deep in the water."

"I can't go into that water," she said, her voice dropping and fear turning to a cold terror that shut out everything else. She looked up at him. "Please, Rafferty, I'm terrified of it," she admitted.

His voice softened to a gentle tone she hadn't heard before. "If you learn to swim, you won't ever fear it again. And you'll be safe, Chantal. I swear I won't let you sink. You can learn to survive with your head out of water."

She shivered and stared past him, forgetting him in her fright. "I can't. You can't imagine how fearful it is, because nothing frightens you. You're not afraid of getting hurt or drowning. You're not afraid of water."

He moved to her, his hands touching her, his voice soothing. "I swear to you, your head won't go under unless you want to."

"There could be gators and snakes and turtles and all kinds of crawly things."

"I'll splash around and scare the snakes and turtles away, and there aren't any gators here. I swim here often—I was here yesterday and early this morning, and there hasn't been a gator once. The ground is rocky in this particular part of the creek and it'll be easier to teach you here."

"No, please. You don't know how it frightens me. I feel as if my heart will burst."

"Why don't you just trust me to do what I promised?" He asked this in such gentle tones that her attention returned to him. "Now your dress is all unbuttoned. Why not go in your shift? I promise I won't look when I carry you into the water.''

"No!" To her horror, she burst into tears.

"Hey, love," he said, in a soft voice that comforted her. He pressed her against him and stroked her head.

"You're never afraid, and you don't know what it's like!" she sobbed, mortified and hating her tears and trying to get control of her emotions, suddenly furious with him for being the cause of her trouble. "Damn you, Rafferty O'Brien! I wish I'd never met you!" She flung the words at him and pulled back.

He grinned. "That's my Chantal. Ah, love, I knew the tears wouldn't last.'' In one swift movement, keeping his eyes on hers, he peeled off the green riding habit.

She shrieked and tried to yank it back, but he scooped her into his arms and marched into the creek. The moment the water touched her, rational thought fled. She fought him, but his arms tightened and he waded out until it rose to her breasts. Brown water swirled all around her. Rafferty O'Brien was the only solid thing in the world. She locked her arms around him and buried her face against his neck.

"I hate you, you bastard!"

"Relax," he said, and she could hear his laughter. "You're all right. It's cool and should be refreshing, and it's as safe as if we were standing on dry land. I made you a promise and I'll keep it." He kept talking, and at first she heard only the steady sound of his voice. The words didn't register, but the tenseness went out of her. The water felt cool against her skin, and he was keeping his promise.

She raised her head. "Damn you, you son of a bitch!"

He laughed. "Where did you learn such language?"

"I've never used it before." She had heard Rafferty use it, as well as Lazare and Papa and Grand-père Therrie, and now she understood why they did. "You're a damnable scoundrel!"

"Admit it," he said, and his eyes sparkled. "The water feels good, and you're safe.''

"I hate it. I'm terrified of it."

"No you're not. I know when your fright left. Now I'm going to let you stand. The river bed is solid, I'll hold you, and you're just as safe as ever."

"Damn you, don't . . ."

He released her legs, and she felt sharp rocks beneath her slippers. Water came below her armpits. Rafferty held her, and he kept his gaze above her neck. But all sense of modesty had left her, chased away by terror and anger.

"Now we walk around, so you become accustomed to it."

"I will never in the next million years become accustomed to this. I loathe, hate, and despise it and you, you miserable son of a bitch!"

He laughed, and her anger increased. "Now watch how it's done," he said, splashing away from her, swimming off and leaving her stranded.

"Come back here!" she screamed at him, water splashing her and waves rocking her.

"Watch me!" he called, his arms slicing through the water, and it became easy to watch him, what with the muscles glistening in his shoulders and arms as he swam and circled to come back to her. He disappeared beneath the water.

"Rafferty? *Rafferty!*"

He surfaced in front of her and shook his head to fling water from his face. His shoulders and chest were bare, and drops of water sparkled on him as he waded toward her. His hair was a shiny cap of black curls pressed to his head. White teeth flashed as he grinned and held out his hands. "See, nothing to fear. It's simple."

She became aware of his bare chest, his blatant masculinity, as her gaze roved over him. He waded toward her and her heart pounded as she watched him. His smile faded, and as he studied her he drew a deep breath, causing his chest to expand. Water swirled against him level with his ribs, and his gaze raked over her.

Her nipples grew taut, and the lush fullness of her

breasts was revealed, her shift clinging to her, as his gaze drifted over her.

"You said you wouldn't look," she said in a low voice.

"I'll keep my other promises," he replied in a deeper voice. He moved closer, and water eddied around her.

"Don't!" She turned to rush away from him, but lost her footing. Strong arms caught her, and she was thankful for his strength and aware of his sleek, wet flesh, so warm to the touch even in the cool water. "You promised."

He studied her in silence. "If you can hold your breath and duck your head under the water and lose your fear of it, the rest is simple."

"You said I didn't have to get my head under."

"You don't, but it's a lot easier if you become accustomed to it. I'll hold you," he said, placing his hands firmly on her waist. "Hold your breath and close your eyes, and put your face in."

The first time she panicked, and would have fallen if he hadn't held her. But after a few more tries it was not as frightening, and finally she could hold her breath and submerge. The first time she did, and came up to rub water away from her eyes, she opened them to find him grinning, his teeth gleaming white against his skin.

"I knew you wouldn't stay afraid! That's good! Let's do it again." Feeling pleased by his praise, she went under with him. He showed her how to blow out her breath, and they laughed over the bubbles. Soon he was holding her middle with his hands, while she kicked her legs and moved her arms and put her face in the water. And the only thing she was aware of was Rafferty's hands moving upward ever so slightly to brush the underside of her breasts. She knew her filmy underclothes were plastered to her body, but his voice sounded normal and he kept giving her instructions as if she were buttoned up to the chin.

Finally he stood her up. "We can stop for today."

"No, let me try, and you catch me if I sink."

"Better yet, plan to sink. Try to touch the bottom. I'll pull you up if you don't come right back to the surface."

She followed his directions, then felt a momentary panic as she neared the bottom. Strong arms scooped her up and she clung to Rafferty, her heart pounding. As she opened her eyes, fear vanished. She stood in his arms, her breasts touching his chest.

"I got scared," she whispered, and something flickered in his eyes. He drew a deep breath. She thought he was going to kiss her and she raised her face, only to realize he was holding back.

"I'll try again," she said in haste, feeling foolish, yet engulfed in longing to feel his hard body pressed against hers, his mouth on hers.

He caught her. "It's getting late, and you have to dry your clothes before you go home."

She hadn't thought about drying. "You have to get out and turn your back and keep your promise."

As his brows arched in a wicked manner, he smiled. "You want me to get out first and leave you here?"

"No! I'll follow you."

He laughed and shrugged. "Have it your way."

Blushing furiously, she placed her hands on his waist and waded out behind him. His pants were wet, clinging to him as if he wore nothing at all, and her gaze drifted down over his firm buttocks and long, well-muscled legs, his body that was fit and virile.

"Now close your eyes!" she gasped, feeling her heart pound and a warmth curl inside her. She should take her eyes away; she didn't want *him* to look, yet he stood only a few feet away with his back turned and she couldn't stop gazing at a body that made her pulse race.

"It'll take you half an hour to dry your things, so we might as well sit down and be comfortable."

"You keep your back turned!"

He chuckled. "If you'll take off your wet clothes and wrap in my horse blanket, you could hang the clothes to dry."

"I'd do that, except I can't trust you to keep your word one minute!"

He laughed again, increasing her annoyance. "I'll keep my back turned. Take them off and wring them out."

She glared at the back of his head, and then once again her gaze ran down over him swiftly. She felt heat rise in her cheeks as she walked away. Behind a bush she pulled off her underthings and wrung them out, spreading them out on a log in the sunshine. She glanced at Rafferty, who sat cross-legged with his back to her.

"Are you all right?" he asked.

"Don't you dare turn around!" she snapped, jumping back behind the bush and trying to cross her hands over herself.

He took down the horse blanket. "Chantal, come get this so we can talk. My back is turned." He flung the blanket over his shoulder, and it fell in a heap yards from her.

She scurried out and snatched it up, half expecting him to break another promise, but he remained with his back to her. Leaving her shoulders bare, she wrapped herself in the blanket and sat down.

"You can turn around now," she said. She sounded prim; it made her nervous to sit with him while she wore only a blanket and all he wore was wet trousers.

He looked amused, and took his time studying her in the blanket. "Now, why did you want to know about my weekend?"

"I told you," she began, then saw the cynical gaze that indicated he knew she was lying. She lifted her chin. "I don't want you to get hurt, but I don't want my brother hurt either. And if I tell you, you'll warn your friends and Alain could be hurt."

His amusement vanished. "You might as well tell me now. The Vigilantes are going to do something, aren't they?"

"It isn't Vigilantes. It's probably the Know-Nothings, but Alain will be with them. They're going to try to drive some of the Irish out of the city on

Friday night. Will you stay at Belle Destin this week-end?'' The last came out in a rush. She was embarrassed, but she wanted an answer and she wanted reassurance that he would stay home.

His gaze was intense, holding hers. ''Do you care, Chantal?''

She looked away. ''I don't want you to get hurt.''

Silence lengthened between them, and finally she faced him. He studied her with an enigmatic expression.

''I'm going to town Friday,'' he said.

She closed her eyes. ''I shouldn't have warned you! You'll tell the others, and Alain will be hurt.''

''Doesn't he know there are twenty thousand Irish in the city now? They won't be driven out by an angry mob.''

''It's the ones in the Irish Channel they dislike,'' she said, glancing at his bare shoulders. Sunlight was dappled on his skin, and the sight of his bare chest disturbed her.

''Tell your brother that word is out about his plans. Maybe that will change them.''

''Please stay at Belle Destin!''

''I'd planned to go to town Friday. I'm meeting Touzet.''

''He'll be with you?''

''Probably, although I'll warn him to stay away. Touzet doesn't enjoy brawls. Chantal, I'll try to get Alain out of it if I can.''

She drew a deep breath. ''I'm frightened for him. Diantha is wild with fear for him.''

''Go to your father about it. He'd stop it fast enough.''

''Papa will be up north. Maman is urging Alain to do this, because she loves trouble.'' Rafe frowned, rubbing his knuckles on the grass.

''My things might be slightly dry now,'' she said hopefully, moving away, aware her bare legs were revealed with each step as the blanket swung open. She felt her thin batiste underclothes, which were still wet. She glanced at him to find him watching her, and knew that if she was going to leave this place it would have to be in wet clothes.

"Turn your back again while I dress."

With a lithe unfolding of limbs, he stood up and turned around. Strong back, slim hips, well-shaped buttocks beneath the clinging damp trousers—his was a body that was perfectly proportioned. She drew a deep breath, her nipples taut against the scratchy blanket. She dropped it to dress swiftly.

"I have to go home now," she said when she was dressed in her riding habit.

He picked up his shirt and pulled it over his head. Her gaze traveled over his chest, then she looked up to catch him watching her and she blushed.

"Meet me here tomorrow afternoon at the same time," he said as they rode home. "You can bring dry clothes, and that way you won't have to wait after we swim. By next week, or even sooner, you'll be swimming as easily as I do."

"Never like you do! But it wasn't as frightening as I thought," she said, grateful that he had helped her to overcome her worst fear.

"You'll enjoy it someday," he said, watching her. "We're almost to the house, so we part ways here."

She reined in and looked at him, and her pulse skipped. His hair had dried and was an unruly tangle, but it gave him a rakish air that was as appealing as when he was groomed and neat.

"I'm probably the only woman west of the Mississippi who can swim," she said.

"No. There are other women who can swim."

She wondered if he had taught someone else, and it gave her a pang. "Have you taught others?"

The moment she asked she wished she could take back the question, for a sardonic gleam appeared in his eyes. "Yes, Chantal. I've taught others. Want to know who?"

"No, I don't!"

He laughed and touched her chin, lifting her face until she looked at him. "I'm glad," he said, the rest remaining unspoken, but she knew what he left unsaid.

"Please don't go to town Friday night."

"Thank you for telling me." He straightened her collar, his hands brushing over her and then his gaze following. "Better go in a back way. You look as if you've been in the water. But no one will know you've been running around without a stitch."

"You don't need to mention that!"

He chuckled. "Meet me tomorrow," he said, wheeling his horse around and riding away, urging his horse to a trot. Remembering his bare chest, his hands moving on her when he'd held her in the water, she felt longing stir. With a ripple of excitement when she thought about tomorrow's meeting she turned her horse for home.

That night Chantal took Amity with her to call on Alain. Without wasting words, she asked upon arrival if she could talk to him alone.

He led her to his front parlor, which was filled with somber mahogany furniture and dark colors that made Chantal feel as if she were inside a cave.

"Now, what brings you rushing over here on a matter of such secrecy and importance?" he asked, sitting down, crossing one leg over the other, and swinging his foot.

"It'll make you angry. You have to promise you won't hurt me when I tell you."

"Good Lord, you'll forever hold that last talk against me! How many times have I hurt you?"

She gave him a look, and he shrugged.

"I haven't really hurt you, and you know it. I promise I'll sit right here in my chair. Chantal, you poke your nose into too many places it shouldn't go."

"I don't want you hurt, and I know you have a wife who fears for your welfare."

"Women are chronic worriers, and Diantha fears her shadow. Will you get to whatever it is?"

"I've heard some men plan to attack the Irish Friday night."

"That's absurd!" He laughed and continued to swing one foot. "Did you hear that from Papa?"

"No. Captain Alworth stopped his steamboat at the landing and told Amity. He didn't approve."

"Captain Alworth is a stuffy old codger and full of nonsense. How could a few men drive the Irish out of New Orleans? The city is overrun with the bastards."

Alain was lying. He stared at her too long, probably thinking that would convince her of his honesty.

"Alain, tell your friends to be careful. Captain Alworth said the Irish will be expecting a fight. You know they're tough."

"Did that damned Irish overseer tell you this?" Alain asked, sitting up straighter, and she felt cold.

"No, he didn't! How often do you think I talk to Belle Destin's overseer?"

Alain's foot commenced swinging again. "I suppose that's true enough. I still can't believe Papa would hire an Irishman. Lazare despises him as much as I do."

"You know he's capable."

"That's because he came from wealth and not peasant stock."

"What a snob you are!"

"Better that than to consort with common trash." He stood up and held out his hands. "Thanks anyway, and you owe me an apology. I didn't even raise my voice."

As Chantal rode home later, Amity failed to cheer her up.

"Chantal, tell me what's bothering you."

She stared at Amity's pale face in the darkened carriage. They were close and shared secrets, and sometimes Chantal felt as if she were more a mother to Amity than Maman was.

"Diantha is terrified for Alain. Some men plan to attack the Irish Friday night. I tried to talk to Alain about it."

"Papa will be furious if Alain does that. Mr. O'Brien goes to town most Friday nights. You should warn him!"

"I know I can't keep Lazare from going, any more than Diantha can stop Alain. I've warned Mr. O'Brien."

"Thank goodness! Chantal, I'll tell you a secret that only Mr. O'Brien knows."

"What is it?" Chantal frowned. What secret was shared between Amity and Rafferty O'Brien?

"I've ridden Daedalus!" Amity said with joy in her voice.

"He allowed you to ride that stallion, when Papa—"

"No! He discovered me on the horse's back and he promised he wouldn't tell."

"Amity, you could be hurt! No one rides him except Mr. O'Brien!"

"Mr. O'Brien made me promise that unless he was with me, I wouldn't ride Daedalus again. Chantal, he's a marvelous horse, and he responds to every command."

Amazed, Chantal stared at Amity, and then she laughed. "You have a way with animals no one else does."

"I showed Mr. O'Brien my raccoons. And he took me way up the bayou and showed me a pair of snowy egrets. They're beautiful."

"You like Mr. O'Brien," Chantal said, seeing he had won Amity's heart.

"Oh, yes! He's the nicest overseer we've ever had, and I hope he stays forever. Maman doesn't like him though."

"How do you know that?"

"I know. I heard her discuss him with Papa. She hates him. He's done something to displease her, but when I asked him about it he changed the subject."

Chantal drew a sharp breath and felt anger, because it was too easy to guess why Maman was displeased with him. Then she realized what it would have meant if Maman had been pleased. . . . Had Rafferty refused her? Chantal felt a rush of pleasure at the thought. Yet if he had, Maman would keep after Papa until he let Rafferty go.

The next morning all thoughts about the Know-

Nothings had been replaced by seething turmoil over that day's swimming lesson.

She dressed in dainty batiste underclothes, leaving her corset at home and thankful she had done so yesterday. How she hated its constraints! She rolled up an extra pair of underclothes and pulled on her blue riding dress and soon she was riding down the lane, her pulse skittering like rain on the roof, knowing she was doing something that was wild and scandalous and delicious and fun.

Chapter 11

Waiting in dark shadows Friday night, Chantal heard the approach of a horse. Moonlight splashed over the lane and Rafe appeared, his broad-brimmed black hat square on his head.

She urged her horse forward into his path. "Are you going to town?"

"Yes. I'm glad you happened along," he said, producing a folded piece of paper. He rode close beside her, facing her. "I want you to have this."

"What is it?" she asked, taken aback, having rehearsed what she would say to him.

"My will. I have a little savings in the bank, and my—"

"Oh, no! Please don't go!" She felt a wrench of pain and fear. "Please stay here tonight!" She clasped his arm.

"By heaven, you sound as if you mean it," he said, studying her. His faint smile vanished. "Chantal, tell me just this once, let me hear you say it—tell me you'll miss me."

"I'll miss you. Please don't go into town! I don't want your will, I want you to stay here. Lazare promised me he wouldn't go."

"Dammit," Rafferty said, leaning away. "For a moment, I thought you cared whether or not I'm beaten to death."

"I do care! I don't want anyone hurt!"

"Take this, Chantal," he said, pressing the folded paper into her hand. "If something happens to me I want you to have my possessions, and I know you'll take good care of my horse, Finnian."

Her throat felt as if there were a knot in it.

"Kiss me good-bye," Rafferty added. His voice was deep, the words slow, making her pulse race.

He was going to town to a terrible fight. She held his will in her hands, so he expected something dreadful to happen. It might be his last night. She slid her hand along his arm, feeling the hard muscles. She felt a leaden weight close around her heart. She looked up at him, biting her lip. He waited, and in the shadows she couldn't see his expression. She leaned forward to kiss his cheek.

His arm went around her waist. "Such a chaste kiss," he drawled. "So cool and proper. Is that the way to bid farewell to a man riding to his death?"

"You're too hard-headed and stubborn to let him kill you!" she rejoined, but the snap was gone. Still only inches away from him, she was breathless. For weeks she had ridden with him, hours filled with provocative moments and constant touches that had been twigs heaped on a fire that burned steadily. Every afternoon this week she had been swimming with him, touched by him constantly, yet he hadn't kissed her. But her awareness of him, rather than diminishing, had grown and burned in a steady flame. She looked at his full underlip and sighed, leaning forward. It was wrong, forbidden, but he *was* going into terrible danger.

Her mouth pressed his, her tongue touching his lips. His arm tightened, crushing her against his chest. With a sob she clung to him and thrust her tongue deep into his mouth. Low inside she felt an ache, a need to press her hips against him, a hunger for more of him. What if something happened to him, this wild, exciting man, who was becoming her friend? Abandoning all reluctance and propriety, she put all of her deep feeling for him into the kiss.

He paused, and she opened her eyes to find him studying her with a solemn, searching expression.

"That's the kiss a woman gives her warrior before battle. You meant that, Chantal."

She wanted him to kiss her. His eyes narrowed and

he dipped his head, obliging her. His hand caressed her breast and she trembled, yet she couldn't stop him. She didn't want his will. She didn't want him to die. He raised his head a fraction.

"There's one way to keep me here," he whispered. "You can stay with me."

"You know I can't!" She pushed back, hurting and worrying, her cheeks flaming at the very thought.

He released her and moved back. "Good-bye, Chantal."

"No! *À bientot*. And please, be careful," she said, leaning over to grasp his hand. She heard him inhale, but she still couldn't see his expression or his eyes. "Please don't hurt my brother or Lazare," she said.

"I won't hurt Alain. Pray he doesn't try to put a blade through me!" He turned his horse.

"If you were to harm Lazare, I could never forgive you."

"So if your precious Lazare tries to kill me, I'm to let him?"

She caught her lip with her teeth. "Please don't go. . . ." He laughed and turned his horse.

She felt a chilling panic that all three of the men in her life would be hurt. All *three* . . . Somehow, in the past few minutes, she had at last faced the fact that Rafferty O'Brien did indeed have a place in her heart. The thought of him in danger frightened her.

She headed toward Belle Destin, her thoughts swirling. *There has to be a way to stop them!* She would find some means, but she had to do it within the hour. As she climbed the stairs to her room, an idea began to form. She moved close to the light to unfold his will and read a scrawling handwriting that was as bold as everything else about him:

May 9, 1858
To Whom It May Concern:

I, Rafferty Michael O'Brien, being of sound mind, do hereby bequeath all my worldly possessions to Chantal Therrie, these possessions being:

one slave, Tobiah Barr, my horse, Finnian, my Colt
.44 revolver, my English twelve-gauge, thirty-inch
shotgun and case, all furniture owned by me, two
deeds to property, and all the monies in my account
at the Louisiana State Bank.

These belongings are to be solely Chantal Therrie's possessions, to do with as she sees fit without
influence of husband or father.

It was signed with Rafferty's signature and witnessed by John Richards, the cashier of the bank, and
Jay Graham, a bank employee.

She stared at the paper and tears brimmed in her
eyes. He had ridden to town Wednesday and had the
will witnessed. She folded it and pressed it to her
heart, her mind racing. *There has to be a way to stop
them!*

An hour later she rushed toward a waiting carriage
where Amity sat.

"Hurry, Giraud! Go as fast as you dare!" Chantal
said, before climbing into the carriage and settling
back. They gained speed and rocked down the road.

"Chantal, are you certain we should do this?" Amity asked, her voice breathless with excitement.

"Yes, I am sure. Do you want Alain hurt?"

"No, but the men may not pay attention to us."

"They'll pay attention if you'll do just as I tell you.
Can you do what we agreed?"

"Yes, I promise!" Amity wriggled on the seat and
Chantal reached across to squeeze her hand. They had
different mothers, but she felt a bond with Amity that
was stronger than that with her parents. "I don't want
Alain or Lazare or Mr. O'Brien hurt."

"When we get there, there may be others involved
whom we know. I have Papa's pistol."

"You don't know how to fire a pistol!"

"I can shoot into the air and draw attention if necessary."

As the carriage careened around a turn both grew
silent, clinging to the seat.

"I wish we had started earlier."

"If we had, we would have overtaken Mr. O'Brien," Chantal replied. "Giraud is Papa's best driver, he'll get us there in time. They won't start early in the evening."

"How do you know?"

"Diantha overheard Alain talking about it. They want to wait until the Irishmen have had drinks and are enjoying themselves. Now let's go over our plans again."

Hours later, they went over them once more. The carriage stood in a darkened spot across the street from a well-lighted tavern. Music and shouts came. Occasionally a man staggered out and lurched down the street, or men sauntered into the tavern. A few women accompanied men to the tavern. Chantal kept watch in one direction and Amity in another. Amity clutched Chantal's arm.

"Chantal, look! There's Mr. O'Brien!"

At the sight of his familiar broad shoulders, Chantal's pulse skipped. A shorter, thin man was with him, and then she recognized that it was Touzet Lacquement. At the door to the tavern, Touzet left him. Rafferty glanced toward the carriage, and Chantal sank back against the seat.

"Get back, Amity! He has eyes like a hawk!" Her heart pounded while he stared at the carriage. He turned and went inside, and she let out her breath.

"Chantal, I'm frightened."

"I am too, but we have to do this, Amity. I don't want Alain to get killed." *Or Rafferty O'Brien.* "Lazare said he would stay away, but I suspect he tells me those things only to stop my worries, just as Alain tells Diantha only what he thinks she wants to hear."

"I don't think you should carry a pistol."

"I may need it. Giraud promised to look after you, so don't be too frightened. Think of Alain and Lazare and Mr. O'Brien."

"I'll try. I wish we could be done and on our way home. Chantal, if Maman learns about this, she'll be in a rage."

"Papa won't let her lay a hand on you."

"Papa is up north."

"Well then *I* won't let her lay a hand on you—or me. If I threaten to tell him, she won't." It had been years since one of Maman's beatings. Papa had put a stop to them. Chantal could recall her parents' shouts after he had returned home from the northern plantation. Maman had beaten Amity and Chantal for climbing a tree, and she had whipped one of the house servants for allowing them to climb it.

Maman had stayed in her room for days and had food sent up, and then climbed into the carriage to go to the townhouse for a month. After that the beatings had ceased and Chantal had felt a grim satisfaction, because Maman could be cruel.

Men poured into the tavern until Chantal could see the crowd through the open doors and lighted windows. Some men stood outside on the banquette. When Chantal noticed that Amity was napping, she let her sleep.

A few blocks down the street something moved, and her heart jumped. Dark shadows shifted as a large group of men approached.

"Miss Chantal," came Giraud's voice. He appeared at the window of the carriage, placing his hand on the sill.

"Miss Chantal, you know I have to do what you tell me to do, but your papa wouldn't want you here, and it isn't safe. I wouldn't want my child here."

She patted his hand. "Giraud, you just stay with Miss Amity and take care of her. I promise I'll be careful. You don't want Mr. Alain or Mr. Galliard or Mr. O'Brien killed, do you?"

"No, ma'am, but begging your pardon, ma'am, you don't know much about angry men. A mob isn't like one man or two. They don't listen to reason."

"It's still my brother and my fiancé and our overseer. They won't hurt me. Now you do just what I told you. Hurry, Giraud! Amity!"

"What is it?"

"Here they come! Giraud will be with you. Get out, and let's fix the carriage."

They watched as Giraud manipulated the team until the carriage had scraped the wall of the darkened, shuttered building. Then he removed a carriage wheel and dropped it to the ground. "Ma'am, I don't like any of this. You should let me take you and Miss Amity home."

"Whatever happens, you won't be blamed. Papa will know you did what I told you. Get down, Amity."

Amity stretched out on the bricked street. Chantal leaned down to push her bonnet awry and smudge dirt onto her bodice. "Now both of you do what we planned," she said, standing up.

"Miss Chantal, I wish you'd change your mind," Giraud pleaded, and she patted his arm.

"You protect Amity."

"Please be careful, Chantal," Amity implored.

Chantal took a deep breath. Her heart pounded with fear as she moved to the corner of the building. The men were closer now, light from the tavern playing over their faces, and she spotted Lazare's broad shoulders. He stood inches above the others, a tall man, big through the chest and shoulders. Alain was at his side and they carried clubs. A knife glinted beneath the street lamp.

Her heart pounded with fear at the sight of all the men. There were so many of them. She had expected ten or fifteen, but it looked as if there were thirty or forty.

They were only yards from the tavern. It was now or not at all. She wanted to run back into the dark and get Amity and go home, but instead she looked at Lazare and Alain and then glanced at the tavern. Rafferty was inside. She dashed forward across the lane toward the tavern, and she screamed.

Chapter 12

Over the notes of the Irish ballad Rafferty O'Brien heard the high-pitched woman's scream, and hair prickled on his nape. He had heard a scream like that twice before, high and shrill and ear-piercing, when Chantal had been around water.

He pushed through the crowd, moving faster than could be believed, shouldering people out of his way and dashing through the door. Men milled about outside; two men were fighting along the banquette, and there was a mob in the street. A mob that included Lazare and Alain Therrie.

"Chantal!"

She stood in the center of the street, screaming and waving her hands and babbling like a madwoman. Frowning, he remembered the carriage he had seen across the street. Now he knew why the carriage had looked familiar.

"Alain, Lazare, help us!" she screeched. "*Au secours! Arrête! Pouvez-vous m'aider?* Mr. Merriman! M'sieu Charboneau!"

The mob shifted, some men's voices sounding like low growls, yet she had stopped them and for the moment held their attention.

Time was critical, and curious men were emerging from the saloon behind Rafe. Men who had been drinking and enjoyed a good fight.

"Get out of here," Rafe said in a low voice, pushing a friend on the shoulder. "We don't want the lady hurt. Take others with you and go!" He heard Alain Therrie shouting at his sister and Lazare talking to her, and every nerve in Rafe's body tingled. He wanted to rush her out of danger, but he knew she was trying to prevent the fight and would be in the middle of it if it got started.

"Get out of here before she's hurt," he kept saying to men pouring out of the tavern. "Get your woman and go home, before there's trouble."

"I ain't afraid of trouble, lad," a man said, doubling his fists.

Rafe caught him. "You don't want the women hurt, do you?"

"No. No." He turned to help Rafe as Rafe strained to hear Chantal, who was screeching and crying and calling more of the men by names.

"M'sieu Brierre, Alain—you must help!" she cried.

"Chantal, for God's sake, what are you doing here?" Lazare snapped. "What's happened?"

"We've had a wreck! Amity is injured."

"Amity! My God, why didn't you tell me!" Alain cried. "Where the devil is she?"

Drawing a deep breath, Rafe turned to look at Chantal, who had gone into another spasm of crying. He wanted to wade through the crowd and scoop her up and take her out and shake her. He thought about the carriage waiting across the road, and knew that Amity wasn't hurt. Chantal ran a damnable risk. A man passed him, marching toward the mob. Rafe caught him and yanked him back.

The man swung and Rafe ducked, yanking out the bowie knife from his boot and placing it against the man's throat. "Go now. I don't want my woman hurt."

The man blinked and stepped back. "I'm going, O'Brien." Rafe kept moving men, trying to get them to disperse, seeing that the mob was breaking up. A block away down the street a fight had broken out, but it involved only three men.

Rafe pushed men away. "Go home." He glanced down the street again. The three men fought, and a boy stood watching. Rafe looked at the broad shoulders of one of the men. With curly hair and several inches under six feet, he was trying to ward off two men with clubs. He was unarmed, and the boy stood swinging his fists in support of the outnumbered man, who looked familiar.

Suddenly Rafe felt as if his heart had stopped. He forgot the mob and everything else around him. He strained to see, his heart pounding in his chest. He didn't dare to hope, but it looked like Caleb. *"Caleb! Darcy!"* Without realizing what he was doing, he pushed men out of his way as he moved forward, and then he was running and shouting. It *was* them! Joy surged in him, bringing tears and a knot in his chest. *They made it!* He had known they would. Except in the darkest moments of doubt, he had clung to his faith that they would appear. He waved his arms wildly as he became more certain.

"Caleb! Darce! Cal!"

As Caleb O'Brien turned, a man clubbed him in the stomach.

Furious that anyone was trying to hurt his brother, Rafe barreled into the man, knocking him flat. The second one swung a club. Rafe grabbed it and yanked it away, slugging the man, who fell back and slid across the road. Rafe turned around as his brother ran into his arms and he hugged Caleb, feeling the breath squeezed from his lungs. "Thank God! Oh, thank God!"

And then Darcy's thin arms were also wrapped around him.

Rafe scooped him up and all three hugged. Salty tears streaked his cheeks, but he didn't care. "Damn, it took you a hell of a long time to get here!" he exclaimed, laughing and brushing his cheeks as he set Darcy down. He looked around and fear squeezed his heart.

"Where's Fortune?"

Caleb's smile faded. "We don't know. We lost you and Mother and Fortune. We thought they might have been with you."

"Is Mother all right?" Darcy asked.

Rafe looked into Caleb's eyes and saw that his brother had already guessed the answer. "No, Darcy. Our mother's dead." He squeezed Darcy's shoulder.

"Mother isn't here?" Darcy asked in his high voice,

his eyes blinking, and Rafe hurt for him. Caleb must
have kept his hope alive. "No, she isn't," he said, hun-
kering down to look into Darcy's eyes. "I'm sorry."

"I wanted her to be here," Darcy said, tears spilling over as Rafe put his arms around him and pulled
him close. Finally Darcy pulled away and wiped his
eyes. "Fortune will come, won't he?"

Rafe raised his head to stare at Caleb. "Well, you
and Darcy made it, so Fortune will too."

Caleb looked down and gave Darcy a squeeze. He
clung to Rafe and cried, "I want Mother!"

"I know you do," Rafferty answered. "We all do,
Darcy."

"I'm not surprised," Caleb said, and Rafe knew he was
talking about their mother. "Where have you been?"

"Ha! Where have *I* been? Where have *you two*
been?" Rafe flung his arm around Caleb's shoulders
and took Darcy's hand. "Come on, we'll buy some
ale and you can tell me. Then you two come home
with me." He glanced over his shoulder. Men were
milling about in the street, but the crowd was dispers-
ing and the tavern had few customers.

He saw the carriage jammed up against a wall. Men
were kneeling down around a figure stretched on the
ground. Chantal stood with Lazare's arm around her,
and Giraud stood off to one side. "Let's go," he said
tersely, unable to bear the sight of her with Lazare.
"I'll take you home with me."

A carriage careened around the corner and reached
the crowd, the driver pulling on the reins. The moment
the carriage slowed the door burst open, and a man
jumped out to run toward Chantal and the crowd.

"There's Ormonde Therrie!" Rafe exclaimed, feeling relieved. Chantal would get the lecture she deserved, but now Lazare wouldn't be allowed to escort
her home, for Rafe knew how closely they chaperoned
Chantal.

"Come along, Caleb, Darcy, and I'll introduce you
to my employer and part of his family."

Chapter 13

"Chantal! What the devil's happening here? Amity?"

"Papa!" Chantal's heart lurched. How had Papa discovered their plans and found them? Why was he here, and not up north as he had said he would be?

"*Merde alors!* Alain, is this part of your damnable politics?" Ormonde Therrie snapped.

"No, sir! I don't know why the girls are here. All I know is Chantal was screaming for help and we found Amity unconscious, lying in the road. Giraud can't talk and just keeps muttering, 'Lawsy me,' and Chantal—" He broke off and turned to look at her.

"Chantal," Ormonde demanded, "explain at once why you and your sister are on the street at this hour!"

"Papa, I heard Alain might be involved in something where he would get hurt."

"Dammit! Why the—"

"Alain!" Ormonde Therrie snapped, and Alain closed his mouth but continued to glare at Chantal.

"And so you came to town to mix in this?" her father asked, in the tone she hated to hear. It was low and quiet, and held the same terror for her as a snake slithering around her ankles.

"Papa, something had to be done, and you were up north, so Amity came with me and we were going to get Grand-père and—"

"Grand-père! *Mon dieu,* he hasn't been on a horse in two years! What did you think your poor grandfather could have done? At this hour of the night he would be fast asleep in his bed!"

"I thought Alain and Lazare would listen to him. They planned something frightful."

"I'm going to have Giraud's hide!"

"No! Papa, I told him he had to take us to Grand-père's. I ordered him to do this, and he pleaded with me not to go. Amity can tell you that."

"And just where the devil *is* Amity?"

"Someone carried her to the carriage, and she's inside," Alain answered. "And if anyone deserves a beating, it isn't Giraud," he said, looking meaningfully at Chantal.

Lazare stood in silence at Chantal's side, and she knew he seethed with an anger that matched Papa's. As her gaze swept the circle of men listening to their conversation, she caught her breath. Rafferty O'Brien stood only a few feet from her, and he was holding a small boy's hand. Why would Rafferty be holding the hand of a child? The child had such blue eyes. . . .

"Chantal, I want—" Ormonde began.

"Mr. O'Brien! Could that possibly be your brother who was lost at sea?" Feeling excitement and joy for Rafferty, because she knew how worried he had been and she knew how she would have felt if she'd been in his place, Chantal rushed to kneel down in front of Darcy, who looked just as she imagined Rafferty must have looked as a child. His eyes were the same compelling blue with the same thick black lashes, and now they were wide and focused on her with obvious curiosity.

"Yes, Miss Therrie, this is Darcy O'Brien, my youngest brother. And this is Caleb O'Brien, another brother. Boys, meet Miss Therrie," Rafe drawled in a dry voice.

"Papa, he's found his brothers who were lost at sea! Come meet them. Alain, Lazare!" she exclaimed, excited for Rafferty, but also mightily relieved to have found this momentary respite from her father's wrath. Perhaps he would cool down if he thought about something else, and he had always seemed interested in his overseer.

"Mr. Therrie, sorry to interrupt a family gathering. This is Caleb and Darcy. Boys, this is my employer, Mr. Therrie. This is his son Alain, and Mr. Galliard."

Terse greetings were exchanged, and Rafferty faced Ormonde.

"No one was seriously hurt here, I trust," he said, turning to look at Chantal. She shifted her gaze away. She could detect the sardonic tone in his voice. Then she remembered that there was another brother. *Where is he? Thank heavens Papa has been distracted by all this!*

"Papa, I'm frightened and exhausted," she said. "May we go home and discuss this?"

"Chantal, I want to see you and Amity in my study at eight in the morning. Alain, ride home with the girls. It will be on your way." He turned to Lazare. "I expect you to bid Chantal farewell now." Next he faced Rafferty.

"Mr. O'Brien, take your brothers to Belle Destin with you. Caleb, I can find work for you, and we'll keep Darcy busy if you boys choose to live at Belle Destin. Come see me at ten in the morning."

"Yes, sir," Rafferty answered. "Thank you, Mr. Therrie." With a glance at Chantal he turned away, and she watched them cross the dark street.

"Everyone go home," Ormonde said, climbing back into his carriage.

Four mornings later, Amity tugged on the reins. "We have gone quite far enough," she said, rubbing the nose of Moonlight, the black mare. "Papa must never know I ride you, and you won't tell."

"*I* might tell," came a deep voice, and she whirled around. Rafferty O'Brien was urging his horse forward from the cool green shadows beneath the oaks. "And why *shouldn't* your father know?"

"Papa said we can't ride for two weeks."

"Is that why I haven't seen Chantal?" he asked.

"Yes. I've only ridden this once, but I just had to see my animals. You won't tell, please?"

He smiled. "No, I won't tell. I miss seeing Chantal. You can tell her that."

"Papa was in a rage."

"As he had every right to be. You two had no cause to mix in something that violent and dangerous."

"But it was exciting! And Chantal said it stopped the fight."

"Yes it did, but it wouldn't have been worth the two of you getting hurt. Men will always fight, and it's not as bad as you might think when we do."

"Chantal says you're bloodthirsty brutes who enjoy it!"

He laughed. "Maybe she's right. I'm going to work now. Amity, tell her I'll be waiting where we usually meet this afternoon."

"Maman is angry with you."

He shrugged. "Stay out of mischief." He rode away and she continued her ride, relishing the pristine solitude of early morning, when the air was still cool and dew sparkled the leaves. Stopping at a familiar spot and giving a whistle as she slid off the mare's bare back, Amity sat on a log, and shortly two raccoons ambled through the brush. Amity drew open a bag she carried and tossed tidbits of sweetmeats to the animals.

As she watched the raccoons eat, a shot broke the stillness. It was a sharp bang that made her jump, while the raccoons dashed for the underbrush and birds flew out of the trees.

"Mon dieu!" She stood up and looked around. *Who is shooting? Papa is gone, and Mr. O'Brien is at work. None of the slaves is allowed to own firearms.* The shot had been close. She moved in the direction of the shot and pushed aside branches. A man stood at the edge of the bayou, rifle at his shoulder, taking aim at a duck flying overhead.

"Tiens! Non! Arrêtez-vous!" She threw herself at the man's back, careening into him. The rifle fired, its report deafening, as they both pitched forward into the bayou. Amity scrambled up the bank and picked up the rifle with both hands, to fling it into deep water.

"Damnation!" He tackled her around her middle, knocking her to the ground. She fought wildly, but in seconds he had locked her wrists together in the grip of one hand while he straddled her middle. "What the hell was that for?"

"You might have killed Benoit!" she answered, looking up into angry eyes the color of summer grass. Thick brown curls dripping with water were plastered to his head, locks curling over a forehead that was creased in a frown.

"Damn, I was shooting at birds, not people!"

"Benoit is a *duck*, you murderer!" She struggled and he tightened his grip. His face was inches away as he leaned over her.

"I'll let you go, if you'll just get up and stop fighting me!"

"Did you kill him?" she asked, holding her breath. He blinked and looked annoyed with her.

"I shot him. I don't often miss, unless someone lands on my back."

"Oh!" she gasped, and turned away. She didn't want to cry in front of the horrible man, but Benoit was a beautiful duck and she loved to feed him and watch him swim. "Did you get Odile as well?"

"No, thanks to you, if you refer to my second shot."

"Now Odile will be all alone!"

"Odile can find another duck."

"They don't do that," she replied, as he stood up and pulled her to her feet. She was wet and bedraggled and couldn't stop crying over Benoit, and she hated the stranger standing in front of her. It seemed to be mutual, as he put his hands on his hips and glared at her.

"Has it occurred to you that you just tossed away a hell of a valuable rifle?"

"Good riddance!"

She sat down and put her face in her hands to cry for her beautiful Benoit. When she had at last wiped her eyes and glanced up, she saw that the stranger had yanked off his shirt and was removing his boots. He threw them down and waded into the water, striding out while ripples moved away from him. He moved back and forth, casting angry glances her way whenever he turned in her direction.

"What are you doing? Is Benoit's body there?"

"No. I'm not hunting for the body of a duck. I'm trying to find a damned good Ferguson. And a Ferguson is a hell of a lot more important than a Benoit! Lord, there weren't many Fergusons made!"

"You're horrible!" Angry with him, she wanted to shove him under. When his back was turned she snatched up his shirt and boots and moved to the water's edge. Just as she heaved them at him, he turned.

"Hey, dammit!"

She held her skirts up and ran, glancing back as he waded out with his boots. "I hope you drown, and I hope your old Ferguson rusts! *Dingue!*"

He ran after her and she lengthened her stride, her heart pounding, because he looked angry and strong. Hands caught her and yanked her back. She turned to bite his arm.

"Dammit!" He plopped down on the ground, pulling her across his lap. She struggled while he reached up to yank down a long oak switch, break it off, and bring it down in a whack across her backside.

In a rage she kicked, but in minutes she was crying and her struggles had ended. He finally dumped her on the ground and stood over her, as she continued to berate him.

"You're horrible. *Cochon-dilatant!*"

"You're a silly, spoiled child! You ruined a damned good rifle. The more I think about it . . ."

He stepped toward her again. With a screech she bounded to her feet and ran, racing through the woods back to Moonlight.

Caleb O'Brien dropped his boots on the porch. His stomach growled with hunger as tempting smells of chicken came. As he turned to the door, Rafe appeared.

"You're wet and covered with mud. Even your hair's muddy! What the devil happened to you?"

Caleb glared at him. "I'll tell you, but I'd like to eat."

"I'll listen while you wash up."

"I want to eat, and then I'll wash up."

"Not in my house. You look as if you've been wallowing with the pigs."

"I damn well wouldn't be any muddier." As Caleb started into the house, Rafe's hand clamped on his shoulder, yanking him back.

"You get around to the pump and wash off before you go inside!"

"Dammit, Rafe . . ." They strode around the house and Caleb began to pump, taking his anger out on the pump. "I shot a duck. Just a damned little duck that would be good to eat. You said I'm allowed to hunt."

"Yes you are, in the areas I showed you."

"I was there," he said, yanking off his shirt. "I was getting ready for a second shot when this child slammed into my back and knocked me into the bayou. Just flat knocked me into the water!"

Rafe chuckled, and Caleb's anger grew. "It wasn't a damned bit funny. She tossed my rifle into the bayou."

"Your Ferguson?" Rafe's eyes widened.

"Yes, dammit! I hunted the whole blasted day and I never found it. She cried and carried on about her precious 'Benoit' and his 'Odile' who now will be alone. As if a duck cared, or knew."

"*Whose* precious Benoit? Caleb, who was this child?"

"I don't know, but she's spoiled and silly."

"That sounds like Amity Therrie, and she's not spoiled or silly. She has a marvelous way with animals and birds that's a rare gift."

"The hell you say! A duck is a duck is a duck. Since when did you become a duck defender? I'll tell you, your precious Amity Therrie won't sit down as well tonight." Caleb bent down to wash his face, the cold water refreshing on his skin. A hand clamped on his shoulder and he was spun around.

"What did you do?"

"I taught her not to toss a man's rifle into a bayou."

"Amity Therrie is special, and don't you ever hurt her again!"

Caleb glared at Rafe as water dripped off his face. But he knew that Rafe's temper was about to snap, and when that happened it meant a hell of a storm. Would he ever get tough enough to whip his brother in a fight? He could beat anyone else in a one-on-one fight ever since he was ten years old, but he could never take Rafe. Damn that bit of baggage! And all over a damned bird!

"You owe her an apology!" Rafe snapped.

"The hell you say! The sun will come up at midnight first."

"You're coming with me and you're apologizing." Rafe yanked him by the back of his shirt, catching skin as well.

"Damn!"

Rafe pulled him along, charging toward the big house, oblivious to Caleb's struggles as they reached a path and a horseman loomed in front of them.

"Good evening, Rafferty, Caleb," Ormonde Therrie said, raising his eyebrows in curiosity.

"Sir, you're just the man I wanted to talk to for a moment. Actually we're on our way to your house, because my brother has something to say to your daughter," Rafe said, releasing Caleb, who rubbed the back of his neck and glared at him.

"Well, we'll go up to the house," Ormonde said.

Caleb wanted to swear, but he held his tongue. The little witch wasn't worth all the trouble. When they had reached the house Ormonde dismounted and handed the reins to a boy who led his horse toward the stable.

"Come in, Mr. O'Brien, Caleb," he said, his gaze going back and forth between them.

"Sir, I would like to talk with you a few minutes first, if I may," Rafe said. Rafe and Mr. Therrie disappeared into the house and Caleb waited. In minutes they returned. Rafe's anger simmered, obvious to Caleb, who had learned even as a toddler to read his brother's emotions. Ormonde Therrie appeared solemn and stern, but he gazed at Caleb without obvious rancor.

One look at Rafe's snapping blue eyes, and Caleb knew what was expected of him. "Mr. Therrie, I'm sorry I lost my temper with your daughter," Caleb said stiffly.

"I've summoned Amity, and she'll be right down," he replied in a calm voice, as if it were not of great importance to him. And then there she was. Her cheeks were pink, her black eyes dancing with fire, and Caleb felt anger rise in him again. He wanted to shake her.

Instead, he faced her. "Miss Therrie, I apologize for my conduct today."

"You should, sir. It was abominable."

"Amity . . ." Ormonde Therrie cautioned in a quiet tone.

"I accept your apology," she said in a stiff reply, raising her chin. She turned and left. *Baggage,* thought Caleb.

"It won't happen again," Rafe said. Ormonde Therrie nodded, and Rafe took Caleb's arm as they descended the steps to return to Rafe's house.

Chantal stood on the upper gallery and watched Rafe and Caleb cross the yard. Rafe held his brother, who staggered and stumbled until they had disappeared inside Rafe's house. What had that been about? Something to do with Amity, because Papa had sent William to fetch her.

Chantal went down the hall and saw Amity's closed door. She knocked lightly and opened it. Amity was stretched across her bed on her stomach. She wiped red eyes. "Amity! What happened?" Chantal asked.

"I hate Caleb O'Brien! I hate and despise him. He's as dreadful as his brother is nice!"

"What did he do to you?" To her surprise, Amity turned crimson.

"I hate him! He shot Benoit, and he tried to kill Odile, only I caused him to miss. Now Odile will be all alone."

"I'm sorry, Amity. I know how you love your birds and animals, but in fairness Caleb O'Brien didn't know he was shooting at anything except a wild duck."

"I hate men! They want to shoot and kill things, and fight."

"You'll like them better someday," Chantal said dryly. "And there will be more ducks. So dry your tears and come for a walk."

Amity wiped her eyes. "Very well, but we'll walk far from the overseer's house. I don't want to see that horrid man again!"

Chantal never had seen her sister as angry with someone as she was with Caleb, and as the next days passed her smoldering fury didn't abate. Chantal missed her rides, and she was afraid to risk meeting Rafe for a swim. As Friday approached she forgot about her rides, because the Galliards were coming to spend an evening and both families would go to look at Soleil.

Friday afternoon the yard was filled with smells of a hog roasting in a pit, simmering jambalaya, red beans, corn, hot bread, and bread pudding with whiskey sauce. Loretta was better than the hairdresser in the Vieux Carré, and by late afternoon Chantal was staring at her image and thought about Lazare.

Her yellow hair was rolled in sausage curls behind her ears, long ringlets down the back of her neck. Her emerald grosgrain dress had rosettes of pink ribbon at the waist and near the hem of the full skirt that stood out over her hooped skirt. The puff sleeves left her arms bare, and the low-cut square bodice revealed her slender throat and the rise of her breasts.

She was waiting in the cool front parlor when she heard William announce the arrival of the Galliards. And then Lazare entered the room, his hazel eyes sweeping over her as he crossed the room to her. As he caught her hands in his, she thought of laughing blue eyes and Rafferty O'Brien.

"I want you to myself," Lazare said over an hour later, turning his cabriolet off the lane as the other carriages disappeared around the bend. "God knows, your father sees to it I never get you alone."

"And if he loses us this time, he won't allow me to

ride alone with you again,'' she said, gazing at Lazare's strong features, his full lips and slightly hooked
nose. He slid his arm around her waist and pulled her
close. "Lazare, if you wrinkle me, we'll both be in
trouble with Papa!''

"I know," he said, slowing as they passed a grove
of sweet gum. "I would like to peel away that dress,
Chantal," he said in a husky voice, looking down at
her. "One kiss . . .''

"We'll lose them."

"You know I can catch up. My horses can outrun
any ahead of us.''

"Lazare, I think you're taking a dreadful ri—'' At
that moment, to her horror, Rafferty came into view,
riding across the field.

"Lazare, we're not alone. There's our overseer.''

"To hell with him.''

"No! Please, I feel like we're standing in the middle
of the square. . . .''

"Chantal,'' Lazare murmured as he pulled her to
him, kissing her and crushing her against him.

She resisted, her emotions churning, realizing her
reactions to Lazare had changed. He leaned over her
and pushed her down onto the seat of the buggy.

She struggled wildly, turning her head. "Lazare!''

He sat up, then caught her wrists and held them with
one hand over her head. He glanced across the field
and back to her. "He can't see you. He can see only
me.''

"I'll look disheveled when we join our parents, and
we'll never catch up. My father will be livid. Let me
up!'' Arguing, she struggled, angry with Lazare, who
watched her with a heated, heavy-lidded gaze. Chantal
knew Rafferty O'Brien could see Lazare but not her.
He would think she was enjoying Lazare's caresses.
"Lazare, I insist!''

"Chantal, when women say 'I insist!' it simply
goads me to the opposite course of action.''

"Please!''

He pulled her up against him and kissed her again,
until she responded to him. Finally he released her.

She fought the urge to look over her shoulder to see if Rafferty was still there. If she did, it would enrage Lazare.

"My father is probably searching for us now!"

"We'll catch up." As Lazare turned the carriage, she straightened her clothes and hair. Finally she couldn't resist turning around to look at the empty field. In minutes they were careening down the road, until Lazare slowed his team of matched grays and grinned at her. "I don't want to overtake them. We can't be far behind."

"Lazare, you are a devil."

"Devils have more fun."

As they caught up with the others and rode with them, she was in torment. Rafferty had seen them clearly. And while Lazare had kissed her she'd thought of Rafferty's laughter, his teasing, his smoldering glances, his kisses that had been more exciting than Lazare's!

She slid her arm through Lazare's and leaned against him. He looked down at her quizzically. "So I'm forgiven?" he asked.

"Perhaps. There's Soleil," she said, feeling better.

They climbed out with the others and marched through the house, Lazare, Ormonde, and Andreas Galliard discussing the construction while Lazare kept his arm around Chantal. Later he took her to one side and they climbed the curving central stairs to the upper floor and walked into the large room that would be their bedroom. He placed his hands on her shoulders.

"This will be our home, our room. I've ordered a bed from Paris."

"The house is going to be grand, Lazare."

He tilted her chin up, bending his head to kiss her. Before his lips touched hers, she remembered standing on the gallery and Rafferty pulling her into his arms. She threw her arms around Lazare and kissed him, wanting him to shut out memories of the man who could ruin everything, wanting Lazare's kisses to make her feel faint. Alas, she was far too aware that his kisses paled in comparison. *What had Rafferty O'Brien done to her?*

When he had released her, Lazare arched his brows and studied her. "Maybe you're getting anxious, eh?"

"Yes. They'll know we've kissed." She tried to straighten her clothing. "We'd better join them."

He took her arm, and they found the families waiting in the carriages for the ride home.

As the drive to Belle Destin curved within view of the overseer's house, she glimpsed Rafferty and Darcy standing on the porch. Rafferty was bent over something Darcy held in his hands. Caleb came around the cabin to join them. In her father's carriage, Chantal saw Amity's cheeks flush and her chin rise into the air. If Caleb noticed, he didn't give any indication.

"Do you see him often?" Lazare asked in a cold tone.

She glanced up. "Pardon?"

"If I thought you were alone with him . . ."

Her gaze went past him. "I rarely see Belle Destin's overseers, except in the distance when they're working in the fields. You should know that." She stared straight ahead as she answered, but a voice screamed that she was lying to her fiancé. Feeling guilt and turmoil, she bit her lip.

Lazare caught her chin in his hand, pinching her. "If I thought you were . . ."

"I'm not! Don't spoil the evening, Lazare. It isn't necessary."

He glanced at Rafferty. "When I remember finding him holding you against him on the ground that day, I want to tear him apart with my bare hands."

She laughed and linked her arm through his. "You don't need to worry about Belle Destin's overseer. How often do you think Papa would allow him to see me?"

"Never." He put his arm around her waist and squeezed. She sat stiffly beside him. Something had changed. A year ago on an evening like this she would have been filled with joy; now she felt uncertainty, emotions she didn't want to acknowledge or experience. She moved away from Lazare and straightened her skirt. Tomorrow night there was a ball, and the family was going to the Brierres'. She raised her chin and firmed her lips. She *would* stop seeing Rafferty O'Brien. Dozens of times she had met him, moments that were forbidden, exciting, and fun beyond measure. She must stop seeing him now, while she could.

So she stopped seeing him, but she couldn't stop thinking about him. Memories haunted her. On the morning of the third of June, four days before the city elections, a horse pounded up the front drive while the family was seated around the oval rosewood table in the dining room. Loretta was dutifully pulling the string for the cypress punkah to fan the family, as they breakfasted on ham and grits and hot biscuits. With a frown creasing his brow, William entered the dining room. Chantal's curiosity was piqued, for there was a strict rule that family dining was never to be interrupted. When William bent down to speak to her father in a whisper, Chantal caught Alain's name.

"Dammit!" Ormonde said, pushing his spoonback chair away from the table. "Excuse me," he said to Blaise, and left the room.

"William," Blaise said softly, as the butler began to follow his owner from the room. William reappeared.

"Yes, ma'am."

She motioned him to her side. "What was that about?"

William frowned. "Shem's here from Mrs. Diantha. Mr. Alain is with some folks in town; they want to change the way elections are done."

Chantal felt cold, and turned to look at William.

"What do you mean, he's with folks in town, William? That's not enough to send someone galloping here."

"I don't know, Mrs. Therrie. That's all he said. He said Mrs. Diantha sent him here to fetch Mr. Therrie right away. That it was bad trouble."

The women exchanged curious glances, Blaise's eyes

sparkling in a manner that made Chantal angry. Finally Ormonde strode back into the room.

"I'm going to town."

"Ormonde, for heaven's sake, what's happened?"

"Earlier this week the Know-Nothings broke into the office of the Registrar of Voters and stole the roles. In retaliation, last night at midnight the Vigilantes barricaded themselves in the Principal, the jail, and the arsenal, demanding control of the city."

"What's Mayor Watering doing? What are the police doing?"

"Diantha didn't send word about that. I'm going to town and try to get Alain out of there."

"It'll be dangerous."

"I'll be careful. I won't be back, Blaise, until after the election."

"Ormonde, take me to town with you. I don't want to be left here to worry about you."

He nodded. "If you can leave at once, you may come along."

As she moved away from the table and went upstairs, another horse was heard coming up the drive. Ormonde headed toward the front and Chantal followed him, aware that Amity was behind her. They listened as a messenger summoned him to a meeting with the mayor, in town at ten o'clock.

"What'll happen?" Amity asked Chantal. "Do you think Papa would take us along?"

"You know he won't, when he wants to leave right away." As soon as Ormonde had stepped back inside the house, Chantal faced him. "Will you let us know if Alain goes home?"

"Yes, I will. It's folly; the Vigilantes can't change the elections."

When he climbed into his carriage, Blaise rushed out to join him. Chantal watched the carriage roll down the lane out of sight. Her gaze shifted in the direction of the overseer's house, and on impulse she gathered her skirts and descended the steps.

The moment she knocked on Rafferty's door she felt out of place and brazen. Darcy appeared, his resemblance to Rafferty more pronounced as she looked into his blue eyes.

"Is Mr. O'Brien home?" she asked.

He nodded, and in a moment Rafferty stepped onto the porch, his brows arching and amusement dancing in his eyes.

"To what do I owe the honor of this visit, Chantal? Your papa will have apoplexy."

"Papa just left. Diantha sent word that Alain and the Vigilantes have barricaded themselves at the Cabildo."

Rafferty's amusement vanished, and he gazed beyond her down the road. "As soon as I talk to the drivers, I'll ride to town and see what I can find out." He clamped his lips together and jerked his head. "Come here."

Puzzled, she followed him down the steps around the corner of the house. He pointed down the lane away from the house, and she walked with him.

"Where's your stepmother?"

"She went with him."

Where the lane curved into a grove of trees, out of sight of the house and cabins, he turned her to face him and placed his hands on her shoulders. "I know you, my little rooftop climber, and I want you to promise me you won't try to get to Alain."

She shook her head. "If I take Diantha, we might talk some—"

Rafferty's groan interrupted her. "Don't you do anything as dangerous as you did in front of the tavern!" His fingers were tight on her shoulders, and she lifted her chin.

"Chantal," he insisted, placing his finger under her chin, "promise me you won't do anything without telling me first. Promise me."

She blinked. He had no right to demand such a promise. She didn't have to answer to him, but as she gazed into his eyes, she nodded. "All right. I promise."

"As soon as I get back, I'll let you know. Don't worry about your brother," he said, his mellow voice adding that gentle note that made her feel secure from worries. "Now let's go."

As she tried to keep up with his long strides she said, "I want to go with you."

"Oh, how I wish that request was made because you wanted to be in my company!" he exclaimed in mocking tones, then dropped his arm across her shoulders. "Stop worrying until you know you have something to be concerned about," he said gently. "I'll get back as fast as I can."

"Thank you," she said, looking into his eyes but unable to read his expression.

The day seemed interminable, and by nightfall she still hadn't heard from Rafferty. She sat up late but continually dozed off, and so finally went to her room, dressed in her gown, and stretched out on her bed. She tried to stay awake, but it was an effort to keep her eyes open.

She felt a hand touch her shoulder and her eyes flew open. Rafferty sat on the side of the bed.

"I just got back," he whispered. His hand remained on her shoulder, lightly squeezing it, turning a curl in his hand.

"And Alain?" she asked, rising up on her elbows.

"The Vigilantes have barricaded themselves in front of the cathedral. Captain Johnson Kelly Duncan is in command, and they're headquartered in the arsenal. They have cannon."

"No! What can they accomplish?"

"They've made demands on the mayor for weapons, and they're posting proclamations around the city." He placed a piece of paper on the table beside her.

"What does it say?" she asked. Biting her lip, thinking about Alain, she sat up. She was inches from Rafferty. He wound a curl around his fingers, letting her hair slide across his hand.

"In essence they pledge to maintain the rights of law-abiding citizens. They've demanded that the mayor yield his power and allow the Vigilantes to appoint the police. They say that the ruffians who have terrorized the parish must go." He tucked strands behind her ear, his fingers lingering and stroking her shoulder. "I didn't get back until late, because your father has been in meetings all day."

"What happened in the meetings?"

"This afternoon Mayor Waterman called out the militia; Major-General John Lewis is in command. Colonel Forno was sent to arrest Captain Duncan."

"Oh, no! What about Alain?"

"The Vigilantes sent Colonel Forno packing. They wouldn't surrender. Your father didn't know whether Alain's name was on an arrest list or not. He said he had sent a message to Alain to come home, but still hasn't received an answer. He sent another message requesting that he be allowed to talk to Alain, and he hasn't received an answer to that one either."

"So Papa doesn't know whether Alain will talk to him or not?" she said, becoming intensely aware of Rafferty seated beside her, his knee touching her thigh.

"No. Chantal, you have to keep your promise. The Know-Nothings have taken over Lafayette Square, and now picket lines of the opposing factions face each other across Canal Street."

"Tomorrow morning I'll go to town," she said, trying to think about something besides Rafferty.

"Giraud and Remi should go with you. And you be careful—the city is under siege. Send one of the servants to tell me, if you decide to try to see Alain."

"I will," she answered, looking at him in the darkness. He wore a black shirt; moonlight spilling through the windows enabled her to see his searching gaze.

"I haven't seen you with your hair down," Rafferty said in a deep, raspy voice. He tilted her face up, studying her with a leisurely, heated look that made a flame burn low inside her. He caught a handful of her hair to hold it to his face, brushing strands against his jaw.

"Thank you for going to town," she whispered, her breathing quick and shallow, her voice breathless.

His arm slid around her waist and she grasped his

arm, feeling the solid bulge of muscle. "Rafferty, you must go," she whispered, her gaze held by his. Then his gaze lowered to her mouth, and she couldn't speak. Her pulse drummed. He shouldn't be in her room, holding her in his arms. . . .

He bent his head and kissed her, his mouth brushing hers, covering hers, as his tongue went into the deep warmth of her mouth. Desire curled and fanned within her. She moaned as he pressed her back into the pillow and leaned over her. Her hand moved and brushed over his leg, and he groaned. She felt engulfed with a need for him, aching, her hips moving. His hand slid beneath the sheet, over her hip, with only her gown between his hand and her flesh. He unbuttoned the thin batiste, his fingers cupping her breast, and she felt on fire. She moaned, the sound muffled by his kiss. His thumb circled her nipple and wild, sweet tremors came.

With a sob she flung away from him and stepped out on the opposite side of the bed. "You have to go!" She gasped for breath, as if she had run miles.

"You don't love him."

"I do! I'm going to marry him. I love Soleil. Papa wouldn't allow me to wed you and you know it! Don't ruin my life!"

"Do you know what it does to me to see you leave with him? To see you in his arms?"

"Please go!" She stepped back, away from the bed.

Rafferty stood up slowly, and she tried to resist looking at him, but she couldn't. She trembled with an ache low inside. He walked without a sound to the window, stepping over the sill.

"Rafferty . . ."

He paused to look back at her.

"Thank you for going to town."

"You remember your promise to me," he said, in a voice that was deep and gruff and filled with what sounded like anger. He was gone.

She climbed back up into bed and stared at the darkened window. She ached for him. She wanted him to kiss her. But she would have to stop seeing him, no matter what happened. Yet he was the best friend she had, next to Amity. His kisses taunted her; her body ached for him. She wiped away hot tears. Lazare's kisses paled in comparison. Why? What magic did Rafferty O'Brien work so easily, to make her ache and return his wild kisses and dream of him afterwards?

She forced her thoughts to Alain. Tomorrow when she would be in New Orleans she would try to persuade Papa to let her talk to Alain. And she would have to tell Rafferty of her plans.

"No, Chantal! Absolutely, no! Never would I allow you to take such a risk!"

"Papa, please let me talk to Alain! They won't harm me! Neither side will harm a woman, and you know it!" she pleaded.

"Shops are all closed; the situation gets more tense by the hour. I won't consider it! The Council meets in half an hour. I don't know when I'll be home. Damn Alain, for such imprudence!"

"Papa, no one has been hurt yet," she said, looking out the townhouse window and thinking about the turmoil on the streets below.

"No, they haven't, and I'd prefer that it stay that way!"

"It may be the best time to talk to Alain. We're only blocks from the Vigilantes. Can we get Diantha here? If she would go with me . . ."

"Diantha?" He stared at her with an incredulous expression. "She'd faint before you got *close* to the Cabildo."

"Send for her, please! Alain may listen to her if she'll go with me. And I need to send a message to Belle Destin."

His gaze narrowed. "To whom?"

"I promised Mr. O'Brien I would let him know if I was going to talk to Alain."

The words hung in the air, and she wondered what questions they would conjure up. To her amazement, Ormonde simply nodded.

"I'll send that message. He told me you wanted to

try to talk to your brother. He said he would go with you for protection if I gave my permission, so I'll send for him. He's a better choice than one of the servants. Man has a cool head.''

She stared at Ormonde, until she became aware that her mouth was open. "Mr. O'Brien goes with me?"

"Yes. I insist on it. He promised he would see to your safety, and he's a man who keeps his word.''

"Papa, Lazare won't like that.''

"Lazare will never know!" Ormonde snapped. "Lazare wouldn't approve of my folly in allowing my daughter to go into danger." He sighed and rubbed his forehead. "*Damn* Alain for such imprudence! Chantal, we're not going to share this with Maman. It would worry her too much.''

She nodded with relief. It would send Maman into a rage.

"I don't know when I'll return. The aldermen and the assistant aldermen are divided over what action to take. Mayor Waterman doesn't want to take any action. Be careful," he said, giving her a level look. "I'm thankful for my children, although at the moment I'm damned annoyed with Alain.''

She hugged him, and received a cursory pat on the shoulder in return. She spent the rest of the day in turmoil, and she knew it wasn't because of her dangerous mission; it was because of the man who would accompany her, with her father's blessing.

Looking pale as snow, Diantha arrived before sunset. Within the first hour she had burst into tears so many times, Chantal finally turned to her. "Diantha, stop crying! If you burst out like that tonight, we'll be in dreadful danger.''

"It's safe to cry here!" she wailed, covering her face, and Chantal regretted she had been sharp with her. She crossed over to sit beside her.

"I'm sorry, Diantha. I'm worried about Alain, and worried about what we're going to do.''

"I'm terrified! Chantal, you do things like this, but I don't! Alain will be furious with me! I'm afraid I'll faint!''

"If you do, Mr. O'Brien will carry you," Chantal said dryly. "Change into black clothing. Mr. O'Brien should be here soon, and we'll leave at once."

At the door Diantha paused. "Chantal, I haven't told anyone yet, but I've missed my monthly. I might be . . ." She flushed a deep scarlet.

"Diantha! A baby!" Chantal exclaimed, feeling a rush of joy for Diantha and Alain. "How marvelous! I'll be an aunt!"

"I don't know yet. I want a baby, but I'm scared."

"There's nothing to fear. Diantha, does Alain know?"

"No. I'm not certain yet."

"Tell him that's why he must come home with you tonight. That may be the *only* reason we can get him to go with us."

She wondered if Papa had picked this particular night to take Maman to call on the Brouillettes, so they would be away. Whatever the reason, Chantal was thankful Maman was gone. Dusk seemed to stretch endlessly, and then finally darkness came. The gaslights burned, lanterns glowed, and lamps swayed on carriages, as she stood on the gallery and gazed at the Vieux Carré. Shutters were drawn, and no women were to be seen. Bands of armed men roamed the streets and individuals hurried past.

Down Royal, a solitary figure in black rode a bay horse. Her heart leapt. Rafferty O'Brien, summoned by Papa to accompany her. She went inside, and in a short time Rafferty walked through the door.

Chapter 14

"We'll ride another block," Rafe said. "It's close enough to walk, but we may need the carriage."

Silvery moonlight belied the danger, washing St. Anthony's garden in moonbeams. The mansard roof of the Cabildo was a square dark shadow next to the three sharp spires of St. Louis Cathedral. Bales of cotton were stacked as barricades and fires had been built in the streets, their flames dancing over the overturned wagons and bales.

"This is as close as—"

A fusillade of shots rang out, and a cannon boomed. Diantha screeched and slumped down in the seat.

"Dammit! She's fainted. This is no place for women. I'm taking you home."

Chantal gripped his hand. "If you do, the moment you're gone I'll come here alone."

They glared at each other, and tension crackled between them. "Dammit, I wish I could tie you up or lock you away until this is over!"

"I'm going to talk to my brother with your help or without it!" Chantal turned to hold smelling salts beneath Diantha's nose.

"What happened?" she asked, sitting up. "Shots! Chantal, do you think—"

"Alain is safe," Chantal assured her, although she was terrified for him. More shots blasted through the night, and Diantha looked as if she would faint again.

"Diantha, you have to come with us!"

"She can wait in the carriage if she's faint," Rafferty said.

"No," Chantal argued. "We need her to persuade Alain."

He turned to Diantha. "Mrs. Therrie, excuse us a moment, please." His voice was gentle, a tone Chantal had heard him use only a few times.

"You come with me," he ordered Chantal, his voice changing to a no-nonsense manner. As he helped her out of the carriage, men yelled and ran past. Shots punctuated the shouts. Rafe yanked Chantal across the banquette into a recessed doorway, where it was dark. Brandishing pistols, the men ran down the street.

"You stay right here!" Rafferty commanded, and then he ran with the crowd and was lost from sight. Chantal squeezed against the wall, her heart pounding as throngs of men raced past.

As the crowd thinned Rafferty reappeared, sliding into the niche beside her. "Mayor Waterman capitulated to the Vigilance Committee's demands this afternoon. An angry mob stormed the Vigilantes, and that's why we heard shots. The Know-Nothings are running back to Lafayette Square. They say the mayor is shut up in the arsenal with the Vigilantes. Still want to try to talk to your brother?"

"Yes, even if we have to leave Diantha behind."

"Vigilantes have been injured. It's no place for either of you."

"I have to see him."

"Chantal, you would try a saint!"

"You can go home, Rafferty O'Brien!"

"No, I can't, because you're going to get into trouble up to your pretty little ears. I'm always torn between shaking you or kissing you."

She drew herself up. "I'll do this myself!"

"Like hell," he said. "Short of tying you up I can't keep you from trying to get to your brother, so I'll take you. But your poor sister-in-law can't keep from fainting. She's terrified."

"She's the only person who might talk Alain into coming home. Rafferty, she thinks she might be with child."

"Dammit, I won't take a mother-to-be into gun-

fire!'' He glanced at the carriage. ''That's all the more
reason she shouldn't go! Damnation!''

''But he'll listen to her! He wants a son desperately!''

''Can't you tell him?''

''If I were your wife, would you want your brother
to tell you about our baby?'' she snapped. She saw the
white flash of his teeth in the darkness.

''No, love,'' he said in that deep, special tone of
voice that turned the world upside down and made her
forget everything except the two of them. ''When that
time comes, Chantal,'' he said, touching her cheek,
''I want you to tell me.''

His voice was warm, husky, and in spite of the boldness of his statement, the impossibility of it, she
couldn't summon anger. In the midst of danger, desire
burned. She had to be careful around him, so careful.
She shouldn't have a reaction to him that was like setting a flame to dry straw, challenges constantly spark-
ing between them.

''All right, she goes,'' he replied in solemn tones.
''Against my good judgment, and against your father's
good judgment. Now,'' he said, taking her arm and
leaning close, ''you're to do what I say, when I say it,
without arguing. If I tell you to get down, you get
down. Do you understand?''

''Yes,'' she answered with a lift of her chin, thinking there were moments when he was insufferably arrogant.

His eyes rolled heavenward and his lips moved.
''Chantal, do you know what the world 'submissive'
means?''

''Yes. Do you know what the word 'cavalier'
means?''

''Someday, love, I'll show you 'cavalier,' '' he said
in a tone that sent her pulse racing. ''Let's go,'' he
said. He helped Diantha from the carriage and they
went in a line, with Diantha between Chantal and Rafferty, who led the way.

They approached the garden, the traditional spot for
duels. Barricades had been thrown up, including

blocks of stone pried up from the front of the cathedral and stood on end; wagons were overturned, cotton bales stacked high. One shot rang out. Rafferty turned to her. "When I say run, we run. We'll go in between those two calèches," he ordered, pointing at the overturned buggies.

"Chantal!" Diantha whispered and squeezed her hand.

"Now, run!" he ordered, crouching, his pistol in one hand, Diantha's hand in the other with Chantal following.

A shot was fired as they raced between the wagons. "Get down!" he snapped, dropping to the ground. Chantal and Diantha followed suit, Diantha crossing herself and mumbling a prayer. When Rafe started forward, a man stepped into their path.

"Get out of here!" the man snapped, the muzzle of his musket pointed at Rafe's chest.

"I've got Mrs. Therrie and Miss Therrie, his sister, with me. I'm the Belle Destin overseer."

"You're a damned Irishman!" He raised the rifle.

"Sir!" Chantal said. "My father sent him to protect us! Speak to my brother about him!" She tried to move forward, but Rafe's arm held her back.

The man paused, studying Rafferty. He lowered his rifle. "Be quick. You're not wanted."

"Come along." They moved with Rafe through a throng of men. There had to be more than a thousand milling about, manning the barricades, tending wounded. Rafe spoke to a sentry at the arsenal door. Holding Diantha's trembling hand, Chantal stood beside one of the tall pillars of the arsenal, her gaze roaming over the long windows and wondering if Alain was inside.

"They say he's in front," Rafferty said on rejoining them, taking Chantal's arm to lead her through the arcade of the Cabildo to the steps of the cathedral.

"Alain!" Diantha cried, running to him as he turned from a cannon.

"He's hurt," Chantal said, and Rafferty's arm closed around her shoulders.

"It's not bad, Chantal. He's on his feet and working."

Alain's shoulder was indeed bandaged, a crimson stain showing. His shirt was gone and his cheek was bloody. Holding Diantha with his good arm, he frowned at Chantal.

"What the devil! Diantha, you shouldn't be here. Dammit, to hell, Chantal, are you responsible for this?"

"I—"

"I promised her father I'd accompany both of them," Rafferty said, facing Alain.

"Damn you for bringing women into danger! I have a job here!" Alain snapped. "Diantha, I demand you go home! Chantal, I'll speak to Papa about this. You're to go. And you," he said, turning to Rafferty, his voice laced with contempt. "If you ever come near my wife again, I'll have you tied to a post and whipped until you're dead."

As Chantal opened her mouth to retort, Rafferty spoke quietly and firmly. "Mr. Therrie, I give you my word, I didn't want them to do this. It wasn't worth the risk of either one of them suffering a scratch." At his words, Alain's face flushed.

"You damned impudent bastard, I—"

"Alain!" Chantal snapped, her patience shredded. "Diantha, tell him what you have to say, and we'll go." She turned away to rub her temple and saw two men kneeling over another; one of the men placed a coat over the face of the man on the ground.

"Rafferty," she said, gripping his arm. He turned her away from the dead man, his hand squeezing her shoulder. She glanced at Alain to see him with his arms around Diantha's shoulders, their heads together as they talked.

"There he is," a man behind Rafferty snarled.

Two men jumped Rafferty, taking him down and pinioning his arms behind him. Another hit him, pounding him with his fists. Chantal screeched and grabbed the man's arm. He flung her aside and she fell, pain shooting up her arm. Rafferty brought one leg up into his groin, sending him sprawling and groaning in pain.

"Stop it at once!" Alain Therrie ordered, his pistol pointed at one of Rafferty's attackers. "Robert, this man is my father's overseer. He was sent here to protect my wife and sister."

Coming to his feet, Rafferty steadied himself, shaking his head and rubbing his jaw. Chantal wanted to run to him, but it would only increase Alain's hatred of Rafferty. She rubbed her arm where she had fallen.

"I'm going with Diantha," Alain said, the anger gone from his voice. "We'll go now."

At the barricade, Rafferty took Chantal's arm. "Run!" he ordered. They dashed across the street, with Alain and Diantha following.

They returned the carriage to the carriage house in back of the Therrie home on Royal, Rafferty climbing down to help Chantal. "I'll leave now for Belle Destin," he said to Alain, looking over her head.

Alain nodded, and Chantal felt a surge of anger. "Alain, this man risked his life to protect us!"

Alain's face flushed, and he flicked Rafferty a glance that chilled her.

"We'll take the carriage and go to Dr. Blair's to see about my shoulder," Alain said, his voice sounding pained, and Chantal's anger evaporated. She watched him and his wife climb into the carriage. When she turned, Rafferty was gone. Farther down the alley she saw him mounting his horse, and she hurried toward him.

"Your lip is bleeding," she said as he stopped beside her. "Come inside and let me tend it."

Rafferty swung down out of the saddle, moving too close. His eyes sparked, and she drew a breath, stepping back and bumping the wall. She touched his cheek. "I'm sorry you were hurt. I feel responsible."

"Do you now? I've been maligned, beaten, and shot at, while I risked life and limb for you and your surly brother."

"I'm sorry!" She touched his arm, and the moment took on new meaning. He moved closer, placing his hands on either side of her, and she felt hemmed in. They stood in the deserted alley behind the Therrie home, the high wall hiding them from the view of those in the house, or neighbors. A lantern flickered, the light playing over his features, and her heart beat faster as he tilted her chin up. "You flirt with trouble the way a fast woman flirts with men in a saloon. Do you have any idea what misery you've caused me, Chantal Therrie?"

"I don't know if it's one bit more than the trouble you've caused me."

"Oh? How have I caused you trouble? This should be revealing."

She bit her lip. "I should go inside."

"Oh, no. You're going to answer my question. How've I caused you trouble?"

She tried to look away, but he turned her chin back to face him. Annoyed, she glared at him. "I don't sleep. My life isn't as peaceful."

"Well, I'll be damned," he answered softly. "Why don't you sleep?"

"I'm going inside!" she snapped, pushing on an arm that was as immovable as a tree.

"You don't sleep for the same reasons I lie awake," he said in a husky voice, and she felt torn between wanting to agree and throw herself into his strong arms and turning and running inside as she should.

As she struggled, his lips brushed her nape. "I've missed seeing you. And I've told you that someday, Chantal, you'll be mine," he said, his voice dropping to that timbre that she enjoyed too much. "That time is getting closer."

"Let me go!" she whispered, emotions warring in her as he slid his arm around her waist and pulled her up against him. His body was hard; he smelled of the cherry-laurel water he used after shaving. Her hands fluttered over his chest and his broad shoulders as he pulled her close. He placed his mouth over hers and parted her lips.

She felt devoured, and she wanted him. Each time with him stirred a bigger tempest than the time before.

She felt the melting heat that started in her loins and spread. Her tongue touched his while she returned his kiss. His manhood pressed against her as his hands slid down her sides.

She wanted him and his kisses, wanted them to go on forever, yet she was engaged to Lazare. She was promised, and this was the wildest folly.

"I mustn't!" she cried, and pushed against him. "We can't marry! We're worlds apart, so all you're doing is hurting me!"

His hand went behind her head, locking his fingers in her hair to pull her head back. "You weren't meant for a loveless marriage. You're a passionate woman, Chantal, and you were meant to take love and give love."

"I don't have a choice!" she cried, suddenly wishing that she did.

He leaned closer, and the look on his face frightened her. His blue eyes blazed, and his voice was inflexible. "You're going to have a choice." He left her and mounted, riding out of sight without looking back, while she shivered and rubbed her arms and stared at his back and broad shoulders. She would never be allowed to marry him. Never. And she didn't want to; all her life she had planned to marry Lazare. For what seemed like the thousandth time, she decided that she would get Rafferty O'Brien out of her thoughts and life forever.

Monday evening, Alain appeared at Ormonde's office in their home in the Vieux Carré. "Papa?"

"Come in," Ormonde said, leaning back in his chair.

"What happened at your meeting today?"

"Any talk of impeaching the mayor has died, particularly since the president of the Council, Summers, has agreed to act as mayor until the new one is sworn in." Ormonde shifted in his chair and waved his hand. "Alain, dammit, you could have been hurt, or worse! Men were killed for nothing. Elections were held today and I cast my vote as always. And don't count on Pierre becoming mayor! Gerald will win.''

Alain ran his fingers through his hair. His face was flushed, and his eyes burned with anger. He pounded his fist against the wall. ''Dammit! We needed reforms—''

Ormonde threw down his pen. ''What you need to worry about are the abolitionists who'll destroy our whole way of life! There's a man up north, he's not an abolitionist; he was born in Kentucky. His public debates have drawn support.''

''That isn't what's important here in our city.''

''You're not listening to men who've been in Washington. Read the *Daily Picayune* or the *Daily Delta*. Lord knows, we've got as many papers as plantations; there's no dearth of news, but I don't think you're reading them.''

''*Our* papers aren't writing about what some Yankee has said.''

''Come back to the Democrats, where you can do some good.''

''Papa, fire that damned overseer. He's Irish.''

''It isn't because he's Irish that you dislike him. John Burnside is Irish, and you would accept an invitation to Houmas Plantation any day.''

''John Burnside is one of the largest sugar producers in America and has one of the finest homes. Rafferty O'Brien is a penniless immigrant, and he's trouble.''

''You and Blaise! She hates him too, although why she—'' He broke off and ran his hand across his brow. ''He's producing the best crop of cotton I've ever had. Have you looked at our fields?''

''You can get a dozen overseers to do the same.''

''You'd better take care of your own place first. You ought to get more cotton per acre than you have the past two years.''

Alain's face flushed, and his anger increased. ''All right, but O'Brien treats Chantal as an equal!''

''The man is well educated. If circumstances in life had been different he would be gentry and have his own place in Ireland. Suppose it were reversed, and *you* were the man whose father had gambled away all you owned and you had to scramble for every penny?''

''You'll regret having hired him.'' Alain gazed outside. ''The Know-Nothings are running the Vigilantes from the city. Some of them have crossed the river and are hiding in bayous below Algiers. I don't know if my party will survive this night.''

''Better for you if it doesn't. Stay here until it calms, then return home. By the time you and Diantha are back in town, it will be forgotten and an old incident. Someday the Democrats will be the party here, Alain.'' He leaned back in his chair. ''My overseer has been to two meetings. He's a good speaker, and men listen to him.''

''He's a Democrat?''

''He's not a citizen yet, so he can't join the party or vote, but he plans to join, and he's articulate.''

''If he weren't your overseer, I'd have him publicly whipped.''

Ormonde straightened up, and Alain felt a stir of alarm. There were moments when his father had been pushed too far, and for all his quiet manner he could be terrifying.

''You won't do that, not when I sent him with them. Chantal would have taken Diantha, and the two gone alone. I wouldn't have let any of them go if I had known shots were fired. But he was under my orders, so you forget retaliation.''

''Yes, sir,'' Alain said, knowing he should drop it. In fact he was willing to stop discussing something as unpleasant as the overseer, when he felt a continual bubble of excitement within him. He shifted, trying to get comfortable because his shoulder ached.

''Papa, Diantha wanted me to wait until we're certain, but she thinks she is in a family way.''

Ormonde looked up at him and blinked, and then for a single rare moment, he laughed out loud. ''A grandchild! How fine! Alain, I'm so pleased! Has she seen Dr. Blair?''

''No, sir. No. She says it's too soon.''

''Nonsense, get her to a doctor. But wait a few days

until it's safe for you to move around the city. So that's why you came so willingly from the barricades?"

"Yes, sir," he said, feeling pleased and amazed that he would become a father. "The escapade frightened her, and she doesn't want to leave her room and this morning she was sick."

"That wasn't because of the Know-Nothings! Good, Alain! Very good! My first grandchild! This calls for a toast!"

He poured claret and turned to Alain. "To my heir and grandson!"

"Papa, it may be a girl like Chantal, and keep us all in a storm," Alain said dryly, and Ormonde laughed. "I still say you should get rid of the overseer."

"The hands work for him and they like him." Ormonde swirled the claret, staring down into the glass. "It's peculiar; he doesn't believe in slavery, yet he gets along better with them than anyone we've had."

"What's so damned peculiar about that? They've heard about that slave he's tried to free, and they work twice as hard for him because of it."

"Perhaps, but he stays, Alain. Let's see what kind of crop he brings in. For a man who doesn't know anything about cotton, he's doing a hell of a job."

"He's a slave-lover, an abolitionist at heart, and an Irishman to boot. You should sleep with a pistol, Papa. Make certain he doesn't cause a revolt. All my life I've heard about the rebellion in St. John the Baptist Parish."

"He's not going to lead a rebellion," Ormonde said, but Alain was glad to see that he frowned as he did so. Ormonde had to be thinking of something he didn't like about the Irish overseer.

"Watch him, Papa. And think about letting him go."

Chapter 15

October 21, 1859

"You look beautiful, ma'am," Loretta said, in a voice filled with awe and pleasure. Chantal studied her reflection in the pier glass.

"Thank you, Loretta," she answered, pleased with her reflection and wondering about Lazare's reaction, which seemed the same every time he saw her: always pleased, yet nothing more. What did she expect, *a reaction like Rafferty O'Brien's?* She pushed the thought aside. She dreaded her talk with Papa, yet she was determined to have one.

Always, when they had a party to attend, Papa was ready a full hour before the rest of the family. The house servants had packed the carriages in the morning. The party was to last all weekend, from Friday afternoon until Sunday night, and trunks were packed with fancy petticoats and gowns and gifts for the Pirious.

With a swirl of petticoats and her emerald silk dress, Chantal went to find Papa.

The house was silent as she descended the curving stairs. "William, where's Papa?"

"He's in his office, Miss Chantal."

She moved down the hall, her slippers a whisper against the polished cypress floor. She rapped lightly on the open door and entered the room. "Papa?"

Her breath caught as Rafferty O'Brien turned and looked into her eyes. His gaze lowered in one of those languorous appraisals, and she saw pleasure light his face. She warmed beneath the look he gave her, and it was an effort to shift her gaze to Papa.

"Papa, I didn't know you weren't alone."

"That's all right, Chantal," he said, looking down at something on his desk, and she was thankful he hadn't noticed Rafferty's perusal. When her gaze slid back to Rafferty's, her heart made another skip at his unfathomable look. His expression was solemn, almost angry, and it startled her.

"I'll go now, sir," Rafferty said, his voice quiet, as unreadable as his expression. "You and your family will be away all weekend," he added, looking into her eyes. Was that why he looked impassive, perhaps angry? *"Do you know how I feel when I see you in his arms or leaving with him?"* She remembered his question; was that why he was solemn? She felt hot and flustered as she watched him.

He held her gaze as he moved toward her, and her heart thudded. Then he passed her and was gone, his boots scraping the boards in the hall as he left. She felt drained, and he had done nothing except greet her and look at her. Nothing! All the more reason to talk to Papa. She closed the door and faced him.

"Is Mr. O'Brien doing a good job?"

"The best. We've never had an overseer as capable as he is, and we're going to have bumper crops this year, cotton and corn. I was afraid that with his inexperience we might have a poor yield, but he gets work out of my hands like no one else has been able to do. And his younger brother is a good farrier. I hired the best overseer this plantation will ever have." Papa glanced at her. "You look pretty, Chantal," he said perfunctorily. "And you're ready early. Punctuality is a virtue. It'll be another hour before Amity and Blaise are ready. Or longer."

"Papa, I want to talk to you."

He nodded. "Yes?"

"Can you talk Mr. Galliard into moving up the wedding date?"

Ormonde frowned, staring at her. "No, of course not!"

"Both of you planned this wedding, and you set a date."

"Yes, we did. Andreas married too young, Chantal.

He was eighteen and Lazare's mother was sixteen. She lost four babies before Lazare was born. Andreas thinks it was a mistake to wed at that age.'' Ormonde looked out the window. ''He isn't a happy man at home.''

Chantal had heard gossip about Andreas Galliard's mistresses, about illegitimate children, mixtures of black and white, who bore Galliard blood. ''It's different for us,'' she said. ''Lazare and I are happy together. Soleil will be finished early next year. I'm getting older. I'm eighteen, and we're supposed to wait until the summer of 1861 when Lazare is twenty-four. I'll be twenty then and *old*!''

Papa smiled. ''Not so old, Chantal. Andreas is adamant. And if anyone is to argue with him, it will have to be Lazare. I'll bring up the matter, but I can't insist. You should know that. I think you'll have a good marriage, Chantal. That's important. Sometimes I don't think young men realize how important,'' he said, looking beyond her out the window again.

She felt surprised. The last statement was an unusual confession from him. Yet she had always suspected that his marriage to Maman was less happy than it appeared to be. Papa would hide it from the world, just as he hid his innermost feelings. Her thoughts shifted back to Rafferty O'Brien and the past few minutes.

''Papa, please discuss the wedding with him.''

He smiled. ''I will, Chantal. I'm happy you're anxious.''

''Soleil will be beautiful. I'm so pleased with it.''

''Good. We have to bring Grand-père out and show it to him soon.''

''Yes. Thank you, Papa,'' she said. ''I'm ready when the others are.''

He nodded, bending over papers on his desk. Before she turned away, he glanced up again. ''Chantal, when you wed, I'll give you two slaves to take with you. You can think about whom you'd like to have, or if you'd rather I bought two new ones for you.''

"I can answer now. I want Loretta, and I'll think about the other."

"Fine. There are a few I won't allow you to take, and I know you're not interested in the field hands."

"Yes, Papa. Thank you." She left the room and walked to the music room, which overlooked one of the gardens. She stood in the slanting western sun, looking down the sloping lawn to the glimmer through the trees which was the river, but she didn't see butterflies swooping in lazy arcs over yellow lilies or pink crape myrtle. She saw solemn blue eyes gazing at her, and she felt afraid. What would have happened if she had told the truth? *Papa, move the wedding up, because Rafferty O'Brien is becoming too important. I see him constantly, and he's becoming my best friend. When he kisses me, I almost faint.* She leaned her forehead against the cool glass and closed her eyes. He must not interfere! She conjured up the image of Soleil bathed in sunshine, imagining how it would look when finished and flowers bloomed in the yard and she could spend nights of love in Lazare's arms. Rafferty's image, bending close to kiss her, drifted into consciousness.

"No!" she exclaimed aloud, closing her mind to unbidden, breathtaking memories.

Later, as they were winding down the drive in two carriages laden with trunks and belongings, she rode in the open carriage. As they turned a bend, she saw Rafferty on horseback, a field hand beside him on a mule. She turned her head quickly and lifted her chin, determined she would forget him for the weekend.

They were an hour late arriving at Great Oaks, which Papa considered as prompt as the Therrie family could be. As she alighted from the carriage she saw Lazare lounging with a group of men on the gallery, and he came down the steps to greet her.

It wasn't until late that night, after a sumptuous banquet, that she was alone with Lazare. As they waltzed in the grand ballroom, he swept through the open doors and waltzed outside, where a few other couples danced.

"Papa will look for us."

"Your father has left the ballroom. No doubt to smoke a cigar with Emile Piriou and some of the men. Let's walk out to the gazebo." He linked his arm in hers and they strolled down the steps and followed the winding brick walk. They passed a wide circle, set back off the lane, where there were marble benches. Stepping into the shadows to a bench, Lazare pulled her down beside him.

"I've wanted you all to myself," he said, putting his arms around her and pulling her close. "You look beautiful, Chantal."

"I wish we were marrying sooner, Lazare. Much sooner."

"So do I, but you know my father thinks a man should be mature before settling. Love, I'd marry you tomorrow if I could without losing my inheritance."

"Have you talked to him again about it, Lazare?"

"Not for the past few months, but I know how he feels. Actually, I know my parents stopped caring for each other long ago. Maman has her friends and parties. Papa has his hunts and gambling and"—he paused—"his amusements."

He meant his women. "Lazare, I've heard rumors. . . ." She blushed. Why was it easier to talk to Rafferty O'Brien than her own fiancé? "Some men have mistresses. Quadroon mistresses. I've heard about the quadroon balls. Does your father?"

"Yes, I think so. It's not something he's announced to the family." She heard the amusement in Lazare's voice, and although she'd already suspected that Andreas Galliard had a quadroon mistress, hearing Lazare admit it so casually gave her a small shock.

"I couldn't bear to share you with a mistress," she said vehemently.

He chuckled and kissed her throat. "You won't have to share me, Chantal. I expect you to keep me very happy at home." His kisses trailed lower, and she forgot the conversation as he pushed her dress down, his big fingers reaching beneath the taffeta and her thin shift to touch the curve of her breast above her stiff corset.

"Lazare," she gasped, closing her eyes and winding her fingers in the hair at the back of his neck.

Saturday afternoon Rafe sat in Jolie's parlor. "Thank you for this introduction."

She smiled at him. "I've followed your progress, and I'm glad to help. Edwin Rosenkrantz wants to get out of the shipping business, and this is the first of his ships he is selling. It should be a good one. I've heard men talk about his ships through the years."

"Tobiah Barr is waiting outside. He is going with me to look at it. He builds furniture, but he understands much more about the soundness of a ship and how it's constructed than I will."

"Edwin should be here any time now," Jolie said, looking composed, her pink taffeta dress a complement to her pink cheeks and creamy skin.

"You've been kind to me, Jolie. You're good to people," he said, knowing from Touzet that Jolie still contributed to Sharon's care, even though the aunt had claimed the little girl and taken her to Texas.

There was a knock, and a servant opened the door. "Mr. Rosenkrantz, ma'am."

"Send him in," Jolie said, moving toward the door as Rafe stood and waited. He felt a hum of excitement. He owned the small house in the Vieux Carré, and now he was going to buy a ship. He had been looking for months, until Jolie made her recommendation. A man came through the door, and all of Rafe's notions vanished of how a shipowner should look. He had imagined a weathered, forceful man who loved to sail and enjoyed the outdoors. Edwin Rosenkrantz was only inches over five feet, with wisps of gray hair and a thick black beard. His blue eyes were round, with high, bushy black eyebrows that gave him a surprised look.

"Edwin! This is my friend, Rafferty O'Brien. Rafferty, I would like you to meet Edwin Rosenkrantz."

"How do you do," Rafe said, shaking hands as Rosenkrantz looked up at him.

"So you're interested in shipping?"

"Yes, sir. And Jolie said you have a ship you want to sell."

"That's right. We might as well talk while we look at it. Jolie, will you join us?"

She smiled. "Thank you, Edwin, no. I don't have much interest in a ship loaded with bales of cotton."

"Then if you'll excuse us?"

Rafe held the door and winked at Jolie as they left the room. "Thanks," he said, knowing he would be back that night and could tell her about the ship then.

"Mr. Rosenkrantz, I know a man, Tobiah Barr. I've asked him to join us in looking at the ship. He builds furniture and is a craftsman, and he'll know more about some things than I will."

"Fine. But what you need, O'Brien, is a good captain. A man who knows the business. I can give you two names, two men who are available now or will be soon."

They stepped outside where Tobiah came forward.

"Mr. Rosenkrantz, this is Tobiah Barr. Tobiah, meet Edwin Rosenkrantz."

Tobiah nodded and said, "Sir."

Tobiah rode with the driver of Rosenkrantz's carriage as they went to the wharf. Rafe gazed with pleasure at the sleek lines of the full-rigged clipper, its tall masts dark against the blue sky. Gulls circled endlessly, their cries mingling with the jingle of halyards.

"She's two hundred and thirty feet by forty-two feet, with a registered tonnage of two thousand. That long hull gives you speed," Rosenkrantz said. "This one can carry a sizeable cargo."

To Rafe's satisfaction, the deck gleamed and lines were coiled neatly or secured, everything in place. Tobiah poked and climbed over the ship, finally nodding his approval to Rafe.

Two hours later Rafe was seated across the desk in Edwin Rosenkrantz's office, signing the papers that made him the owner of *The Swan*.

"Here are the names of the two captains. If you can hire either one, you'll have a damned good man you can depend upon to do the best job possible."

"Thank you. I appreciate this, sir."

"I envy you, starting a new business, but I'm tired of being tied to this. I want to settle—at least I'm going to try it, and see if I like it."

Rafe stood up while Edwin Rosenkrantz pocketed the draft written on Rafe's account. "Thank you, sir," Rafe said. "I know I'm going to like it."

"Better than that, you should make money. Handle *The Swan* right and you will." He tilted his head and peered up at Rafe. "What are you going to do with her?"

"Sell cotton."

"Can't beat that. That's what *The Swan* can do best. Ship it to England and bring back goods from their mills. Good luck."

Rafe stepped into the sunshine and grinned at Tobiah, who stood waiting. "Thanks for giving me your opinion."

"And now you own it?"

"Yes, I do," Rafe said. "I have the names of two captains to contact."

"Congratulations, Mr. O'Brien."

"Always so formal, Tobiah. I've only heard you call me Rafferty that night we went to look at my little swamp."

Tobiah shook his head. "It's habit now."

"Thanks again. See you tonight, Tobiah." Rafe turned to head to Touzet's to tell him the news. He grinned and whistled, feeling happy. He would have to have his own prosperous business before he could gain permission to court Chantal, and with the delayed plans Lazare had it was giving him time to acquire property and the means to acquire more. He would name his ship the *Annora*. He sobered as he walked. He and Caleb had talked about Fortune. After this much time, they knew they should give up. Fortune must have drowned, yet Rafferty couldn't accept that in his heart.

He was learning the cotton business from Ormonde Therrie, and from men Ormonde Therrie had introduced him to. The next purchase would be a warehouse. He wanted to become a factor, for he had been learning about it by dealing with factors for the Therries. Rafe knew the warehouse he wanted, had the funds for the purchase, and had an attorney talking to the owner. The warehouse was by the dock, and if he could hire someone to run it as he planned to hire someone to captain his ship, he could stay at Belle Destin near Chantal. *Chantal* . . .

Chapter 16

March 1860

"Caleb?" Chantal stepped beneath the shade of the shed as Caleb O'Brien rose up. He wore a leather apron. His chest was bare, revealing hard muscles that flexed and rippled with his movements. He held a bellows in his hand and had a piece of iron on the anvil. Even in the shade it was steaming hot, with the fire glowing red. Sweat glistened on Caleb's face and shoulders.

"I'm trying to find your brother," she said.

"Rafe's either at the cotton press or the gin house, I think. He said he needs to fix something."

"Thank you," she replied and moved away, riding toward the cotton buildings. Wondering if she would find him with a roomful of men, she bit her lip. Her night had been sleepless and miserable, when it should have been one of the happiest nights in her life. And there was only one reason for this: At her own urging, the engagement party had been moved up. Why did the prospect now sit like a leaden weight on her heart? Would she feel relief after she had told Rafferty?

No more swims, no more rides and long talks. No more of those forbidden kisses and shared looks that were becoming more important by the day. She groaned aloud and ran her fingers over her heated brow. As she neared the cotton press she could look through the shed and see that it was empty. This screw press could compress the lint into bales, and Papa worked with Rafferty to oversee it all. She heard hammering coming from the gin house, the building where the seeds and hulls were removed. She dismounted

and moved inside, and found Rafferty in the lint room
where the cleaned cotton was stored.

"Mr. O'Brien?"

He straightened up. He was stripped to the waist,
his chest and shoulders covered in sweat, the black
curls on his chest matted and damp. His pants rode
low on his narrow hips and he held a hammer in his
hands. Behind him cotton hung off boards like white
icicles, seeming to drip from the walls, draped in loops
at the ceiling and along the boards of the press. Great
white mounds lay like banks of snow in the corners of
the room. Rafferty had fluffs in his dark hair. She
stared at him, knowing that the next few moments
would be embedded in her mind forever.

"To what do I owe the honor?" he asked in sardonic
tones, studying her.

"I wanted to talk to you." She glanced around.

He threw down the hammer. "We're alone, but it's
three hundred degrees in here. Let's get down to the
creek."

"I have to get back."

"Come on, Chantal. It's only minutes away, and I
might burst into flames if we don't." He took her arm.
Everything inside her screamed no. *Tell him now! Tell
him and go home and be done with it!* She bit her lip.

"Rafferty . . ."

He looked down at her and grinned. "Come on.
You look hot too."

She pressed her lips together. *Just this once! Coward! Coward! Tell him and get it over with and say
good-bye! Kiss him good-bye! I suppose one last kiss
couldn't hurt. Last kiss . . .*

It hurt. Everything hurt, and it shouldn't have. She
swayed between anger at him for the disruption he had
brought to her peaceful life and a hot, wild longing
that threatened to smash her world to millions of
pieces.

At the isolated creek he tethered her horse and lifted
her down. "We're getting summer instead of spring."
He bent down and splashed water on his face, his cotton trousers outlining his muscled thighs.

"My back is turned," he said, removing his boots. "Let's swim, Chantal. It's beastly hot."

"I need to talk to you."

"Fine, only let's do it after a quick dip. Don't tell me you wouldn't feel better as well."

She glared at his back in consternation. Always he presented choices. *Say it to him now, quickly, while his back is turned and he's yards away! You can't swim with him and then tell him!*

"Rafferty . . ."

He turned to study her, his brows arching. "This looks serious." He stood up and pulled off his belt, and suddenly she couldn't breathe. Her gaze drifted down over his narrow hips and legs, and then she blushed when his eyes caught hers. Giving his belt a toss, he walked to her. "What the hell is wrong, Chantal?"

Her heart lurched. It wasn't supposed to be this way. A hundred times during the night she had envisioned telling him about her engagement party, and always she had been on her horse, Rafferty either on his bay or at the stable door when she told him. But never like this, when he was half-naked and standing only inches away while he studied her with a solemn, inscrutable expression after asking her what was wrong. *He knew without my telling him that I had something to say. "What the hell is wrong?" Does it look that bad to him?*

She hurt, and she closed her eyes. "Andreas Galliard has moved up our engagement party. Maman and Papa will give the party here in September."

There was silence, and she opened her eyes to meet a fiery gaze. "You don't love him! You can break it off now!"

"I do! I *do* love him, and I *can't* break it off!" she exclaimed, feeling panic rise. She wouldn't let Rafferty O'Brien interfere in her life or destroy her peace. She was promised to Lazare, and she must not forget it for a moment. It had been arranged, planned for years.

"Chantal," Rafferty said in a husky, seductive voice that made something burn inside.

Hard arms caught her and she fought him, trying to unclasp his hands and break free. He spun her around, yanking her to his chest. She pounded against him, thrashing her head back and forth so that he couldn't kiss her. "No! Let me go! No! They'd never allow us to wed!"

"You don't love him!" Rafferty wound his fingers in her hair and held her head, his mouth finding hers.

His arms were tight and hard, like fetters binding her, but his kisses were soft, hot, and tantalizing, melting her resistance. Her mouth opened beneath his, his tongue going deep as he kissed her hard, and her thoughts and her anger and her hurt spun away.

She yielded, clinging to him.

He spread his legs, pulling her to him, pressing her hips against his. His fingers moved to her nape as he bent over her and kissed her. He pushed her down on the grass, coming down with her to stretch out over her as he kissed her. She slid her arms around his neck and returned his kisses.

The last time, the last time . . .

His hands stroked her breast and she moaned, feeling his fingers everywhere, and then his hand was on her thigh and he shifted beside her, rolling her to face him while he continued to kiss her.

Tears streaked her cheeks. She should stop, should say good-bye. She had to stop, but she wanted him. She wanted his wild kisses, wanted Rafferty. Her father would not allow her to marry anyone except Lazare. The thought faded and she yielded, seizing the moment, clinging to him, telling herself she would never be able to have his kisses again.

"Rafferty," she whispered.

His fingers drifted higher between her thighs. She gasped with pleasure, feeling sensations she had never known.

"We shouldn't, because I have to tell you good-bye. . . ."

He kissed her ear, his tongue tracing circles as his hand moved between her legs. She moaned softly.

While he kissed her he unbuttoned her dimity dress and peeled it down, pushing it and her chemise to her waist. He swung his leg over her and sat up astride her, his thumbs drawing circles over her pink nipples. She looked up at him and saw the thick bulge in his tight pants, then reached out, unable to resist touching him. He caught her hand and held it against him while he closed his eyes and groaned. He was big and hard and she shifted, aching and wanting him.

"Rafferty," she whispered, tears stinging her cheeks, sorrow mingling with passion.

He bent down to kiss her breast, his tongue tracing her nipple while she closed her eyes.

"Rafferty . . ." Her voice was a raspy whisper as he stood up and looked down at her. She felt on fire, and he wasn't even touching her. She lay sprawled beneath his intent gaze.

He dropped down beside her, winding his fingers in her hair and working out the pins and plaits until it spilled over her shoulders. Then he knelt at her foot to kiss her ankle, caressing her leg, his gaze hot and languorous as he bent her leg and kissed the back of her thigh.

"When we marry, we can do this . . . nights and nights of love," he whispered. "No man will ever love you like I will, Chantal," he said.

Her pulse drowned out his words and her fingertips trailed over his hard shoulders. He moved his hand between her legs to her hot moistness, touching the bud that throbbed and making her arch her hips. His hand moved on her and sensations rocked her. She grasped him, clinging to him, closing her eyes as he kissed her while she writhed and felt tension build. Sensation engulfed her, exploding in spasms of release. She ached for more, wanting him, wanting what she didn't know. "Oh, Rafferty, I shouldn't. I can't. I have to marry him. And yet . . ."

"Say it!" he said, his voice deep and demanding.

"Say it, Chantal!" He wound his fingers in her hair. "*Look* at me!"

She opened her eyes and felt her heart thud. He looked as if he needed her for his very life. Never had a man looked at her with such an expression of—only one thing—love.

She tingled with sensations she had never experienced before. But there was more than passion, and they both knew it.

"*Say* it, dammit!"

"I love you," she whispered, then closed her eyes and felt the hot tears sting them. "But it doesn't matter. I'll forget and—"

"The hell!" He bent to kiss her hard, his tongue thrusting deep, his weight moving over her, his manhood hard against her. "I want you. I love you. You can't marry him and be bound in a loveless marriage all your life."

"No! The law says I have to obey Papa."

"To hell with the law! You're mine, Chantal, and you'll always be mine. When I take you, Chantal," he said, looking at her solemnly, "I want you to want me without reservation. As badly as I want you, I want you to know it's right."

"I can't!" she gasped, rolling away, feeling as if her heart were being torn from her body. She did love Rafferty, but she was eternally bound to Lazare Galliard.

"Break your engagement now. I'll give you as good a life as he will. I promise you, Chantal."

"I can't," she said, closing her eyes because she hurt more than she had ever hurt in her life. Rafferty's blazing blue gaze burned like hot steel through her heart.

"You don't love him. Vows can be broken. You can't imagine how empty Soleil will be without love."

"I'm pledged, and I can't change it. Papa would never allow me to see you." As she pushed away and mounted her horse to race away from Rafferty O'Brien, she wondered if she would ever stop hurting. Tears

blinded her eyes, and her body throbbed with scalding
desire for him.

She raced up the stairs at home and almost collided
with Maman. Chantal gasped, because she had thought
the hall was empty when she came inside. Maman
caught her shoulders and looked at her. Chantal
wanted to jerk away, but she couldn't. Her cheeks
flamed in embarrassment as Maman marched her into
Chantal's room. "Get in here, Chantal! You're going
to answer my questions!"

The next morning, Rafferty strolled into the plantation office and closed the door.

"Sit down," Ormonde said in a pleasant voice, his
gaze full of curiosity. "I expect another bumper crop
this year. And cotton and corn prices are better. You're
due for a raise, Mr. O'Brien."

Rafe sat in the leather chair and gazed at his employer. "Thank you, sir, but I have to give notice. I'm
quitting."

Ormonde's brows arched. "If you have a better offer, give me a chance to match it. Word gets around,
and everyone in these parts knows you're the best
damned overseer in Louisiana."

"Thank you, but I'm not going to be an overseer."

Ormonde leaned back, and a crooked smile tugged
one corner of his mouth up. "I might have known.
You've become a citizen, and a power in the Democratic Party. Going into politics?"

"I might, but that would be secondary."

"I'm curious what your plans are. You're a damned
fine planter, but I haven't heard of your buying any
land."

"I've bought a warehouse and opened an office on
Gravier, near Benjamin Florence's office. And I now
own a Baltimore clipper, the *Annora*. I'm going to be
a factor." Ormonde's eyes grew round, and then he
smiled. Rafe tilted his head. "Sir? You find that amus-
ing?"

"Yes. You learned the business from me, from my
taking you to talk to my factor, to see how it's done

and what he does. And now I'll have to pay you to sell my cotton."

"I don't expect you to leave your factor," Rafe said.

"You know I've been displeased with his service. I think the man takes advantage of me, but I'm at his mercy."

Surprised and pleased, Rafe smiled. "You trust me to be fair?"

"Of course I do. You won't change from the man you are here. A ship and a warehouse. I'm surprised. You Irish like land, and respect it. You're a farmer, and land is important. It's in a man's blood, and it's more permanent than ships and warehouses."

"Yes, sir, but every month the storm brews stronger over the question of slavery. We've got a presidential election coming up. From what I hear, sentiment is still running high up north over the hanging of John Brown. Slavery is a custom that may run out of time. If it does, I don't want to be caught up in it."

"As a cotton broker, you'd be caught up in it anyway."

"Not in the same manner. With a ship—and I plan to buy another ship as soon as possible—I'll be more fluid. I can move merchandise. And I intend to do more than be a broker. I own three houses in the Vieux Carré now."

For the first time since Rafe had met Ormonde Therrie, the man looked genuinely shocked. He stared at Rafe. "Where the hell did you get the funds?" Instantly his face flushed. "I beg your pardon, Mr. O'Brien. It's just that you caught me by surprise. That's none of my affair, and I apologize for the question."

Rafe smiled. "Don't apologize. If you were in town more and moved in my circle, you'd know. I gamble, and I bank my winnings. I've done so since shortly after my arrival in New Orleans. They're put away in the Louisiana State Bank in its fire-repellent brick vaults," he added dryly.

"You win that often?"

"Sir, my father was as close to a professional gambler as a man can get and still have a farm and another income. Caleb and I know how to gamble; we know how to win, and when we lose we're smart enough to fold. I could have lived on my winnings instead of taking this job, but I wanted to learn about cotton.''

"By heaven, now I'm curious! I can take a guest to the Elkins Club. Hell, if you're going to be a factor, you'll be invited to join. Come with me Saturday night.''

"Thank you. I'd enjoy that.''

"What about your brothers? Caleb is a damned good worker, and I'd be happy to keep him on.'' He sighed. "Now I'll have to train another overseer. I'll discuss it with Caleb. What about the youngest brother?''

"Darcy will spend his time back and forth between us.''

"You've never heard from the other brother, have you?''

"No, sir, but I haven't given up hope.''

"You're going to live in three houses?''

Rafe smiled. "No, sir. I'll rent two, and live in the one on Esplanade.''

"Are we going to be neighbors?''

"We'll be close.''

"I'm surprised you didn't pick the American sector.''

"The French Quarter holds a distinct charm,'' he said, knowing he would be closer to Chantal and the Therrie townhouse.

"Well, Mr. O'Brien, I hate to see you go, but I wish you good fortune and I'll send my business your way.''

"Thank you,'' Rafferty said, standing and extending his hand. "Thank you for giving me a job. Your family is special.''

When Rafe stepped into the hall, Chantal was standing in the library doorway. Her eyes were wide, full of curiosity. Her cheeks went pink, and she nodded. His heartbeat quickened, and he hoped he was doing the right thing. By now he was wildly in love with her, and he needed to make changes now so that he could move on her social level.

"Miss Therrie,'' he said, acknowledging her in a

brief greeting. He crossed the hall, pausing a few yards from her. "I just talked to your father. I'm leaving."

"Leaving?" Chantal blinked, as if his announcement were incomprehensible. He stood so near, yet her family were all present in the house, as well as the servants. The moment held a sense of unreality, as if she couldn't comprehend what he was saying.

"I've quit your father's employ, and I'm moving back to the city. I'll see you again." He turned and left, striding out the door.

She felt as if she were losing a part of herself. Stunned, she followed, watching him go down the wide steps in his long, easy stride, looking as if he owned Belle Destin.

"I've lost the best damned overseer I'll ever have," Ormonde said, moving to her side in the doorway and watching Rafferty.

"Why is he leaving?" she asked, feeling shocked by the news. "What's he going to do? Is he going back to Ireland?"

"Far from it. He's bought a ship and a warehouse, and he's my new cotton factor. As a matter of fact he'll live on Esplanade, near our house."

Stunned by the sudden changes, Chantal watched him stride away. "A cotton factor?" she repeated, feeling shock, but pleasantly aware that Rafferty had just shot up in the social scale. Hereafter he would be almost on an equal footing with Lazare. *A house on Esplanade. A ship.* When did he do this? And why hadn't he told her? Yet all the wealth in the world wouldn't change Papa's stand on her engagement. Rafferty had moved up in life, but Papa was a man of principle and kept promises.

"What's happening?" Blaise said, joining them.

"You wanted to talk to me. I'm free now," Ormonde said, turning to her.

She gave Chantal an angry glance. "Yes, Ormonde, we have something to discuss."

"Our overseer just quit," Chantal announced.

Blaise frowned, glancing from Chantal to Ormonde. "Is that right? Mr. O'Brien is leaving?"

"Yes. I damned well hate to see him go, too. But the man has his mind made up and his future laid out. He already has another business."

Blaise blinked, staring at Ormonde and then looking at Chantal. Chantal felt a swift rush of satisfaction. Maman had intended to talk Papa into letting Rafferty go. Now it would make no difference that Maman knew Rafferty was the man Chantal had been with yesterday afternoon. He was gone out of their lives, out of hers forever. She felt tears threaten and turned away, heading for her room.

"You wanted to see me, Blaise," Ormonde said.

"It was nothing, my dear," Blaise answered smoothly, her mind racing to make sense of this new turn of events. Rafferty O'Brien had quit his job. Chantal couldn't see him now. Ormonde was watching her. "I had thought I would go to the city, but on second thought I think I won't."

Blaise went upstairs to find Chantal. When she opened the door to her room, Chantal looked up from the windowseat. Blaise stepped inside and closed the door.

"If you ever see him alone again, I'll tell Ormonde and Lazare. If anyone had caught you with him yesterday, you would have been ruined. Now he's going to move in the same social circle as Lazare," she added softly. "I wonder how long before Lazare calls him out."

"Don't stir Lazare to a duel! I want to marry him and live at Soleil."

"You know Lazare wouldn't be the one to die."

"You don't have a guarantee of that; I've seen Rafferty O'Brien shoot," Chantal said. "He doesn't miss. Just think of Daedalus, before you get Lazare into his line of fire. No one thought that horse could be ridden. I don't want my fiancé killed!"

Blaise frowned. O'Brien was an unpredictable, intrepid man. "No, none of us wants that. Just don't do something foolish to ruin your marriage to Lazare. He's going to be the most powerful man in the state of Louisiana."

"I told you, I want to marry him. Please don't goad him into a duel when we're on the brink of our engagement party. Mr. O'Brien has gone out of our lives."

Does Chantal mean what she says? Blaise wondered. *She's too strong-willed and impulsive, as unpredictable as O'Brien. What a pair those two would make! Neither would have a moment's peace.*

"Very well, but don't you ever allow him to touch you again! If you're deflowered, Lazare won't marry you!" She moved a step closer and lowered her voice. "Chantal, you *will* marry Lazare, or I'll ruin your life."

Chantal blinked and nodded, finally looking afraid. Feeling impatient, Blaise left the room.

She closed the door and stood in the hall, her thoughts on Chantal. In a union with Chantal, Lazare would add more wealth and more power to the Therries, and more nights of searing passion for her.

If Chantal were such a silly little fool to throw over Lazare for an Irish overseer, Blaise would destroy her. Her heart beat faster at the thought of the secret she harbored; the dark knowledge Ormonde thought he had concealed so well, a secret she would use only if necessary. It could bring down all of them, but it would be the cruelest blow to Chantal. Blaise locked her fingers together as she thought about it. Long ago she had followed Ormonde on his regular trip up north; she knew where he went, and what he did there.

Perhaps Rafferty O'Brien was gone from their lives forever. Blaise felt a smoldering fire of hatred toward him. Someday she would get her revenge and ruin him. No man had ever spurned her—none. With a last glance at Chantal's door, Blaise hurried to her room.

Inside her room Chantal leaned her head forward on her knees and cried silently. *I should be glad,* she thought. *It's right that he's going.* "Rafferty," she whispered, remembering lying in the grass with his hands on her, his long body beside her, his mouth on hers. "Rafferty O'Brien, I love you. . . ."

Chapter 17

August 1860

Rafe woke, staring into darkness and wondering what had brought him out of sleep. There was a clattering sound on the polished oak floor of his new townhouse on Esplanade. Pushing aside the mosquito bar, Rafe swung out of his rosewood half-tester bed. There were pebbles on the floor. The night was dark as he stepped into his pants and reached for his Colt.

Another flurry of pebbles struck the floor. He moved swiftly to the door and flattened against the wall beside it, revolver ready as he peered out. Below in the courtyard he saw a man's silhouette. Only one man of his acquaintance was that tall and broad-shouldered; lowering the Colt, Rafe leaned out.

"I'll have a gravel road in here if you throw much more. I'll be right down."

When he reached the back door and opened it, Tobiah stepped inside. As they stood in the dark, Rafe wondered how many of his servants had heard the commotion. "What's happened, Tobiah?"

"Mr. O'Brien, I'm in love."

"Did you get me up for this? Do I offer congratulations or condolences?"

Tobiah remained solemn, and Rafe sobered. "She's a slave," Tobiah said, and Rafe could feel trouble stirring like storm winds rising off the sea. "I want you to buy her. I have my savings, and if it takes more, if you'll make me a loan, I'll repay every cent plus whatever interest you charge."

"To hell with that. I'll buy her if I can, but her owner may not want to part with her," Rafe said.

"Her owner doesn't want to part with her. He wants

her in his bed, and it's only a matter of time until she'll be there one way or another,'' Tobiah said in a tight voice. ''And if he forces her, I'll kill him.''

''You know what would happen to you, and to her, if you harmed her master.''

''She doesn't like him. He frightens her. He's moved into the family's garçonniér and moved her there with him. There are other servants, his valet, his cook, but she's alone with him too much. I want her out of there as soon as possible.''

''All right. I'll try to buy her, but if he's set on bedding her, he may not yield,'' Rafe said tersely, feeling frustration kindle.

Tobiah held out a box. ''Here's my savings since we arrived. I have over three thousand dollars there.''

As he accepted the box, Rafe grinned. ''You haven't been limiting yourself to your salary for income either. How the hell did you accumulate three thousand?''

''Same way you did, sir, working and gambling. Plus fighting.''

''Fighting?''

''I bet men they can't last five minutes with me. I make a tidy sum on my fights. I fight up around Congo Square, but not on Sundays. White men aren't often there.''

Rafe laughed. ''All right, Tobiah. Who is she, and to whom does she belong?''

''Mr. O'Brien, this isn't going to be easy,'' he said solemnly, and Rafe felt a hearty agreement.

''Who is she?'' Rafe repeated, his sense of calamity growing over Tobiah's reluctance to say the name.

''Her name is Lenora. She belongs to Lazare Galliard.''

''Damn! You know he wouldn't sell a bucket of Mississippi mud to me. I'll get an agent, someone to keep my name and yours out of the transaction.''

''Yes, sir. Get someone persuasive. And do it tomorrow. She's terrified.''

''That bastard. I don't think Chan—'' He broke off. ''I'll do it.''

"If he takes my Lenora against her will, master or not, I'll kill him."

"And then they'll lynch you. She's his as much as a horse. I'll get someone to call on him tomorrow. There's a man who moves in Galliard's circle, and I've become friends with this man. He's a banker from Virginia. I'll see if he'll do it."

"Thanks, Mr. O'Brien."

"I'll do my best, Tobiah. I swear."

Three weeks later, Rafe walked into the furniture store where Tobiah worked and asked if he could see him. He was directed to the alley behind the store, where Tobiah was carving a rosewood table.

"Can we talk here?" Rafe asked, dreading the next few minutes and feeling a sense of helplessness.

"Yes, sir. I take it the news isn't good."

"No, and I sent the best man I could find. Justin Herbert is a persuasive man. He's a man Galliard respects. Galliard refuses to consider selling her." Rafe didn't want to repeat the whole of the conversation he'd had with Herbert, who'd told him that Lazare Galliard intended to bed Lenora, wouldn't sell her until he had, and expected to do so within the next couple of months.

"Damn him!" Tobiah said, in a quiet voice that sent a chill down Rafe's spine.

"Tobiah. I don't want Galliard dead for Miss Therrie to mourn over. And above all, I don't want you lynched because you killed him." Black eyes pierced him, and Rafe felt another chill. "Tobiah, please."

"Sir, I love her, and you should understand."

Rafe drew a deep breath and turned away, looking down the alley, yet seeing only Chantal in his mind. "I told Justin to keep trying, and to talk to Lazare's father."

"Thank you, sir. Keep my money and persist with offers."

Rafe nodded, and he hurt for his friend, because he knew how he would feel if it were Chantal. And knew that if it *had* been Chantal, and Lazare had forced her, he would kill Lazare.

Chapter 18

Amity Therrie's skin prickled at the high squeals she heard. She turned the stallion to veer through the brush toward the river in the direction of the noise.

On a slab of rock near the river's edge, a cotton-mouth water moccasin was trying to swallow a rabbit.

"No!" Amity dropped to the ground and searched with frantic haste for a weapon. "Stop! No! Get away!" she yelled, hoping to frighten the snake.

Her heart pounded, and her hands shook in her haste. She yanked up a long stick and ran to beat the snake's flat head. The body was thick, covered with scales the color of the dried mud on the rock.

"No! Monster! No! Let him go!"

The snake thrashed and writhed and the rabbit was free, the snake twisting, opening its mouth wide.

Immobile, Amity stared into the white throat a moment before it struck. Needle-like pain shot up Amity's arm, and then the snake started to slither away. Blood showed through the pricks on her arm below her elbow.

A shot blasted the air, and the snake's head splattered.

"Don't move!" Caleb O'Brien snapped, pulling a knife from his belt. He took her arm. "That's a bad one. Turn your head and yell all you want, but I have to get the poison out."

Feeling terrified, Amity held her breath. The knife cut, and pain enveloped her. She wanted to scream, but she clamped her jaws shut and drew a deep breath, tears burning her eyes. She felt Caleb's mouth on her arm and turned to see him sucking the blood from the wound. He spit it on the ground and sucked again. Her arm throbbed; beyond Caleb the rabbit lay bleeding and panting, on the rock next to the headless snake.

"The rabbit . . ."

Caleb finally raised his head. "Don't move. The quieter you can be, the less it will circulate. A cottonmouth isn't as quick and deadly as a rattler, but we've got to get out the poison."

"The rabbit's hurt!" she said, crying and hurting.

Drawing his revolver, Caleb glanced at her. "There's no reason for the rabbit to suffer, and he won't get better." His arm was steady, the back of his hand sprinkled with pale hair and freckles.

She looked away and he fired, the shot deafening. He thrust the revolver into his belt and wiped the knife on leaves.

"Mr. O'Brien," she said, fighting a faintness and hurting more than she had ever hurt in her life. "I'm not supposed to ride the stallion, and he won't let you ride him. I don't want Papa to see me on him."

"You're not riding anywhere now." He looked at her solemnly. "That was a cotton-mouth water moccasin."

"I know. A congo."

"That wound should be cauterized. I should heat my knife and put it in the wound."

She blinked and stared at him, terrified.

"You don't want to lose your arm."

She nodded, fear enveloping her. She had never been hurt, more than scratches. She watched him gather twigs and start a fire, then place the knife in the tiny blaze.

"I don't know if I can stand that," she whispered.

His eyes narrowed and he walked out of sight, leaving the knife in the fire. The flames became blue, the steel glowing red. *He'll thrust that into my arm, into the bite,* Amity thought, horrified. Caleb strode back through the bushes and held out a bottle.

"Here. Drink it down fast."

"What is it?" she asked, lifting it to her lips. She gagged and coughed.

"Drink it!" he snapped. He stood with his feet apart, arms akimbo, his hands on his slender hips.

She blinked back tears and poured the horrible burning liquid down her throat. Her stomach felt on fire. He was waiting, so she held her breath and tried to drink it all.

"Ugh!" she coughed, feeling her stomach heave and her head spin. "What was it?"

"Giraud and I brewed it. I can't wait for it to take full effect. Sit on the grass and turn your head away. Grab something to squeeze, because this will hurt like hell. And go ahead and scream. Don't be as damn stoic as you were before."

She sat down and her head swam, the pain diminishing a fraction. She felt hot and wondered if it was the poison in her system or that ghastly drink.

He took her arm and she looked away, inhaling sharply.

"God," he mumbled and she turned, looking into his eyes. "I'm sorry," he said. "I don't want to hurt you like this. Go ahead and squeeze something."

Placing her head on her knee, she clasped the twig of a sweet gum thrusting up through the tangled grass. When the hot knife touched her, her scream ripped through the clearing. The stench of burning flesh made it worse. White-hot agony seared into her arm and through her being. Her head reeled and she wanted to faint, anything to escape the horrible hurt that tore at her.

"Dammit!" Caleb threw down the knife and drew her against his chest. She cried, her head spinning. Burning and throbbing, her arm took all of her attention, until the pain had subsided to a level she could endure without crying. She became aware of Caleb O'Brien holding her close, stroking her head and talking to her without stopping.

"You're a wee lassie and I'm sorry. So sorry. Go ahead and cry. I didn't want to hurt you, lass. You're a brave one. Cry until it stops hurting. Sorry. I'm damned sorry." His voice was deep, soothing to her.

She could hear his heart beating, and she realized her hands were against his chest.

She raised her head. "I'll be all right."

Caleb O'Brien held her in his arms and looked down at her, and Amity's heart missed a beat. He had deep green eyes with curly brown lashes. His hair tangled over his forehead, and all her spiteful thoughts toward him, her hatred and anger from the duck incident, evaporated. She had never been held in a man's arms. Her head spun, and she clung to him with her good arm.

"I shou' thank you for taking care of me," she said, finding the words difficult to say and her speech sounding slurred. "But I don' think I shou' thank you for the drink."

He grinned, revealing even white teeth. "If we had done this without the drink, you'd know to thank me for the brew. It helped. Take my word for it. It dulled the pain a little."

She shook her head. "No, it didn't. And I'll be in trouble at home. I'm not supposed to ride the stallion. Only your brother rides him. I'm not allowed to taste strong drink. I'll be in trouble for all of this."

"Shh. Don't worry. I'll take care of the horse. I'm going to get you home now."

She bit her lip. "I'm sorry I threw your gun in the bayou."

He nodded and stood up, scooping her into his arms.

"You can't ride the horse."

"Miss Therrie, if my brother can ride him, I can."

"He'll throw us both if you get on him."

"No, he won't." He lifted her into the saddle and kept a hand on her, as he swung up and eased himself into the saddle. He held her close as Daedalus moved at a sedate pace for home.

Her head reeled; she hurt, and yet she felt giddy and light. To her horror, tears threatened. "Tha' poor rabbit," she said, wiping her eyes. "I shall have nigh'mares about the rabbit an' the snake. I'm glad you sho' its ugly head off."

"Next time scream for help, and do *not* attack a snake!" he ordered her.

"I just wanted to save that poor little rabbit." She put her head against Caleb O'Brien's broad chest and cried.

She felt his hand on her back again, and she wiped her eyes, "You're a ver' kind man. And you're ver' handsome," she said, looking at him. He grinned and leaned forward to kiss her cheek.

"You're drunk, begging your pardon, Miss Therrie."

"Me?"

"It's okay. I'll explain to your father. Believe me, he'll forgive you."

"Tha's first time a man has ever kissed me," she said, touching her cheek. Caleb looked down at her.

"Well let me tell you, Miss Therrie, it can be done a whole lot better than that, and someday it will be. That kind of kiss is called friendship."

"Wha's the other kind?" she asked owlishly, and he grinned.

"The other kind," he said in a voice that stirred a tingle inside her, "is the best kind."

"Hmmpf. I don' know. . . ."

"You will."

"Will *you* show me the bes' kind?" She ran her finger along his jaw.

He grinned down at her and shook his head. "No, ma'am! My brother would whip me from here to Pointe Coupée Parish if I took advantage of your being slightly under the influence."

"Daedalus lets you ride him. Tha's 'mazing, Mr. O'Brien."

"Call me Caleb."

"Caleb O'Bien. I thou' you were so horrid, but you're ver' nice."

"Tomorrow you may have another thought on the matter," he said.

She reached up to twist a lock of his curly hair. It was soft and curled around her finger. "Pretty hair."

He laughed. "That's the first time anyone has ever told me I'm pretty!"

She studied him. "Your hair's pretty. You're ver' han'some," she said, trailing her fingers along his broad throat and touching a tuft of hair at the neck of his shirt.

"I won't hold you responsible for this conversation, so tomorrow you can forget what you said. Don't worry about it."

"Why wou' I worry? You're a ver' han'some, nice, man. Ver' nice. You killed the hor'ble snake."

"Here we are." He slowed at the stable and Giraud appeared, his brows arching and his eyes going round with curiosity. Caleb dismounted and lifted her gently down into his arms, turning to Giraud.

"Take the horse. Cotton-mouth bit her."

"Holy sakes! Doc isn't here."

"I cut it open and sucked out the blood and cauterized it."

"Afternoon, Giraud," she said happily.

"Afternoon, ma'am. Sorry about the bite." He looked at Caleb. "What else did you do?"

"I gave her a bottle of our brew."

"Oh, sakes! Poor little thing. A whole bottle, Caleb?"

"It might've taken an edge off the pain. I'll carry her to the house." He left, striding the long walk to the big house while Amity sang and played with his curls. Someone must have seen them from a window, for before they'd reached the house Chantal, Mrs. Therrie, and William came out, rushing down the steps.

"She's had a snake bite."

"Oh, my heavens!" Blaise Therrie exclaimed. "William, get Remi to ride for Dr. Baines!"

"Yes, ma'am."

"Mrs. Therrie, I cut open the wound and tried to suck out the poison, and I've cauterized it," Caleb said.

"Maman, doesn't he have pretty hair?"

Caleb blushed, and Chantal and Blaise Therrie both

looked at him. "Good Lord," Blaise exclaimed,
"Amity's foxed!"

"That's my fault, ma'am. It hurts to put a hot knife
in a wound, so I gave her something to drink."

"Thank you, Caleb," Chantal said.

"Where's her room?" he asked.

"This way," Chantal said, as she hurried to lead
the way. "To the right at the head of the stairs." Caleb
carried Amity up the stairs with ease, placing her on
a soft canopied bed. She caught his arm.

"Are you leaving me?"

"Yes. Your family will take care of you now." He
turned away and Blaise moved to the bed, talking softly
to Amity while Chantal followed him into the hall.

"Caleb, thank you. You may have saved her life."

"Yes, ma'am. I tried to tell her she shouldn't attack
snakes with sticks. Need a revolver for that."

"What was she doing?" Chantal asked, descending
the curving steps with him.

"Trying to save a rabbit the snake was eating." He
grinned. "She took a stick after that snake and tried
to beat it away. I guess it takes a he—a lot to frighten
the Therrie women."

Chantal slanted him a curious look.

"I'm going. I hope she's all right. I did all I knew
how to do."

"Thank you."

Caleb hurried down the steps, heading home.

"Come in!" Ormonde Therrie called, and Amity
entered his office and crossed the room to kiss Grand-
père's withered cheek. He sat with his hands folded
on the cane that stood between his bony knees. His
curly white beard trailed on his thin chest, and he
shifted the cigar in his mouth. Foul-smelling smoke
circled his head.

"What's this I hear about your getting snakebit?"
he asked in a raspy voice.

"I did, Grand-père, but I'm almost well now," she
said, sitting in a black leather wingback chair, twisting
to show him her bandaged arm. She turned to Or-

monde and took a deep breath, feeling a cold dread at the thought of what she had to do. "Papa, the Ferguson I threw in the bayou is gone."

"What Ferguson?" he asked.

"You threw Ferguson in the bayou?" Grand-père snapped.

"*A* Ferguson, Grand-père."

"Did he drown?"

"She didn't drown anyone, Papa. Let her answer. Amity, what is this? What Ferguson?"

"I tossed Caleb O'Brien's Ferguson into the bayou."

"Sounds to me like you tried to drown someone," Grand-père grumbled. "If you threw a man into the bayou . . ." He turned to Amity. "Did you push someone into the bayou?"

"Yes, sir, I did," she admitted, wishing she had caught Papa alone, "but that's not the Ferguson."

"Amity, please!" Ormonde cried in exasperation. "What's this about a Ferguson? And whom did you throw into the bayou? Why wasn't I told about this?"

She locked her fingers together. "Well, when Caleb O'Brien shot Benoit, I—"

"Good God, a duel!" Grand-père exclaimed.

"Papa, for God's sake, let us talk!" Ormonde snapped. "One of the men shot a duck."

"A duel between a man and a duck? That's a bunch of damn foolery."

"No, Grand-père. Caleb O'Brien shot one of my ducks named Benoit, and I threw his Ferguson rifle into the bayou."

Grand-père's thin shoulders shook with laughter. "What kind of poufa would allow a chit of a girl to take his rifle and toss it into the bayou? Serves the man right, I'd say!"

"Amity, what's this? All I know is what Mr. O'Brien said about his brother, that he shot your duck and intimidated you."

She blushed at the remembrance, yet Caleb O'Brien had saved her life and been as kind as possible after the snake bite. She raised her chin.

"I pushed Caleb O'Brien into the bayou and took

his Ferguson and flung it into deep water and he never did find it.'' To her consternation Grand-père continued to chuckle, while Ormonde's scowl grew fierce.

"Dammit, why didn't you tell me this that night?''

"Because I was angry over Benoit.''

"Do you know what a good Ferguson costs? Dammit! There weren't more than a hundred in existence! The entire duck population of Belle Destin isn't worth a Ferguson!''

"I *would* like to get him another gun,'' she said, feeling miserable.

"Come here at once.'' Ormonde stood up and her heart beat with fear, for she had seldom seen her father look so angry. She followed him through the office into his library, to the walnut armoire. He opened it and selected a rifle, lifting it to his shoulder and then lowering it and holding it out to her.

"The Ferguson was a repeating rifle used at the Battle of Kings Mountain in our Revolutionary War by a Scotsman, Ferguson. Unfortunately for him, the Pennsylvania rifles picked off his men one by one.'' Papa turned the rifle in his hands. "I got this rifle recently from a man in town. He'd been to Kansas. Actually, I won it from him in a card game,'' he said, bringing it to his shoulder again. "You tell Caleb it's a breech-loading rifle. It's a .52-caliber New Model Sharps carbine, with a paper cartridge. As the underlever is raised, the breech-block moves vertically up. The percussion cap is fired by an external hammer. The man called it a 'Beecher Bible,' a nickname from Kansas because Henry Beecher, a Kansas preacher, says this rifle contains more moral power than a hundred Bibles.''

"I don't think I can remember all that,'' she said.

"Caleb knows guns,'' Ormonde added. "He may be familiar with one of these.'' He ran his hand along the barrel.

"Papa, you don't have to give him your favorite!''

"My squirrel rifle is my favorite, but I like this one. Caleb saved your life, Amity. You might have lost your arm or even your life, if Caleb O'Brien hadn't taken care of you. And you were unfair to keep silent about what you did to him. Can you carry this?''

"Yes, sir.''

"You give this to Caleb O'Brien with your apologies. Amity, the man saved your life! He came to this country with nothing, and a Ferguson not only cost him a small fortune, it was a repeating rifle and a very special weapon.''

"Yes, sir.''

"He was hunting where I allow men to hunt. As far as he knew it was just another wild duck. Great heavens, we owe him! You take this to him today. And next time, young lady, you tell me if you've been partly to blame!''

"Yes, sir.'' Her father placed the rifle and its accouterments in her hands, and she turned away. "Thank you, Papa.''

She went upstairs to look at herself in the mirror. Loretta had fixed her hair, parting it in the middle and braiding it in loops over each ear with curls over her forehead. She wore a deep blue grosgrain dress.

She rode past outbuildings to the forge where she found him alone. His shoulders were beaded with sweat, and his hair curled in damp ringlets on his forehead as he bent over one of the smaller geldings and hammered a shoe in place.

"Mr. O'Brien?'' As she dismounted, her heart pounded, and she felt nervous.

Caleb turned around and nodded, finishing his task and leading the horse outside while she entered and waited. He returned, wiping his hands on his pants beneath his leather apron.

She reached up to her saddle and removed the rifle, swinging it down. Suddenly arms had locked around her, and the rifle was being yanked from her hands.

"What the devil!'' he snapped. "I saved you from snake bite. I wasn't the varmint that bit you!''

She looked up at him. He was hot, his body hard against hers, the smells of wood smoke and sweat and leather part of him. Her heart pounded as she gazed into his snapping green eyes.

"I brought the rifle to you for a gift. It's yours."

His brows arched in surprise and his mouth opened. He blinked and looked down at the rifle in his hands. He released her so swiftly she almost fell and wrenched her arm. She gasped from the pain, and his arm shot around her waist to steady her.

"Sorry! Are you all right?" He smiled at her. "This is a damned—excuse, me miss—a mighty fine rifle. Sorry if I misunderstood. We'll have to end our misunderstandings and be friends, Miss Therrie. All right?"

"Yes, it is all right," she said, smiling back. "And you should call me Amity if we're to be friends."

"Fine. And you can call me Caleb," he said, squinting along the barrel of the rifle. "This is a beauty!"

She laughed. "If I can't bear to see a duck shot, do you think I would shoot you?"

He grinned and shrugged. "I had a feeling you would have shot me with joy."

"I'm sorry about your Ferguson. I told Papa I wanted to get you another rifle."

"Did you now?" he asked, looking amused. "Did you tell him you sunk mine in the bayou?"

"Yes, I did," she said, blushing. "I'm sorry."

"Well, I'm sorry I shot your duck. I didn't know it was a special duck. It just looked like all other ducks to me, not particularly like a Benoit. You should've bought Benoit a hat or little jacket, so I would have known."

She wondered if he was making fun of her; but his green eyes sparkled, and she couldn't stay angry.

"He was a special duck, but you couldn't have known that. I told Papa and he said to give you this rifle instead, that he thought you might like it just as well." Caleb didn't look much like his brothers, who had longer faces and blue eyes and black hair. Caleb was stockier, square-jawed, with a crook in his nose and thick brown curls above devilish green eyes. He turned the rifle in his hands, and she wondered if he had forgotten her.

"I can't remember all the things Papa told me about it, but you can ask him and he'll love telling you. Papa could talk about guns forever."

"I know something about it. I met a man on my way to New Orleans, and he had one of these and let me fire it. It can be used as a muzzle-loader if the powder fouling builds up to the point where the breech can no longer be opened."

She listened, feeling better and pleased that he liked it, but not understanding a word of what he'd told her about the gun.

"This is a dandy. It's short and light. I can carry it when I ride." He lifted the rifle to his shoulder and looked down the barrel. He didn't have long, slender fingers like Rafferty; instead Caleb's fingers were blunt, his knuckles large.

"Your father is right. This is a mighty fine rifle, and I'm happy to have it. Thank you."

"Thank you for saving my life." He was studying the rifle, and she wondered whether he had even heard her. "Would you like to take it out and try it?" she asked.

"Yes, I'd like that. I can leave. Just a minute here."

In a few minutes they were riding side by side, and she glanced at him. "Let me show you my animals."

He grinned. "Fine, but I'm still going to hunt."

To her surprise, he took to the raccoons as readily as they did to him, clambering over his shoulders and onto his head while he fed them tidbits she had given him.

"They like you. And Daedalus let you ride him. Papa is going to race him at Metarie in three weeks."

"That'll be a race to watch and to wager on. I've seen Rafe run him. There's not a horse in Louisiana to beat him." Caleb pulled a raccoon off his head and set it on the ground. "Okay, I won't shoot these fellows, but I don't know how I'll recognize your pet ducks."

"It would be nice if you didn't shoot anything."

"Amity, I've hunted all my life."

"You get along so well with them," she said, watching him feed a raccoon.

"I've raised animals all my life, too. But I like to hunt and I like to eat what I hunt."

She stood up. "Come along, and I'll show you where you can try your rifle."

When they had reached a meadow, she dismounted. "Here. You have plenty of space." While she talked he swung out of the saddle and set up empty bottles. He took her arm and led the horses away, stopping far from the bottles. "Want to try it?" he asked, loading the rifle.

"Good heavens, no! I detest guns."

He grinned and continued to work in silence. Finally he turned and fired, and a bottle shattered. She watched while he reloaded and hit each one without a single miss. Next he began to name his targets.

"See that branch to the right of the rock, the tip where the leaf hangs down?" He shot it and each target he named, taking time to reload with deliberation.

"The rifle is grand." He walked to her and rubbed his fingers on her arm above the wound. "How's your arm?"

"It's healing, thanks to you."

"You were brave."

"Thank you, Caleb. I'm going home now, because I don't want to watch you kill something."

Sunlight made his eyes even more green. He smiled at her and gave her a quick, impersonal squeeze. "We're friends?"

"Yes, we're friends," she replied, suddenly liking him very much and glad she would be his friend, but wishing he didn't want to hunt because he knew how to win the trust of the raccoons.

Thinking about Caleb she headed for home, her thoughts shifting to Chantal's engagement party.

Chapter 19

September 29, 1860

Chantal clung to the bedpost as Loretta laced the white coutil corset. Next came the batiste drawers Blaise had ordered from Paris, and her jaconet petticoat. The underskirt with its stiff hoops came next. Two servants helped lower the dress of rustling red moiré over Chantal's head. The low-cut bodice, trimmed in Maline's lace, had short puffed sleeves that revealed Chantal's slender arms. The hem and neckline were ruched, and the full skirt was caught in puffs with silk roses. Silk roses were twined in her hair, which was pinned in a crimped chignon down the back of her head, with curls over her forehead. She fastened the ruby necklace that was a gift from her father, and ruby earrings dangled in her ears.

"You look beautiful!" Loretta exclaimed.

"Yes, ma'am, you do," Addie said, her dark eyes shining as she looked at her mistress, and Chantal stared at her image. For years she had dreamed of this night. Since she was ten she had been promised to Lazare, yet now the night was here and she felt reluctant and worried, emotions she had never dreamed she would feel. There was only one reason for her unhappiness.

"Thank you, Loretta, Addie. I want to be alone."

"Yes, ma'am."

Chantal didn't want to go downstairs. She walked to the window and looked at the overseer's house, where a light burned in a window. Rafferty didn't live there now, although he visited his brothers occasionally. She seldom saw him now that he had moved to town, but even a glimpse of him down a city street set her pulse racing. She dreamed about him; she missed him, yet she had to marry Lazare. Papa never would allow her to wed Rafferty. Why couldn't she forget him? Why did it hurt so much?

And it was more than a physical longing. Rafferty could take her breath away, melt her with his kisses, but it went beyond that. She could tell him anything; his teasing fun could bring her to laughter and his calming influence could put an end to her fears. Both men were intelligent, tough, confident; both could be cavalier, dashing. But Rafferty had a special flair for listening, and a sense of fairness that Lazare lacked. And Rafferty had none of Lazare's vanity. Yet did that really matter? And Lazare was a man with a background the same as her own. He wouldn't care a fig about things that would stir Rafferty's wrath.

Rafferty O'Brien could cause her as much trouble as joy—making her learn to swim when she was terrified of water. Her arguments might as well have been whispered to Caesar for all that Rafferty listened to them. Rafferty was more unpredictable, more undaunted, more stubborn. Not to mention more exciting, more appealing . . .

All she had to do was step out onto the gallery, climb down the tree, and run away. She could marry Rafferty O'Brien instead of Lazare. The mere thought made her heart race. She thought of Soleil, Lazare, all their plans, her dreams for the future. *"I want you. You can't marry him and be bound in a loveless marriage all your life."*

"Rafferty," she whispered. The door opened behind her and Blaise stood there in a daring green satin dress, trimmed in black ostrich feathers and cut low to reveal her full breasts.

Emeralds and diamonds glittered at her throat and ears, and Chantal knew every man present would notice Maman and want to dance with her. She avoided the sun at all costs, and her skin was creamy, pale, and flawless. She looked far younger than her years, yet for all her beauty Chantal wondered how Papa could love her. Maman's cheeks were unduly flushed, and her eyes snapped with anger, causing Chantal to study her with curiosity.

"This is your night with Lazare. After tonight you'll be officially engaged. But your father has been witless enough to invite Rafferty O'Brien."

"No!" Chantal's eyes widened. *Rafferty at my party! He will be here tonight! I can dance with him. He will talk to me, touch me. . . .*

"Yes. Your father—men can be so dense—didn't realize."

"You told him Rafferty and I have—" She blushed furiously, angry with Maman.

"Yes, I told him Rafferty O'Brien had kissed you."

Terrified her father would call him out, Chantal closed her eyes. Her face burned with embarrassment. "What did he say? What will he do?"

"As I just said, men are very dense about matters of the heart. He thinks it was nothing. He thinks you must be wildly in love with Lazare, because you begged them to move up this party."

As Chantal sighed with relief, Maman approached and lowered her voice to say, "I can guess why you wanted the party as soon as possible. You're in love with Rafferty O'Brien, yet you want to marry Lazare because you have the good sense to know which man can bring you happiness."

Chantal drew a deep breath and firmed her lips. She had no intention of discussing Rafferty with Maman.

"You're a bright child and you've made the wise decision, but don't change it. Rafferty O'Brien could never give you what Lazare will. Never. And if you do one thing to destroy this marriage, I'll ruin your life. Don't underestimate what I can do, Chantal! You've won battles between us with your father, but they've been small battles. Not big ones. I promise you, you'll regret it with all your heart if you throw aside Lazare."

"I *love* Lazare, and I *wanted* our wedding date moved earlier," she said stiffly, as anger, fear, and hurt warred within her. *Rafferty will be here tonight. . . .*

"Shall we go?"

"I'll be along," Chantal said, and Blaise smiled.

"I can't wait for your marriage. You're the luckiest woman in the South, and you don't even know it."

"I know Lazare will be a good husband."

Maman laughed, leaving the room and closing the door. Chantal turned to the mirror again, to reassure herself how she looked. *Rafferty will be here.* . . . It made her knees weak to think about seeing him.

Feeling fluttery inside, she took a deep breath and left her room, going into the hall to go downstairs. Her father approached from his room.

"How beautiful you look, Chantal!" he exclaimed, gazing at her, and she felt pleased by his warm compliment.

"Thank you, Papa."

"Tonight I'm aware of time. My children have grown up. Amity will attend the ball, and she looks like a woman, not a child. And you'll be engaged to Lazare. I want you to be happy," he said, and Chantal wondered if Maman's talk had influenced his remarks.

She nodded. "I think I'll be very happy."

He studied her with a solemn expression. "I hope so. Sometimes we're so caught up in honor, we lose sight of our hearts. Are you ready to go downstairs?"

"Yes, Papa," she said, wondering about him and what he had meant by that last remark. Nothing had forced him into marrying Maman. Quite to the contrary, he had brought her home from Paris with him, and Chantal knew it had taken a good bit of persuasion to get her to leave her precious France. Now he linked Chantal's arm through his and looked at her.

"Do you love Lazare?"

"Papa, I wouldn't have asked you to move this party up if I didn't want to marry him. Of course I love him." How hollow the words sounded! It wasn't Lazare's image that danced in her vision. It was one of cool Irish eyes and thick black hair, the image of a man who could make her heart race. "I would marry Lazare tomorrow if I could. I wish we could move up the wedding date as well."

"Thank heaven you and Amity won't be trapped in unhappy marriages! And thank God, Alain is happy with Diantha! If only she could carry a baby to full term! She's lost two now, and I pray they can have a child."

"I know, Papa. Both of them want a family."

"No sad thoughts now. This is your night, your party. Shall we go downstairs?"

She smiled, but at the head of the stairs her smile faded. Below, coming through the doorway, was Rafferty. He looked up, his gaze meeting hers and stopping her breath, burning into her.

Looking incredibly handsome in his black tail coat and trousers, he moved to the foot of the stairs and stood waiting, and she was aware with every step of his eyes on her. When Chantal and her father had reached the bottom, he came forward to greet them.

"Good evening, Miss Therrie, Mr. Therrie. This is quite an occasion."

"I'm glad you could come," Ormonde said. "I missed the meeting with Senator Benjamin last week. You'll have to tell me about it."

"How beautiful you look, Miss Therrie," Rafferty said in a formal, impassive tone.

"Thank you, Mr. O'Brien." *Miss Therrie, Mr. O'Brien.* She hurt all over. But she had come too far to turn back now and break her engagement. *It will stop hurting. Soon I will seldom see him. He looks so handsome. . . .*

"Word is rampant in the East that if Lincoln wins the election, southern states should secede," Rafferty said. "Governor Gist of South Carolina wants to renounce the Union if Lincoln is elected." He glanced at Chantal and then beyond her. "If you both will excuse me, I see a friend." He moved away, and Chantal longed to reach out and catch his arm and pull him back. Beyond him she saw Lazare approach.

"There you are, and looking lovely! This is our night, eh, Ormonde?" Lazare said, dropping his arm around Chantal's shoulders. His black coat was as elegant as Rafferty's. He wore a white silk cravat around his thick neck, and she knew she was the envy of her friends to have Lazare.

"Yes it is," Ormonde answered.

"Did I see Rafferty O'Brien here?"

"Yes you did," Ormonde said. "He's my factor, as you know, and I invited him. Lazare, he should mean nothing to you."

Lazare shrugged. "I'm happy to have him hear the announcement of our engagement."

"Excuse me. I see the Hausers, and I want to greet them." Ormonde moved away, and Chantal looked up into Lazare's sleepy-eyed gaze.

"You look beautiful," he said, "and I want you to myself; I want to kiss you, but I'll wait until our announcement." He smiled at her and took her arm to move into the ballroom.

She felt dazzled as she looked at the crowd of friends and at the elaborate ballroom. For weeks they had been getting ready, and now banks of pink roses decorated the walls, while masses of English ivy were draped from the ceiling and the chandeliers burned with flickering candles. The party would last through the night and the guests would stay two more days for hunts, for another ball, for lavish dinners, but tonight was the announcement, her moment with Lazare.

For over an hour she greeted guests, and then she and Lazare moved to the dance floor. As she danced she saw Rafferty dancing with Eugenia Perret, who lived at Belle Rose, a neighboring plantation. A year older than Chantal, Eugenia was Chantal's idea of beauty, with her willowy height and dark beauty, olive skin and shiny, midnight hair. It hurt to watch Rafe laugh at something Eugenia had said, to watch him smile at her, hold her hand, his other hand on her waist. As Eugenia's dark eyes flashed at him she laughed, and Chantal felt a twist of pain.

"If you don't stop watching him, I'll call him out," Lazare said softly.

"Don't be ridiculous! I've waited years for this night!" Lazare studied her and she gazed back at him. "Don't frighten me, and please don't fight any duels.

I don't know what I would do if something happened to you.''

"I'm not afraid of the Irishman."

"I meant *any* duels with *anyone*. Please, Lazare."

He smiled. "Don't worry. I have no intention of dying." He swept her in a turn and their conversation ended.

She danced with her cousin Emile and with Alain, and then suddenly she was looking into Rafferty's eyes as he took her hand in his and turned her onto the dance floor.

He gazed at her solemnly without speaking, and she couldn't talk.

"You're the most beautiful woman in all of Louisiana," he said.

"Thank you."

"You're making it hard for both of us. It'll be more difficult to break off with him after this engagement is announced."

"Stop it, Rafferty. I love him, and I intend to marry him."

"No, you don't love him. You would never have spent hours riding or swimming with me, you wouldn't have let me kiss you as you did if Lazare Galliard held your heart."

"You're as arrogant as ever—so sure of yourself and your charms!" she snapped, wanting to get away from him and yet wanting to dance the rest of the night with him.

"It isn't arrogance, and you know it. A man knows when a woman loves him, just as a woman knows when a man truly loves her. When he will sacrifice anything for her. Would your precious Lazare risk his life for you?"

"Yes, he would!" Rafferty's response was a cynical smile that made her angry. "I asked them to move up the date for this party, and I'm asking him to move up the date for the wedding! I'll forget you, Rafferty O'Brien! I've dreamed for years of Soleil, and you would take that from me!"

"Chantal, a house can't make you happy."

"It isn't just a house. Our families are alike. We're French."

"Oh? You were born in France?"

"You know I was born right here, but we're of French descent. We've known each other all our lives. I know what my life will be like with Lazare, and it's what I want."

"You and I have spent hours together, riding, talking, swimming. We know each other. I wouldn't push, Chantal, if I didn't love you with all my heart. And I don't think you love Lazare."

"That was a solitary moment, when we were by the river. You know I succumbed to your charms only because it seemed natural. It didn't mean anything."

"Look at me and say that," he said quietly, but his voice held a note of steel that made his words an irresistible command.

She gazed into his blue eyes and felt as if he could discern every thought in her head. She couldn't imagine giving up Lazare and the life she had always known, much less fighting her parents. She knew they wouldn't allow it. "The moments with you didn't mean anything," she said in a rush.

"You're lying to yourself and to me. And after you're engaged to your precious Lazare, when I kiss you, you won't stop me."

"Yes, I will! You are arrogant and cavalier, and I want to stop dancing!"

"All of this hurts, Chantal, but someday you'll be mine. I'll win your heart, and I'll be more important than Soleil." He stood still, gazing down at her while dancers swirled around them. "I love you, and I'll fight to my last breath to win your love."

He left her and moved through the crowd. Her heart pounded as she looked at the back of his head, and she had never hurt so badly. Was she wrong? Was she making a dreadful mistake she would regret forever? She had wanted him to dance through the wide doors outside into the shadows and kiss her. And if it were Rafferty O'Brien who would stand beside her when Papa announced her engagement, what would she feel?

"If I thought you cared about him . . ." Somehow
Lazare had appeared at her side, to whisper in her ear.

"I care about *you*! And you've waited far too long
to dance with me," she said to Lazare, forcing a smile.
"And far too long to kiss me."

"After this dance your father will make the announcement, and then I shall remedy everything,"
Lazare said, gazing at her with a look that once would
have set her pulse racing, but now did not. Was their
engagement a mistake? She had these few minutes to
stop the announcement, to stop the engagement. What
kind of life would she have with Rafferty O'Brien? She
knew so little about his plans, and she knew all of
Lazare's. Papa wouldn't allow her to marry Rafferty.
And all these people were here, waiting for the announcement of her engagement to Lazare.

Lazare took her arm and they moved to the platform
that held the musicians. As she stood between her father and Lazare her head spun, and she didn't hear
Papa's words. All she could do was stare ahead. Across
the crowd, at the far end of the ballroom, taller than
most of the guests, stood Rafferty, staring back at her
without taking his gaze away even for a moment.

". . . the wedding to be June 22, 1861." There was
applause, and she hurt so badly. She looked up at Lazare, pulling him down to whisper into his ear.

"I don't care about propriety. Kiss me now."

His brows arched and he pulled her against him, his
mouth covering hers as he kissed her.

"Lazare . . ." she heard Papa say, and Lazare released her. People laughed and surged forward, to
congratulate Lazare and give Chantal their best wishes.
The next time she glanced at the end of the ballroom,
Rafferty was gone.

The music started, and as she danced she couldn't
spot Rafferty O'Brien anywhere. She felt a tight knot
of pain in her heart that wouldn't go away. *Tomorrow
will be better,* she assured herself. He had upset her
tonight, but eventually she would forget her feelings
for him. She had to forget him *now*, because she was
engaged, yet as she danced the evening dulled. She

moved woodenly, trying to listen to Lazare, trying to answer, and reassuring herself that over time she would forget.

Hearing the music drift over the grounds, Caleb glanced toward the big house, where lights glowed through the trees. He felt restless, penned down by his job as overseer. He wanted to travel, to see the country that he heard so much about from men just off the riverboats that stopped at Belle Destin.

The lights were off, and he crossed the porch to pull off his boots, knowing Darcy probably was asleep in the backyard where it was cool. They had rigged up cots with mosquito netting so they could sleep outside. He moved through the darkened living room.

"You're late," came a deep voice.

"Jesus! Rafe?" Caleb queried.

"I'm here. Sorry if I startled you."

"I thought you were going to the party."

"I did go to the party. I saw Chantal become engaged to Lazare Galliard, and then I left."

"You should have stayed and had fun. If I had been invited, I would have stayed."

"No thanks." Caleb's eyes had adjusted to the darkness in the house, but he still couldn't see Rafe where he sat in the shadows of the tall wingback chair. Then Rafe stood, tilting a bottle to drink. He threw it into the hearth and it splintered into pieces.

"You're drunk!" Caleb exclaimed in surprise, for usually Rafe could hold his liquor.

"Not enough," Rafe answered. "Do you know how difficult it is to break an engagement announced before hundreds of people?" He grabbed the poker from beside the hearth and raised it high, then swung it down. It smashed a small table in two, and Caleb blinked. He had never seen Rafe in such a state.

"Jesus, Rafe! What's wrong?" And then he knew. So many things fell into place. "You're in love with Chantal Therrie!"

"Ah, my astute brother."

"I knew there was a woman, but I thought it was someone in town. *Chantal?* Jesus, Rafe . . ."

"Stop blaspheming."

"Chantal! Rafe, there are lots of other beautiful women."

"You couldn't begin to understand, because you've never been in love. She doesn't love Galliard, and he doesn't love her."

"Why is she marrying him if she doesn't love him?"

"Their fathers arranged it, and she's been taught to obey her parents."

"Lord, that's a terrible custom!" Frowning, Caleb studied him. "How you hold your liquor is more than I'll ever understand. You don't sound drunk."

"I'm not as drunk as I'm going to be."

Feeling at a loss, Caleb stared at him. "I'm going to bed outside."

Rafe watched him go, then crossed to the cabinet to withdraw another bottle and uncork it. He drank deeply and went out through the front door, to mount his horse to ride to town. He hurt all over; he hadn't believed it was possible to hurt as much as he did tonight. He would never forget the sight of Chantal as Ormonde announced her engagement, or of Lazare Galliard as he pulled her into his arms and kissed her. He groaned, remembering her sprawled on the grass beside him, half-naked, trembling with passion, responding to his every touch. He could have taken her, and then would there have been an engagement announced? *Should have. Should have slid between her legs and possessed her.*

He shook his head. "No," he said aloud. "Will not ruin the reputation of the woman I love. She has to say yes and mean it." He took a long pull on the bottle. *Lord, it hurts.* And could he ever get her to break the engagement? Now he would never see her, except at parties or as she rode by in her carriage. He couldn't swim with her, he couldn't ride with her. He hurt more than he had ever hurt in his life. "Chantal, I love you," he whispered.

November 11, 1860

Rafferty O'Brien stood on the loading dock at his warehouse. The *Annora* bobbed in the water, its three tall masts dark against the blue sky. The Baltimore clipper had a length-to-beam ratio of six to one, with a pointed, hollow bow, and an overhanging counter-stern with a depth of twenty-seven feet. He had been promised the ship could achieve a speed of twenty knots, and he felt pleased every time he looked at her sleek lines.

A man strode around the corner of the warehouse and stopped at the foot of the steps to the platform. "Mr. O'Brien, sir, may I talk with you a moment?"

Rafe looked down at Tobiah and nodded. "Come up here." He led him back to his office. Rafe sat behind his wide oak desk and leaned back in his chair.

"Mr. O'Brien." Tobiah faced him. "I'm sorry to come to your place of business, but I figured your warehouse would be better than your brokerage office. I don't think many people saw me."

"Forget it, Tobiah. I don't mind your coming here."

Tobiah's frown vanished for a moment as he looked at the wide office, whose long window provided a view of the dock and the ships beyond. "You've done well." His attention returned to Rafe. "I need your help. Lenora and I are going to run away tomorrow night."

Rafe felt a sense of impending doom. Runaways were hunted and punished, and feelings were running particularly high now, just after the presidential election. "Give me some more time. My friend is going back to Galliard to increase his offer."

Tobiah shook his head. "Lenora is terrified of Mr. Galliard. He's tried to seduce her, and she thinks any time now he'll force her. I'd like to put a knife in him, but it would make it more difficult for us to escape."

"They'll come after you because of her. She'll still be a slave up north, and they can bring her back here. The Supreme Court ruled in the Dred Scott case that the government is pledged to protect the owner in his property rights, in both territories and states. Are you sure you want to take such risks?''

"Yes, I'm sure. I love her. We'll find sanctuary."

Rafe understood how Tobiah felt about Lenora. He himself would have run anywhere if it meant having Chantal. "Last year the abolitionist John Brown raided Harper's Ferry. They hanged him, but the unrest he stirred up hasn't died down. I've heard some of the men back from Washington talk. Men are angry. You'll whip up a hornet's nest here if you take her with you." Rafe looked into implacable black eyes.

"Yes, sir, but this is what we have to do. Sir, how would you like to be Galliard's slave?''

Rafe glanced out the window at the busy wharf. Last week Abraham Lincoln had won the election. Breckenridge won Louisiana's electoral vote but Lincoln was elected, and men were in a ferment over his victory, the governor calling for a secession convention. What change would Lincoln bring? The Republican platform was for protective tariffs and a railroad to the Pacific, and it opposed the extension of slavery into new territories. Everywhere Rafe went, men were confident that cotton would protect New Orleans. Ninety percent of the cotton purchased in Europe last year had come from the South. It was an extremely dangerous time for Tobiah and Lenora to run away, but Galliard was reason enough to go. He turned back to Tobiah and nodded. "I'll get you horses."

"If they trace the horses to you, you'll be in trouble.''

"I'll worry about that," he said, thinking about what he could do. "The horses will be at a vacant plantation up north, along the river road on the west bank of the river. The place is called Soleil Plantation, and it's—''

"I know. It's to be Galliard's home, with his new wife. We would all be happier if I put a knife through his heart.''

"No, we wouldn't. I'll leave two horses by the back of the house tomorrow night. I can't get them there until after dark.''

"I can't get her away until late in the night. She'll tell him she's ill."

"You know what will happen if you're caught."

"I'm willing to take the chance. And I know what a risk you're taking for me." He stood up. "I'll get out of here now, and I won't come back. Thank you, Rafferty." He held out his hand. "And good luck. You've given me everything."

"Thanks, Tobiah. You saved my life back there, so maybe we're even now. Ride with care."

Tobiah paused. "Sometimes we hear things white folks don't. There's not much talk, but I've heard Mr. Therrie has a mistress hidden away on land he owns up north."

Rafe was only mildly surprised. "I know he goes there once a month; the family said it was to see to the crops there, but that isn't necessary."

Tobiah shrugged. "If you ever come to Baltimore . . ."

Rafe nodded. "Good luck."

Tobiah nodded and left the office. Rafe moved to the window and watched him go out the back. Lazare would hang Tobiah if he could. Or beat him to death. *So, Ormonde Therrie had had a mistress on his northern plantation all these years.* Rafe hadn't heard the slightest rumor, but Tobiah would know. If Ormonde kept a mistress, she would have servants and word would get out. Rafe rubbed the back of his neck. The men in town had an unspoken code to keep all talk of mistresses from wives and families.

Going outside again, he picked up a sheaf of papers and looked over the cargo list for his ship that was set to sail. He ran his finger down the list of products he would sell on consignment or under contract: rice, ten quintals; millstones, three pair; whetstones, one dozen; deerskins, four hundred pounds; fox and raccoon, five pounds; beaver, five pounds; otter, fifty pounds; flour, fifty barrels; hams, fifty-eight pounds; molasses casks, twenty-eight. The rest of the available space would be filled with bales of cotton.

When the cargo was sold in England, the ship would load with new cargo to be sold in Louisiana. When this voyage was over and his ship had returned home, he could deduct his commissions and expenses and the balance would be credited to his clients. He suspected that Ormonde Therrie's recommendation had brought him customers. He had made five loans at twenty percent interest, and he had a captain he felt he could trust. With fifteen years' experience as a captain, Matthew Thomas, who had recently lost his own ship, came with high letters of recommendation. Short, stocky, looking more like a stevedore than a captain with his bushy black hair and beard, Matthew was eager to sail, and Rafe hoped he had made a wise choice in hiring him.

As he checked off the list, Rafe pondered where he would get the horses for Tobiah. He would send someone he could trust to Algiers that afternoon to purchase four horses. Two he could keep until the furor over Tobiah died down, and then he would sell them. Two he would take to Soleil tomorrow night. Thoughts of Soleil conjured up Chantal, and he inhaled sharply. He ached to see her; he missed the daily contact, the dawn rides, the swims that she couldn't resist. He felt hurt and frustrated at not seeing her. He was aware of every day that passed without a change in her status.

That night, two hours before midnight, he strode into Jolie's to play faro. As he walked down the hall, she appeared. She wore a green crepe de Chine dress, and to his eye she looked not a day older than the first time he had seen her.

"Mr. O'Brien!" she called out in her lilting voice. "I haven't seen you for a while."

"I've been here, Jolie. You're the one who's always busy."

"Come have a drink and tell me what's happening— or are you in a rush to get to the tables?"

He laughed and shook his head. "I always have time for a drink with a beautiful woman, Jolie."

She smiled and led the way to her quarters. "Still prefer whiskey?"

"Tonight I'll take claret, please."

"I hear the engagement has been announced between Chantal Therrie and Lazare Galliard. And that you are now a very busy cotton factor, and you own your own ship and warehouse.''

"Partially thanks to your tables.''

"You've probably won more than any man who frequents my house," she said gazing at him. "And I've heard there's no woman in your life.''

"You always know what's happening in the city,'' he said lightly, feeling uncomfortable with talk that centered on his life. "You know about everyone, Jolie, and no one knows about you.''

She laughed. "I lead a simple life right here. I run my gambling house and stay home. I don't irritate the ladies in town, because I stay out of their way. I don't become involved with the men in town, so no duels are fought over me and no scandal or gossip stirs. I'm of no more interest than the peddlers who ply the docks. We're part of the scenery. I'm glad you and Lazare haven't come to blows. She'll wed him, and I hope someday you'll meet a woman you can truly love.''

"I have met her, Jolie,'' he said. "I love Chantal and I always will, even if I have to spend my life here watching her grow old as the wife of Galliard.''

"Touzet was right. You *are* the most stubborn man who's ever played my tables!''

Rafe felt as if he were silently fencing with her. He didn't understand the contest of wills that was taking place, but she irritated him with her observations and he suspected he was annoying her in turn.

"The heart is not something one can control with cool logic, like the brain.''

She blinked and looked away. "Touzet also may be right that he'll have to visit you in St. Louis Cemetery. Lazare is not a man to be crossed. Yet I suspect Miss Therrie will be true to the man she weds.''

"Of course she will. I just intend to see that that man is me.'' He stood up abruptly. Jolie was disturbing him, and he couldn't say why. "You don't approve of my love for her.''

"No, I don't. But you're losing her—next year she'll

be wed. You're wasting your life, and you're too interesting and virile a man to spend it in such a manner.''

Her words startled him, and he turned to look at
her. His gaze drifted down over her and then back to
meet her cool blue gaze. "Thank you for the claret,
Jolie." She nodded as he left and strode down her
hall. He paused a moment in the busy front room, then
turned for the craps table.

Long past midnight, he rode to his house. As he rode
down Royal, past the corner of Royal and Conti, banker's
corner, he inhaled deeply and looked around. He
loved this city. When they had sailed from Ireland,
he'd felt as if his heart was being torn from his
body. Ireland was special; it was the home of his boyhood. Always in his heart Ireland and his mother and
father would be tied together, and he felt that if heaven
was a place it must be a bit of green Ireland. But from
the first moment he had rounded the bend of the Mississippi on the packet he had fallen in love with this
steamy, thriving, passionate city of men with flawless
manners and high tempers, women with spirits like
Chantal's, the most beautiful women he had ever seen.
New Orleans was a beautiful lady with come-hither
glances, saucy seduction, and heart-winning charm.
The buildings—the St. Charles Hotel, the St. Louis
Hotel, City Hall, the elegant homes, St. Louis Cathedral—all the architecture was fascinating, a mixture of
French and Spanish and American. The food was the
best in the world. And while Ireland would forever be
tied up with his parents and boyhood, New Orleans
would be linked forever with Chantal. He saw her everywhere he looked. She *had* to feel what he did; he
knew she must love him. She *had* to see that a pledge
made by her father when she was a child was not as
binding as what was in her heart today.

And if she didn't? He constantly thought about trying to carry her away a few nights before her wedding.
He didn't think she would protest for more than a mo-

ment. "Dammit," he said under his breath. That wasn't the way he wanted to win her hand.

He reached his house, riding down the alley behind it toward the carriage-house gate. He had servants quarters, a carriage house, and rooms above it for a stableboy. He dismounted to open the gate. Something rustled beside him, and someone stepped out of the shadows. A black man faced him, and Rafe's hand went beneath his coat to his revolver.

"Mr. O'Brien, I'm a friend of Tobiah's," he said. "Tobiah sent me to tell you that Lenora ran away from her master, so they had to leave New Orleans. He couldn't wait for horses."

"How long ago was that?" Rafe asked, worried now because Tobiah and Lenora were on foot.

"Two hours. He said to thank you."

"Damn." Rafe raked his fingers through his hair and peered down the empty alley. When he looked around, the stranger was gone and he was alone.

Rafe led his horse inside the two-stall stable and carriage house, leaving the horse saddled. With his mind racing over what to do, he hurried to change to riding clothes. He strode across the flower-filled court-yard and climbed the curving stairs, to enter the living quarters on the second floor.

When he had bought the house he'd hoped that someday he would bring Chantal here, and everytime he entered the spacious parlor, he thought of her.

He moved with ease in the darkened house, for faint light from street lamps shone through the French doors to the gallery. His gaze roamed over the swag-and-jabot pale yellow moiré drapes, a Mallard rosewood armoire, his mahogany drop-front desk, and the bro-caded satin camelback sofa Tobiah had made. Tobiah had a talent for furniture-making, yet it would be of no use to him if he was caught.

In the bedroom Rafe glanced briefly at the rosewood half-tester bed he had built for Chantal, and imagined her in it. *Where is she now? At home at Belle Destin, or out with Galliard?* Bringing his thoughts back to

Tobiah, he changed to dark clothes and took his revolver and his knife.

In minutes he was riding out of the Vieux Carré.
Tobiah might have gone to Caleb. Rafe felt a tight knot
of fear. Without horses, Tobiah stood little chance. He
was a man of cities. He didn't know how to get through
swamps and across wilderness. Rafe urged his horse
to a gallop, and prayed Tobiah was safe.

"I'll saddle up and ride with you," Ormonde Therrie said, striding out of the library beside Lazare.

"Good morning," Chantal said, descending the
stairs. It was too early for a morning call from Lazare.
"Is something wrong?"

"Runaway slaves," Lazare said. He moved to her
side while her father went to get his pistol and his hat.
"My Lenora is gone, and I think she went with that
Tobiah, Rafferty O'Brien's slave. Not that O'Brien
would care."

"Does Mr. O'Brien know?"

"There's little he would do about it if he did. We'll
find them, and then that slave of his will wish he had
stayed on the ship instead of coming to New Orleans
with O'Brien."

Ormonde appeared, and Lazare left with him.
Chantal saw a group of men on horseback milling in
the front yard. "They'll catch both of them," Blaise
said, and went upstairs.

The modiste was coming to Belle Destin to take
measurements and discuss Chantal's wedding dress,
and she had little time to think about the runaways
until that night, when they all sat down to dinner.

"We didn't find them, but we found tracks," Ormonde said, buttering golden cornbread. "The dogs
lost the scent only a mile out of town, but we'll find
them. We think they're still in the area."

"Where's Rafferty O'Brien?" Blaise asked.

"He was here today," Ormonde answered Blaise.
"He rode with us part of the time."

"Is he distraught to lose the slave he has tried to
free?"

Ormonde's dark eyes rested on Blaise. "I think he hopes they get away, but the man has the good sense to keep his mouth shut. He doesn't understand slavery," Ormonde said, cutting into a succulent piece of turkey. "And he told me that when the slaver picked him up after his shipwreck he thought he might be sold into slavery. I think it put a fear into him that will prevent him from ever owning slaves with a clear conscience. As a factor he doesn't have to own slaves to run his business, which is just as well. Man has lost weight since he worked here. I don't think brokering is as good for him as farming."

Chantal didn't hear the rest of the conversation, and she had lost any appetite she'd had. Rafferty had been at Belle Destin today, and she hadn't known it. She had thought with time she would get over her hurt, but instead she thought about him more and hurt more. She lost sleep; she missed him. And today he had been right here at her home and she could have seen him. She pushed her food about on her plate but didn't take another bite.

When dinner was over, the family assembled in the parlor. Chantal felt restless and wanted to escape, but beneath Blaise's watchful eyes she sat and tended her embroidery. When they heard horses, her head rose; in minutes William appeared, summoning Ormonde.

Chantal followed the men into the hall as Lazare greeted William.

"Mr. Therrie, we've picked up the trail. We found a little scrap of Lenora's dress caught on a bush."

"I'll be right there."

Chantal followed him outside, her gaze racing over the mounted men until she was sure Rafferty was not one of them. They turned and rode down the lane. She knew that if they caught Tobiah, Rafferty would try to defend him. She hoped he stayed away, and knew nothing about it until they had meted out the punishment.

It was a still, hot night and she sat on the upstairs gallery, listening to the baying of hounds in the distance. She saw the door of the overseer's house open, and her heart missed a beat as Rafferty emerged.

She raced down the stairs and outside, running down the lane. He was mounted, riding away.

"Rafferty!"

He turned his horse and came back, gazing down at her from the saddle. He wore a black coat, dark trousers, and black boots, and he looked marvelous to her. She was breathless and she felt ridiculous, yet she wanted to reach out and throw herself into his arms. She wished he would dismount to talk to her.

"I didn't know you were here today," she said, the words popping out. She locked her fingers together so she wouldn't reach to touch him. He gazed at her solemnly. "They're searching for your man and Lazare's slave," she added.

"Tobiah is in love with her. I hope they get away."

"You don't know where they are?"

He smiled. "Miss Therrie, you're engaged to the man who is hunting them. Do you think I would answer your question if I could? I know where your loyalty lies. And I know what your fiancé will do to them if he catches them."

His caustic reply hurt. "The men have found a piece of material on a bush that looks like part of Lenora's dress," she said.

"I need to catch up with them. Tobiah doesn't deserve a beating, and neither does Lenora. All they did was fall in love."

"No. They ran away. That's against the law." Why was she arguing with him? She wanted him to stay. Was he really angry with her, or using anger to hide hurt?

"Perhaps, Miss Therrie, you don't understand affairs of the heart," he said in a cold voice. He turned his horse and she watched him ride away. She hurt, and wanted to call to him to come back. Instead she bit her lip and cried, hot tears streaming down her cheeks. When he was gone from sight, she covered her face to cry. Never before had he been cold or harsh with her, and it hurt.

"Miss Therrie?"

She whirled around and wiped her eyes as Caleb O'Brien approached. He could move through the woods without a sound. He frowned as he studied her, and she knew it was impossible to hide her tears.

"Did Rafe just leave?" he asked.

"Yes, he's gone." She had tried to answer in a normal tone but her voice had wavered, and she sniffled.

"Holy Mary!" Caleb said softly. "Why're you marrying Galliard if you love Rafe?"

"I don't know what you're talking about!" She hurried past him. She stopped to wipe her eyes again, and turned around. "I've been engaged to Lazare for years."

"Does that mean you can't marry the man you love?"

"I love Lazare Galliard."

Caleb's scowl deepened. "Seems like your damned tears are over someone else. Lord, I hope I don't ever fall in love! You're going to marry a man you don't love? You're crying, and Rafe's hell to live with!" Caleb turned away, and then he was gone as silently as he had come.

He seemed to vanish into the bushes without a sound or stir of leaves. She covered her face and cried. She had been unkind and rude to Caleb, and she wanted Rafe to come back.

She turned away from the house, taking a lane, refusing to go home and have Blaise question her about her tears. She had no wish to see anyone and so headed toward the creek, remembering her swimming lessons, her laughter and kisses with Rafe. She pushed through bushes at the water's edge to bend down and splash water on her face. As she parted reeds, she saw a face in the reflection of the water. Chantal gasped, and jumped back.

A man loomed over her, and a young woman stood close to him. The man held a pistol. "Ma'am, don't scream, or I'll have to hurt you."

She looked at both of them. "You're Tobiah. I'm Miss Therrie." From the look on their faces, Chantal knew she had only added to their worries. "I just left Mr. O'Brien."

"He doesn't have a thing to do with this. I don't want to bring trouble down on his head."

She looked from one to the other, thinking about what both of them were risking for their love. "They're hunting you on Belle Destin. They can't be far away."

"Yes, ma'am. We heard the hounds. Without horses, and with men hunting day and night, we haven't gotten far." He faced Chantal defiantly. "Ma'am, I don't want you to start hollering and alert the search party about us. Lenora, you go now. I'll catch up."

"Wait!" Chantal said. She knew how much Tobiah meant to Rafe, and the girl looked young and terrified. She was slender and beautiful, with large black eyes and a thick cap of black curls. And Rafferty was right. If Lazare caught them, he would beat Tobiah to death. Chantal's mind raced, but finally she stopped wrestling with the choices. "I'll get you horses and show you where you can hide until I get back."

Tobiah and Lenora looked at each other, and he lowered the pistol. "Why would you do that, ma'am? Your father is hunting me, and your fiancé is after both of us."

She stared at him. "I know what you mean to Mr. O'Brien. Come with me." The woman looked at him and Tobiah nodded.

Chantal led them along the bayou, walking in water until the bayou began to spread and get deeper. She continued east, skirting the bayou, and in minutes saw the oak outlined against the sky. Once, years ago, Alain and Chantal and Amity had tried to hold hands and reach around its trunk, but they had needed a fourth person. Papa said it was probably the oldest tree at Belle Destin. Long limbs stretched out parallel to the ground and ivy fluttered on the trunk.

"Climb up there. I'll go home and get horses, but they'll think you stole them. I can't tell them I took them."

"No, ma'm," he answered solemnly, and she wondered if he would trust her or if they would both be gone when she came back.

"It'll be almost dawn, because I have to make an appearance at the house again or my stepmother will wonder what I'm doing."

She hurried home, running through the darkness, wishing she could take Amity with her but knowing it would be better if no one knew what she planned.

Long after midnight, and after her father had returned, Chantal slipped out to the stable and unlocked the heavy padlock, whispering to the dogs and opening the door. With her heart pounding in fear of discovery, she led out two horses and headed off for the tree.

"Tobiah?" she called softly as she neared it. Her skin prickled when only silence came. Had he gone? Was there anyone else around to hear her?

"Tobiah?"

"Over here," he said, stepping out of bushes behind her.

She slid off the horse as Lenora appeared, and Tobiah swung Lenora up on a horse.

"I brought the padlock from the stable," Chantal said. "Can you smash it, so it'll look as if you broke into the stable and stole the horses?"

His white teeth showed in a broad smile. He swung the butt of the pistol and smashed the lock. He picked up the lock and pulled it between his hands until it snapped. He handed it back to her.

"I think that'll be sufficient. Thank you, ma'am. Oh, and Miss Therrie? He loves you as much as a man can love a woman."

The statement was strong and positive, and she felt a strange stirring and deep longing, a great sense of loss. She drew a deep breath. "I hope you get away."

"Thank you, ma'am," Lenora added. "I don't know Mr. O'Brien, but he sounds like a fine man."

Chantal gave them directions to get out of the parish and then she raced for home, wanting to be back in the safety of her room. Her heart pounding in fear, aware of the stableboys sleeping in the loft, she ran across the yard to drop the lock at the open door of the stable. As she turned around, a man emerged from the shadows.

Caleb O'Brien faced her. "Miss Therrie?" There was an awkward silence while he studied her. "Two horses are gone," he said in a questioning tone.

She bit her lip. "Are you going to tell Papa?"

"Hell, no—beg your pardon. No, it's your home. I just thought you might want some help."

"Someone stole the two horses," she said, not wanting to admit to anyone what she had done. They stared at each other another long moment in silence.

"I'll walk you home," he said.

"You don't need to. I'm safe anywhere on Belle Destin."

He motioned toward the house and she didn't argue, because she wanted to be back in the haven of her room as soon as possible. As they neared the house, she turned to him. "You can watch me from here. I go up that tree to my room. You'd better go home too."

"Yes, ma'am. Thanks, Miss Therrie," he said in a soft voice. "Rafe will appreciate what you did."

She nodded and hurried toward the oak, clinging to the shadows and then clambering up to her room. She fell back on the bed with a sigh. What she had done was wrong. It went against everything she had been taught. It wronged Papa, wronged Lazare, wronged everyone she had known all her life. Yet she knew she would never tell Lazare. Guilt plagued her, yet she would do it again, for it would make Rafferty O'Brien happy.

"He loves you as much as a man can love a woman." The words ran through her thoughts, and tears stung her eyes.

While Chantal kept quiet and tried to stay out of the way, the household was in an uproar over the stolen horses. Her father sent servants to neighboring plantations to warn them about the theft. Men rode away in search of them. Blaise, bored with the search, decided to go to the Vieux Carré.

Ormonde returned after dark, rumpled, dusty, and handing his hat to William. When he learned Blaise had gone to town, he ordered that a carriage be readied to go into town.

"Papa, what about the horse thieves?" Chantal asked, aware that Amity had come downstairs as well.

"They think it's the runaways. Reward has been posted, and word telegraphed to states north of here. We'll send word west through the territories by Pony Express. We'll get them and our horses back."

Chantal turned away. Her guilt was terrible, for she felt she had betrayed both her father and Lazare. But later that night it wasn't guilt that kept her staring into the darkness, long hours after the house was quiet. Rafferty had sounded cold and angry with her, so *hurt*. She had never guessed that telling Rafferty good-bye would hurt both of them this badly. She ached for him, her pulse skipping at the mere mention of his name, her heart pounding at the glimpse of him. Would she ever stop hurting?

"Psst!" came a sound from the window, where a man's dark head and broad shoulders were framed.

Chapter 20

Clinging to the oak tree, Caleb O'Brien was framed in the window. She stepped out of bed and pulled the covers around her.

"Merciful angels, Caleb, what are you doing?"

"Rafe wants to see you, and he said I should come get you unless you want him to come up here."

"No! I'll be down in a moment."

"Yes, ma'am." He vanished from sight.

Her heart fluttered and her fingers shook. In the soft glow of moonlight she pulled out her chemise, under-drawers, and a blue dimity dress, dressing hastily and stepping into her slippers. What could he want at this hour of the night?

She caught her hair and tied it behind her head with a blue ribbon. Pulling a black cape around her shoulders, she scampered down the tree, expecting to find Rafferty waiting at the bottom. He wasn't there.

With a frown she headed toward the overseer's house. As she hurried along the path, Rafferty rode out of the shadows.

"Chantal," he whispered.

Her heart and breathing stopped. Dressed all in black, he blended into shadows. He bent down to catch her and swing her up on the horse in front of him.

She was against him, his arms around her, and her heart thudded. She wanted to wrap her arms around him and cling to him, but she simply stared straight ahead. Why this visit in the dead of night? Was he as angry as before? Surely he knew she had helped Tobiah.

For the moment it didn't matter. *He is here, holding*

me. She inhaled the fresh scent of cherry-laurel water he used after shaving, which was familiar now. She wanted him to pull her into his arms and kiss her, yet earlier he had treated her with a cold fury that kept a distance between them.

He rode in silence; no more teasing and flirting as he had always done in the past. They stopped at the place where he had taught her to swim. He climbed down and pulled her down, tossing aside his hat.

"Thank you, Chantal. Caleb told me what you did for Tobiah and Lenora."

Moonlight showed through dappled shadows, and she could see his blue eyes. She barely heard what he said. All she could think about was being with him. He stood only inches away, and if he reached for her she would be in his arms.

He arched his brows. "Chantal?" He took a step closer and tilted up her face. He inhaled deeply, studying her while he reached out slowly and untied the ribbon that held her hair. He drew it away, freeing her hair. It fell in a golden cascade over her shoulders and he caught a lock in his fingers, letting it slide over his hand.

"I really didn't do anything," she said, her heart fluttering as she noted that his anger was gone.

"I know your aiding them to escape went against all you've been taught. And I know it's something you can't share with your fiancé," Rafferty said, tilting her face up with his finger beneath her jaw. "I could have said thank you back there at the house."

Just the faint touch of his finger on her chin made her weak with longing.

"What I want to hear," he asked, and his voice was husky, "is why you did it."

She looked into his eyes, answers swirling and then gone, knowing only one thing. "Because I love you," she said, words coming out in a rush, and she stepped forward to slide her arms around him.

"My God, Chantal . . ." He groaned and wrapped his arms around her, crushing the breath from her lungs. He kissed her and she pressed against him,

winding her slender arms around his neck, clinging to
him with a sob as she thrust her tongue over his, drinking him in, wanting his hard body, wanting his love.

She hadn't known it was possible to want a man's
body the way she wanted Rafferty. She wanted to touch
him, wanted him to kiss her and love her. Her hands
moved to unfasten his belt.

He caught her wrists, his strong hands holding hers
as he leaned back to look down at her. "You're engaged, Chantal," he whispered hoarsely.

She felt as if she stood at a brink, a turning point
in her life where she must make a final choice for all
time. She had thought she was making it at her announcement party. Before that party Rafferty had been
the Belle Destin overseer, and she had seen him constantly. There had been no long separations, no time
to be without him and see what it was like. Now she
knew exactly what it was like to be apart. It was un-
bearable. And Soleil wasn't what kept her awake at
night and made her lose her appetite.

"You were right," she said, knowing the choice was
already made. "Soleil doesn't mean anything," she
whispered, tugging free his belt. He caught her hands
again.

"You don't know what this is doing to me, but I
won't compromise you. And I won't share you. Will
you marry me?"

The question hung in the air like a glittering moon-
beam caught on the wind, unforgettable, forever etched
in her memory, words she hadn't expected to hear tonight. Words that made her tremble with eagerness.

"Yes," she answered. "Yes, of course, Rafferty."

He crushed her in his arms, his kiss making her hot
and faint, his strong arms holding her so close she
could barely breathe. He trailed kisses to her throat,
his fingers moving to her buttons. While her pulse
drummed her dress fell away, drifting in a cloud
around her ankles.

His eyes feeding on her with a searing hunger, Rafferty stepped back to pull his shirt free of his pants
and yank the shirt over his head to toss it aside. She

stroked her fingers across his muscled chest as he removed her chemise, his hands cupping her full breasts, his thumb drawing circles over her taut nipples. She gasped with blinding pleasure, her head feeling heavy, her fingers moving through the matted curls on his chest.

Kneeling, he peeled down her underdrawers to shower kisses on her while she wound her fingers in his hair. His kisses were hot, intimate, exploring her soft body until he stood to remove the rest of his clothes.

She caressed him, blushing in the darkness, yet wanting to touch him, her fingers moving over his muscled thighs. "I didn't know it could be like this," she whispered. "Marriage was a house and a family, but this was no part of my dream. You were right when you told me that."

"This isn't half what it will be, Chantal," he said. "You should have a man who adores you, who wants to kiss and love you every waking minute."

When she caressed his throbbing manhood, he groaned and pushed her down on the grass.

As he moved between her legs, he caught her chin. He was on his knees between her legs, his body lean and powerful, his shaft dark and hard and ready. Rafferty looked into her eyes.

"There'll be no turning back. Is this what you want?"

"Yes, with all my heart." She stroked him, her fingers moving on his hard shaft. He inhaled as he came down over her. "Love, I'll try to keep from hurting you."

"Rafferty . . ." His back was smooth as satin, his buttocks hard. His shaft thrust against her and she felt too tight, and then pain came.

"Hold me, love. Wrap your legs around me," he whispered.

She moved with him, lost in sensation, hurting yet wanting him in a way she had never known. She felt possessed by him, complete with him, belonging to him heart and body. "Rafferty!"

"Chantal!" he cried, his mouth covering hers as he thrust his hips. She hurt and yet she wanted him. Her cry of pain was muffled and finally he shuddered with release. He crushed her to him, his hips moving until he was quiet. Their bodies were hot and damp, their breathing ragged.

"Love, my love," he whispered, showering her with kisses, his hands stroking her. "Chantal, I hurt you. I promise it will be better, so much better. I've dreamed of you. You can't imagine how much I want you, how often I think about you."

She clung to him, tears welling, because it seemed right to be in his arms. Right and exciting and perfect.

He raised his head. "Lord, you're crying! Did I hurt you badly? I'm sorry. It'll be better next time. I swear I'll make it better. I wouldn't hurt you. . . ."

She placed her hand on his mouth. "I'm all right. I'm crying because I'm happy now, and I haven't been."

He groaned and buried his face against her neck, to crush her against him. He turned his head and kissed her and finally rolled on his side, turning her to face him. He propped himself on his elbow, and gazed down at her. "We have to talk about what we're going to do."

"I have to tell Papa first. With him riding out constantly to hunt for Tobiah and Lenora, I don't know when I'll get a chance to talk to him, but I must tell him before I tell Lazare."

"He may call me out."

"No!" she cried. "I couldn't bear it if you and Papa faced each other in a duel. You mustn't kill him."

"Your family won't be happy over this turn of events."

"*Please* don't fight Papa," she said, stroking Rafferty's jaw and feeling the tiny stubble of his dark beard, running her fingers along his ear.

"I won't, Chantal. I'm sure I'll have to fight Lazare. He'll be enraged, and you know it."

She closed her eyes and leaned her forehead against Rafferty's chest. "I should have listened to you and listened to my heart. You tried to keep my from getting engaged.''

He raised her face. ''Breaking your pledge will be difficult, but engagement isn't marriage. It can be broken if we have to leave the state to do it. And I won't fight your father, I promise.'' He twisted to glance over his shoulder. ''Let's swim, Chantal.''

She raised herself up to look at the river, moonlight streaming over its onyx surface. ''I've lost my fear in sunshine, but not at night. I can imagine crawly things.''

He laughed and picked her up, scooping her up against his chest and striding toward the river.

''Cavalier brute!'' she teased, and he looked at her, his face only inches away. ''Rafferty,'' she said, forgetting the water and winding her arms around his neck to kiss him.

Finally he raised his head. ''Chantal, I love you.''

She squeezed him, her face against his throat. He strode to the water, and they swam until Rafe caught her to carry her back to the shore. ''See, you won't have to risk stepping on a crawly thing.''

''Don't talk about it until we're out of the water.'' On the bank he lowered her slowly, their bodies slippery and wet and cool. And she felt him throb with desire, hard again as he bent his head to kiss her.

She hurt from before, and she tensed when he moved between her legs. ''Chantal,'' he whispered, ''this will be better.'' He stretched beside her, his hand moving between her legs. He shifted position so that his tongue touched her cool wet belly, then moved down to the heated softness at the juncture of her thighs to arouse her. When he could wait no longer, he moved over her.

He thrust slowly, his hips moving, and she felt torn apart. He felt huge, filling her, and then suddenly the sensations changed. Her hips moved, the need becoming intense, pain filtered away by desire, bursting into ecstasy as she cried out while waves of pleasure washed over her. She wound her arms tightly around him.

"Love," he whispered, the sound muffled as his control vanished. His hips moved, thrusting until he reached release, his hot seed filling her, both of them moving in unison as one, hearts beating together.

When their breathing had returned to normal, Rafferty turned his head to look at her. "We'll tell your father as soon as possible, Chantal. And I'll have to fight Lazare."

"No!" She flung her arm across his chest to hold him close.

"He'll be enraged, and his pride will be at stake. He'll lose a lot of land if he loses you."

"Lazare and you dueling! You frighten me now."

"Stop worrying. You can't change men."

She played with a lock of his black hair. "I love you, Rafferty O'Brien."

"If you want, I'll buy the land and build you another Soleil."

"You can do this? You came to New Orleans without anything. I saw the small room where you lived."

"Yes, love, but that was a long time ago, and I've worked for your father."

"You couldn't build another Soleil on overseer's wages."

"No, I couldn't, but I'm a gambler and I've won often over the years. I've won a great deal."

"And you can build a house like Soleil? You keep things to yourself," she said, propping herself on her elbow to study him.

He stroked her cheek. "I won't keep anything from you," he said softly, and she wrapped her arms around him to hug him, placing her head against his chest.

"Papa is going to go into shock."

"Let me talk to him first, and save you some of his anger." With her ear against his chest his voice was a deep rumble. She sat up to look down at him again, thinking about telling Papa. She looked away, watching silvery streamers of moonlight play over the surface of the river while shadows undulated beneath overhanging tree branches.

"That seems cowardly."

"We know you're not a little coward, Chantal," he said with amusement. "I'll make an appointment to talk to your father, and then you can see him. It'll be better that way, love."

"You make life easy for me, Rafferty."

"Try Rafe."

"Rafe. I think of you as Rafferty." She leaned over to kiss him and then pulled away. "Maman threatened to ruin my life if I didn't marry Lazare."

"We won't worry about your stepmother. She can't hurt us."

Chantal touched his lips. "I haven't slept nights." He turned his head to kiss her fingers.

"Do you think I have?" He stroked her bare back, lifting her hair away from her nape as his fingers played lightly over her. "I've waited so long," he said, his voice becoming husky in that tone that started a fire within her.

Two days later, on the nineteenth of November, Chantal paced her room. Rafferty was talking to Papa in his office. Her palms were clammy, and she felt as if she couldn't get her breath. And between worries and fears, she kept thinking of Rafferty and their night together by the river. She wanted to be with him, to be in his arms, to have him love her again as he had that night. It made her cheeks turn pink to remember, but it also made a sweet, hot ache start low within her. She longed for him in a way she had never wanted Lazare.

She prayed she didn't have to encounter Maman until she had talked to Papa. He had said that when he was finished talking to Rafferty, he would send William to fetch Chantal. Papa had looked at her quizzically when he'd told her about his appointment with Rafferty.

If Papa were to call out Rafferty, she couldn't bear it. They would have to run away, and that frightened her. She opened her door. The hall was empty, and she tiptoed down the stairs and toward the office. The door was closed. No voices were raised in shouts, a hopeful sign. Suddenly the door swung open and Rafferty emerged. He closed the door behind him and glanced her way.

As he approached, her gaze raked over his black frock coat, the brocaded vest, his tucked white shirt, and black trousers. He was flawlessly dressed, but she remembered how he had looked naked, hard and ready, standing over her. One look at his frown and her heart dropped. She felt an ominous foreboding.

"What did Papa do?" she whispered when Rafferty reached her.

"He's sending for you now," Rafferty said, holding her hands and standing close, his thumbs moving back and forth over her knuckles. He looked over her head. "Here comes William. Your father's in shock, Chantal. He had no idea this might happen."

"What did he say?"

William passed them with a nod and entered the office. In seconds he reappeared, closing the door behind him. "Miss Chantal, your papa wants me to fetch you. He wants to see you."

"Thank you, William. I'll be right there."

"Yes, ma'am," he said and went down the hall, leaving her alone with Rafferty.

"Your father is going to want you to wait," Rafferty said. He touched her cheek, drawing his finger along her jaw. "He said he would talk to me again. He's not happy, but then I knew he wouldn't be." Rafe took her hand and looked at her solemnly, and her heart missed a beat.

"I can give you a lot, Chantal, but I don't have the Galliard wealth. I won't be governor someday; I don't want some of the things Lazare wants that would make you very prominent."

She smiled, standing on tiptoe to kiss his cheek. She looked into his eyes. "I want *you*, Rafferty O'Brien. I want you to love me like you did the other night."

"Oh, Lord, Chantal." His gaze burned with hungry desire. "I made a promise to your father."

"What promise?" she asked, dreading to hear the answer.

"That I won't see you for six weeks."

"No!"

"Chantal, I want you for the rest of our lives. I can give on this one point. Your father has had a terrible shock. He's planned this wedding since you were a small child. This will bring the wrath of his society down on his head."

"I can't bear to go six weeks without you!" she said in a low voice.

"Lord, Chantal, we have to cooperate with your father. Remember that. Don't keep him waiting, love. I'll be outside." Rafferty winked at her and then he was gone, striding down the hall. She took a deep breath and went to her father's office.

He gazed out the window and turned to watch her as she entered and closed the door. She crossed the room to stand on the other side of his desk and face him.

"I'm sorry, Papa, but I don't want to marry Lazare. I love Rafferty O'Brien."

"Chantal, engagements are binding. You have been pledged through the years to Lazare. It will be disastrous to break it off now."

Her heart constricted, and her hope that this might be resolved with a minimum of difficulty was shattered.

She placed her hands on his desk and leaned forward. "Please. I love Rafferty. I don't love Lazare, and I don't want to marry him. It would only bring both of us unhappiness."

"I think you're too young to know what you really want," he said. His skin was white, his lips thin and pressed together, and his fists clenched. His controlled fury shocked her.

"Papa, I *do* know! I tried to go ahead with my engagement to Lazare, and it's been dreadful. I've known this for a long time, and I've fought with what I felt. I tried to go ahead with the engagement and I felt more miserable. I love Rafferty. I want to be his wife, not Lazare's! If you've been so happy all these years then you know what I feel, and if you haven't, then spare me going through what you've experienced."

"Chantal!"

"I'm sorry, but I love him. I don't feel pain at the thought of saying good-bye to Lazare. When I just said it to Rafferty, I felt as if I were losing part of myself."

"Chantal, that's the foolish dream of a young woman! You're too young to make a wise choice. Lazare will be the most powerful man in Louisiana. He can give you every luxury, every comfort. He can give you more than I have, more than Rafferty O'Brien will ever give you. O'Brien is a gambler, a will-o'-the-wisp Irish, so different from your French heritage."

"It isn't that important. Not any of it. You know Rafferty will provide well for me."

Ormonde rubbed his head. "Dammit, Chantal, this is a kettle of snakes. Lazare will kill him."

"Lazare *has* to accept this."

"No, he doesn't! And the man has never lost anything he wanted. Never! He'll kill Rafferty O'Brien, and you'll lose both of them. Can't you see that?"

"If Lazare has any feelings for me, he won't challenge Rafferty. I'm sorry for what this is causing you, but I can't marry a man I don't love and spend a lifetime of unhappiness."

"I don't think you know what you're doing!" Ormonde snapped, his voice rising. His face was red, and her heart raced with fear.

"Dammit!" He hit the desk with his fist. "Can't you see that you're decreeing O'Brien's death?"

She turned to ice and stared at him. "We talked about Lazare, and Rafferty didn't worry."

"Neither have eight others. By heaven, you didn't think! You're marking him for death."

"No!"

"I want six weeks from you to reconsider," he said, regaining his composure. "You're to wait until after the holidays." He looked at a calendar. "You will wait until the twenty-eighth of December to break off with Lazare."

"Papa, that's forever! I'd have to go to parties with Lazare, and it would only make things worse when I do break the engagement!" Ormonde's head came up, and his dark eyes were filled with a cold fury that made her quail inwardly.

"You're to wait until the twenty-eighth of December. I don't know that I'll consent at that time but I'll consider it, and I'll feel better about the situation if I feel you've given some thought to what you're doing. I think you're rushing into something you'll regret the rest of your life. If you think you love Rafferty O'Brien, you'll love him a month from now."

"Very well, Papa. I'll wait to tell Lazare."

"And during the intervening time, you must promise you won't see Rafferty O'Brien."

"He's often here with his brothers. I may not be able to avoid seeing him."

"You promise me you won't go out with him. And you'll go out with Lazare as you have been."

"It'll be difficult."

"Chantal! I don't have to consent at all! I can force you to wed Lazare!"

"Yes, Papa, I promise. Maman will be furious."

"You're going to have to face the wrath of our friends and relatives as well. You may decide O'Brien's not worth it. And men may stop doing business with O'Brien. Chantal, you're throwing away a golden future. Every available woman would give the world to have Lazare's pledge. Rafferty O'Brien will never give you the life of luxury and prominence that Lazare will."

She lifted her chin. "Rafferty's here now. May I tell him what I've promised you?"

"No. I'll tell him. And you'd better think and think hard about causing his death."

She left her father with a mixture of emotions. She wanted to be with Rafferty, in his arms, but now they couldn't talk to each other. She was also deeply frightened for him. *"Would he risk his life for you?"* Rafferty had asked her this about Lazare, yet could she give up her future with Rafferty if it would save him from Lazare?

Upstairs, she stepped onto the gallery and saw Papa with his hat pulled low, striding toward the overseer's house. As she watched his purposeful walk, she seemed to see disaster looming.

Within the next quarter of an hour, as Chantal sat and watched for either Rafferty or Papa to reappear, William stepped onto the gallery.

"Miss Therrie, your momma wants to see you. She's in your room."

Chantal inhaled deeply and walked to her room, knowing a storm would break when Maman confronted her. She opened the door and her heartbeat raced. Maman's pale skin was white, splotched with red, a sign of her rage. Her mouth was drawn down and her eyes were slits, and Chantal thought of the harpies she had read about in mythology.

Maman crossed the room and with a full swing of her arm, slapped Chantal. The stinging blow made a sharp crack. With a cry Chantal fell back against the wall.

Maman leaned close. "This time it'll do you no good to run to your father, because he agrees with me! And he feels part of this is his fault for hiring Rafferty O'Brien!"

Chantal fought back tears from the blow and touched her aching cheek, looking into green eyes that burned with rage.

"Ormonde told me he's required six weeks of you before you make a decision." Her hands gripped Chantal's shoulders, long fingernails digging into her flesh, and Chantal bit back a cry.

"Before that time is over, you will choose to remain engaged to Lazare and you will marry him. Do you understand?"

"I love Raf—"

Maman struck her on the other side of her head, a blow to her ear that made a ringing noise in her head. *"You'll marry Lazare, do you understand?"*

Chantal couldn't hold back tears this time as she stared at Blaise.

"If you don't wed Lazare, Chantal, I'll ruin your life. And I swear, you'll never marry Rafferty O'Brien."

Chantal's blood ran cold, because Maman sounded so positive. She knew Maman was capable of hiring ruffians to kill Rafferty, and now she feared for his life. "Don't kill Rafferty O'Brien!" she gasped, and at the flare of satisfaction on Maman's face Chantal wished she hadn't shown her fear.

"You're stubborn and foolhardy, Chantal," Maman said, leaning close again and glaring at Chantal. "Listen to me: I'll carry out my threat if you break your engagement. You'll never marry *any* man—no one! I'll ruin your life. Do you understand my threat?"

"Yes, Maman," she whispered.

"You've won your last argument with me; your father will support whatever I want. I've told him I'm locking you in your room tonight and tomorrow. I intend to make certain you don't see Rafferty O'Brien."

If Papa really had allowed Maman to lock her in her room for a night and day, he was truly enraged. Never had he been so cruel.

"You won't marry *any* man if you persist, and Rafferty O'Brien won't live."

"Don't harm him!"

Maman straightened up and walked to the bedroom door. "If I had my way, you would be locked in the root cellar."

"Maman!" Chantal said. Blaise turned, and her eyes narrowed. "Don't harm Mr. O'Brien! If anything happens to him, I'll break my engagement!"

"Don't threaten me, Chantal! It will only make things worse for you. You don't get any food today."

"Papa agreed to that?" Chantal asked, startled at the harshness of the order.

Maman gave her a level look. "He doesn't know, and you won't tell him." She left, closing the door and turning the key. Chantal was terrified for Rafferty's welfare. If she broke the engagement, it was the same as issuing an order for his death. She would talk to him about their predicament the first chance she got—but when would that be?

* * *

"Bravo!" Lazare exclaimed, as the gold velvet curtains came down after the first act. He stood to applaud as the gas jets came on and gaslights fluttered across the foot of the stage. He stepped back to allow Chantal to pass in front of him. Her blue faille dress rustled as she closed her fan and stepped out of the box with Ormonde. When they were gone Lazare looked over at Blaise, who gazed at him with glittering eyes.

"What's wrong with Chantal? She acts as if she has the ague. And you look as if you're sitting on needles. I think you have something to tell me," he said, suspecting that Blaise was furious with him.

"Yes I do, and you wouldn't answer my note last Wednesday night."

"No. I'm engaged now, and I can't run such risks," he said, looking over the audience and seeing Rafferty O'Brien's dark head as he went up the aisle. Lazare's expert eye went over O'Brien's elegant black clothes, the ruffled white shirt beneath a red moiré vest, his black satin cravat. The man had learned how to dress and was wearing the best. Lazare gritted his teeth and felt a knot of fury. O'Brien belonged to the Elkins, and to the yacht club at Lake Pontchartrain, and he was becoming a strong Democrat, quoted in political discussions.

Wondering how difficult she was going to be, he shifted his attention to Blaise. Women were so demanding when it came to parting. Time now to end his affair with her forever. "The opera is good, but you don't look as if you're enjoying it."

"You won't either in a moment. Chantal has been seeing Rafferty O'Brien."

Lazare swiveled around to study her. For the first time, he paid attention to her. "What do you mean 'seeing him'?" he asked, a slow-burning anger starting.

"I just know she's been with him. Lazare, she's young and can be swayed by a charming, handsome man."

"He's here at the opera, and they've barely glanced

at each other. They didn't acknowledge each other when they did.''

''Surely you don't think that means there's no feeling between them? Lazare, really, coming from you! Besides, he's cast her more than one glance, and she him.''

''She won't care. Men stare at her and try to flirt with her.''

''Has she acted the same lately? Is she as eager and affectionate?''

He stopped to think; Blaise was right. Chantal had been cool and elusive when he tried to get her alone or steal a kiss.

''Great God, Lazare, you take her for granted so much you don't notice!''

''Dammit! I'll kill the son of a bitch!''

''So there *is* a difference. You'd better sit up and take notice. And think twice before you challenge the man to a duel. He's not your average citizen. He's a deadly shot, as good as you are.''

''I doubt it, Blaise,'' Lazare said dryly, his fury increasing.

''I don't want you hurt. There's another solution, and one I think would please everyone.''

He wondered what was in it for Blaise. ''What's that?''

''You and Chantal will attend the ball Friday night at the St. Louis Hotel. Afterwards, take her to our townhouse. We'll go back to Belle Destin, and I'll keep Ormonde occupied. Seduce her, Lazare, and Ormonde will have no choice but to move up the wedding date.''

''That would compromise Chantal, and it would be a scandal.''

''Only if it's known, which it won't be. And you'll have some good reason to give your father and Ormonde for moving up the wedding. Besides, scandal never really hurts a man.''

He mulled it over in his mind. It was distasteful, because Chantal was proper and chaste. ''I want my bride chaste. We'll have a wedding that will outdo anything ever seen in New Orleans society.''

''Men and their standards!'' Blaise wrinkled her nose in disgust. ''Don't be an ass, Lazare! She's as pure as snow, and if you seduce her a few months early, what difference will that make? You'll still be the only man who has touched her. If you wait, you may be the second man.''

''Damn you, Blaise! If I thought that, I'd kill him tonight. And if he's possessed her, I won't marry her.''

''And lose all that fine cotton land and a claim to one third of the Therrie wealth? You're letting passion rule instead of your head.''

He rubbed his jaw and thought about it. How taken with O'Brien was Chantal? Would she mourn and build him into some saint in her memory if he were killed? It would be satisfactory to call him out and blast the devil to Hell. He glanced up to see Chantal return with Ormonde. When the curtain rose, he twisted slightly in his seat to watch her.

He followed her gaze to the dark head facing the stage, and rage burned in him. His gaze raked over her. Her cheeks were pink, her lips full. The scoop neckline of the deep blue dress revealed the soft curve of her lush breasts, and he felt desire stir. *Saturday night. Take her to the townhouse and seduce her.* He imagined Chantal in his arms, yielding to him. *Damn, I wish I could ride home with her tonight, without the Therries along!*

He didn't hear any of the second act, and as Rafferty O'Brien went down the aisle Lazare felt a stab of hatred.

The ride home was interminable, but finally he had Chantal to himself on the Belle Destin lawn. ''I've asked your father if I may escort you to the ball Friday night, just the two of us, and he has agreed.''

''He has? That doesn't sound like Papa,'' she said, frowning. Lazare wondered where his mind had been the past few weeks. Why hadn't he noticed the change, the uncustomary coolness, in Chantal? He pulled her to him and felt resistance as she stood stiffly in his arms.

"Lazare, Maman and Papa could come back outside."

"They won't, and you know it. And we're in the dark, with my carriage between us and the house." He bent his head, kissing her hard, feeling anger and passion stir. He wanted to push her down in the grass and possess her, then tell her he would beat her if he ever caught her with O'Brien. Instead he kissed her throat and pushed down the neckline of her dress. She caught his hands, but he took her wrists and held them behind her back with one hand while he kissed her and muffled her protests, his other hand plunging beneath her dress to fondle her. The more she struggled, the more his anger grew. Why hadn't he noticed the change in her?

She pushed and he released her, both of them breathing hard.

"Lazare, I'll have to face Maman and Papa when I go inside!" She straightened her clothes. "I'll look a fright."

"Until Friday night, Chantal." He brushed her cheek and walked with her to the door, to kiss her again briefly before he turned to go.

As he rode home, his rage increased. Friday night, he would make Chantal his for once and forever. And he would ask to move up the wedding date. Then he would find O'Brien and challenge him. Damned if he cared how much she would mourn.

Chapter 21

December 14, 1860

"As conservative as Senator Benjamin is, he's urging secession," Alain said, standing in a large circle of couples, the men talking politics. The ballroom was warm and crowded, and Chantal tried to pay attention to the talk. "President Buchanan has declared secession unconstitutional."

"As if he could stop the states!" Lazare said. "Federal office-holders have resigned. Judge Magrath of the U.S. District Court in South Carolina resigned. The Secretary of the Treasury just resigned to go home to Georgia. And we have a new president-elect, so Buchanan's declaration means nothing."

"Georgia has already voted one million dollars to arm the state," Simon added.

"We need the union for our sugar; the federal tariff would be gone if we withdrew," Charles Boer said.

"You're a sugar planter, looking after your own interests," Lazare said.

"We *all* have to look after our own interests!" John Maltby said, and Chantal thought of his bank. "We've got strong ties with the North; this city and this state depend on the northern commerce."

"Nonsense. We have cotton," Lazare argued. Chantal's thoughts wandered, and it was difficult to keep from searching for a glimpse of Rafferty. Her gaze drifted over the room.

Showing above most of the crowd, his black hair was easy to spot. It was an effort to avoid staring at him. He wore a ruffled white shirt and dark cravat, and his black clothes and dark hair made him the most attractive man at the ball. She ached to be with him, if only for a few minutes, yet she was afraid to do anything that might stir Lazare's wrath or curiosity and she had to abide by her promise to Papa.

"You've been nominated as a delegate to the secession convention, along with your future father-in-law," Charles said.

"Most of you know how I feel. I'm an Immediate Secessionist," Lazare answered. "I think we should break away from the North. We'll still have commerce with the North, just as we do with England and France. We'll control the Mississippi River."

"And your father?" Simon asked, looking at Alain. "How does he feel?"

"He's a Cooperationist. He's worried about ties to the North. And my father is a deliberate, cautious man. He thinks before he acts, and says more of us should do the same," Alain said with a laugh.

"Perhaps that's why your father has adroitly avoided duels and still kept men's respect."

"That, and his deadly aim," Alain replied dryly.

"It looks as if your opponents will campaign under one banner, Cooperationist, to prevent immediate secession," John Maltby said to Lazare.

"If the Unconditional Unionists campaigned under their true colors, they wouldn't get a vote!" Simon exclaimed, and several laughed. "And the Conditional Unionists are stalling for time as far as I'm concerned."

"I understand David Adams is a secessionist in the second district and Robert Evans in the third district," Alain said.

"One of our new Democrats, Rafferty O'Brien, has been nominated. I've heard rumors he's an Unconditional Unionist," John said, and Chantal felt as if she had received a jolt. She hadn't known Rafferty had been nominated as a candidate for the secession convention. An Unconditional Unionist. She wasn't surprised. He wasn't in favor of slavery; he was new to the South. But this would serve to pit him against Lazare in another area, and add fuel to the fires of hate already between them.

"They'll be lumped under the Cooperationist name, so we should learn how each one feels before we vote," Simon stated.

"I say vote for Lazare and Daniel and the Immediate Secessionists and be done with it," Alain urged. "Just before the presidential election the *Bee* proclaimed its unionism, but as soon as the election was over the *Bee* began to change. The *Daily Picayune* is moderate, but the *Daily Delta* is fiery about what we need to do. If we do go to war, we'll whip the North in months."

Lazare's hand stroked her arm, and Chantal looked up to find him watching her. She wondered now how she could ever have thought she was in love with him. But whatever she had felt, it was over and gone. Only a few more weeks now, and she and Rafferty would have abided by their promises to Papa to avoid seeing each other. If anything, the separation had made her all the more certain of her feelings for him.

"If y'all will excuse us, Chantal and I will dance," Lazare said and took her arm to lead her to the dance floor. The hoops beneath the skirt of her dress of rose silk kept a distance between them as they moved across the floor. "You're quiet tonight, Chantal," Lazare said, watching her through half-closed eyes.

"There are so many things to do to get ready for a wedding," she said. She needed to pay more attention to Lazare; he was being his most charming, and far more attentive than he had been in months, but it was difficult to feign an interest in anything he said.

Maman watched her constantly. It was the first ball Chantal could remember where Maman had sat on the sidelines with the matrons and hadn't danced all evening. Lazare whirled her around, his long legs stretching out. Her gaze swept over the sixty-six-foot-wide rotunda with its Corinthian columns that were forty feet high with capitals of black cypress. At the foot of one of the columns stood Rafferty, gazing back at her with a solemn expression. Their eyes locked and held, her heart racing; intense longing making her want to run to him. And then people danced between them;

Lazare turned, and Rafferty was gone from view. Only two more weeks, fourteen days, and she could formally break with Lazare.

An hour later, as she danced with Lazare, he gazed over her head. "Your parents are leaving," he said, and Chantal felt a flutter as she watched them go. She had always been strictly chaperoned with Lazare, seldom being alone with him more than a few minutes at a time, and for years not even that. Suddenly, tonight, she was allowed to go to the ball with him, and he would accompany her home alone. She was astounded Maman had allowed it.

"We were to leave when your parents were," Lazare said. "I told your father we would follow them home, but I asked for two more dances with you after they left, and he consented."

Two dances, and she would go home to Belle Destin without touching Rafferty, without talking to him, without dancing with him. She hurt, and wished there were some way to slip out for only minutes, but her promise was binding.

After the two dances Lazare took her arm as they moved through the crowd. When they reached the door, she felt compelled to turn.

Rafferty stood across the wide vestibule. His blue eyes were focused on her intently, but without a flicker of acknowledgment. As he leaned against a column he looked relaxed, solemn. She longed to hear his deep voice, to touch him, but she could do nothing but go with Lazare. She was unaware of what she did or said until they were blocks away from the hotel, and then she realized Lazare was headed up Royal instead of turning toward St. Charles and the river road home.

Lazare drove his elegant new buggy with panels inlaid in silver. At one time she would have been impressed and delighted to be seen in it, but now all she wanted was to jump down and run back to the ball.

"Lazare, where are you going?" she asked, still thinking about Rafferty. He had looked more handsome than ever, yet so solemn.

"I'm taking you home."

"But you're going to the townhouse, and we're supposed to go to Belle Destin."

He laughed. "No we're not. Your mother said they'll be at the townhouse tonight."

Chantal barely heard him, and paid little attention as he took her arm and entered the house. Lights glowed in the front hall and parlor, and not until they had stepped into the parlor did she wonder where her parents were. Lazare removed his coat and closed the tall double doors.

"Lazare, if Papa comes in he'll be furious to find the doors closed."

Lazare smiled, crossing the room to pour two glasses of brandy and bring one to her. "We'll drink to our engagement, Chantal."

As she accepted the glass, all she could think about was that first time with Rafferty in his small room, when he had poured glasses of brandy.

"Here's to a wedding that will be the envy of all Louisiana," Lazare said, touching her glass and drinking deeply.

She drank and felt the hot brandy warm her insides. She sat down on the sofa and watched Lazare put out the lamps until only one glowed. He came to sit beside her.

"You're quiet. Let's drink to the most beautiful bride in Louisiana."

She sipped the brandy and gazed over the rim at him. He finished his brandy and set the glass on the marble-topped table. Watching her with a smile, he unfastened his cravat.

"Lazare, should you do that? If Papa comes in he—"

"Let me worry. They know we'll be husband and wife. I've waited all evening to kiss you." He took her glass of brandy and she felt a sense of dread. He pulled her to him, and everything in her screamed out to push him away. She didn't want to be in his arms, to feel his mouth on hers, to dream of Rafferty, to ache for him and despise Lazare's kisses.

Lazare's mouth pressed against hers bruisingly, and he pushed her back against the pillows on the sofa, crushing her against his chest with his arm around her waist, pressing down her hoops and crinoline. He paused to look at her, and his gaze frightened her.

"You're cold as ice, Chantal. What's wrong?"

"Perhaps I'm catching something," she whispered. "Lazare, I should say good night now," she said, wriggling to get free.

"In a moment, my darling. I get so few chances to be with you." He pulled her to him, his mouth hard on hers. As his hands moved on her back, she tried to push him away. He was not the man she wanted, not the man she loved.

Her thoughts swirled around Rafferty and her predicament, and the brandy took the edge off awareness. As Lazare bent his head to kiss her throat and her breast he pushed her dress to her waist, lifting her full breasts above the corset.

"Lazare!" She hadn't realized he had unfastened the row of buttons down the back of her dress. While he cupped her breasts, she pushed against his chest, loathing him and afraid her parents would walk into the room.

"Confound women's clothes!" Lazare pulled her up, holding her easily, his mouth on hers, smothering her protests. She struggled uselessly while his hand went beneath her skirt to unfasten her hoop skirt and push it away, shoving her down again on the sofa. Chantal twisted away and pushed with all her strength as he kissed her breast.

"Lazare, stop! Stop at once! I'll be compromised!"

She went cold, suddenly realizing that might be what he wanted. Until minutes ago she had been lost in thoughts about Rafferty, when she should have firmly told Lazare good-bye.

Her eyes flew wide, and she felt rage and a strong determination to get away from him. Now, when it was only two weeks until she could dissolve the engagement, she wasn't going to be forced to wed Lazare.

"Let me go at once! Papa will kill you for this!"

Lazare slanted her a look and smiled, his fingers

caressing her as he raised his head. His touch, instead of stirring passion, revolted her and was an invasion.

"We're going to be man and wife, Chantal. He'll understand we couldn't wait."

"You know he'd never understand!" she snapped, as Lazare offered the glass of brandy. "No, I don't want any brandy," she said, pushing his hand away.

"It would make the evening less painful," he said. "Take a drink."

She struggled to get free of him, but he was a large and strong man and it was useless to try to break away. "Lazare, I can't bear this. I'll be humiliated," she said, feeling a suffocating panic.

"No you won't. You'll marry me, and it won't matter," he said, leaning forward to kiss her. She tried to turn her head, but he caught her and held her with his hand at the back of her head. Then his hand was gone, moving beneath her skirts, pushing them up to her waist.

"No!" she gasped, struggling as he raised his hips to unbutton his trousers and free his thick shaft. She wriggled out of his grasp and turned to run for the door, yanking her silk dress up as she went. She reached the door and pulled.

Shock chilled her when she found she couldn't open the doors. She whirled around. Lazare had pulled off his trousers. He yanked his shirt away and looked at her, smiling, yet she saw the anger and determination in his eyes. Removing the last of his underclothes, his gaze raked over her.

She cried out. "Papa!"

Lazare's smile didn't waver. *We are alone. Why didn't she realize it? Maman and Papa are on their way to Belle Destin, and when I don't return I'll be compromised. Papa will force me to marry Lazare right away.*

"You can make this difficult and painful, or pleasant and something to remember," Lazare drawled. "We have all night, Chantal. Or at least until early hours, when your Papa misses you and rides back here." Nude, Lazare looked more overwhelming and powerful than before. Six and a half feet tall, he had a thick chest covered with a mat of brown hair. His arms and legs bulged with muscles, and her strength would be no match for his. She felt a wave of revulsion and anger, her mind working swiftly. He poured more brandy and came toward her.

"You planned this all along. Maman—" She broke off.

"Yes, your stepmother aided me in this small deception. We'll marry sooner this way, Chantal."

"This isn't right, Lazare. It isn't honorable, and after all this time you can wait."

"No, I can't wait. You should be able to see how eager I am. You can scream yourself silly, and it'll do you no good. You can fight, and it'll only cause you pain. I'll make you mine tonight, Chantal, and it'll be forever."

"You will lose any shred of respect and affection I ever felt toward you."

His smile was harsh and cynical. "How much does love enter into any marriage you know? We were pledged as children. Love has nothing to do with it."

"I won't marry you! I don't love you!"

"Do you want your brandy?"

"No!"

With an angry scowl he swung his arm and tossed the glass onto the hearth, where it shattered, golden drops of brandy shining on the stones. "Chantal, you might as well learn now, you will *always* do as I say."

Lazare moved closer, reaching out to yank her to him with such swiftness it made her gasp. His mouth closed on hers and his arms locked like bands around her, crushing the breath from her lungs. He was bare, his body pressing hers, and she sobbed as she struggled uselessly against him. He pushed her to the floor and she struggled to break free as he straddled her and pulled up her skirts.

She twisted her head. "No! Lazare, I want the brandy! Please!"

He paused and looked at her. "Please!" she begged.

"You'll hurt me! I want a glass of brandy! Please! You said the night can be pleasant, or it can be painful!"

His breathing was ragged, and she watched him gain control long enough to get up and move to the decanter. She was up in one swift movement, snatching up a desk chair. She swung it with all her strength, striking the locked glass doors leading to the gallery.

She managed to squirm through an opening, pieces of jagged glass in the frame tearing at her dress. Suddenly there were fingers clamped onto her shoulder. Knowing that if he pulled her back inside she wouldn't get another chance for escape, she bit his hand.

"Dammit, Chantal!" he snapped. His hand unclenched, and she broke free. Still in her chemise with her dress around her waist, she scrambled down the iron post and dropped to the ground to run. She caught up her skirts and ran down Royal, turning at the first corner.

Lazare was naked and would have to take time to dress, but then he would be after her. If she ran to Rafe's house, Rafe would kill Lazare. The livery stable was only blocks away, but she couldn't go there in her disheveled state. Touzet Lacquement! She didn't know where he lived, only Exchange Alley, but he was Rafe's friend and might help her.

Terrified Lazare would spot her, she raced toward Exchange. She ran past the corner, where light spilled from halfway down the block at the Orleans ballroom. Men and carriages milled in the street. Suddenly a hand closed on her wrist.

Chantal spun around to look into the eyes of a stranger who smiled at her. He was well dressed in elegant clothes and a white silk cravat, and she guessed he had come from the ballroom.

"What have we here, a half-dressed beauty running through the night! Tell me your name, my pretty."

"Please, I'm going to be betrothed!" she gasped, pulling her dress higher. Her mind raced, for the man had taken her by the wrist and was drawing her toward the dark garden behind the cathedral.

"Come here. The evening is early."

"We're eloping tonight. My fiancé waits for me, and my father is after me."

The man's smile faded, and he looked over his shoulder. "Who's your father?"

"I'm marrying Touzet Lacquement, a *maître d'armes.*"

The man dropped her wrist. "Go quickly. If your father appears, I'll send him that way," he said, pointing over his shoulder.

"Thank you, m'sieu. My darling Touzet will thank you."

"Just go!" he said, hurrying back toward the Orleans ballroom. She ran, racing past the garden, running to Bienville. She entered the first house with a light in the window, going upstairs to knock at a door. She felt terror at being alone in such a situation, and in the darkened hall she slipped her arms through the tiny puff sleeves of her dress and fastened the top button.

"Ma'am?" A servant opened the door, staring with round eyes at her.

"I need to find the house of Touzet Lacquement. Can someone help me?"

She prayed it was no one who knew her or her family. The butler nodded. "Just a minute, ma'am. Would you care to come inside?"

"No, I'll wait here," she said, her heart thudding with fear.

In minutes a man in a dressing gown appeared. "May I help you, miss?"

"I need to find M'sieu Touzet Lacquement as quickly as possible. It's very important."

"He lives in the first apartment in the next block. But he may not be home. Would you care to come inside? I'll be glad to give my assistance."

"Non, merci. Au revoir," she said, already going down the stairs. She opened the door and peered out cautiously. A man strolled down the opposite side of the street, but otherwise it was empty. She stepped out, heard hoofbeats, and rushed back inside. The man

upstairs had closed his door, and once again the hall-way was dark.

Through the glass doors she saw Lazare riding up the street. His hat was pulled low and a slave rode beside him. Holding her breath, she leaned back in the dark hallway until he was gone from sight.

Her heart pounded with fear, and she reached be-hind her to button her dress. She had to get home. As soon as Papa discovered her absence, she could be compromised.

When she stepped outside she felt vulnerable and exposed, but the only man in sight was on foot and far too thin to be Lazare. Racing to the next block she ran upstairs, praying Touzet was home. She knocked on the door and gasped for breath.

The door opened, and Touzet stood staring at her. He blinked, and raked his fingers through unruly black hair.

"Mam'selle Therrie!"

"Please help me!" she said swiftly in French. "I have to get to Belle Destin as fast as possible."

To her relief he simply nodded, pulling her inside and closing the door. "I'll get my coat and sword. We'll go at once."

She wanted to faint with relief. He brought a cape to her and swung it over her shoulders. "Should we fetch my friend?"

"No! He would kill Lazare if he knew. Please, just help me get home. Lazare is searching for me."

"*Merde alors!* You wear my hat and try to hide your hair."

Within minutes they were on board a boat, steaming up the river. He had pulled out a bulging bag of jin-gling coins to give to the captain, and as she sat hud-dled in the bow Touzet was laughing and talking to their rotund captain. In minutes Touzet appeared with a glass he held out to her. "It's rum. Take a drink, Miss Therrie, and calm your nerves."

"M'sieu Lacquement, I can never thank you enough."

"You don't need to thank me. I know what you mean

to my wild Irish friend. And he would kill Lazare if he knew what had transpired.''

"But you don't even know what it is Lazare did," she said, drinking the rum.

"No, perhaps you should tell me, and then I could call him out.''

"I can't bear duels! They're barbaric.''

"Women don't understand affairs of honor. They are necessary.'' He grinned. "And they are great excitement for the winners.''

She couldn't smile. The night had been harrowing, and she ached for Rafferty. "M'sieu Lacquement, please give Rafferty a message. My parents won't allow me to talk to him. Please tell him that if I break my engagement, Lazare will kill him.''

"Perhaps after tonight, my Irish friend will challenge Lazare anyway.''

She felt cold, because Touzet was probably correct. He disappeared inside with the captain, and while they rode upriver she had time to think. By now, if Papa had discovered that she had not returned home, she was already compromised, and he would force her to marry Lazare. And she was certain Maman would see to it that he discovered Chantal's absence.

She bit her lip and stared at the black waters that parted ahead of them, listening to the chug of the engine. She had imagined a galloping ride home, and the possibility of a steamboat hadn't occurred. *Rafferty.* She longed for the haven of his strong arms, his help, his cool thinking, because it might already be too late to save herself from marriage to Lazare. Her mind worried with the problem, and then when a possibility came, she began to unpin her hair.

As they turned into the darkened, deserted landing at Belle Destin, she faced Touzet and gripped his hand.

"M'sieu Lacquement, I suspect my stepmother has already alerted my father to my absence, because this would bring about my marriage to M'sieu Galliard.''

"Mon Dieu!"

"I have a plan. I'll tell you as we go.''

"And you need me for this plan,'' he said with a

long sigh. "Very well." He spoke to the captain, and took her arm to go ashore. As they stepped onto land, Chantal caught his wrist.

"Wait a moment." She walked to the river's edge and ducked her head into the muddy water, withdrawing it instantly. Touzet caught her around the waist, yanking her away from the water.

"*Sacrebleu!* I thought you were going to drown yourself!" he exclaimed, clutching his heart. "Your head is hot?"

"I'm all right. I wanted my hair wet with river water," she said. "Now here's what we'll do." As she talked they approached the house, where lights shone in all the windows. Touzet wrung his hands.

"*Mon dieu!* My Irish friend has put me here!" he exclaimed, pausing a moment while he stared at the house.

"M'sieu Lacquement, I'll be in your debt forever."

"Do not concern yourself, *ma chèrie*, I will do this for you, and then M'sieu O'Brien can buy me a round of drinks tomorrow night. If I live to see him again . . ."

"There's the tree." She leaned forward and kissed his cheek and squeezed his hand. *"Merci."*

"Dépêches-toi," he said, and placed his hands over his eyes and turned his back. She pulled off her clothes quickly and dropped them, stepping behind a bush.

"I'm ready."

He gathered up the clothing. *"Un instant, je vous prie, ma chèrie,"* he said without looking her way. Then he was gone at a trot, and seconds later went up the tree with the agility of a wiry monkey. Chantal looked at the lights and saw Maman cross the parlor. Amity's room was dark, and she wondered whether Amity was in bed or in the parlor with Maman. And where was Papa? That was the question of importance.

Touzet came down the tree and ran around the corner of the house; he went to the rain barrel as she had instructed, and within minutes he had returned and dropped a bundle with a plop. He was off and running. *"Au revoir!"*

She grabbed up the wet clothes to pull them on with

shaking hands. He had followed her directions, and she had what she needed. She threw the dry cape around her shoulders and ran toward the front of the house and up the stairs, trailing water across the floor, knowing traces of mud would show in her hair from the dip in the river. She rushed inside the parlor.

Maman, Amity, and William turned to stare at her.

"Chantal!" Maman exclaimed, her gaze going over Chantal. "What on earth?" she asked, sounding shocked.

Amity recovered first. "Chantal, what happened? Papa has gone to town to search for you."

"To town? Why would he go to town? I was in bed until a short time ago," she said, as William left the room. He glanced at her as he passed, and his eyes were round and full of curiosity.

"Where have you been?" Maman snapped. Her face was white, all color drained from it, and she stared at Chantal with an open mouth.

"It was hot, and I've been to the river to swim."

"To swim!" Maman exclaimed, blinking. It was the first time Chantal had ever seen her at a loss.

"You don't know how to swim! And it's not hot!" Amity exclaimed, then bit her lip.

"Yes, I do know how to swim. I learned a while back when I fell into the river on a morning ride. I just swam out, and so I tried again. Now I'm not afraid of water."

"Where's Lazare?" Maman asked.

"He brought me home behind you and Papa. I went to bed and couldn't sleep, so I went for a swim."

"A gator could get you!" Maman said, still staring at Chantal, her voice puzzled.

"You swim with snakes, like the one that bit me," Amity said.

"You were beating that snake with a stick," Chantal replied dryly. "When I splash around, snakes go away."

"What about gators?" Maman asked, and shivered. "You *swim,* Chantal? Your father will have apoplexy!

And it's December! My God, you're with snakes and gators and fish and turtles in that filthy river!''

"Anything could happen in the dark," Amity said while Maman stared at her.

"Lazare brought you straight home?" she said, sounding puzzled. "We should have seen you."

"He wanted to take me to the townhouse, but I insisted that you and Papa were returning here, so he brought me home."

Maman bit her lip and frowned, color returning, and an angry spark came into her eyes. "Lord, you're trouble!" Maman snapped.

"Then I shall stop being trouble. I'll go upstairs to bed. I'm cool, and it's a pleasant night, and I'm very tired now. I'm sorry Papa had to go to town for no purpose."

She went past Maman quickly and to her room, to change to a cotton gown and climb into bed. William and Amity, as well as Maman, had seen her come in dripping wet. Lazare wouldn't dare to tell what he had done, or how badly it had ended. But he would hate her for this night.

With her damp hair spread on the pillow, Chantal lay in the dark and listened to sounds. In minutes she heard a horse go down the drive, and guessed that Maman had sent word to town that she was home.

She sighed with relief when she thought of how close she had come to having to marry Lazare. And now she couldn't bear to wed him. His very touch made her flesh crawl. Her heart was completely Rafferty O'Brien's. And fear filled her for Rafferty, because now Lazare would try to kill him.

She bit her lip and turned to the window, longing desperately to talk to Rafferty, wishing she could be in the haven of his strong arms.

Chapter 22

"I'll raise you," Rafe drawled, looking at his hand of three tens. The last two hands had been a straight flush and a full house and he had won; he intended to bluff his way through this one, and the only other man still playing was Fermin. Rafe forced his attention to his cards, but the flesh on the back of his neck crawled, and every muscle tensed in readiness for a fight. He wore his Colt Dragoon .44-caliber six-shot revolver, with its eight-inch barrel and wood grip. It was tucked into a special shoulder holster he had designed and then had made by a harness maker. He added a clip spring around the cylinder of the revolver, to hold the Colt in place. The seam was open on the holster so he could withdraw the revolver in one quick movement, and he had spent hours practicing firing it. Now he had to fight the urge to reach under his coat and touch it.

For ten minutes Lazare Galliard and two of his friends had been in Jolie's place. They were to Rafe's left at the bar. For the past four nights, since Touzet had told him about Chantal, Rafe had gambled at the Elkins and Jolie's, both of them Lazare's haunts, hoping Lazare would challenge him. Twice Lazare had been at the Elkins, but across the room and involved in vingt-et-un, and he had ignored Rafe. With a deep breath Rafe moved his arm and felt the bulge of the pistol in his holster beneath his coat. The bowie knife was strapped inside his boot, but he wanted to fight Lazare with his fists.

Fermin studied his hand, glancing at Rafe, clamping his lips together. Rafe inhaled and relaxed, looking at the pile of money in the center of the table, glancing at the men waiting.

"I'll fold," Fermin said in a reluctant tone.

Rafe folded his hand and scooped up his winnings. Anger boiled, and he fought the urge to cross the few yards and slam his fist into Galliard's face. When Touzet had told him what Lazare had attempted with Chantal, Rafe had found it difficult to bide his time.

"Jolie, you're getting careless," Lazare began, in a loud voice that carried above the noise of the men and the piano. Rafe felt a tingle of anticipation. "Letting such riffraff in your place—an Irishman factor who cheats, and who's an abolitionist to boot."

Rafe pushed back his chair and stood, pocketing his winnings. Touzet moved beside Rafe, while men around them grew silent. The piano made the only sound as talk died all over the room.

"Mr. Galliard, I don't want a fight," Jolie said.

"You won't have a fight, Jolie sweet. The man's a coward as well."

"My friend, come away with me," Touzet urged Rafe.

"I'm enjoying myself, Touzet, and I'm in no danger," Rafe said, turning to face Galliard, looking into his pale eyes. "There are men in town who never issue challenges, because they fear their opponent may name a weapon other than their favorite," he said in a quiet voice.

Lazare's face was suffused with crimson, and he stalked over to Rafe to slap him with the back of his hand. "Under the oaks, Sunday morning at dawn. *Name* your weapon!" he snapped. "Unless you're too cowardly to do anything except use your fists."

"I'll be there," Rafe said, and heard Touzet groan. He saw the glitter of triumph in Lazare's eyes.

"And the weapons? Pistols or rapiers? Broadswords or knives?"

Rafe had long ago decided what weapon he would name when Lazare challenged him—one long familiar to Irishmen who didn't relish fancy footwork with swords. "Clubs, Galliard."

"Mon dieu!" Touzet cried behind him, as Lazare frowned.

"So we will fight our duel," Rafe said. "Until then . . ."

Stepping forward, Rafe clenched his fist and hit Lazare as hard as he could, slamming his fist into Lazare's jaw.

Lazare crashed back over a table and chairs, scattering men and cards.

Ignoring him, Rafe winked at Jolie and left, feeling a grim satisfaction at the momentary shock he had seen on his adversary's face. It was a brief triumph. Lazare Galliard was taller, had a longer reach, and outweighed him. But each would fight with equal anger and hatred. Rafe and Touzet strode outside and turned down the street.

"Rafferty!" Jolie held her skirts and ran to him, placing her hand on his arm. "Please reconsider this folly!"

He was touched by her concern. "Jolie, I've waited for this since my first month in New Orleans. Don't worry about me."

"I will worry! And Chantal will be sick with worry! You told me she intends to break the engagement. Don't do this when you are on the verge of winning her! You will both be hurt!"

He hugged Jolie, feeling a knot in his chest. "Jolie, friends like you are one of the best parts of a man's life. Thank you for your concern. I'll be all right. Now don't worry."

"Jolie!" a woman who worked for Jolie called from the doorway.

She sighed and turned to go back inside, while Rafe strode away, glancing at Touzet. "She's right," Touzet said. "Now you have done it, my foolish friend," he added, dancing alongside him and trying to keep pace with Rafe's angry strides. "Clubs! *Merde alors,* the town will reel with shock! No one fights with clubs!"

"He didn't say no."

"But it simply isn't done! It isn't a gentleman's weapon!"

"To hell with that. The whole point of a duel is to try to kill each other. You can do that with a club, and if you've spent much time in the Irish Channel you know we're accustomed to fists and clubs. Fancy swords are for the French. The Irish get right to it."

"*Mon dieu!* I cannot believe you would do this! My pupil! My reputation! With rapiers, you could win! You fence as well as Galliard!"

Rafe looked at him, his anger momentarily abating. "You've never told me you thought I could hold my own with him."

"I wanted you to keep trying. You must not get cocky. *Mon dieu,* clubs! That's barbaric!"

"Killing isn't? The bastard deserves what he's going to get."

"*Mon dieu!* The whole town will be there. Perhaps I could charge them to watch!"

Rafe glanced at him, and Touzet shrugged. "I'm not serious. I have to be your second. Where will you get a club?"

"I'll break a table leg," Rafe said grimly, and Touzet clutched his head and moaned as he continued to trot alongside Rafe.

"There are no rules for clubs. Suppose he takes a piano leg?"

"A club is a club. If he has a piano leg and I have a table leg, I'll still take on the son of a bitch."

"It is so messy, so ungentlemanly, so primitive! People will love it. You will be famous all up and down the river: The Man Who Duelled with Clubs. We can put it on your tombstone. You must ask that the first drop of blood ends the duel. If he agrees, then as soon as one of you bashes the other, it is over. I don't think Lazare will want to battle to the death when it is clubs."

"I'll battle until he apologizes."

"*Merde alors!* No! He never will."

"Then we'll bury him."

"And Chantal Therrie will despise you!"

"You think that, after what he tried to do to her?"

"When a man dies, he becomes a saint. I've had more experience with women than you."

"Dammit, she should know I don't have any choice." He raked his fingers through his hair. "I have to kill Galliard or he will kill me."

"Ah, my poor friend, you've got yourself into it this time! If you kill him, she will hate you. If you don't kill him, he will kill you. I will visit you in St. Louis Cemetery. Or I can help you pack and flee. Or you can change to rapiers, and ask that the first drawing of blood ends the affair."

"No, I'll fight with a club. She isn't in love with him, so I'll win her forgiveness."

"If you're alive to do so. Clubs! The weapon of barbarians! *Mon dieu,* my reputation is ruined, because the town knows you're my pupil!"

Rafe rubbed his knuckles. "Whatever happens, it felt damned good to hit him. Now I'm going to send a message to Ormonde Therrie. I don't want Chantal to get word about the duel until it's over. I think her father will agree."

"With Mam'selle Therrie, I think you do the right thing. Most women would sit home and cry and faint and wring their hands, but this one—ayee!"

Rafe's smile was fleeting. "Lord, I miss seeing her, Touzet."

Sunday morning, mist rose and swirled, and the sky was overcast, rain threatening. Rafe and Touzet rode in Rafe's new G. & D. Cook & Company buggy, the Pride of the South. Touzet had insisted they take the carriage rather than ride their horses, because if Rafe was badly injured they might need the carriage to get him to a hospital. Touzet had brought along his doctor.

As the carriage swayed, Touzet clutched his sword and a box with a brace of pistols. Rafe held the club in his hand; he had bought a sideboard from someone in the Irish Channel and hauled it home and cut off one leg. He had grooved out an indentation for his hand to give him a firm grip. Now he ran his hand over the smooth, dark brown walnut; the leg was thicker than

Touzet's arm and fully three feet long, with three balls along its length. Rafe shifted his attention outside, thinking that he had met Chantal while working on this very road so long ago. He would duel with the fiancé of the woman he loved; yet he couldn't believe that Chantal felt even a hint of love for Lazare now.

Chantal. Lord, how he missed her—her hot kisses, her softness, her laughter, her dimples, her sparkling black eyes that a man could lose himself in when passion heated their dark depths. He looked outside but saw only her soft lips, her eyes looking at him with heated desire. For once, all sides were in agreement that Chantal shouldn't know about this duel.

Life would never be commonplace for the man who won Chantal's love. Thank God he could trust Ormonde Therrie to keep her shut away at Belle Destin.

Sleep wouldn't come, and Chantal stared into darkness. The night was cloudy, mist rising and surrounding the house. She was to go on a sortie Friday night with Lazare. Papa and Maman would accompany them; since Papa's midnight ride to town, Chantal suspected she would not have to concern herself about being alone with Lazare again.

Even so, she dreaded every moment she would have to spend with him. And now it would be worse, because he knew she did not love him. Lazare frightened her now, because he would get his revenge for her rejection. He was arrogant and strong-willed and demanding. She felt tense as she stared into darkness, the outlines of furniture blurred through mosquito netting. She didn't love him and she never would. Never. Her heart long ago had been won by Rafferty.

A key scraped in the lock. Chantal frowned and sat up in bed, staring at the door. Someone had just locked her door. She stared at the door for minutes, but there wasn't another sound. She pushed back the covers and climbed out of bed, moving soundlessly on bare feet. With care she turned the porcelain knob and pulled.

She frowned and stared at it. Why would anyone lock her in her room in the dead of night? Papa clearly would have declared his purpose if he had done it. *Maman*—this was her devious doing, but why? What was her purpose?

She pulled again, as if to reassure herself it had not been her imagination. She moved to the windows, walking slowly past them and gazing out at the misty yard. Fog hung over Belle Destin, obliterating everything except the oak beside her window.

Why had she been locked in her room at night? Something was happening, yet everything was quiet outside. There were no horses, no voices, no men. Tomorrow was Sunday morning. Chantal sat down to think about it.

Why would Maman lock me in my room? Tomorrow when it is time for the family to assemble for prayer, Papa will send for me. Why, between now and that time, would Maman want me locked in my room? Papa isn't up north. He's right here in the house. If I scream someone will come, and Maman has to be aware of that. Unless Papa has agreed I should be locked up. Why? What reason could they both have to slip up in the dead of night and lock me in when I shouldn't have known about it? What could they hope to hide from me in the few hours of night that remain?

She stared at the mist, wondering where Rafferty was and what he was doing. Had Touzet told him about the evening with Lazare? Had he given Rafferty the message that if she broke her engagement, Lazare would try to kill him?

Ten minutes later her head came up. She jumped up and ran to the wardrobe to throw open the doors and find what she wanted to wear, selecting her blue riding dress. If Lazare or Rafferty had challenged the other to a duel, Papa and Maman would not want her to witness it.

She dressed swiftly, brushing and tying her hair behind her head with a blue silk ribbon, not taking the time to fasten a bonnet on her head.

Within minutes she was climbing down the oak, then moving to the window to push it open and climb into

Papa's office. She moved to the desk and opened it, taking out his brace of dueling pistols.

She slipped out of the window and ran away from the house, taking a circuitous route to the overseer's house and running across the porch to knock on the door.

It opened, and Caleb faced her. His chest and feet were bare, the top button of his pants unfastened. He raked his hand through his hair and frowned.

"Miss Therrie!" He looked toward the big house and pulled her inside to close the door.

"Where's Rafferty?"

He stared at her and shifted. "Ma'am, does your father know you're here?"

"Caleb, please! Maman locked me in my room. I heard the key. I know the only reason they would do this is a duel."

"I'm not supposed to tell you," he said in a low voice. "Your father told me not to tell you, and Rafferty told me not to."

"Get me a horse or carriage."

He groaned. "Damn—sorry—no. I'd lose my job, and Rafferty would whip me to jelly."

"Are you going to sit by and let your brother die?"

"Miss Therrie, I don't expect Rafe to be the one to lose."

"Are you going?"

"Yes, ma'am."

She turned to yank open the door, and he slammed it shut. "Ma'am, I have to agree with your father. Go back to the house."

"No! I'm going to the duel! Lazare duels under the oaks. If you or Papa won't go with me, I'll go alone."

Caleb stared at her. "Miss Chantal, you can't go alone at night on the river road. Sit down here and let me get a carriage, and I'll take you to see him."

"How early are they fighting?"

"At dawn, when it's light enough to see."

She nodded and moved to a chair. "Please hurry, Caleb."

"Yes, ma'am. Let me get my shirt."

Minutes later he walked through the room. "I'll be back with the carriage. It'll take some time, ma'am, to get the horses hitched."

She nodded while he went outside and closed the door. As soon as he was gone, she went to the window. Mist swallowed him up, and she couldn't see him. She stared with an uneasy feeling. Had he gone to get a carriage, or gone to get her father? Caleb clearly didn't approve of her going to the duel either, but suddenly he had capitulated, offering to escort her without argument.

She left the house, closing the door quietly and going down the steps.

It was dark and quiet, and she felt a prickle of apprehension. She was now sure that Caleb had gone for her father, and she knew she would have only a few minutes' start on them. She hurried to the stable to get her horse, slipping on the halter with shaking hands.

She was leading him toward the door when a man loomed in front of her.

"Get out of my way!"

"Miss Therrie!"

"Giraud, thank heavens! Help me!"

"Sakes, Miss Therrie, what are you up to at this time of night?"

"I have to get to town. Get a fast horse and come with me."

"Ma'am, your father told me I'm not to obey you and go against my good judgment hereafter when—"

"Are you sending me out in the night alone?"

"Oh, my sakes, ma'am!"

"Get out of the way! I have a pistol, Giraud!"

"Yes, ma'am. I'll get a horse. I can't allow you to go alone."

"You get him fast and catch up with me. I'm not waiting, Giraud. Papa won't be far behind."

"Oh, my sakes! Please, Miss Therrie—"

Riding astride she passed him, turning Caesar for the road and urging him to a gallop, one pistol tucked into the waistband of her skirt beneath her jacket, the other clutched in her hand. In minutes she heard hoof-beats, and Giraud caught up with her. They raced along the Belle Destin road until they turned onto the river road. Both had horses that could maintain a killing pace, and Papa wasn't going to catch her. Finally she slowed.

"Ma'am. We should take a carriage. All those men are going to be in a fit if they see you ride up like this."

"I'm not going back, Giraud. Mister Caleb has gone to tell Papa that I'm going to the duel."

"Oh, Lordy! How I wish you'd go back and talk to your Papa about this. Miss Chantal, you're putting years on me."

"I don't want to hear another word about it!" She wheeled her horse to face him. "I'd hate to hurt you, but I have a pistol. I'll tell Papa I ordered you to accompany me."

"Thank you, ma'am."

"You can get me there if we cut across country, instead of taking the river road."

"Ma'am, we're going to be early anyway."

"Giraud, my father and Lazare's father and possibly Lazare will be on this road. We're going across country and you're to lead the way, because I know you can do it. I'll go alone if you won't do this."

"Supposin' I get lost?"

"You won't."

He turned his horse and moved ahead of her, and they left the river road.

Rafe's carriage slowed as it crossed Bayou St. John and headed toward the oaks. When it stopped, Rafe emerged with Touzet and the doctor following, Touzet carrying the club that was to be Rafe's weapon. A few spectators had already arrived, waiting in silence, reminding Rafe of vultures perched high waiting for a kill.

Rafe pulled off his coat and removed his collar and silk tie. He wore a full-sleeved white shirt which he opened at the collar, then ripped open across his chest to give him freedom of movement. He inhaled deeply, feeling a steady undercurrent of excitement. He had waited since the afternoon he had stepped in front of Chantal's horse to get a chance at Lazare Galliard.

Carriage wheels rumbled and harnesses jingled as three carriages rolled through the mist into view. The first phaeton had a leaping brass lion on the side, with brass trim and red wheels. Lazare Galliard stepped down and glanced at Rafe. Dressed in fawn-colored trousers and a dark brown frock coat with a red silk cravat, he looked ready for a night on the town rather than a duel. He removed his top hat and cape, his coat and cravat, handing them to a waiting servant. He picked up a gnarled club and glanced across the field at Rafe.

Rafe guessed the club was oak, and it looked fully three feet long. Galliard handed the club to his second. A white-haired man moved to Lazare's side. He was inches shorter than Galliard but with the same prominent features, the same large head, white muttonchops, protruding eyes, and bulbous nose above thick lips. The elder Galliard. Rafe hated them all, for they stood in the way of his marriage to Chantal.

As the formal procedures were followed, the seconds conferring, Rafe heard the approach of more carriages. While an audience gathered, a familiar carriage and two men on horseback came into sight. Caleb rode to Rafe as the Therrie carriage halted near the Galliards.

Caleb's face was flushed, his hair a tangle of curls, and the instant Rafe looked into his brother's eyes he knew something was wrong.

"She knows you're going to fight, and she left ahead of us," Caleb said.

Rafe felt a tingle of apprehension, his gaze sweeping the scene—the majestic oaks with their long-reaching limbs, the carriages and men standing in hushed clusters, the damnable swirling fog that could hide anyone or anything beyond the immediate circle of vision.

"Where the hell is she then, if she left ahead? Is she alone, Caleb?" he said, fear tightening in him as he thought about Chantal on the river road alone in the dark.

"No. When we saddled the horses, Giraud was gone. She's on Caesar, Giraud is on Thor."

"She's had time to get here, unless Giraud misled her," he said, his gaze sweeping the area once more. Relief came, because Rafe suspected Giraud was following his owner's orders and Giraud and Chantal would appear long after the duel had ended.

"He's a slave. Why wouldn't he obey her and bring her here?"

"He was miserable after the incident in town. Ormonde Therrie told him to use his own good judgment the next time she tried to involve him in something dangerous, and to keep her out of trouble."

"I wish I'd known! I ran the legs off Odin."

"How the hell did she learn about this?"

"Mrs. Therrie locked her in her room. Chantal heard the key turn and finally guessed the reason. When she came to me, I told her to wait while I got a carriage. I went to get Mr. Therrie and when we got back, she was gone."

"Just pray Giraud keeps her riding in circles. I don't want her to witness this."

The crowd was growing larger; Ormonde Therrie stood talking to the Galliard men.

"I thought he would stop over here with you," Caleb said, his hands on his hips.

"At the moment, that's his future son-in-law. He's where he should be, and I don't hold any animosity for it."

"I wish I could join you in the fight."

Rafe looked at Caleb, and they both grinned. Touzet walked up and slapped his forehead. "Ayee, *merde alors*, don't laugh! It's bad luck! But I'm glad you're here," he said to Caleb, then turned to Rafe.

"I've talked to Lazare Galliard's second, Phillipe Duval. He will not consent to end this with the first bloodshed." Touzet's face was creased in a frown, his eyes full of worry. "*Mon compère*, I beg of you to change this choice of weapons! It is not too late to

request pistols or rapiers. This will be a slow, agoniz-
ing, and painful matter.''

Rafe looked at Touzet, and the Frenchman clamped
his lips shut. He turned to walk to Lazare's second. In
minutes he was back.

''It is time, my Irish friend. You will stand with
your back to Lazare Galliard. We will call out five
paces and then you turn and the duel begins. Both of
you have stated the duel will be until death.''

Rafe glanced around the ring of men and then looked
over Touzet's head at Caleb, who gave him a cocky,
crooked smile. Through the mist Rafe walked out to
meet Lazare and let go all the pent-up rage and anger.
He thought about Lazare's attempt to take Chantal by
force, to compromise her, and of all the times he had
wanted to fight Lazare.

As they came face to face only inches apart, he
looked into pale eyes that held the same contempt and
hatred that he felt.

''Remember, Galliard, the first blow is for what you
tried after the ball.''

''You filthy scum. I shall bash out your brains and
bed Chantal, and she will pay a hundred times over
for that night.'' Rafe drew his breath and turned his
back. At last he could take on Galliard.

''One!'' Touzet called, and they took a long step.

''Two, three, four, five! Now, commence!''

Rafe turned, to see that they were yards apart. He
crouched, the club held up, moving in, as Lazare also
came forward cautiously. Suddenly Lazare lunged forward and swung the club.

Rafe ducked and jerked away, feeling the wind whip
past as the club raked across his cheekbone and ripped
away flesh.

Rafe swung upward, catching Lazare solidly on the
hip, hearing the slam of the club against Lazare's bone,
a grunt of pain. Lazare's club swung again, coming
down. Rafe twisted and the blow caught him on the
shoulder. Pain shot down his arm.

He waded into Lazare, swinging the club and
knocking him off his feet, hitting him across the chest.

With a bellow Lazare lunged up, striking at Rafe, who twisted and used his weapon with the agility of a rapier. Club struck club with a bang that echoed in the stillness.

A shot rang out. "Stop the duel!"

Lazare turned his head, and Rafe glanced in the direction of the voice. He didn't know whether to laugh or swear, but he did know that his rage at Lazare was finally finding an outlet, and he had no intention of stopping the duel to please Chantal.

"Stop at once!" she said. Wearing her blue riding dress and with her hair tied behind her head, Chantal sat astride Caesar and held two pistols pointed at them. She had chosen her place well. Caleb couldn't get to her easily; Ormonde was across the clearing.

"Chantal, this is none of your affair, and I demand you go home!" Lazare snapped.

"I agree," Rafe said. "This isn't your fight or your place, and every man here wants you to return to Belle Destin," he said, looking into her eyes and wanting to shake her for interfering. "Stop protecting him, Chantal!"

"Dammit!" Lazare snapped and jerked his head at Ormonde. "Get her out of here!"

"Chantal, go home at once," Ormonde said, his quiet voice carrying authority.

To Rafe's irritation, she raised her chin. "Very well, Papa, I'll go. But first . . ." She looked at Rafe, and he braced for what was coming.

"The man who loves me, who wants my love"—her voice came loud and clear in the stillness—"will put down his weapon and go."

No one murmured or moved. Rafe looked into her eyes and felt the old tension crackling between them. She meant it, yet if he dropped the club he would be branded a coward forever.

"So it seems I have the love of neither one of you," she said, and there was a waver in her voice for the first time.

"This is not a woman's place or her affair, and it

has nothing to do with what we have pledged, Chantal!'' Lazare snapped. ''Now get the hell out of here!''

She gazed at Rafe and lifted her chin. He inhaled deeply and felt regret fill him. He dropped the club, and several men murmured.

''You filthy coward!'' Lazare's voice was the lash of a whip.

''Papa!'' Chantal's voice rose. ''It's plain which man loves me! I beg you to cancel my pledge to marry Lazare Galliard!''

With a snarl Lazare lunged at Rafe, swinging his club. A pistol fired, and dirt kicked up beside Rafe's foot. He felt a sharp sting in his toe.

''Dammit!'' he said under his breath. Lazare stopped and looked at her.

''Get back, or I will shoot you the next time.''

''Gentlemen!'' Ormonde Therrie said, raising his voice so that it carried clearly. ''To my regret, the engagement of Chantal and Lazare, as well as this affair of honor, are over. We'll go home now.''

Rafe glanced at Lazare and knew they would meet on a killing field yet again, but that the next time it wouldn't be an affair of honor, but a swift and violent end for one of them.

''Until next time,'' Rafe said.

''Coward!''

Rafe turned and walked to Chantal. He took the reins of Caleb's horse and swung into the saddle to ride beside her. They turned away together, the mist closing around them as they rode away from the silent men who were climbing back into carriages or mounting horses.

She handed him both pistols, and he tucked them both into the back of his belt. They rode until Rafe felt they were alone and there was no danger anyone had followed them. He reined his horse and swung down, pulling out the pistols to place them on the ground. He felt a cold rage that he tried to control.

''Get down!'' he commanded, taking her reins.

Chapter 23

"I had to stop you." Her heart thudded, because his blue eyes were fiery. She didn't want to get down, because there was a hot rage in his eyes that made her tremble.

"Dammit!" he snapped, and reached up. An arm like steel wrapped around her waist and yanked her off the horse. In a flash she was over Rafe's knees on the ground, his hand coming down on her backside. Fear changed to fury, and she bit his thigh.

"Blast!" he growled, and gave her another whack. Within minutes tears were spilling from her eyes, and finally he stopped and she rolled away, coming up on her knees, both of them gasping for breath.

"I hate you, Rafferty O'Brien!" she cried, looking at the fierce expression on his face, her own anger tempered by fear. This was a man she hadn't seen before, with his glare of rage and his heaving broad chest.

"You trouble-making harridan! You're a meddling little witch, and that's what you deserve!"

"You're a ruffian and a bully!" she snapped back. "You can go straight to hell, Rafferty O'Brien, for all the trouble and heartache you've caused! You're the Devil himself!" She jumped up and ran for her horse, trying to swing her leg up, but without a step or fence she was unable to reach Caesar's back.

Arms closed around her and she was yanked back. She fought wildly, crying, tears blurring her eyes while she kicked and bit and scratched.

"Dammit to hell!" he snapped, but she heard a change in his voice, and then he turned her. His eyes

sparked with anger and with something else, a look
that made her feel hot. She looked at his full underlip
as his head lowered. And then his mouth was on hers
and he kissed her, wrapping his arms around her and
crushing her to him. She tried to break free, to keep
her mouth closed. She bit his lip and he growled, a
deep sound in his throat.

She twisted away and reached for the horse again.
Rafferty caught her. "Come here, Chantal. We'll settle this."

She kicked him, her toe hitting his shin. "That's
enough!" he roared. He yanked her feet out from under her and she went down. Before she could move he
had caught her dress and ripped it open. He pinned
both wrists above her head, holding them with one
hand, while he knelt to kiss her breasts. Her heart
pounded wildly, feeling as if it would burst against her
rib cage as she looked at his lean hard body, his eyes
that were filled with determination. She felt caught in
a clash of wills, furious with him, *wanting him.* His
shirt was open, and the dark mat of hair across his
muscled chest was inches away as he leaned over her.
He straddled her, her efforts and struggles futile while
she fought the sensations coursing through her.

"I hate you!" she cried, her eyes squeezed shut.

"I adore you, Chantal," he drawled in a husky
voice. "You're a beautiful interfering meddler, and I
absolutely adore you. . . ."

Her fighting stopped, and with a sob she reached for
him. He released her hands and she stroked his shoulders, winding her fingers in his soft black hair as his
mouth covered hers and he kissed her deeply, his
tongue hot, demanding. He bent his head to take her
breast in his mouth, sucking and teasing her nipple
with his tongue, sending fiery sensations coursing
through her.

With a final sob all the anger left her, burned away
to desire and relief that he was safe from the duel. She
clung to him, and then her hands moved down on him,
pulling his shirt free of his trousers while they kissed.
She unfastened his belt and unbuttoned his trousers to

free him from their constraint, while he pushed her
skirts up and opened her batiste Parisian underdrawers
and pulled them down over her pale hips.

He thrust his hard shaft into her, both of them gasping, moving with desperate hunger. She wanted him,
desire burning into ecstasy, consuming her while
Catherine wheels of light danced in her closed eyes
and sensations rocked her.

They clung together and gasped for breath.

"You beat me," she said.

"You deserved it," he whispered. "You shot me in
the foot."

She opened her eyes and stared at the mist hovering
above them. She pushed at him and he turned to look
at her, his mouth curving in a crooked grin.

"I shot you in the foot?" she asked, aghast.

"Yes, love," he answered dryly. "Because of you I
have been run down by a horse, beaten, lost countless
nights of sleep, challenged to a duel, declared a coward in the eyes of all the males of New Orleans, probably of Louisiana, and shot in the foot."

"Rafferty!" she cried, tears spilling over as she
grabbed him and hugged him to her, all the horror and
fright of the past few hours catching up with her. She
shook with sobs and clung to him, realizing after a
moment that he was shaking with suppressed laughter.

"Why are you laughing?" she asked, trying to wipe
her eyes and control her emotions.

"*I'm* the one who was shot, and *you're* the one
who's crying! That's a hell of a turn of events."

"You're too much of a scoundrel! I don't believe
you."

"My sweetness, shall I show you blood?" He rolled
over and sat up, pulling off his boot.

"*Mon dieu!*" she cried. The black stocking was
ripped; both his stocking and foot were red with the
blood that was now oozing from the wound.

"I'm so sorry!" she gasped. "Oh, Rafferty, I'm
sorry! I didn't mean to shoot you!" She threw her
arms around his neck and he toppled backwards, taking her down with him.

"I didn't mean to hurt you. I've never fired a pistol before. And your face! I could kill Lazare for this," she said, looking at Rafferty's skinned cheek.

He grinned. "I think I've fallen in love with ninety pounds of trouble. Let me bind up the wound, and we'll go back to Belle Destin."

"I don't think I can ride back," she said in as haughty a tone as possible, blushing and feeling a ripple of anger toward him. "You've ripped my dress! I'm not certain I want to marry a man who will be so . . ."

He looked at her, and his blue eyes were solemn. "You deserved what you got," he said quietly. "And if you think Lazare Galliard would have resisted beating you, you don't know him at all, Chantal."

She leaned close to him, feeling a fiery anger, "Perhaps I don't regret so much that I shot you!"

"Chantal!"

She jumped up and ran away from him, looking back at him. He glowered at her, then bent his head to work on his foot.

"Look at me, Rafferty O'Brien!" she snapped, struggling to pull her torn bodice together. "How can I go home!"

He raised his head and his gaze moved down slowly over her throat to her breasts. She felt her nipples tauten beneath his gaze. He stood up and walked to her, bending his head to kiss her throat, to push open the bodice and cup her breast and kiss her, and desire was a scalding heat in the center of her being.

In a moment he raised his head. "As much as I'd like to spend the morning here," he said in a raspy voice, "I'd better get you home. And we'll pray this mist holds and you can slip into your room and put on another dress."

She listened to him, but all she could think about was that she was free now to marry Rafferty. She would be able to spend night upon night in his arms; she would be able to touch and kiss him and he would touch and kiss her.

"Ready to go?"

"Now I'm free," she whispered, running her hand along his cheek below ripped flesh.

Something flickered in the depths of his eyes. "We'll marry soon, Chantal," he said in that voice that was so deep and arousing, a tone she could listen to forever. "And when we do, I'll spend the nights kissing and touching you, hour upon hour."

"Rafferty, please . . ." Again she was in his arms.

An hour later he helped her onto her horse and urged Finnian to a fast pace, taking off across open ground the way she had come.

In minutes it hurt to sit in the saddle, and she glared at him.

He glanced at her a few times and when they slowed, he moved closer. "What's wrong, Chantal? If looks could deliver a blow, I would be lying back there on the ground."

"It hurts to ride, and that's your fault."

He arched his brow. "Just remember that the next time you try to stop a duel."

She lifted her chin and urged Caesar to a gallop, clamping her jaw shut as her discomfort increased. They went across the Belle Destin grounds, and he waited several yards from the house while she climbed to her room and returned in a different dress. He left the sycamore he had been leaning against and moved forward to her, placing his hands on her waist.

"I'll talk to your father," Rafferty said.

"Please be careful. Lazare may try to kill you." Fog had changed to light mist; Rafferty's black lashes were damp, and the moisture had tightened the curls in his thick hair. She felt a ripple of fear for the moment when they would part and he would ride back to town. She stood on tiptoe and wound her arms around his neck.

Pulling her into his arms, he kissed her passionately. Minutes passed before she at last pushed against him. "My dress shouldn't look wrinkled. Shall we go find Papa?"

They held hands, and had started toward the front

of the house when they heard shots fired on the road.
A horse pounded up the drive. Rafe's hand went to the
pistol in his belt and he withdrew one, loading it
swiftly. As they drew close to the house, Ormonde
Therrie stepped outside.

Alain reined his prancing horse. "Papa! Papa! I just
got word—South Carolina seceded from the Union
Thursday!"

"My God," Rafferty whispered, slipping his arm
around her waist and pulling her closer.

Chantal looked up at his solemn features and felt a
chill, pressing against him. "Alain looks as if he's just
won a victory, and you look as if you just lost."

"You can't allow it!" Blaise snapped, fighting to
control her blinding rage as she strode back and forth
in the closed parlor while rain drummed against the
window. Her nerves felt stretched raw. "She has to
marry Lazare!"

"I *have* to allow it! It's too late to turn back now.
In front of fifty men, she declared she was not marrying him. There is no way Lazare or his father would
want her now," Ormonde said, raking his fingers
through his hair. He slumped on the sofa, taking a
long drink of whiskey.

"Ormonde, she has thrown away a fortune! Lazare
is the prize catch of all time! He will be governor
someday, possibly more! He could give her the world!
The silly little baggage! You should beat her senseless!"

"It's done, and we'll have to live with it," he said,
standing up. "And the sooner they're married, the
sooner talk will die. February twenty-third is the date
I've set." He poured another drink and threw it down.

"Ormonde, you've allowed this catastrophe! You
hired him! You brought this down on us!"

"Enough!" he yelled, slamming down his empty
glass on the table with a bang. "I've heard enough,
Blaise. It isn't as if she were marrying some penniless
beggar! Dammit, the man is rising in society like a
shooting star. And he's a fine man."

"He can never attain the status of a Galliard! You've ruined everything!" she screeched at him. "She'll be nothing, nobody! She could have had the world. And you helped do this when you brought him to Belle Destin!"

Ormonde crossed the room and slapped her. "Shut your mouth!" he snapped in a quiet voice.

She blinked, placing her hand on her cheek. She glared at him, hating him, shaking with rage for what Chantal had done. Lazare was gone, and the Galliard fortune with it. And the man who had spurned her was entirely to blame.

"You'd better forget Chantal; the South is clamoring for all states to secede, the city is wild with secession talk. If Louisiana leaves the Union, our lives may change. And more immediately, you'd better worry about the rain," Ormonde said, striding past her and picking up his coat. "I haven't seen it rain like this since 1840. Lafourche and Concordia were underwater then. The river took houses in its course."

He slammed the door, and she picked up a vase to heave it after him. It crashed against the wood and broke into pieces. She wanted to scream and break everything in the room.

She rubbed her cheek. "Damn you, Ormonde! You'll regret this!" she said. She picked up another vase to smash it, next yanking up a pillow to rip it to shreds. "Damn you," she said, as feathers floated to the rug around her feet. She looked at the ceiling, thinking about Chantal in her room upstairs.

"I warned you," she said, glaring at the ceiling, seeing Chantal in her mind, "if you didn't marry Lazare, you'd never wed any man. I warned you!" Striding toward the door, she decided she would reveal the secret she had harbored for so many years. It would be revenge to Ormonde as well. God, how could they have let Lazare go?

Blaise paused, her hand on the porcelain doorknob. *Not this way. Let her become engaged to him. Let them think they will find happiness.* Then *tell Chantal.* Blaise laughed aloud, the sound dying in a guttural sound that was almost a sob. *Wait, then tell Chantal. That will be true revenge, when they have more to lose. Yes, that's the way—when learning the truth will hurt Chantal the most. Wait until the news will be the most devastating.*

She heard a hissing noise and turned her head, taking a moment to place the sound. Rain came in driving sheets against the windows. She moved to the window and looked out. Lightning flashed, lending a silvery brilliance to the yard, which was grooved by rivulets of water streaming down the slope toward the river. In the next flash she saw the glitter of the river higher than ever, and she felt a cold fear. If Belle Destin was wiped away it would hurt Ormonde, and consequently she would suffer. She had heard talk about the plantations the river had completely swallowed in years past. They were gone forever, their wealth obliterated by the raging torrent.

Belle Destin was built too near the river's edge. She had seen the Mississippi spread out over the low country for miles. She hugged her arms around her body and shivered, suddenly feeling afraid for herself. There would be time enough later for Chantal.

Caleb swung the shovel, pitching gummy mud onto the levee, swinging back to scoop up more earth, working with rhythm and sweating in spite of the cold rain. The Mississippi was running, rippling and swirling, whole trees and bits of cabins floating past.

Rafe joined them, after staying in town to vote on the secession election the day before on the seventh of January. Rafe, Ormonde, and Lazare had won parish seats to the convention. Orleans Parish's left bank had twenty representative parish seats. Ascension Parish had two representative seats, and one senatorial. Now oozing mud drew Caleb's thoughts back to the levee.

Since the day after Christmas and the Therries' celebration all available men had worked on the levee, but as Caleb looked at the swollen black waters he felt a sense of desperation. The levee was too high, too soft. They were trying to complete another reserve to fall back on if the first gave way, but unless the rain stopped Caleb didn't think the soft mud would hold.

In Ireland they had lived on the sea, on cliffs high above the water. He had seen wild storms and raging waters, but never a swollen river that looked as if it would become a sea from Ascension Parish to Lake Pontchartrain to the Gulf. For days the rising bayou had shifted from green to muddy brown while Spider Creek looked like a raging torrent, cutting new paths on its way to the river. All hands had rushed to strengthen the levee, but it became only a matter of time before it would be impossible to hold back the Mississippi.

"O'Brien!" Ormonde Therrie had a shovel in his hand. "I'm taking ten men and going to the stable! We're not going to hold the river much longer! When it begins to go, get the hands to safety! I'm moving the horses and checking on the women!" he shouted above the noise of rain and rushing water.

He turned away to mount his horse. Caleb looked at Rafferty, who was working as diligently as the rest of them. In minutes a crevasse opened, and water swirled through.

In another ten minutes it broke in three places, and water gushed through the opening until Caleb was ankle-deep in swirling water.

"Get back to the cabins! Get to higher ground! Pass the word!" Caleb shouted and Rafe called downriver, the shouts soon lost from hearing. Caleb and Rafe mounted horses and plodded through water and mud.

Two days later the rain stopped and the waters subsided, and work commenced to repair all the damage. Cotton had already been harvested and it wasn't time yet to plant the new crop, so Belle Destin escaped suffering a crop loss. The landing had broken loose and washed away and would have to be rebuilt, but all the animals and people on Belle Destin had survived the storm.

The roads were rivers of mud, and Saturday night Caleb flagged a sternwheeler and climbed on board to ride downriver to the city. Standing in the wheelhouse with Captain Jefferson, he watched the river swirling around them, the water up and running.

"Have you heard?" Captain Jefferson asked, his blue eyes sparkling with excitement and his black beard bobbing up and down as he talked. "Word's all up and down the river! This week Governor Moore seized federal property in Louisiana!"

"Then we're going to secede. I'm in the militia and we're ready to go. My brother's going to the secession convention."

"I'd place my bets on secession. Mississippi seceded on the ninth, Florida on Thursday. There are fifteen slave states, and I'd think all of them would go together." He was quiet as he navigated past a jam of logs. "Want to give it a try?" he asked Caleb.

"I'll have us on a sandbar within five minutes," Caleb said, crossing to the wheel.

"No, you won't. I'll show you how, and now the river's up. I know this river like I know my own hands. Here, take the wheel. Do you know where we are now?"

Caleb calculated. "We're still in Ascension Parish, about one mile from where the Belle Destin landing was."

"Good. Turn the wheel."

Caleb followed instructions, relishing the feel of the river and the ship, feeling excitement grow as he concentrated on learning what Captain Jefferson told him. This was a big country and he wanted to travel and see it; Rafe had arrived, fallen in love with Chantal and New Orleans, and was ready to put down roots, but Caleb wanted to see other cities.

Would Captain take him on his steamboat? Would he teach him how to pilot a riverboat? If so he would have to tell Rafe good-bye, and Darcy, although Darcy might be allowed to go with him. And would Rafe need him to fight Lazare Galliard? What would happen when both Rafe and Lazare were in Baton Rouge for the secession convention? With a mixed feeling of re-

luctance and eagerness, Caleb decided to give Ormonde Therrie his resignation.

Alain closed the door, shutting out the noise from
the three-story-high trading room in the center of the
Merchants' Exchange. He joined a group of men in
the room on the second floor. Cigar smoke was a haze
in the air as he leaned back in his chair.

"How many men do you think we'll have voting for
immediate secession?"

"We hold eighty seats; the opponents control fifty,
but some of the Cooperationists will be swayed to vote
for secession. There's no question about Jason Hale's
vote, or Patrick LeBlanc, or Benjamin Bonviliau,"
Lazare answered.

"My father will urge caution," Alain said. "And
Rafferty O'Brien will urge remaining with the Union."

Lazare barely heard the conversation swirling around
him as he gazed out one of the long windows. On the
road home from the convention, he would kill Rafferty
O'Brien. God, how he hated him! When he thought of
all the Therrie land he could strangle O'Brien with joy.
Instead, it would be over and done far too quickly—a
shot through the back where the road crossed Bayou
Manchac, then weight the body and push it into the
bayou. If not there, then any likely place would do.

He felt an eager anticipation. He wished he could
be the one to tell Chantal that O'Brien was dead, but
that would be impossible. Let O'Brien wonder all
through the convention when it was coming. Lazare
rubbed his shoulder, which still ached from a blow
from O'Brien's club. Damned barbarian! He would be
out of the way soon enough.

As the first rosy light of dawn warmed the day, Caleb
gathered his things. A knock sounded, and he went
down to find Amity standing outside. Surprised, he
glanced around, knowing her parents wouldn't approve. "Come inside." No one was in sight, and he
closed the door behind her.

Her black hair was brushed and shining, tied with a

pink ribbon behind her head. She wore a pale pink dress and she looked beautiful. He felt a twist of longing as he looked at her.

"Maman told me you were going, that you had quit," she said.

"I was going to tell you good-bye, Amity," he said solemnly. "We'll see each other again. I'll be back, and I'll see you. Rafe and Chantal will marry, so we'll always see each other."

"I brought you a present," she said softly and held out a wooden box tied with a blue silk ribbon. He gazed at it awkwardly, feeling embarrassed. He tugged the silk bow free and pulled away the ribbon to raise the lid of the box. He lifted out a pocket watch with a gold chain and an ornate T engraved on its golden back.

"Amity, this is a fine watch!"

"It was Grand-père's and I loved it as a child, so on my fourteenth birthday he gave it to me and said I could keep it. I want you to have it, Caleb. You're one of my best friends," she said shyly.

"I don't know what to say," he said, blushing and staring at it. "It's an elegant watch, and it was your grandfather's. You should keep it."

"No. It's important to me."

"Thank you," he said, hugging her. "I'll treasure it." He looked around at his things. "Want to walk down to the dock with me?"

"Yes, I planned to see you go."

He nodded and tied up his belongings in a bandanna. He thrust his pistol into his belt, tucked the watch into his pocket, and looked at Amity with a sheepish grin. "I'll have to get a vest to wear the watch."

They walked down the lane to the new landing, which smelled of fresh-cut cypress. In minutes they heard the whistle of the boat and Ormonde Therrie rode into view. Caleb looked at Amity.

"I'll be back before you know it."

"I'm glad." Her father joined them, extending his hand to Caleb.

"Good luck, Caleb," he said as they shook hands. "You've been a good worker, and I'll always be glad to take you back. You take this with you." He thrust a leather packet into Caleb's hands.

Surprised, Caleb looked down and opened it to find it full of money. "Thank you, sir!"

"You've been a big help to me. I suppose you'll be back for the wedding?"

"Yes, sir!"

The whistle blew and the sternwheeler slowed and turned toward the landing, the big paddlewheel churning the water to white froth and black smoke billowing from the two smokestacks.

"Good luck, Caleb," Ormonde Therrie said.

"Good-bye, Mr. Therrie." Caleb looked at Amity, who smiled at him. "Good-bye, Amity. Stay away from water moccasins." Caleb strode up the plank and turned at the rail to wave to Amity and Ormonde.

"Sure you want to leave here?" Captain Jefferson asked Caleb as he came up the stageplank.

"Yes, sir. I'm sure," he answered.

The whistle blew, and Caleb followed Captain Jefferson atop the hurricane deck to the pilothouse. Captain took ahold of the big wheel that was ten feet in diameter and pulled away from the landing. In front of the texas, the quarters for the captain and deck hands, were the twin stacks, belching wood smoke into the air. As they rounded the bend Caleb looked back to see Amity still standing alone on the landing, watching him till he was out of sight, her pink skirt whipping around her slender legs as the wind blew, the opaque brown water of the Mississippi flowing past her. He waved and she waved in return, and then they rounded a bend and she was lost from sight.

Chapter 24

Before she extinguished the lamp and went to bed Chantal touched her wedding dress, with its tiny pearls sewn into the white satin bodice trimmed in Valenciennes lace. She would wear this for Rafferty next month. Her heart beat with eagerness, and she longed to be with him.

An hour later, as she still lay awake in bed, thinking about Rafe, the knob turned, and her door swung open.

"Chantal? Are you asleep?" Maman entered the room. She moved around the room, lighting a lamp. "I want to talk."

Chantal felt a chill of apprehension, because Maman never came to her room late at night. It had to be something urgent. Maman's face was flushed, and Chantal's wariness deepened. Papa was in the city, or Maman wouldn't have come to talk at such a strange hour.

"Your wedding to Rafferty O'Brien is approaching," Maman said, turning at the mantelpiece to face Chantal. "You don't have regrets yet, do you?"

"No. I love him very much," she said, sitting up.

"And you don't realize what you gave up in Lazare. You're so foolish, Chantal, but then I shouldn't have expected any more from you. Your father should have known and been more careful. He's to blame, as surely as there is air to breathe."

Chantal wondered what Maman was leading up to. She waited as Maman looked at her.

"Do you remember, Chantal, when I warned you that if you broke your engagement to Lazare you would never marry anyone?"

"Yes, I remember," she said, frowning because Maman usually carried out her threats.

"Well," Maman said, and her voice became syrupy with a sweetness that seemed all the more evil because of the malice it coated, "I meant what I said. I'm going to share a secret with you, and when I do you won't want to marry Rafferty O'Brien."

Chantal felt cold. Maman looked too smug. Whatever the secret was, it must be dreadful and powerful. Determined she would remain composed, Chantal sat up straighter and clenched her fists.

"Your father goes to our northern plantation almost every month. Do you really think he goes there for business?"

"Yes . . ." Chantal answered cautiously. She had never questioned her father's actions. She couldn't believe there was a mistress, but even if there was, that wouldn't prevent her from marrying Rafferty. "Of course I believe it. That's what he's always said he does."

"Well, he's lying. All these years, he has lied to you."

"I don't believe you," Chantal said, anger kindling. "Why would he lie?"

"There's the important thing, Chantal," Maman said softly, and her eyes were filled with malevolence. "Because, Chantal, he goes to *visit your mother.*"

Chantal felt her heart thud. "My mother is dead! She died in the fire when Belle Destin burned and my sister died!"

"No, Celine didn't die." Maman walked closer and stood over Chantal, placing her hands on her hips. "Your mother was mad. She set fire to Belle Destin, and your sister Honoria perished in the fire, and Ormonde knew he would have to put Celine away. He couldn't bear to place her in an asylum. And he wouldn't have been able to remarry. So he told the world that she had died. And he put her in a house north of here, secluded and fenced with caretakers for her. She's mad, and he has her imprisoned there."

My mother is alive! All these years, my mother has

been alive! "Papa is still married to her?" Chantal whispered, looking up at Maman.

"I'm sure your father got a divorce. It would be so unlike him not to."

"You don't know?"

She shrugged. "We were married in the church. I'm married to him. He would have had grounds to have his marriage to Celine dissolved."

"What did Papa tell you?"

"He didn't tell me anything. I followed him and learned it." Maman leaned close. "If your father learns you know the truth, he'll be devastated. He doesn't know anyone knows. He doesn't know I've learned the truth. Grand-père doesn't know. No one does, except the people who care for Celine. Do you know what it will do to your father if you reveal what I've told you?"

Chantal's head swirled. *My mother is alive. All these years, my mother has lived only a few miles north of here. Papa goes to see her once a month. She is mad. . . .*

"Does Alain know this?"

"No. I'd guess her parents knew, but they're both dead now."

Chantal stood up and rubbed her forehead. She felt hot, suffocating. *My mother is alive. She is mad, and I could inherit it, my children could inherit her madness.* She looked at Maman.

"That's why you've told me, isn't it? Because I could go mad; because I could have children like her."

"Yes. That's a risk you and your precious Rafferty O'Brien will take. Ormonde should have put her in the asylum, but I'm sure he didn't have the heart to do so."

"You were willing for me to take a chance with Lazare."

"I'm willing for you to take it with Rafferty O'Brien," Maman answered with cool satisfaction.

"Suppose you're lying. What proof do I have?"

"You can do just as I did, and follow your father. Only be careful, Chantal, that he doesn't see you, be-

cause it would be a crushing blow to him if he thought
others knew what he had done. He'll go to see her this
Friday.''

"Where is the place?''

"North of Baton Rouge, on the river. Here, Chantal, I've drawn you a map," she said slyly. "You can
see her walk with him on the grounds.''

Maman wasn't lying, that now seemed certain. Rafferty wanted a family more than anything, and if she
had inherited her mother's madness, or if she would
pass it on to her children . . . Chantal closed her eyes.
She felt a tight knot of pain in her heart.

"I don't think you'll want to risk having children
who are mad,'' Maman said softly.

"What about Alain?''

"Diantha has miscarried two babies. Perhaps it's
nature's way of keeping order.''

Chantal moved to the French doors to stare into the
darkness.

"Good night, Chantal.''

"Are you happy now?'' Chantal asked, staring at
Maman and wondering about her stepmother.

"You were so foolish to toss aside Lazare. If Lazare's children had been afflicted, he still would have
showered you with wealth.'' She closed the door.

Chantal felt chilled as she put out the lights. She sat
in the darkness of the gallery looking at the stars overhead, glimpsing the river running past Belle Destin,
thinking about Rafferty. He wanted a family like the
one he now had. Her mother was alive, and mad. How
had her father hidden Celine all these years? As quickly
as the question came, the answer followed. Her father
hid most everything he did. He was taciturn and kept
his affairs to himself. He was willing for all three
of his children to risk marriage, even knowing what he
did. And perhaps it would be safe—but if it wasn't, it
could ruin the lives of all concerned.

She was still on the gallery when dawn came. She
wondered if she would ever sleep again. She went inside and penned a note to Rafferty.

For all formal occasions they were chaperoned now,

but they both knew their favorite places on Belle Destin and they could meet and be alone for a brief time without fear of discovery.

She knew he was trying to cooperate with her father before the wedding, to do what was proper and right so that scandal and talk would die as quickly as possible. She placed her head in her hands and cried, wanting him, but afraid now and wanting to avoid hurting him.

The next morning she waited on the path to the river, and in minutes heard his horse. She wanted one last time with him before she broke their engagement.

He wore an elegant dark brown coat and fawn trousers. Her heart pounded as she dismounted, and when he swung down she ran to throw her arms around him, wanting him this last time with a desperation that made her shake. *The rest of my life I will be without him.*

She turned her head to kiss him, her tongue thrusting over his, tasting him, wanting him to touch and kiss her and wipe out for a few moments the terrible thing that lay between them. She needed to give him freedom.

He raised his head to look at her. "Chantal, you're crying!"

"I haven't seen you for days," she whispered, her throat raw. She hurt so badly. "Kiss me, please, Rafferty. Kiss me."

He bent his head and crushed her in his arms, kissing her. In minutes she felt his hands at the buttons of her dress and when he raised his head, she unfastened his belt.

"Make it last," she whispered, memorizing every feature, the scars, his thick lashes, the mat of hair on his chest. Finally she lay in his arms as he kissed her, moving down her belly, moving between her legs. She moaned, clinging to him, aching to keep him in her arms forever.

When he thrust into her softness, she wrapped her long shapely legs around him and clung to him, running her hands over his strong body, moving with him. "Please, Rafferty . . . I love you. . . ."

"Ahh, Chantal. My love."

Their cries mingled as rapture burst, and for a brief moment she was able to shut out the dark cloud that hovered over them. But as they relaxed, their bodies damp with perspiration, all her worries came rushing back.

As she dressed, she turned to find him watching her. He had pulled on his boots and trousers and held his shirt in his hands. "What is it, Chantal?" His hair was an unruly tangle, his skin copper over taut muscles, and he looked marvelous.

She raised her chin, hurting so badly she could barely breathe. "We can't marry. There's no use arguing with me, Rafferty. I don't want to marry you."

"You don't mean one damn word of what you're saying! You're about to cry, and you've been crying." His voice softened and he moved toward her. "Now, honey, tell me what it is. What's wrong?"

"No. I'm not going to tell you because it would hurt my family dreadfully, it would hurt you and it would hurt me. Don't pursue it, Rafferty. You'll forget, and you'll love someone else and you'll be happy."

"That's a bunch of damned nonsense!" He placed his hands on her shoulders and tilted her face up. She closed her eyes so she wouldn't have to look at him.

"Chantal, you can't break the engagement without telling me why. And I *won't* forget, and I *won't* love someone else. Now what *is* all this?"

"Leave me alone, Rafferty! I mean what I say. The engagement is over." She looked up at him. "I made a mistake when we got engaged."

He frowned. "What're you talking about?"

"This isn't what I want."

"Are you going back to Lazare?"

"I don't want to discuss this."

"I don't believe you! You just begged me to love you—you asked, Chantal, you kissed me. After what we just did, can you stand there and say you don't love me? Or want me to love you?"

"That *is* what I'm saying. I wanted one more time, but as far as marriage . . . I made a terrible mistake."

He clamped his lips closed. "You have a hell of a peculiar way of showing me. Are you going back to Lazare? Is your father forcing you to do this?"

She raised her chin. "I don't want to discuss it." She moved away from him and mounted her horse, her back tingling because she expected him to yank her back at any moment.

"Are you riding away just like that? This is it—good-bye?"

She couldn't look back at him, but kicked Caesar and they bounded forward. She rode home at a gallop, right up to the back door, then flung herself off the horse to race inside and tell Loretta to get someone to take care of Caesar and take him to the barn. She raced through the hall and stopped. Maman stood at the foot of the stairs.

She arched her brows and looked at Chantal. "Rafferty O'Brien must be at Belle Destin."

"We're no longer engaged."

"You'll have to explain that to Ormonde, Chantal."

Chantal ran to her room and shut the door. She had done the right thing, but she would have to face Rafferty again. He would never accept the few protests she had just given him. Would she be strong enough to let him go? She sank down on the floor and put her head in her hands.

That night she asked her father if she could see him, and when he had shut the door to his study, she drew a deep breath.

"I've broken off my engagement to Rafferty O'Brien."

His mouth dropped open. "Good God, Chantal! This great love that you threw over Lazare for, and now you don't want Rafferty O'Brien?" Papa's face drained of color, and then the blood rushed back. His cheeks were florid as his temper snapped. "Damnation!"

She raised her chin and stared at him, thinking about

all the years he had hidden her mother away. *Has he hurt over it all this time? Does he still love her, or did their love die years ago?*

"Papa, I can't marry him. Not Rafferty, and not Lazare."

"Why in hell not?"

"There are better uses for my life. I don't want to marry Rafferty O'Brien."

"We'll lose all our friends! You've made a scandal of us already; now the gossips will reel with this bit of news. Dammit, what's wrong with you?"

"I realize I've made terrible mistakes."

"I don't think you can get Lazare back, Chantal."

"I don't want him back."

He frowned and stared at her. "What the devil brought this about?"

"I don't want to marry either man."

"That doesn't make sense! Surely you don't want the life of a spinster."

"At this moment, I do. May I be excused, Papa?"

"Hell, no! Sit down, Chantal. I demand that you tell me what brought about this change."

"I just know what's in my heart. I'm making a mistake."

"We're not going to tell anyone about this yet. God, you could change your mind in three more days!"

"I won't, Papa."

He stared at her a moment, and she could feel the waves of anger. He clenched his fists and turned his back. "Get out!"

She fled to her room and flung herself into the rocker to cry.

Hours later, Amity opened the door. "Chantal? What's wrong? Papa is furious, and won't say why. He left, riding away from here without telling anyone where he was going."

Amity closed the door and moved through the dark room to sit near Chantal. "Chantal, what happened?"

"Amity, if I tell you, will you swear you won't tell? You can't tell Mr. O'Brien or Papa or anyone."

"I won't."

"Are you sure you want to know?" When Amity nodded, Chantal stared beyond her, wiping her eyes. "Maman told me that when Papa goes north, he goes to see Celine, my real mother."

"She's dead!"

"No, she's not. He's hidden her and locked her away. She's mad, and she burned Belle Destin when Honoria died." Chantal told Amity all this rapidly, and when she had finished she looked at her. "So you see why I can't marry Rafferty O'Brien. He's always said a family is the most important thing to him. Suppose I were to marry him, and our children turned out to be like my mother?"

"Oh, Chantal! I can't believe Papa could hide her all this time!"

"It's better than sending her to an institution. You've heard Annette talk about her grandmother. They put her in the asylum, and it was dreadful."

"Alain is married. Papa was willing for you to marry."

"I'm sure he was willing for me to risk marriage. Perhaps it's safe, but we don't know. I just can't do that to Rafferty. He wouldn't do that to me."

Suddenly Amity hugged Chantal. "I'm so sorry!"

Chantal clung to her and cried. "I love him, Amity. It hurts so badly."

Amity leaned away. "You're sure Maman is telling the truth?"

"Yes. She said if I didn't believe her to follow him and I would see, because he walks outside with my mother. I know Maman is telling the truth. She warned me long ago that she knew something that would keep me from marrying if I displeased her. Papa has never once offered to take any of us with him up north, but time and again he has offered to take us with him to the city."

"Chantal, I'm sorry."

"I want a true answer. If you had to make this decision, what would you do?"

Amity turned her head to stare into the darkness.

Finally she looked back. "I would do the same as you have. You can't marry him, not if what Maman says is true."

"But I don't want to live without him!"

They sat in silence, and Chantal wiped tears away. "My mother's parents died years ago; I wonder if they knew what Papa has done. All these years my mother has been alive!"

"Alain's memories of her are good, except that time he got lost along Bayou Canouet. Remember, Chantal?"

"Yes. He said they always told him he wandered off and got lost, and they were frantic searching for him," Chantal said. "Do you suppose she took him there and left him? He remembers going with her, and he's always said she left him and he couldn't find her, and was lost, and everyone told him he had wandered away. Oh, Amity, I can't bear to think I might have children that would have to be put in an institution all their lives!"

"Do you think you can discuss it with Papa?"

"What do *you* think?"

"I suppose not."

"Papa is in a rage. Friends will gossip, and they'll think I'm mad. To be engaged to two men and break both engagements in the same year—I will sound mad."

"Chantal, have you ever seen the asylum? I've heard such dreadful things."

"Annette went once with her mother to visit her grandmother, and later she cried and cried."

"Our poor father! Suppose he's loved her all this time? I know he loves Maman, but suppose he still loves your mother?"

"I've thought of that, Amity. Maybe that's why Papa keeps so much to himself."

"I'm sorry. Maybe we're wrong. Maybe you should tell Mr. O'Brien, and let him make the choice."

"Would you tell the man you love?"

Amity thought it over. "No, I wouldn't. A man would say it doesn't matter, but it could matter dreadfully later. Look at Papa. Oh, Chantal, all these years, every month he goes to see her! Think how that must hurt him! I wonder if Maman hates him for it."

"I don't think so. If she did, she would have done something long ago to stop him."

"That's true. She wasn't going to tell you if you married Lazare. And Alain doesn't know."

"We're not going to tell him, Amity. He and Diantha have lost two babies now, and maybe there will never be one to survive. I don't think we should tell him." They talked about it until the first faint light of dawn, when Amity fell asleep on the floor. Chantal put her head in her arms and cried. "Rafferty, my love. Rafferty . . ."

William stood in the doorway, and Chantal turned away. "Tell Mr. O'Brien that I can't come downstairs and receive company."

"Yes, ma'am," William said. "But he looks as if he might come up here anyway," he added under his breath. As soon as he was gone, Chantal ran for the stairs to the attic. She wouldn't put it past Rafferty to force his way upstairs, and she couldn't bear another confrontation. She hurt so badly, and she loved him and wanted him, and she would never be strong enough again to deny him to his face. Never.

When she had returned to her room, her father was waiting. "Chantal, where the devil have you been?"

"I was in the attic."

"My God! What's going on? Mr. O'Brien is like a wild man! You won't see him, you won't go to town, you look as if you haven't eaten in days!"

"I don't want to marry him," she said stiffly, then clamped her mouth closed. She hurt as if someone had thrust a knife into her.

"Chantal, this isn't the behavior of a normal young woman," he said. His face was ashen and his voice strained. "If you don't give me a logical reason for your actions, I will have to assume . . ." He paused and turned away. "I'll have to assume your mind is going, and I'll get a nurse to stay with you so you won't harm yourself.''

"Papa!'' She stared at him in horror. She took a deep breath and stared at him, wanting to blurt out that she knew the truth. Yet she held back, knowing it would hurt him.

''There's a reason, and a sound one. There's nothing wrong with my mind, but it will hurt someone in the family if I reveal my reason to you. Give me some time to think it over.''

He stared at her with a scowl. ''Chantal, if you would tell me or Rafferty, perhaps we could help. Has Lazare threatened you?''

''Give me some time before we discuss it. I want to make sure I'm doing the right thing.''

''I'll give you time, but if you or Rafferty has been threatened, tell us. Let us help you. Rafferty is sick with worry and hurt. And if you're afraid for him to know, tell me.''

''I'll think about it, Papa,'' she said, and realized she had gained some time. As soon as he had left she moved to the gallery and saw Rafferty riding away. He was tall, his back straight, his hat at an angle. She cried out and clamped her hand over her mouth. Her pulse raced and she wanted to run downstairs and grab the reins and stop him. She wanted to be held in his arms, to have his kisses. Instead she ran to her room and threw herself over her bed to cry.

On Friday afternoon she sat on a horse in a copse of trees, yards from a Louisiana plantation house built on piers with wide stairs leading to the front door. Branches of trees touched the roof, and vines overgrew the gallery. The house had a wide central hall and twin chimneys.

Chantal was taken aback by the bars over the windows. Celine was a prisoner, yet Papa walked with her. A stout fence surrounded grounds that were untended and weed-filled, and Chantal had waited almost a quarter of an hour before continuing behind

Ormonde through the unlocked gate onto the grounds. He had been inside the house for two hours now.

She shifted in the saddle and wondered about her mother, her curiosity having grown each day. Two people came out of the back and descended the stairs. A small pond was behind the house, and a stretch of land between the house, the pond, and the walk had been cleared.

Chantal narrowed her eyes and stared at a woman who was slender and short, with black hair fastened behind her head. She wore a simple brown dress that looked as if it had been made for a servant. Chantal moved with caution, edging closer and finally dismounting, to venture through the trees as close as she dared.

As the couple walked to a bench and sat down, she could hear their voices but she couldn't distinguish their words. Papa's voice was a deep rumble, Celine's light. Once Celine kissed him on the cheek, and Chantal frowned. Did she know who he was? How clear was her mind? Did she still love him? Had Celine done anything violent after the attempt to burn down Belle Destin?

She looked normal and harmless. Chantal moved closer and studied her features intently. Celine was beautiful, with pale skin, large dark brown eyes, and black hair. If she herself looked like her mother, it was impossible for her to discern it. She saw only a faint resemblance to Alain, perhaps in the eyes and cheekbones.

Chantal crept closer, hugging her skirt around her legs, moving with care and crouching down, feeling a guilty twinge for spying on Papa. Yet here was her mother, her real mother, hidden away from her all these years! Celine's voice was high and childish, like a young girl's. "The white bird is the prettiest one on the river, but sometimes when I sit here I see the redbirds, and think they're just as pretty."

"I'll bring another pair of swans when spring comes, Celine. We'll put them here on the pond."

"I'd like that. I'll think of names for them. Help

me name them, Ormonde. There was an old poem I'll have to remember. Part of it went, 'Sabrina fair, listen where thou art sitting, under the glassy, cool, translucent wave, in twisted braids of lilies knitting.' " She turned to Ormonde. "I'll name one Sabrina and name the other Troilus."

As Chantal listened to them talk about the swans, she decided that Celine sounded as rational as Maman or Papa. Could he have put her away because he wanted Blaise? She dismissed the notion as swiftly as it had come. Papa wouldn't have done that, for he had told everyone that Celine and Honoria had both perished in the fire long before he ever met Maman.

As Chantal listened to Celine and Papa, she felt a growing ache. Celine sounded normal. If only she could have visited her occasionally during the years, just known her real mother! There were moments she caught Papa with a faraway, despondent look on his face. Was he thinking about Celine? Did he have regrets about locking her away?

They moved, and Chantal couldn't risk following because the trees thinned in that direction. It was too late to ride back the long miles to Belle Destin. She pulled a blanket off Caesar's back and found a place to sleep for the night. She had brought a small bundle of cold ham and biscuits. By the first light of dawn she mounted and rode home alone, her thoughts in a turmoil. She longed to talk to Celine, just once to talk to her real mother, to get to know her. Would it be impossible? Would it be so wrong?

The next week Papa stopped at the conservatory door as she watered plants. "I'm leaving for the secession convention, Chantal. Rafferty is going with me."

"Take care, Papa." Once she would have raced to him to kiss his cheek and tell him good-bye. Now she stood and gazed at him, her thoughts on Rafferty. He was going to Baton Rouge as a delegate.

"Rafferty is here. I'm leaving now."

As if she had no will of her own, she followed Papa

to the porch. Looking thin and solemn and so handsome, Rafferty sat on his bay with his black hat
squarely on his head. The moment she stepped through
the door, his blue eyes met hers and she couldn't look
away. He stared at her and she felt impaled by his
gaze. Her eyes brimmed with tears and she turned,
groping for the door and running inside, hearing him
call her name.

"Chantal!"

She ran upstairs to her room.

In a few minutes Amity opened the door. "They're
gone, Chantal. I think you're going to have to tell Mr.
O'Brien."

"I'm going to tell Papa, Amity. He said if I don't
give him a logical reason for my actions, my mind
must be going."

"Papa can't think that!"

"Why wouldn't he? He threatened to get a nurse. I
told him I had a good reason, but that someone in the
family will be hurt if I reveal it. He thinks Lazare has
threatened me or Rafferty." She looked outside, aware
that Rafferty was riding north with her father. "I'm
going to have to tell Papa that I know about her, and
I dread doing it. Amity, she's my real mother. I want
to go see her, just see her."

"Do you think she's—" Amity stopped and
frowned.

"Violent? Papa goes to see her every month. I saw
them walking together, and she acted normal and
sounded normal. I just want to talk to her a few minutes."

"I guess I would too. Do you want me to go with
you?"

"You may have to keep Maman occupied. I'll take
William with me to drive the buggy."

"William doesn't know how."

"He'll manage. I'll be careful. This is my chance
to go, while Papa is in Baton Rouge."

Chapter 25

"Abraham Lincoln was elected as a representative of a sectional party opposed to slavery. He seized the opportunity for power, while our Democratic Party is split between the North and the South. Now we have a president-elect who'll push to abolish slavery and abolish the economy of the South! He'll abolish states' rights!" Lazare's voice rang in the chamber.

Rafe shifted in his seat, his gaze going over the fluted and square oak columns. Completed in the fifties, the gothic capitol building was intricate and ornate. He had heard rumors that the architect and the chief mason had had a fist fight on the grounds, and he wondered if it was over the ornate interior. When he returned home, he would force Chantal to see him. Ormonde suspected she was afraid and had been threatened by Lazare. She was so on edge, it shouldn't take much pressure for her to capitulate and reveal what was frightening her. Rafe studied Lazare with his fuzzy muttonchops, and he knew Lazare would try to kill him.

"In 1859, the South furnished almost ninety percent of the cotton on the European market," Lazare continued. "Our production was over four million bales that year, and it keeps growing. Senator James Hammond has said that no one will dare make war on cotton. Without firing a gun and without swords, we'll bring the world to our feet." Lazare waved his hand and looked at the members. "To quote the Senator: 'Cotton is king!' "

There were cheers and claps and thunderous applause. If Lazare had hurt her or threatened her, Rafe

knew he would kill him with joy. He had listened to
Lazare long enough. Rafe stood and was acknowledged by the president of the convention, former Governor Alexander Mouton of Lafayette.

"Cotton *is* king, but cotton depends on a market.
How many miles of rail do we have in the South? About
ten thousand; the North has double the miles. Where
is the coal, the iron, the copper? In the North. Cotton
is king, but we can't eat cotton. Louisiana depends on
the commerce of the Mississippi Valley, on the products and supplies from the Valley. Louisiana is tied
more closely with the states north of here than the
other southern states. Why rush into secession at the
first heated moment, and suffer the consequences of
acting rashly? Already rumors of war are flying. If
war should come, only five states have seceded and
one third of their population is slaves. How many sol-
diers would five states be able to put into the field
against the remaining twenty-eight states in the Union?
I would also remind my colleagues that the United
States Constitution does not grant the right of secession."

There were boos and jeers, led by Lazare standing
up and waving his arm. "Abolitionist! Foreigner!"

James Taliaferro of Catahoula Parish rose to Rafe's
defense. President Mouton banged a gavel for order
and recognized Ormonde Therrie.

"I'm here as a Conditional Unionist. We need to
send the South's grievances to the North, give the
North a chance to meet our demands. I urge you to
consider proposing an amendment to the United States
Constitution to secure the rights of the slave states. If
we can guarantee our rights and remain in the Union,
Louisiana will fare better. Our sugar planters need the
federal tariff; our state needs the Mississippi Valley
commerce; forty percent of the white residents of New
Orleans are immigrants. Another large segment are
northerners who have moved to the city, bankers, brokers, businessmen who do not want to break with the
Union because it will hurt the economy. I urge this

convention to try to secure states' rights and remain in the Union, where we can prosper.''

"I make a motion for a convention in Nashville, Tennessee, of slaveholding state representatives," said Joseph Rozier of New Orleans. "This will be for the purpose of proposing amendments to the United States Constitution for protecting slavery."

While the motion was seconded and the floor opened for discussion, Rafe looked across the room at Lazare. They stared at each other, and Rafe felt a ripple of cold fury. Hatred was still unsettled between them; there would be a time and place. And there would be no more affairs of honor. He wore a pistol beneath his coat and he practiced daily. Judging from the looks Lazare gave him, it wouldn't be long before he gave vent to his rage.

He stared back until Lazare looked away. Lazare's big fist was clenched on the table, and Rafe wished they could have five minutes alone.

His thoughts shifted to Chantal, and what Ormonde Therrie had said to him last night. Had Lazare threatened her? Was that why she had broken the engagement? If that was all, there was a simple solution and one he would welcome. He couldn't understand the change in her, but after talking to Ormonde he felt better. She loved him. He knew that, as surely as he knew he needed air. It was a matter of finding out what she feared and then dealing with it. He could barely go an hour without losing himself in thoughts about her. He longed to hold her and kiss her, feeling an aching void, a physical hunger that swamped him. He remembered loving her on the grass by the river, Chantal in his arms, her long bare legs around him.

His body reacted to his thoughts and he forced his attention to the speaker, another Immediate Secessionist. This group of men would decide the fate of a state. They would vote whether to take Louisiana into secession or keep her in the Union.

By the time of the fourth roll call, this group had defeated delaying motions for amendments to the U.S. Constitution, a second motion by James Fuqua of East

Feliciana Parish calling for an Alabama convention to consider a union of all slaveholding states, and a final motion by Charles Bienvenu that the decision of the convention be submitted to a vote of the people. This was defeated eighty-four to forty-five, with Lazare voting in the opposite camp as Rafe. On the final call on January twenty-sixth, the convention voted for secession by one hundred and thirteen to seventeen. Rafe noted that Ormonde had joined him in voting against secession.

When Rafe went down the steep steps, he was surprised to see Caleb waiting.

"What're you doing here?"

Caleb shrugged. "The boat stopped here and I got off. I thought you might need someone to ride home with you."

Rafe grinned. "I watched my back all the way up here. I plan to do the same going home."

"What was the vote?"

Rafe's grin and good humor at seeing Caleb evaporated. "Louisiana secedes from the Union on the vote of a handful of men. I think it's revolution, and it'll lead to war."

"That's all I hear on the river."

"Now I go home," he said, feeling a pang. "How's Chantal?"

"She's fine, I suppose."

Caleb glanced around and frowned. "You suppose?"

"She told me we can't marry, and she won't tell me why. She won't tell Ormonde, but just before he left home he talked to her, and he thinks Lazare has threatened her life or mine."

"Maybe this trip home will end the problem."

"I wish he would try something and I could end it. It's only four weeks until the date we had planned for our wedding. It seems close, and it seems endlessly far away. I've waited so long for Chantal," he said, determined on the way home to stop at Belle Destin and see her, even if he had to hunt over the entire plantation to find her. She had avoided him for the last time, and he suspected from what Ormonde had told him that once he had the truth from her, they could deal with it and go ahead with their wedding plans.

"Sorry things aren't what they were when I left," Caleb said.

"I think we'll work it out when I get home. I hope I can work it out before we get into war."

"Do you really think war is coming?"

"I don't know. If it does, Caleb, what will you do?"

He grinned. "Get in it, I suppose. Think the South will have a navy?"

"You'd go with the South?"

"Yes. That's all I know. What would you do?"

"I don't know. I don't want to face it until I have to. Maybe the day won't come. Caleb, it'll be dangerous going home. You don't have to come with me."

Caleb grinned. "I wouldn't miss it. I think he'll come after you. Now's the perfect time, when you're traveling."

Rafe shrugged. "You were warned."

They heard hoofbeats, and looked around to see Ormonde Therrie.

"Rafferty, wait a moment. Caleb! I'm glad to see you," he said, dismounting to shake Caleb's hand. "I hope you're returning to Belle Destin."

"Sorry, sir. I thought my brother might like company going home, but the boat will be back to pick me up in a few days."

"If you two don't mind, I'll join you on the ride home too."

Rafe looked at him and met a cool, black-eyed gaze that made him think of Chantal. "Sir, there are ruffians on the road. You might be safer if—"

"I want to see you arrive home safely, and you might be better off if I ride with you. If I may join you two?"

"Yes, of course," Rafe said, wondering if Ormonde Therrie's presence would make any difference to Lazare. He didn't think it would, nor Caleb's for that matter. "I don't want either of you hurt. And riding with me might bring that about."

"We're going to ride home with you," Ormonde said cheerfully. "Right, Caleb?"

"Right, sir," Caleb answered. Rafe smiled, but he felt a knot of worry. Lazare might be bitter enough that he didn't care whether he harmed Ormonde or not. He would cheerfully kill both Caleb and Rafe, and Rafe wished Caleb had stayed on the boat. Darcy was home with servants at Rafe's house, and Rafe had made arrangements through a lawyer for a fund for Darcy, but Darcy needed more than a lawyer and funds at his age. He needed his brothers. Running his finger along the scar on his jaw, Rafe frowned. He had to get Chantal to talk to him. He had to make her reveal the reason she wanted to break their engagement. One thing he knew—he still had her love. Time and again he had remembered the last moments with her and their lovemaking, her desperation that should have warned him she was terrified and hurting over something. She cried constantly, and only a woman in love would have acted the way she did.

He felt better, because there had to be a solution if they both loved each other. Her black eyes and merry laugh danced in his vision, and he wanted to hold her and kiss her. *Chantal, How I miss you. . . .*

As they left Baton Rouge they fanned out, riding far apart, Ormonde and Caleb yards in front of Rafe. Their conversation died and they rode in silence, Rafe straining for any unusual sound, watching the road for any point where ambush would be likely, finding too many places where underbrush and trees were thick on either side of the road.

A bird's call came, high and clear, and the hair on his nape prickled. Ahead was the dark shade beneath the thick trees along Bayou Manchac.

Rafe gave three short, low whistles and Caleb turned to look at him. They exchanged a look and Caleb drew his pistol. Ormonde turned to glance at them. Rafe moved up, closing in closer to Caleb and Ormonde. Ormonde also brandished a pistol now, and all of them continually watched the woods. In minutes the green waters of the bayou came into view, and tall cypresses

draped with moss standing in the quiet water. A snake
rippled through the water, only its head showing, leaving V-shaped waves in its trail. Rafe turned in the
saddle so that he could ride looking behind him. Ahead
the road curved, and he shifted. The bayou thinned,
looking as if it were solid ground, yet he knew it was
water beneath the green. Dark woods were still, with
no leaves stirring and no sounds except occasional bird
whistles far away. They rode back into the sunshine
and Rafe relaxed, placing his pistol in his belt again.

"There isn't another likely spot, and we should get
home safely now," Ormonde said.

As the three men entered Belle Destin, Blaise stood
in the front hall and Amity behind her. Blaise's face
was flushed and her eyes wide.

"You're home earlier than we thought you would be.
Come into the parlor and—"

"Blaise, where is Chantal?" Ormonde asked. Blaise
blinked and glanced at Rafe and Caleb.

"She doesn't feel like seeing company," Blaise answered.

"Get her right now, Amity," Ormonde ordered.
Rafe watched Blaise and saw her eyes widen. She
looked afraid, and he felt a sense of foreboding.

"I can't get her, Papa."

"Ormonde, I need to talk to you in private about
this. If you gentlemen will—"

"Blaise," Ormonde said, his voice cutting across
her words. "I want Chantal here now. Amity, why
can't you get her?"

Blaise looked like a cornered animal, and Rafe's
nape prickled. She stared at Ormonde and bit her lip.

"Blaise," Ormonde said again, and Rafe heard the
quiet threat in his voice.

"She's gone to see her mother," she whispered. "I
wanted to talk to you alone about it, Ormonde," she
said, backing up.

Rafe felt at a loss as he looked first at one, then the
other. Shock coursed through him like a streak of
lightning at the sight of the rage on Ormonde's face.

"She's *where*? She's gone to see *Celine*?"

For one moment Blaise looked into Rafe's eyes, and he realized that whatever had happened to Chantal, Blaise's part in it had been to get at him.

"Dammit, answer me!" Ormonde demanded. Blaise's face drained of color and Amity stepped back, her face pale as snow.

"My God! Rafferty!" Ormonde snapped, and then he was striding for the door. Rafe rushed after him, growing cold with fear at Ormonde's reaction. He didn't understand anything that had happened, but whatever it was, it was terrible. His long strides matched Ormonde's, who talked as they crossed the porch.

"We need fast horses. We'll take fresh ones," he said, turning for the stable and breaking into a run. Rafe glanced at Caleb and ran. Whatever had happened, Chantal must be in terrible danger.

As they saddled the horses, Ormonde explained in terse sentences. "We don't have a moment to lose. Celine is mad, and I put her away up north. I'll explain it all later, but we have to go now. Celine was my first wife. She tried to kill Alain once; she set fire to Belle Destin and Honoria, our second child, died."

They mounted and galloped away, Rafe feeling a cold knot of worry for Chantal, who he knew would want to know her real mother and who would be unafraid to visit her and talk to her. And Blaise wouldn't have warned her of the danger.

His thoughts swirled as he leaned over Finnian: Chantal's mother Celine was alive. And mad. And Blaise had told Chantal without Ormonde's knowledge. Now Rafe felt he knew why she had told him she couldn't marry him. He wanted to crush her in his arms and tell her it didn't matter. That he wasn't afraid. Chantal was normal, Alain had married and led a normal life.

He rode Daedalus; Ormonde and Caleb had the next-best Belle Destin horses and they rode as fast as possible, pushing the animals. But the distance was great, and Ormonde's grim countenance drove Rafe faster. Ormonde knew Celine, and clearly he was in the grip

of fear for Chantal's safety. Rafe prayed that she would
be careful.

Lazare sat in the shadows along the river road, yards
from the turning to Belle Destin. He had followed the
O'Briens and Ormonde from Baton Rouge. He couldn't
take three men without putting himself in danger. He
didn't know about the young O'Brien, but Rafferty was
rumored to be a deadly shot and Ormonde was one
without question.

Either one O'Brien or both would come back down
the road and turn toward the city. O'Brien had probably gone to see Chantal, but sometime today or tonight he would ride past.

Lazare ran his fingers over the butt of his pistol.
What pleasure he would take in killing O'Brien! He
was tempted to give the man a chance to draw on him,
but decided he would get it over and done with. He
shifted in the saddle. For the quarry he hunted, he
could wait hours.

Within the hour he heard horses coming at a gallop.
He drew his pistol and backed his horse farther into
the shadows.

Ormonde and the O'Briens galloped down the Belle
Destin road and turned north, pounding the road.
Where could they be going at such breakneck speed?
Was the South at war? Why would they ride back to
the Capitol? He frowned and replaced his pistol in his
belt. Flicking the reins, he urged his horse after them.

Chapter 26

In the pink light of dawn, Chantal rode in the buggy and stared at the countryside. William would drive her home tonight. He had shuffled his feet, and said he was uncertain about driving the buggy, but he'd had no choice except to obey her.

Sun shone on the dry fields, and as they drove through Baton Rouge they passed the Capitol. Rafferty was inside along with Lazare and Papa, deciding the fate of Louisiana. Rafferty. She couldn't keep running from him, yet she still didn't feel strong enough to face him and tell him why she had broken their engagement. He would never agree with her solution.

After hearing Celine talk to Papa, Chantal had lain awake the past nights questioning her decision. Suppose Celine were normal now? Suppose Papa had put her away too swiftly? Once it had been done and he'd wed Maman, he would have had to keep Celine in the northern house.

Frowning, Chantal stared at houses as they rode out of Baton Rouge. Suppose she didn't need to break her engagement with Rafferty? Papa had to tell her the truth about Celine's condition. When he returned from Baton Rouge, she would ask him. If Celine lived harmlessly, shut away from society yet without any signs of madness through the years . . . Chantal's pulse raced at the thought. If so, she could marry Rafferty. She didn't want to think about it until she knew, because all her hope and joy might be dashed to pieces.

Finally they turned down the narrow lane and, at Chantal's insistence, William broke the lock on the big gates. The lane wound through thick trees and tangles

of weeds, and within minutes she had lost sight of the
road. She was afraid, but if she didn't see Celine now
while Papa was gone he might never allow her to talk
to her mother. She had to, if just once in her life.
Chantal's hands were ice as she stepped out of the
carriage and looked into William's troubled eyes.

"Miss Chantal, your papa sure wouldn't want you
to be at this place. No, ma'am, and he wouldn't want
ol' William here either. Miss Chantal, we should go
home."

"William, I'll tell my father I made you bring me
here. You take the buggy around back and wait. I've
come all this way. I'm not turning around now and
going home," she said, even though her heartbeat had
quickened, and she was frightened.

"Yes, ma'am. But Mista Therrie won't like this at
all."

She patted William's arm. "He'll know I told you
to bring me here. Stop worrying, William." She gazed
into his dark eyes. "I had to come."

"Yes, ma'am, but some things is better left alone."

"You take the buggy around back while I go inside."

"Yes, ma'am."

She climbed the steep steps to the door and raised
the knocker to let it fall. In minutes a black woman
opened it. She wore an apron and a black linsey-
woolsey dress, and Chantal knew she was one of Papa's slaves.

"I'm Miss Therrie. I've come in place of my father.
Mrs. Therrie is my mother, and I want to see her."

The woman stared at her, then looked past her at
the carriage.

"I want to see Mrs. Therrie!" Chantal said sharply.
"She's my mother."

"Yes, ma'am." The woman stepped back, and
Chantal entered the house. It was devoid of the vases
and crystal and ornaments Belle Destin held. Furniture was plain, surfaces polished and bare. "The front
parlor is here," she said, gesturing to her right.

Chantal entered a room that held ornate, heavily

carved furniture, but there were no small vases or fig-
urines or pictures, and this gave her the forlorn feeling
of a house that was being emptied for a move. The
bars on the windows were even more disconcerting.
Feeling uncertain, and fighting an urge to run back to
William, she sat down. This was her mother's home,
and she wanted to see her and talk to her if only once
in her life.

With a faint swish of her brown muslin skirt, Celine
entered the room with the servant behind her. Chantal
stood up. "I'm Chantal Therrie."

"Chantal?" She frowned and moved to a chair with
a graceful, gliding walk. Her plain muslin dress was
clean, worn without hoops, and her dark hair was
parted in the center and caught in a net behind her
head. She was as beautiful as Blaise, but in an entirely
different and more delicate way. Her body was as thin
as a child's. "Won't you sit down? I don't have many
visitors."

"Papa comes to see you."

"Your father?" Celine asked, looking puzzled.

"Yes. My father is Ormonde Therrie."

"You're Ormonde's child," she said, as if she had
never heard of Chantal. You're a half-sister to my Alain
and Honoria. How is Alain?"

"Alain's fine," Chantal said, a tight feeling in her
chest. Celine didn't know her, and while it shouldn't
hurt, it did.

"How's Diantha?"

"She's fine, too," Chantal said, worrying because
Celine didn't know her even as she knew to ask about
Diantha. Yet Celine was able to converse with her, and
in minutes she was telling Celine about her engagement to Lazare.

"Papa pledged that I would marry him when we
were children, but now there is another man I love,
Rafferty O'Brien, so I broke my pledge to Lazare Galliard."

"I remember Andreas Galliard—he liked to dance.
He always smiled."

"He's Lazare's father." As they talked Chantal's curiosity grew, for Celine was easy to talk to and she remembered people. Had Ormonde acted too swiftly and then been unable to reverse his decision? Or was Celine's madness something that came and went in cycles? Or did it underlie an appearance of normalcy? Only Papa had the answers, and it was going to be difficult to confront him, because he wouldn't want to discuss it.

"Ormonde is getting swans for my lake. Would you like to see the lake?"

"Yes," Chantal answered. As they walked to the back door, the servant followed them outside. She kept a constant, close watch on Celine. Were they Ormonde's orders that she stay with Celine?

Chantal's first fears were gone, but as she talked to Celine she felt as if she were talking to a complete stranger instead of her real mother. Beside the small pond where her father had sat and talked to Celine, Chantal seated herself on an iron bench and turned to face Celine. Four ducks swam back and forth, and Celine told her their names.

Celine was so beautiful, with no wrinkles in her skin, yet there was a blankness to her when Chantal talked to her. Conversation centered around the pond, the ducks, the flowers. Perhaps it was because Celine had been shut away from the world for so many years. Chantal felt no tie to her at all. *This is my mother, yet she's a stranger.*

Celine reached up to place her hand against Chantal's cheek. "You're my daughter?"

Chantal nodded, feeling a tight knot in her chest. "Yes, ma'am." She glanced beyond Celine and saw the servant move closer when Celine touched Chantal.

"Here's where Ormonde will bring the swans. I'm glad you came. I haven't seen you for so very long. I'm glad you're here."

"I'm glad I came, too," Chantal said, thinking of how she had dreamed of this woman so many times in the past.

"Would you like to see more of the grounds? I'll show them to you. We have a landing on the river.

Perhaps sometimes you can come with Ormonde by boat. Come with me. Wait until I tell Reseda where we're going,'' Celine said, returning to talk to the servant. Reseda looked at Chantal, who smiled in return. Celine motioned to Chantal to join them, and as she started toward the house Celine turned to talk to Reseda again. Reseda went into the house as Celine returned to Chantal.

"Reseda will be with us in a moment. She's gone to get her shawl. She knows the way. The pond runs into a small creek and it winds to the river,'' Celine said, holding out her hand. Closing over Chantal's hand, Celine's fingers were cool and slender.

They walked along the path around the pond, and as it curved out of sight of the house Chantal glanced back over her shoulder for Reseda. The path was wide and graveled, and she felt secure. They weren't far from the house. Reseda was supposed to follow and Chantal assumed she would, since she had watched them constantly since Chantal's arrival.

The weeds were trimmed back from the path, as if someone regularly used the lane from the river to the house, but bordering the winding path all was wild undergrowth and thick forest.

"Sometimes I sit and watch the boats as they come down the river. I remember watching the boats at Belle Destin. I would take you with me and we would sit on the landing and hear their whistles blow, and you would laugh and want to see them.''

"I was too young to remember.'' Chantal glanced over her shoulder again, wondering what was keeping Reseda, and the first glimmer of worry came. "I think we should go back. They may be looking for us.''

"Come see the landing,'' Celine said, walking faster. "You haven't been with me in so long. You're my baby, and I want to show you the wide river where the big boats travel.''

Chantal went with her. She had no memories of Celine, but she had been only a year old when Belle Destin had burned. "I want you to see the river,'' Celine said.

"I think we should go back. William is waiting."

"Who's William?"

"He drove the buggy, and he'll take me home."

"You belong here," Celine said, smiling at her. "You're my baby. Come look at the river."

"As soon as I look at it, we'll go back," Chantal said firmly, determined she would please Celine with a glimpse of the river, then insist on returning to the house.

"Come with me," Celine said, taking her by the hand. Her voice was cajoling, as if she were talking to a small child.

Brown water swirled past yards beyond them, down a slight slope. The landing was of aged wood and it stood only inches above the river, with a handrail along the walk from the bank. They walked out on the landing until they stood in the open, surrounded by water except for the narrow walk to the bank.

"The river's more narrow here than at Belle Destin," Chantal said. "We have to go back now." She turned to go, but Celine's grip on her hand tightened.

"You said we'd go back to the house as soon as we saw the river." Chantal tried to extract her hand, but Celine held it tightly. Wind blew against her, and she felt alone and uncertain.

"You always like to look at the river, Honoria. Alain should be with us. I want you to see it. Remember when I used to take you to the river?"

Chantal felt cold as Celine smiled at her. "Yes, I remember," Chantal replied. She couldn't pull her hand free.

"We've looked at the water; we must go back now," she said, amazed at Celine's strength.

"I've searched for you, Honoria."

"I have to go back to the house. They're waiting for us, and William will be looking for me," Chantal insisted, trying to keep her voice calm.

"Mrs. Therrie! Mrs. Therrie!" came a call, and Chantal guessed it was Reseda.

"Down here at the river!" Chantal shouted.

"No!" Celine exclaimed. Her smile faded, and she

glanced around. "I'll tell William where you've gone, Honoria. Do you know how long I've waited for you to come see me? It's been so long. You were a naughty child to wait so long, to run and hide from me. I've hunted for you, Honoria."

"I'm not Honoria! I'm Chantal!"

"I want you to stay with me. I want you to stay here at the river, so I'll always know where to find you."

Chantal tried to break free, but Celine's grip was as strong as a man's. She looked fragile and weak but she wasn't, and she was slowly pulling Chantal toward the edge of the landing.

"Celine, don't! I'm not Honoria!" Chantal cried as she struggled.

"Mrs. Therrie!" Reseda called, running into sight along the path, her white apron visible through the trees.

"You're staying here where I can find you, Honoria!" Celine exclaimed. "I won't let them take you from me again!" She released Chantal abruptly, shoving her into the water.

Chantal sank, but she had spent hours in the water with Rafferty. She stopped fighting the water and shot to the top, letting the current carry her, debating whether to strip off the clothes that were dragging her down or try to get to the bank wearing them.

"Honoria, you won't leave me now! You'll be here where I can find you!" Celine cried.

Reseda reached Celine and tried to grab her. Celine pushed Reseda and turned, running toward the water. "Honoria!"

She screamed as she stepped off the landing. Her arms flailed the air and she toppled into the river, dropping out of sight beneath the swirling brown water.

The current was carrying Chantal swiftly downstream. Frightened for Celine, Chantal struggled against the water. She yanked off her skirt and let it go, ripping loose the hoop skirt and pulling off her silk jacket. She fought the current as Celine bobbed to the surface only a few yards back.

As Celine floundered and screamed, Chantal
strained against the current. Celine disappeared beneath the water and then surfaced once more, this time
almost within reach. Chantal plunged through the water and grasped Celine's collar while Celine fought her.
Celine would drown them both if she got a good hold
on her.

Clutching Celine's dress, Chantal towed Celine, letting the current carry them downriver and trying to
work her way toward the shore. She glanced back to
see Reseda running along the bank, but far behind
them. As they swept around a bend, she was lost from
sight.

Celine no longer struggled, so Chantal shifted to
hold Celine beneath her arms. A log was thrust out a
few feet into the river and Chantal swam across the
current to reach it. Her fingers caught on the end and
she pulled. Clinging to it, she worked her way to the
muddy bank. It took long minutes to climb out and
pull Celine out. She lay unconscious, and Chantal
rolled her over and pushed on her back, trying to get
river water from her lungs.

"Reseda, help!" Chantal shouted, seeing Celine
stir.

The woman ran into view and Chantal stood up.
"I'll get help. You watch her," she gasped.

"Yes, ma'am. I can't swim," Reseda said, rolling
her eyes at the river, and Chantal saw she was terrified
of the water.

"Just watch her. I'll hurry." She ran through the
trees to get back to the path to the house. Wondering
if she had lost her way, she looked around, unable to
spot the path or the river or the house.

"Help! Please, help!" she cried.

"Chantal!" The deep voice that called to her made
her stop in shock.

Rafferty! "Here I am!" she cried, running toward
the sound of his voice, and then he was there. Through
the trees he hurried toward her.

"Rafferty!" Pushing aside brambles, she threw herself into his arms. He crushed her to him, bending his

head to kiss her. For a moment she forgot everything else except him. She clung to his strong shoulders, weeping, wanting to hold him and never let go.

Then she remembered Celine and looked up at him. "Rafferty, Celine's down by the river. She may go back in the water. . . ."

"Where, Chantal?" Ormonde asked, and she looked up as Papa and Caleb pushed their way through the bushes behind Rafferty.

"Straight down there through the trees," she said, pointing as Papa and Caleb moved past her. She turned to look at Rafferty and then she was pressed against him, kissing him, winding her fingers in his hair. "I love you," she whispered.

He held her away. "Your father will be back with her in a minute. I don't care, Chantal. I don't care who your mother is, or what happened when you were a baby. We rode like hell and I haven't had a chance to talk to him, but Blaise said you were with your mother. And Ormonde said she's mad, that she's dangerous."

"She thought I was Honoria. She pushed me into the river."

"Thank God you know how to swim!" Rafferty exclaimed. "I don't care who your mother is. I want you to understand. I'll take my chances. Alain took his."

"He doesn't know about her. Papa's never told anyone unless it was my grandparents, Celine's mother and father. Blaise discovered her, because she followed Papa and learned he was hiding Celine here. Papa has kept this to himself all these years." She placed her hands on his cheeks, framing his face. "Rafferty, you've always said a family is the most important thing."

"*You're* the most important thing," he said gruffly, making her heart pound as he crushed her to him to kiss her again.

"Chantal!"

She turned to face Papa, who was scowling, his expression full of concern. "We can't find Celine. She's gone."

"I pulled her up away from the water, and Reseda was with her."

"Reseda said Celine pushed her and she almost went into the river. Woman is terrified of the river, and Celine slipped away from her. I've sent Reseda to the house. Celine's footprints lead toward the house. Caleb is trying to track where she went, and Reseda will get the servants to join in the search. Are you all right?"

"Yes, I am. I'm sorry, Papa. Blaise told me about Celine. I had to come see my mother."

"I need to talk to you and Rafferty, but right now we must find Celine." He raked his fingers through his hair. "Take her to the house, Rafferty, where she'll be safe, and then you can help in the hunt. We have to find her quickly." He looked back over his shoulder and rubbed his forehead, and Chantal felt an ache for him.

"Celine's dangerous, so be careful," Ormonde cautioned.

Rafferty nodded and placed his arm around Chantal's shoulders, holding her close against him. Twigs crackled behind Rafferty. They turned as one, and found themselves looking into the muzzle of a pistol.

Chapter 27

"Stay where you are," Lazare Galliard drawled, his gaze raking over Chantal. "You really are shameless, Chantal," he said, and Rafe glanced at her, aware for the first time of her appearance. The wet cambric underdrawers left nothing to the imagination. Her wet silk blouse clung to her, and only the corset gave her a degree of modesty. He had been so thankful to find her that he hadn't stopped to look at what she wore. Now he tightened his hand on her shoulder as she lifted her chin and glared at Lazare.

Emotions churned in Rafe as he watched her; she was more trouble than a band of wild horses, but he was proud of her for her bravery. Now that he knew what worried her he felt as if a weight had been lifted from his heart, for he didn't care what was wrong with Celine. He wanted Chantal, and he was willing to risk all to have her.

All he had to do was convince her of that—and live through the next few minutes with Lazare.

"Ormonde, what is all this?" Lazare demanded, his voice having lost its usual arrogant tone. "What's happening here?"

The muzzle of the pistol was pointed squarely at Rafe's chest. Rafe's arm was around Chantal and he held her close to his side, close enough that she could be in danger if Lazare fired.

"Lazare, this is a private matter!" Ormonde snapped. "And there are laws against shooting an unarmed man."

"So there are. Chantal, move away from him. From

that first afternoon he's hidden behind you, and you
have protected him," Lazare drawled. Rafe seethed,
and wanted nothing but a chance to get his hands
around Lazare's neck.

His pistol was primed and ready, yet against Lazare,
who already had his aimed, he wouldn't stand a
chance. His mind raced while he released her.

"Lazare, leave us alone!" Ormonde demanded.
"There are ways to settle accounts, and this isn't one
of them. I'm giving my coat to my daughter." Ormonde handed his coat to Chantal. Rafe could see the
movement out of the corner of his eye, but he wouldn't
take his gaze off Lazare. If Lazare looked away even
for the flicker of an eye, he was going for his pistol.

"I'm sorry, Mr. Therrie, but there is a score to settle, and Chantal thoughtlessly deprived me of the
chance to do it on the field of honor. Now, who is
Celine?"

Silence lengthened between them. "I'll find out
anyway, so you may as well tell me. If you want my
silence, you'd better cooperate with me."

"She's my first wife," Ormonde said, his voice
sounding pained.

"Celine Therrie?" Lazare said, frowning, still
watching Rafe and holding the pistol without waver-
ing. Rafe had only one thought: *Where is Caleb?*

"Yes. She didn't perish in the fire at Belle Destin,
but I knew I would have to put her away and I couldn't
bear to place her in an asylum."

"My God! So that's where you've gone all these
years." Lazare flicked a glance at Ormonde, and Rafe
reached for his pistol.

The blast shattered the quiet and Rafe inhaled
sharply, his hand stopping in midair.

"Don't go for your pistol," Lazare said coldly. "Get
away from him, Chantal, or I'll shoot him right now."

"Chantal, come here," Ormonde said, and Rafe
pushed her away. He looked into Lazare's pale eyes
and felt the hatred burning between them.

"Celine Therrie is alive," Lazare said, frowning.
He glanced at Ormonde, then back at Rafe before Rafe

could move. *Caleb will have heard the shot.* Rafe tensed, ready to draw at the first chance he got.

"Celine Therrie has been hidden away all these years. You're still married to her."

"No, I'm not. I was granted a divorce long ago," Ormonde answered, and Rafe could hear the pain in his voice. He felt sorry for Ormonde and all he was having to go through now. "Through the years I've cared for her, and I visit her every month; she has everything I can give her for her physical comfort."

"I heard Chantal talking to O'Brien—Celine's mad! If she's mad, Chantal could inherit the same madness. Chantal's children could inherit it," Lazare said, his voice growing louder, his face flushed. "You were going to let me marry Chantal when you had Celine hidden away here, and when you *knew* that—"

"Lazare, I told you before," Ormonde snapped, "this isn't the time or place to discuss it! Celine attempted to drown Chantal, and now Celine has escaped us and we don't know where she is. She's roaming the grounds. She could hurt herself or someone else. Put your pistol away before someone gets hurt."

"Damn you, Ormonde Therrie! You would've let me marry Chantal, knowing we might have children who would be mad. And Blaise knew this as well! Damn you all!" He raised the pistol a fraction, and Rafe was helpless as he looked down the barrel.

All he could hope was to throw himself out of the direct path of the shot—that he would take it in the shoulder or arm.

"Alain!" a woman shrieked.

A woman hurtled toward Lazare as Rafe lunged at him. Lazare fired. Rafe couldn't stop his momentum and he hit them both, all of them sprawling on the ground. He yanked out his pistol.

Another shot rang out and Lazare groaned, holding his arm to his chest. Rafe rolled away and saw Caleb emerge from the trees with his pistol in hand. He turned to see Lazare in the dirt, a woman sprawled across him, a dark stain spreading in her back.

"Celine!" Ormonde cried out, and rushed to her. Rafe trained his pistol on Lazare as he moved to Chantal and put his arm around her.

Ormonde turned her over and placed his hand against her throat. He looked at Lazare. "You killed her."

"I didn't mean to shoot her," Lazare said, sounding dazed. All color had drained from his face, and his arm was bleeding. Caleb held his revolver pointed at Lazare, and he watched Ormonde bend over Celine before looking up at Rafe.

"I should kill you now, so I won't have to continually look over my shoulder," Rafe said, "but I have no stomach for pointless murder. You've just killed a woman, Chantal's mother."

"God, I didn't mean to!" Lazare said, his face going ashen. He scrambled to his feet and looked at Rafe.

Rafe tightened his finger on the trigger and felt Chantal press against his side. Looking into Lazare's eyes, Rafe lowered his pistol. He wondered if Lazare even saw him.

"Mr. Therrie, I didn't mean to—" Lazare insisted. "I didn't mean to hurt her!"

"Get out, Lazare," Ormonde said, bending over Celine's body.

Holding his injured arm, Lazare turned and walked away. Glancing at Caleb, Rafe shook his head, and Caleb put away his pistol.

"I'll take Chantal home," Rafe said to Ormonde.

Nodding, Ormonde picked up Celine's body and strode ahead to the house. Caleb followed him, leaving Chantal and Rafe alone.

"I should stay with Papa."

"Caleb will stay with him," he said, glancing down at the wet clothes that were molded to her figure. She blushed and pulled her father's coat closed.

"You need a dress, and Caleb will be with him."

"William is here with the buggy."

"Your father might want to go home in the buggy. You can ride with me." He turned her to face him. "I'm sorry about Celine."

Chantal gazed off through the trees. Her father and Caleb were already gone from sight. "She was a stranger. I couldn't feel much of anything, because I didn't know her."

"Let's go home," he said, holding her close against him.

In minutes they were headed home, with her riding sidesaddle before him on his horse. She turned to cling to him tightly and he stroked her back, letting her ride in silence. Once she burst into tears, and another time she pulled his head down to kiss him.

At Belle Destin they went in the back door; before she started up the stairs, he caught her hand. "When you're dressed, come downstairs. I want to talk to you."

His heart thudded as he gazed into her black eyes and saw the heated look she gave him. He wasn't going to allow Celine's condition to stand in the way of their love. Chantal turned away, climbing the stairs quickly as a door opened above and Blaise emerged from her room.

"Chantal, what happened?" she asked, moving to the head of the stairs.

Chantal paused only a moment. "I have to get some clothes. Celine is dead; it was an accident."

Rafe looked up at Blaise, wondering how much of the blame for all of this could be laid at her feet. He felt a deep anger as Chantal went to her room, and he stared up into Blaise's green eyes.

"What's she talking about?" Blaise asked. She was pale, her cheeks bright with color. She came down three steps, and Rafe saw her hands were shaking. "What has happened?"

Rafe curbed his temper; still, he felt a contempt that he didn't try to hide. "Celine is dead; Ormonde is there now."

"How'd she die? What happened?"

"Ask Ormonde about it," Rafe said, unable to keep the anger out of his voice.

Blaise's eyes widened and looked full of fear. She backed up a step, and then another. She turned and ran to her room and slammed the door, while Rafe went down the hall to wait for Chantal to return.

Chapter 28

In the last dusky light of day Chantal found Rafe seated outside, looking at the front lawn of Belle Destin. After bathing she had dressed in blue organza, and tied her hair behind her head. Her heart thudded when his dark head turned and she looked into his blue eyes.

He stood up and jerked his head. "Let's get away from the house."

She moved to his side, and he draped his arm across her shoulders as they went down the steps to his horse.

Rafe lifted Chantal to his saddle and swung up behind her, pulling her against him as he turned to ride down the lane and off the path toward a secluded place.

"I want to go where we'll be alone," he said, his breath fanning on her ear.

Her heart pounded. It felt so right to be in his arms. The day had been one shock and then another, but out of it all the truth had come, and Chantal knew now that he wanted her in spite of Celine. He stopped by the creek and lifted her down. In the dusk she could see him clearly, the last light filtering through bare-limbed trees.

He shed his tie and black coat. His white linen shirt and black pants were dusty and rumpled from hours in the saddle, yet he looked appealing and reassuring to her.

"It doesn't matter to me," he said in a husky voice. "I don't give a damn about Celine's condition."

She wanted to faint with joy and relief at his words, yet her experience with Celine made her cautious. "I couldn't bear to hurt you the way Papa's been hurt.

You saw him today, crying over her after all these years. Suppose—''

"I don't want to suppose." Rafe placed his hands on her waist, his gaze going over her features. His voice was low, barely audible. "From that first afternoon, I've been in love with you. There will never be another woman for me, Chantal."

She trembled in his arms, her heart racing. She touched his lips lightly with her fingers. She needed him and loved him, and there wouldn't be anyone else for her, but she couldn't bear to hurt him.

"I can see you getting ready to protest," he said, "but it won't do you any good. Chantal, I'll take the chance that you'll be normal and our children will be all right. Your father is a responsible man, and he was willing for Alain to marry and willing for you to marry."

She stared into his blue eyes and wanted to agree, to fling herself into his arms, but she held back, feeling torn in two. "I couldn't forgive myself if something happened. If you had to take care of me the way Papa has had to hide her and care for her and worry about her . . ."

"Let me take my chances. Hell, life is one chance after another, and you've never been afraid of them before. I've never seen you run from risk. We may be at war in months, and I'll be gone."

"No!" She reached for him and he caught her to him, crushing the breath from her lungs. His kiss was fierce and hungry and ended any holding back. She was starved for him, wanting to kiss and touch and love him.

The stubble on his jaw scraped her skin, but she didn't care. Her head reeled and desire burned high in her. She felt on fire, suffocating with a need for him, relishing every touch, each kiss, needing him and knowing how closely she had come to losing him, scared now by his solemn statement about war.

"I can't bear to lose you," she said, tears brimming over.

His mouth came down on hers, his tongue playing

in her mouth as he kissed her until she was breathless. She didn't feel his hands moving on her buttons until he had peeled away her dress and cupped her breast, looking into her eyes and watching her as he traced circles around her nipple. "You're mine, Chantal. I won't let you go, and I'm not afraid."

She tugged at his belt and he caught her hands. "I'm dusty. I've ridden all day."

She looked up at him and he inhaled deeply, bending his head to kiss her while he pulled off his belt. Next he yanked off his boots and turned to pull her to him, lowering her to the ground and slipping away her chemise. He removed the last of his clothes and stood over her, looking down at her.

She wanted to melt beneath his hungry gaze, and she wanted to caress his hard body and kiss him and make him tremble with desire as she did.

He knelt and bent to kiss her leg, moving slowly, trailing fiery kisses along her thigh. "I love you, Chantal, and I have to have you. I need you. I haven't been able to work or eat or sleep."

She ran her hands over his hard shoulders, feeling the muscles, winding her fingers in his hair, looking at him and pulling him closer.

"Rafe, please. I want you."

Something flickered in his blue eyes; she felt devoured by the look he gave her as he spread her legs and lowered himself between them, easing himself into her soft warmth.

"Chantal, Chantal," he whispered, kissing her throat. He moved slowly, filling her, and what had been painful before now stirred waves of ecstasy and need. She kissed him as their hearts pounded together.

"Chantal!" he gasped her name, winding his fingers in her hair while she arched beneath him, lost, new sensations cascading over her, shutting out the world. Rapture burst in her and she felt release.

Later as she lay in his arms she told him everything, from the moment Blaise had told her about Celine.

"I love you, Chantal. I don't care about your mother. I don't care what happened in the past, and

I'll say it as often as you need to hear it. I want to marry you.''

''How do you know I won't be—''

He placed his hand over her mouth gently and looked down at her. ''I can't live without you. Now, are you going to marry me or not?''

She felt as if chains around her heart had broken away. ''Yes, I'll marry you. Life has been dreadful, Rafferty.''

He pulled her closer, wrapping his arms around her tightly, bending his head to kiss her.

''What happened in Baton Rouge?'' she asked later, and his solemn look frightened her.

''There were one hundred and thirty delegates. By a vote of one hundred and thirteen to seventeen, secession won. On a difference of ninety-six votes, Louisiana seceded from the Union. We're a republic right now, and they're designing a new flag. The convention takes up again in New Orleans on Monday, but your father and I won't be there because of Celine.''

''And what about war?''

''I think it's inevitable.''

''Other nations have divided and haven't gone to war. Papa says if we go to war it'll be brief, and the South will get what it wants because of cotton.''

Rafe looked at the slow-moving creek and its muddy banks. ''You can't eat cotton, Chantal. The North has industry. I haven't traveled this country, but I'm in one of the biggest cities in the South and I read the papers and hear talk from men who are northerners. You can't fight a war with cotton and slaves against men with steel mills and copper mines and iron ore, against an organized army and navy.''

''Papa says more southerners are graduates of West Point and we fight better, that southern men know hunting and shooting. And we have some ironworks.''

''That's true.'' Rafferty rolled over and propped himself on his elbow. ''I want to take you to Ireland for a wedding trip.''

''To see your home! I've never traveled far,'' she said, feeling excited about it.

She gazed into his blue eyes and thought how close she had come to losing him forever. She placed her hand on his cheek. "How did you get the scar? You didn't have it when I first met you."

"I told you, fighting."

"Were you fighting Lazare?"

"What difference would it make?" he asked, kissing her throat. She closed her eyes and inhaled swiftly, sliding her hand over his bony hip, letting her fingers trail down to his muscled thigh, feeling the crisp black curls along his legs, shifting her hand and feeling him grow hard again. She drew a deep breath and wanted him.

"I would hate Lazare more than ever if I thought he had caused that scar."

"Bloodthirsty wench," Rafe whispered in her ear, then traced the curve of her ear with his tongue, sending tingles through her.

She caught his face and turned him to look at her. "I know you don't believe in slavery and you voted to stay in the Union. If we go to war, on which side will you fight?"

His blue eyes were dark as he gazed down at her solemnly. "I can't answer that now. I don't believe in slavery, but I love the South. I love New Orleans and I'll fight to defend it. I hope to God I don't have to make the choice."

"I hope you don't either." She buried her face against his chest. "You'll be all mine; I don't want to lose you!" she whispered, her heart pounding, wanting him again. She caressed him and heard him groan as he turned her and bent his head to kiss her, shifting his body over hers.

"I couldn't give you up, love," he whispered, and kissed away her reply.

Rafe stood beside Chantal as Celine was buried in the Therrie family plot on Belle Destin at mid-morning the next day. Ormonde was quiet, Blaise silent and pale, dressed in black. When the service was over,

Blaise left for town in a carriage that raced away down the long drive.

Chantal and Rafe stood in front of the house as Ormonde stepped outside. "Rafferty, I need to see both you and Chantal as soon as possible," Ormonde said. "Can you meet with me in my office in an hour?"

"Yes, sir," Rafe answered. He looked into Ormonde's solemn black eyes and wondered if another storm was about to break over them.

"Yes, Papa," Chantal answered, her fingers locked in Rafe's. He couldn't bear to turn her loose. All morning he had stood beside her or held her hand. He wanted to get her away to himself and love her again, but he knew he wasn't going to get the chance with Ormonde back at Belle Destin.

Last night Caleb had arrived in the city after midnight, and they'd left at dawn to return to Belle Destin. They brought Darcy with them, and as soon as they reached the plantation Darcy disappeared to find his friends. All the time Caleb and Rafe had worked at Belle Destin Darcy had worked and played alongside slave children, and he was as close to them as to his friends in town.

As Ormonde went inside, Rafe turned to look at Chantal. She wore a black dress, and he hoped she didn't stay in mourning for a year. Her hair was parted in the center, curled and looped up, and he wanted to pull it all down and peel away the black dress. He felt his body responding to just standing close to her and looking at her.

"I wish I could take you home with me," he said softly.

A smile curved her lips. In spite of the somber occasion her eyes sparkled, and every time she looked at him his pulse skipped. Once he caught her gaze going over him in a long, slow appraisal that made him draw a deep breath and clench his fists to keep from reaching for her.

She was all he could want and all he had dreamed about, and he had the hours counted until their wedding. He was having a necklace made as a wedding gift for her.

Her hand was warm and small in his, her bones delicate, yet in lovemaking her soft hands could drive him over a brink, and there was nothing delicate in her scalding responses. "Your father looks worried."

"This is a sad time for him, and he's going through it alone. He keeps to himself."

"Don't shut me out that way, Chantal. Don't keep bad news from me and worry alone. Do you understand?"

"Yes, sir," she answered in a demure voice that made him laugh.

"Have you been trouble all your life?"

"Not until I met you," she answered with twinkling eyes. "You caused most of it, Rafferty O'Brien!"

"Liar! There's a bit of mischief," he said, leaning closer to her, "I wish we could get into now. If only we could be alone . . ."

"We can't, so stop leering at me. Here comes your brother."

Wearing a black coat and pants with a ruffled white shirt, Caleb came around the corner of the house. With surprise Rafe noticed that Caleb was taller. He didn't know when Caleb had grown the extra inches, but he had to be over six feet tall now.

"I'm getting ready to go," Caleb said, and Chantal glanced at Rafe.

"I'll leave you two to say your farewells. Caleb, I'll see you at our wedding." She leaned forward to kiss his cheek lightly and he blushed, grinning at her.

"He better be good to you," he said and she smiled, walking away and leaving them alone. "My boat should be in town, and it leaves tomorrow. I can catch it if I go now."

"Go on to town, but come back the last Saturday in February for our wedding."

"I'll be back. What about Galliard? Am I leaving you unprotected?"

Rafe looked beyond Caleb at the grounds of Belle

Destin. "I don't think he'll cause trouble. He looked as if he may live with regret for a long time."

"A man like Galliard? Regret will ride with him only a mile, and then he'll convince himself he was right."

"Catch your boat. I'll take care of myself."

Caleb grinned. "Sure, big brother—just like you did back there." He became solemn. "Lazare's honor is on the line with you. He'll come after you again. He'll have to, to save face."

"I'll be careful. I'm not afraid of Lazare, and I'm not hiding behind Chantal or you!"

Caleb grinned. Rafe felt a warmth well up in him for his younger brother. He was closest to Caleb and loved him deeply. He reached out, hugging him, feeling his broad, powerful shoulders and amazed at how tall he was. "Damned if you aren't as tall as I am!"

Caleb grinned. "I might be able to whip you now."

"I hope we don't have to find out." Rafe stepped back. "Take care of yourself."

"You take care. And take care of Darcy. We can't let him be an orphan."

"Caleb, when you travel watch for Fortune."

Caleb nodded, his green eyes solemn. "I'll always wonder, Rafe. Until we know for sure, I'll think he's alive."

"I'm sure he is. I was always sure you were."

They gazed into each other's eyes, and then Caleb mounted his horse. Rafe watched him ride down the drive, then turned to go into the house.

"You look solemn," Chantal said, approaching him in the hall.

"I hate to see Caleb go. We were always together growing up," he said, his gaze going over her. "Damn, I wish we were alone," he said gruffly.

She blushed and looked up at him, her eyes getting a lethargic, heated look that made him throb with need.

"Rafferty, I'm worried about Papa. I think there's something besides Celine that's worrying him."

"Chantal," he said, touching her shoulder, unable

to keep his hands away from her. Her mouth looked full, so soft, and he wanted to kiss her.

"Are you listening to me?"

"No, I'm not. I'm thinking about you, wanting you."

"Please," she whispered. "I'm worried about Papa. He seems angry and sad."

"He's a strong man, and he'll be better. Give him a little time, Chantal. He's had some shocks."

"Do you think Lazare will talk about Celine? Will he tell all the people we know?"

Rafe touched a soft lock of her hair. "I don't think he'll talk. He killed her; he isn't going to admit what he did to anyone. Your father hasn't tried to have him arrested or press charges."

"Papa won't do that to Lazare." She ran her fingers along his vest. "Lazare intended to kill you, not Celine. For that Papa should press charges, but he won't. Not unless Lazare does something else."

"Chantal, don't step in front of me again if Lazare does try something." To his annoyance, her solemn expression vanished and her black eyes began to twinkle.

"I'll always try to protect you!"

"You're headstrong, vexatious, exasperating, the most beautiful bit of trouble I've ever seen. And there are some things you're going to have to learn."

"Is that right? And you think you're going to teach me?"

"If we just had more time before we see your father, I'd teach you something."

She laughed, dimples showing, and he wondered if he would spend the rest of his life in turmoil, trying to get her out of predicaments. Her eyes sparkled and he burned with a need to hold her. He glanced over her head at the empty hall.

"Come here. We have a few minutes before we meet your father." He caught her hand and drew her into the library. He closed the library door and leaned against it, pulling her to him.

"Rafferty! Papa is downstairs!"

Rafe bent his head to kiss her, his tongue playing in her mouth, his hand sliding over her. "Dammit," he whispered, frowning at her. "I hate the damned corsets and hoops—don't bring any along on our wedding trip. I'll sink them all in the sea!"

"I shall be hopelessly out of fashion."

"It won't matter," he whispered. "I don't intend for you to be out of bed." He bent to brush her full lips as he unbuttoned the black dress and pushed it open, bending to kiss the soft curve of her breast above the stiff corset. She gasped and pressed against him.

"You can't imagine how much I want you," he whispered. "I want to love you for hours." Her lips were full, tempting, and her languorous gaze scalded him. He framed her face with his hands.

"Chantal, the first thing I want to teach you is that you don't have to solve your problems alone. Trust me, love."

"Whatever you say," she said sweetly, giving him a teasing smile that made him inhale deeply.

"Our wedding is an eternity away," he said, wanting her now.

"No, it's only weeks away. *Yesterday* it was an eternity away," she answered solemnly. He caught her to him again.

"This corset is going, Chantal. It's like hugging a tree."

She laughed. "So I'm like a tree, am I, Rafferty O'Brien? You can keep your busy hands to yourself then! *You're* not soft, but do you hear me complaining?"

He held her, wrapping both arms around her and bending his knees so he could look into her eyes. "No, I'm not soft," he whispered, "and I won't be as long as I have you within reach."

"Rafferty!" she looked into his blue eyes, and they both laughed.

"Chantal, it'll be good between us. I've known that since the afternoon I opened my eyes and looked through a blue veil at the most beautiful face I had ever seen."

"You really thought I was the most beautiful woman you'd ever seen?"

"How many times do I have to tell you?"

"Forever. You were very brave."

"So were you, love," he whispered, kissing her throat, suddenly wanting to keep on holding her, wishing he could take her on his horse, ride to town, marry her, and sail away today. Ormonde had looked too solemn, and Rafe worried about what he had to say. He throbbed with need for her, aching, but he knew that the wedding was still weeks away and that, now that they were engaged, Ormonde wouldn't let him alone with her.

"If your father would just go to town for the day . . ."

She pulled away, straightening her clothes. "If my father knew what you've already done, you'd have to duel again!"

"But you would save me or shoot me again, or do something to interfere," he said, smiling at her and reaching out to button her dress, pushing away her fingers. He longed to unbutton it completely, but it was almost time to see Ormonde.

"That first night in town, you unbuttoned my dress! I may be trouble, Rafferty O'Brien, but you're arrogant and bold beyond words!"

"You liked it, Chantal," he drawled. "You didn't stop me."

"I tried to stop you. You make me sound like a woman off the streets."

"No, love. If you had been that, I would've tried to get you across the room into my bed that night. Now I think you'd better go and leave me alone and let my body cool, or your father will see what effect you have on me."

"Rafferty!" She blushed and stepped back, and then her gaze dropped. Her cheeks became more red but her gaze stayed on him. He drew his breath again, all amusement evaporating.

"Chantal," he said hoarsely.

She reached out to brush her hand against him as

lightly as a breeze, yet he inhaled again. "When you
do that . . ."

"You've made me brazen, Rafferty O'Brien," she
whispered.

"Not as much as you will be," he answered.

She swept past him and into the hall, and he moved
across the room to the window. Soon she would be
his, all his, to love as long and as much as he liked,
to look at and touch whenever he wanted. And his life
would never be dull, not with her. Pray God a war
didn't separate them.

His thoughts shifted to secession and the growing
conflict. Secretary of the Interior Jacob Thompson had
resigned, the Secretary of the Treasury Phillip F.
Thomas had resigned, and Jefferson Davis had resigned from the Senate. The Mississippi River was
blockaded at Vicksburg by an artillery battery of
southerners. The Augusta arsenal had been seized. The
situation changed daily, building toward a major conflict. How could he fight for slavery? Yet married to
Chantal, how could he fight against the South?

He gazed across the gardens of Belle Destin.
Branches were bare in the January weather, but in a
few months there would be a riot of color with azaleas
and camellias in bloom. The Mississippi River would
be one of the main targets, because whoever controlled the Mississippi would control the entire valley.
He felt a ripple of fear for Chantal, wishing he could
take her to Ireland and they could sit out the conflict
if it came, but he knew neither one of them would do
that.

Five minutes later Chantal reappeared. "It's time to
meet Papa," she said. He took her hand, feeling her
slender fingers in his. "I've waited so damned long
for you, Chantal, and now I feel every minute draws
us closer to separation."

"If war comes, everyone says it'll be short." She
smiled. "You're not going to worry about war now,
Rafferty O'Brien. Not when we have a wedding soon!"

"Yes, ma'am," he answered. "Come along. We
don't want to keep your father waiting."

If Ormonde intended to try to talk him out of marrying Chantal, he was in for an argument. Rafe didn't care about Celine. He was willing to take risks, and he wasn't going to listen to arguments from Ormonde about the dangers involved.

When they entered Ormonde's office, Rafe braced for trouble. One look at Ormonde's face and he felt something was amiss. Ormonde's frown cut deep furrows in his forehead. For the first time, he showed his years. He looked defeated, and Rafe remembered his father that last year when they had lost everything.

Rafe put his arm around Chantal's shoulders and when she sat down, he perched on the arm of the chair where he could keep his arm around her. He felt as if he were on the verge of losing her again, and he was determined that when he left the room she would still be his.

Ormonde turned to face them. "This talk is long overdue. I've been guilty of many things. I didn't know Blaise knew about Celine. I didn't know she had told you about her. I could no more understand your break with Rafferty than he understood it, and I never guessed what could be behind it."

"Papa, please," Chantal began, "it's all right."

"Chantal," he said, silencing her. "I have things that need to be said and should have been said long ago. I've made excuses—I was young, I was under duress, I used poor judgment, but those things don't excuse a lifetime of silence that I knew was a mistake."

"Papa, it doesn't matter," Chantal said, and Rafe knew she was hurting for Ormonde and he understood, because he had hurt for his father.

Ormonde waved his hand, as if to dismiss her reassurance. "It does matter, and I should have talked to you years ago." He faced Chantal. "Celine wasn't your mother."

Chapter 29

"I don't understand." Stunned, Chantal stared at him.

"Perhaps I should have told you before now, but it seemed best to leave things alone. Within months after I married Celine, I knew something was wrong with her. Her condition became worse after Alain was born, but I didn't want to acknowledge what was happening. Then Honoria was born. The first time Celine tried to—" He broke off to turn away and look out the window.

Chantal hurt for him, because she knew how difficult it was for her father to express himself, yet she was at a loss. Celine *wasn't* her mother! She glanced up at Rafferty to find him watching her. He winked at her and she felt better. His hand was on her shoulder and he rubbed it back and forth, a constant reminder that he was with her.

She brushed his knee with her hand, grateful for his presence beside her.

Ormonde began again. "Celine tried to drown Alain. When it happened I wanted to think it was an accident, yet I knew it wasn't. And I knew we shouldn't have any more children. Grand-père had arranged our marriage, and when we wed I was happy with her."

He was quiet again and Chantal wanted to go put her arm around him, but she suspected it would be of no comfort to him. Ormonde had always kept a wall around himself, and never let it down for his children. She stroked Rafe's knee and was thankful he was not remote and impossible to talk to. Far from it.

"I was young and unhappy. I . . . found solace elsewhere."

Papa's back was still turned, but his words gave Chantal a jolt. She felt shocked to hear him make such an admission. She wanted to tell him to stop; his life was private and his affairs his own business, but now she had to know about her mother.

"I loved a wonderful woman, but she didn't have the social standing necessary." He turned around to look at Rafe. "When I look back now I realize what I should have done, but at the time society, our social code, seemed important.

"By the time Alain was four we weren't going out or having friends in. People knew Celine was in bad health, but they didn't know it was her mind and not her body. There was a rumor in town she had consumption, and I did nothing to stop the rumor.

"Her parents knew the truth, and they did as much as I did to hide Celine from the world. When you were born, Chantal, I knew I could bring you home and claim you as Celine's. No one would know."

"This woman," Rafe said, "did she know about Celine?"

"Yes. She knows everything. I trust her completely," Ormonde replied. "I brought you home, Chantal," he said, turning to look at her. "I took you from your mother and she let me have you, because she knew what I could give you. Your mother is a beautiful woman and quite normal. You and Rafe have no worries."

She glanced up at Rafe and leaned her forehead against him, feeling relief. In spite of all his protests that he didn't care, she was immensely relieved to know that Celine wasn't her mother.

"Celine became worse, and then the night came when she set fire to Belle Destin and Honoria died. I knew with two small children that I couldn't allow Celine to stay with you and Alain. I couldn't bear to place her in an asylum, so I bought land far enough away where I thought it would be secluded and I put her there. I tried to take good care of her. Chantal, I

ask your forgiveness. You should have known your
mother.

"If I hadn't met Blaise, I wouldn't have Amity.
There have been three women, three mothers to my
children, but one of them I've shut out of my life. I've
tried to provide for her financially, even though she
hasn't needed my help for years. Now she's quite
wealthy and independent. Even though I haven't acknowledged her before now, she's always been important to me. You can't undo the past, you can only live
with it.

"The woman lives in New Orleans," he said, looking again at Rafe. "If you want to meet her, Chantal,
you may. It's long overdue. Rafferty already knows
her."

Startled, Chantal looked up at Rafferty. He frowned
at Papa, and she suspected Rafferty had no idea of the
woman's identity.

"Would you like to meet her, or would you rather
leave the past alone?" Ormonde asked.

Chantal weighed the question in her mind, because
it would be less painful to her father if she left the past
behind and let it all die now. Yet she had spent all her
life dreaming of her real mother, and the need to know
was too strong.

"Does she know me? Do you see her and tell her
about me?"

When he looked away, she felt as if she had pried
too deeply into his private life. "Yes, I see her. Yes,
she knows. She sees you in town, but you don't know
her."

"I'd like to meet her, Papa."

He nodded. "I thought you would. I've made arrangements with her for this afternoon. She's on her
way here. Her name is Jolie Fouquet," he said, looking again at Rafferty. "Chantal, I'm sorry. You should
have known your mother."

Chantal stood up and went around the desk to him,
hugging him. "I love you, Papa. You've been good to
me."

He hugged her lightly, patting her shoulder, and then he moved away.

"I'll leave you two alone. I'll call you when she arrives."

As soon as he had left the room Rafferty stood and drew Chantal into his arms, holding her tightly against him.

"We don't have to worry about my mind," she whispered.

"I never did, Chantal. It seemed a remote risk to me." He raised his head to look at her. "But I'm glad Celine wasn't your mother, because you're free of worries now."

"Papa said you know Jolie."

He nodded. "She's a fine woman. She runs a gambling house. Lazare knows her, most men in town know her."

"How *well* do they know her?" Chantal asked, blushing, wondering if there was more than gambling at Jolie's house.

Rafe shook his head. "She keeps to herself. There are no rumors, nothing. Whatever is between Jolie and your father, they've hidden it well. She looks young, surprisingly young if she's your mother. She gave you up so you would have all this," he said, waving his hand. "Remember that when you talk to her, Chantal. It may have hurt her all these years to lose you and watch you with Blaise."

"She may not have wanted me."

He shook his head. "I think she gave you to Ormonde because it would be best for you. She's a fine person; I like her. I met her soon after I arrived in New Orleans. Touzet introduced us. I think she wanted you to marry Lazare, because he could have given you so much."

"How in the world would you know that?"

"I talk to her sometimes when I go to her place to gamble. She didn't like it when she found out you were the woman I wanted to marry. I didn't understand why, except I guessed she favored Lazare. Most women like Lazare."

"As if most women don't like you! I couldn't bear to watch you dancing with others!"

He looked down at her and frowned. "Is that right? While you waltzed away with Lazare?" Something flickered in the depths of his eyes, and she forgot their conversation. She tilted her head back and closed her eyes, reaching for him, and he leaned forward to kiss her.

She was still in Rafferty's arms when Ormonde rapped on the door. Chantal moved away, straightening her clothes as he opened the door.

"Chantal, come to the front parlor."

"I want you to come with me," she said to Rafferty.

He shook his head. "No. There are things to be said just between the two of you. Go ahead and talk to her, Chantal."

She followed Papa to the front parlor. Beside the marble mantel stood a woman in a royal blue dress of crepe, with a hat of lace and woven straw. Chantal felt surprise, because Jolie looked even younger than Blaise or Celine. And just as beautiful and far more regal, as if she were the true mistress of Belle Destin. She was fair with blue eyes, but Chantal could see a resemblance between them in their straight, thin noses, prominent cheekbones, jaw structure, and fair hair.

"Jolie, this is our daughter, Chantal," Papa said in a gentle tone of voice Chantal had never heard him use. He turned to Chantal. "Chantal, this is your mother, Jolie. I'll leave you two alone."

Chantal was barely aware when he left the room. She motioned with her hand, and Jolie sat down.

"All these years I thought my mother had died when Belle Destin burned."

"We both did what we felt was best for you," Jolie said. "I've watched you when you were in town, and I've heard about you from your father and Lazare. I couldn't have given you all this, Chantal."

"I understand, but I wish it could have been different."

Jolie looked down and drew a deep breath. "As the years have passed I've grown accustomed to my life, but I'm glad to get to know you now. Sometimes I made dresses for you when you were small, and your father told you he'd had them made in town.''

Suddenly tears stung Chantal's eyes, because she realized Jolie must have loved her deeply. They stared at each other and Chantal stood up and crossed the room. Jolie stood to open her arms, and they hugged each other.

''Chantal,'' Jolie said softly, and Chantal realized that here was the mother she had dreamed about, a woman who did love her and who would have cared for her if she could. They moved apart and both wiped their eyes. ''Don't be too harsh on your father. We live in a society where we didn't have good choices, and he did what was best. Anything else would have meant scandal.''

''I glad to know now. I want you to come to my wedding.''

''You have a stepmother, and I can't cause trouble. I'll have to stay out of Ormonde's life, but I want you to come visit me. We can do that without scandal. The man you'll marry is a friend; while people won't understand both of you calling on me, it won't cause talk.''

''Rafferty said you hoped I'd marry Lazare.''

''That was a while back. I know you're marrying a fine man. I like Rafferty very much. He fell in love with you the first time he saw you, and I thought that was impossible, that he would interfere in your life.''

Suddenly Chantal laughed. ''He did interfere! I love him.''

''Then you're very fortunate. Tell me about yourself.''

They sat down again and talked for over an hour. Finally Jolie hugged Chantal and told her good-bye. Chantal followed her to the front door. At the bottom of the wide steps a buggy waited, with Rafferty leaning against it, his long legs crossed at the ankles. Chantal remained in the doorway to allow him to talk to Jolie without her. Jolie paused to wave, and Rafferty helped her into the buggy and climbed in, closing the door.

Chantal's gaze went over Belle Destin. She wouldn't have had any of this if she had stayed with her mother. She wouldn't have known Amity or Papa, yet it hurt to think of the years without her real mother, because she had liked Jolie. She glanced at the buggy and went inside the house.

Rafe climbed into the buggy and folded his long legs in the narrow space. Jolie held a handkerchief to her eyes, dabbing at them and regaining her composure.

"I'm glad you're her mother."

"It will still remain a secret from the world. Ormonde has a wife, and he has his circle of friends. I'm no part of it, and that won't change."

"No, but Chantal can see you, and both of you can get to know each other now."

"I didn't want you to interfere in her engagement; Lazare could have given her so much, but she loves you and you love her. If Ormonde had followed his heart as you have done . . ." She paused and looked away, to glance back in seconds. "You're an exceptional person, Rafferty O'Brien. I underestimated you. I'm glad she's marrying you."

"It makes me feel good knowing that I have your approval," he said, feeling inordinately pleased. "To tell you the truth, I'm delighted to learn you're her mother, and not Celine and not Blaise. And now I know where she gets some of her toughness."

She smiled and patted his knee. "She gets it from Ormonde. He's my strength. He has regrets now, but if we had to do it over we'd make the same choices. It was best for her."

Rafe leaned forward and kissed Jolie's cheek. "You can come to the wedding as my guest. Blaise doesn't know, does she?"

"No, she doesn't, and she doesn't deserve better, but I don't want to cause trouble."

"Come to the wedding. I'll tell people I invited you."

She shook her head. "My child will be a beautiful bride, but I have given up so much of her life, I can give this up, too. You don't need rumors flying about you, either."

"I don't give a damn about rumors."

"There is something you should care about—Lazare. I know everything that happened. Ormonde told me. Lazare's shock and penitence will be brief. He hates you, and you're the only man who has gotten the best of him or caused him real trouble. He'll try to kill you. I've heard him talk, and I know he will."

"I thought that was over."

"It's not over. He hates with a rage that can lead in only one direction. Chantal loves you, and I don't want to see you killed."

"Thanks for the warning."

"And marry her as soon as possible. I'm in town, and I hear many men talk. Men who travel come to my house. I think we're headed for war."

"I agree, after my trip to Baton Rouge. Slave states are taking federal property. When Governor Moore seized the mint, he acquired over half a million in gold and silver. The U.S. government isn't going to let money and forts go without a fight. Louisiana seceded, and next Monday a provisional Congress will meet for a constitutional convention in Montgomery, with delegates from the seceding states. There's only one consequence I can see. We're marrying as soon as Ormonde will allow—February twenty-third."

She looked into his eyes and leaned forward to place her warm palm on his cheek. "That first night, neither Touzet nor I thought it possible you could win her hand. It was like asking for the city to become yours."

He laughed. "I'm a fortunate man. I love her as much as I love life."

"Perhaps I shall get to know my granddaughter."

He nodded and opened the carriage door, hopping to the ground. He turned. "You must have been fourteen years old when you had her."

She laughed. "You're almost right. I was seventeen."

He winked at her before he closed the door and watched the carriage roll away. He glanced back at the big house that looked as if it were a fort against all storms, but he had seen what floods and reversals of fortune could do. If war came, it would change Belle Destin and everyone who lived there.

Chantal stepped outside, looking at him expectantly, and his pulse jumped. All he had to do was look at her and he became hot with desire. He climbed the steps, wishing Ormonde Therrie would get in his buggy and go to town so he could have Chantal to himself.

The next morning in his warehouse, Rafe stood at the window and watched the work on his ship. He had recently purchased it—instead of another clipper, a sloop powered by steam or sail. It couldn't carry as much cargo and it didn't have the speed of a clipper, but he had wanted something small and fast he could arm. He'd had it redone with a special captain's cabin that he and Chantal could use. Now he was having it armed with cannon, because when they returned from their wedding trip he expected to sail back to a country at war.

Not since the night Lazare had given him a beating had he gone unarmed and unprepared for a fight. He wore his Colt in the shoulder holster, except at night when it was beneath his pillow. In a box on the floor of his carriage was another revolver. While he thought about Lazare, Rafe watched the work being done on his ship. Men worked around the clock to make the conversion, installing two eighteen-pound swivel guns fore and aft.

After Captain Thomas had concluded the last voyage, Rafe had told him to look into arming a ship. Rafe had heard of a British naval captain, Cowper Coles, who had applied two years earlier for a patent for a revolving cupola or turret, but so far Rafe hadn't found any for sale.

Until he discovered something better, he was installing regulation thirty-two-pounders amidships. They looked out of place on the sloop, but Rafe felt more secure.

His gaze shifted to his warehouse. Business was booming; his wedding was almost here. Lazare Galliard was the only threat, and Rafe expected Lazare to take action before the wedding. He yanked the revolver from the holster and aimed. Crossing the room, he took his hat from a hook and picked up his coat. He would ride out along a bayou, where he could practice drawing and firing his Colt.

Chapter 30

"Two days until my wedding day, Darcy," Rafe said, sliding the razor over his jaw.

"You sure you want to get married? Caleb says he never does."

"I'm very sure I want to get married. And someday Caleb will change his mind. I promise you, Darcy. He'll want to get married."

"He said Miss Amity and Miss Chantal are trouble, but they seem pretty nice to me. Miss Chantal smells sweet all the time."

"You're right. They're pretty and nice and smell sweet. Sometimes they're trouble, but they're worth it."

"After you marry Miss Chantal, will you be gone long?"

"Yes, I will," he said, looking in the mirror at his younger brother. "Caleb should be here any time now, and he'll stay with you until I get back. He's going to take you upriver on a steamboat."

"Last time he showed me how to turn the wheel! And I caught a fish that was thirteen inches long! And I caught a turtle!"

"You'll have a good time."

"I like it better when Caleb's here and you're here."

Rafe paused to look at Darcy, who stared back with wide blue eyes. "I like it better, too, but we can't always do that. And a wedding is very special."

"Caleb and I could go with you."

"You'll have more fun going upriver on a steamboat with Caleb, and this is a special time for me to be alone with Chantal."

Darcy sighed and slid off the chair. He was short, but none of the brothers had gained their height until they were nearly eighteen. They heard a door bang, and Rafe grinned as Darcy bounded out of the room. It wasn't difficult to tell when Caleb entered a house.

Rafe stepped into the hall and stopped, momentarily taken aback. Caleb came up the stairs and hugged Darcy, glancing at Rafe. He was dressed in a gray uniform.

The stand-up collar bore the two horizontal gold stripes of a first lieutenant. One wale of yellow frogging marked his sleeves. Leather gauntlets were tucked into his belt. He wore a side knife with silver mounts, and a Remington .44-caliber revolver. The gray felt slouch hat was at an angle; his black leather boots were worn with silver spurs.

"I know you've seen volunteers before," Caleb said. "President Jefferson Davis issued a call for one hundred thousand volunteers when he was sworn in last week. I've been in the state militia, so it was a simple step into the Confederacy. Several of us had uniforms made."

"My God, Caleb! You volunteered? It's so early!"

Darcy ran his finger along the saber, encased in a scabbard of russet leather and brass, that rested on Caleb's hip. "You're going to fight someone, Caleb?"

"I might. I will if I have to."

"You didn't have to volunteer," Rafe said solemnly. "You didn't have to join yet." It hurt him to see his younger brother in uniform, and it made the threat of war more imminent.

"Stop worrying!" Caleb said lightly. "I haven't fought anyone, and the Confederacy may never go to war."

"You're an officer."

"They elected me. And it was thanks to my keen shooting," Caleb said and grinned. "How long are you going to stand there staring at me?"

"I wasn't ready for this."

"You're not joining the Union forces, are you?"

"I hoped I wouldn't have to make a decision."

"Then you're like a man standing in a gale hoping he doesn't have to cover his head. Don't look so gloomy. The ladies think I'm brave, and there have been parties celebrating the Confederacy. I'll bet you've been to some."

"I've been invited, but I haven't attended."

"If you weren't getting married, I think you'd be in uniform too. When are we going to Belle Destin?"

"As soon as I get ready. They'll have the first dinner tonight, and the guests arrive today. The parties last until the Monday after the wedding. We'll all come back to town for the wedding Saturday at St. Patrick's and the party at the St. Louis, and then the guests, including you and Darcy, will go back to Belle Destin. Caleb, what about Darcy? Since you've volunteered, should I make arrangements for him to stay at Belle Destin?"

"No. This is a young army, and we're not at war yet. I told them I had to make a trip upriver, and they agreed. If war breaks out, I'll get back as fast as possible and I'll take Darcy to Belle Destin."

"Can I see your sword?" Darcy asked.

Caleb withdrew it. "It's a saber," he said, turning to show Darcy how to handle it while Rafe finished shaving and dressing. Rafe felt sobered by the sight of Caleb in his new uniform. The town was in celebration, as if they had won a war rather than tottering on the brink of one. Banners fluttered proclaiming Louisiana part of the new nation—the Confederate States of America. Posters were up, calling for volunteers for military service. Parties were given to celebrate. Abraham Lincoln was on his way to Washington, to be inaugurated within a week.

Before they left for Belle Destin, Rafe glanced around his house. Everything was changing swiftly. When he returned, he would be a married man. Chantal would be his, mistress of his house. Caleb was a soldier now, and the South stood on the brink of war. He closed the door and followed Caleb downstairs.

Rafe sat across from Chantal at the Therrie table in the big dining room. Forty guests sat the length of the table, which was ladened with turkey, oyster dressing, rice, venison, ambrosia, crab cakes, golden candied yams, damson preserves, crawfish, pecan rum cake, platters heaped with steaming food and glistening crystal filled with wine. In spite of the food, all he could see was Chantal. She met his gaze, and the sparkle in her eyes matched the excitement dancing in him. She was breathtaking in a deep rose silk dress, and he couldn't wait for dinner to end so he could get her alone. *Only hours now, and I'll be holding her.* He looked into her eyes and saw the change in her expression, knew she could see the searing desire he felt, his impatience to hold her and kiss her. *Tomorrow . . . tomorrow. How long I've waited for her, but it will be worth it!*

In a dressing room of St. Patrick's, Chantal gazed at herself in the cheval glass. The white dress was perfection, made of satin with white roses and hundreds of tiny pearls and Valenciennes lace trim. Her golden hair was fastened behind her head in a looped chignon. She never saw Maman except when there were guests present, and Chantal wondered if there had been an additional strain on her marriage since Celine's death.

"Amity, how does it look without hoops?"

Amity giggled. "Maybe you'll set a new trend!"

"Tell me the truth—do I look pretty without them?"

"Of course you do!"

"Amity, it's my wedding day!" Chantal said, her heart pounding with joy.

"You look beautiful! It's time to go." They looked at each other, and Chantal held out her arms to hug Amity.

"I'll miss you, but I'm so glad you're marrying Rafferty. I much prefer him to Lazare. Be happy, Chantal!"

"Thank you. I want you to be happy, too."

Amity nodded and they left to join Papa, who smiled at her and linked her arm in his. "How beautiful you look, Chantal! I sent a carriage for Jolie, and she's consented to sit at the back. She said she won't be at the party afterwards, but she would come to the wedding.''

''I'm glad, Papa. I liked her very much, and Rafferty likes her.''

As father and daughter moved up the nave, Ormonde turned his head to gaze at the rows of guests. Chantal looked up the long aisle at the banks of white roses near the altar and the painted murals behind them. The great Gothic vaulted ceiling, with its reinforced cast-iron rods, curved overhead. As candles flickered in the soft light, all else faded except the sight of Rafferty in his black clothes, white frilly shirt, and black silk cravat, waiting for her at the altar. As she walked the distance between them, she saw that his blue eyes were intent, and she felt as if she would burst with joy.

They stood together in the hush of the church, and she gazed into his blue eyes as he held her hands. His expression was solemn, his deep voice quiet as they repeated vows to love and cherish each other so long as they both should live. Rafferty bent his head and kissed her, pausing to look into her eyes a moment, and she felt as if she wanted to melt into his arms, or run from the crowd so she could be alone with him.

Instead they joined the guests in celebration at the St. Louis hotel, talking to well-wishers and drinking bubbling French champagne Papa had specially ordered. Chantal had no appetite for the feast that was furnished, but feasted her eyes on Rafferty as they danced. By midnight she had finally kissed Maman and Papa good-bye. She hugged Amity and kissed Caleb and Darcy, and then Rafferty helped her into his buggy and they were alone at last.

Rafferty reached for her, pulling her into his arms in the dark seclusion of the closed carriage. His head came down and his kisses burned, igniting flames of passion in the core of her being. She shifted her hips closer, wanting him.

''In minutes we'll be at my ship and under sail. I've

left orders with the captain and crew that they're to stay out of sight until we're in our cabin, and then they're to leave us alone except at mealtimes. I'll have you all to myself."

She barely listened as she kissed his throat and ran her hands along his thighs, feeling the hard muscles, wanting his arms around her.

On the dock the carriage slowed and they stepped out, Rafferty bending down to grasp her legs and swing her into his arms. Lanterns glowed brightly on his ship as he strode toward the plank. He stopped and she looked up, turning her head to follow his gaze. Behind them was the dark shadow of his warehouse, one in a long row of warehouses.

At an upper window of his wooden building, a tongue of flame danced brightly.

A man walked past another window, a dark shadow moving about in the warehouse.

"Dammit!" Rafferty snapped. "Chantal, you stay here!" He set her down and ran across the wharf to the building. She looked at the upper floor, where red flames now flickered in three windows.

Feeling cold with fear, she saw a man's silhouette upstairs as Rafferty raced into the burning warehouse. Broad shoulders were outlined against the orange fire.

From the carriage she took the pistol Rafferty kept in a box. Scooping up her long satin train, she turned to the driver of the carriage. "Get the fire truck! Sound an alert, or the whole town will burn!"

"Yes, ma'am!"

Gripped by fear, she raced after Rafferty. Lazare would try to kill him if they met inside the building. And Rafferty would try to kill Lazare for setting the fire.

The entire upper floor blazed now, and the roof had caught. Sparks dropping to the loading platform below had set it on fire. A gray cloud of smoke, filled with dancing orange sparks, rolled upward into the night sky and spread over the town.

Terrified for Rafferty, wanting him to come out where he would be safe, she ran to the building and raced up the steps. Fire licked down one wall, spreading like a grass fire as she raced inside. Smoke stung her eyes.

A dark shadow emerged through the smoke, and Lazare loomed on the stairs. As he bounded down the stairs and stopped in front of her, she raised the pistol and pointed it at him.

"Get out of here!" she said, waving the pistol.

He glanced over his shoulder. "Where is he? Upstairs?"

"Get out and leave us alone, Lazare!" she demanded, backing up as he came toward her. He held a fiery torch in one hand, a pistol in the other. "Get out, or I swear I'll shoot you!"

He stared at her. "You're so foolish, Chantal. I know how well you shoot. You shot your beloved in the foot that morning under the oaks, when I suspect you meant to hit me. I'm not afraid to take my chances with your aim."

He was closing the gap between them, and she didn't know how to aim the pistol or even if it was loaded. She pulled the trigger. The blast jerked her arm. Lazare sneered as he grabbed her wrist, twisting it painfully. Dropping the pistol, she cried out. He slapped her, knocking her to the floor, where she struck her head.

Chapter 31

Rafferty heard the shot and ran toward the sound. He coughed as he tied his silk cravat over his nose and mouth. Fire crackled around him and he squinted, his eyes burning, a lick of flame searing his hand. Racing down the steps, he saw Chantal sprawled on the floor, her white wedding dress billowing around her, Lazare standing over her.

Enraged, he vaulted the bannister and dropped to his feet.

Lazare spun around to face him, his revolver still pointed at Chantal, who stirred.

"Drop your pistol, or I kill her now!" Lazare ordered.

She sat up and rubbed her cheek. Tears brimmed in her eyes. "Rafferty!"

"Drop it!" Lazare snapped. Rafferty felt a sense of helplessness, but he knew he had no choice. His only chance against Lazare would come if Lazare shifted his aim away from Chantal, but now he couldn't risk having Lazare hurt her.

Determined to spare Chantal at all costs, Rafe released his pistol and it struck the floor. Lazare smiled, and raised his arm with deliberation to aim.

They were only twenty yards apart. Fire crackled behind Rafe now and roared upstairs, burning through the roof. Outside, the platform burned. Out of the corner of his eye Rafe saw Chantal sit up, and his muscles tensed.

She raised his revolver and fired. The blast was shattering inside the room. It blew the pistol from Lazare's hand.

Rafe threw himself against Lazare with all the force he could and both went down.

"Run, Chantal! Get out!" Rafe bellowed, as he struck Lazare in the mouth.

Lazare kicked him and smashed one fist into his stomach, bringing the other up to strike him on the jaw. When Rafe crashed against the wall, Lazare came after him.

Rafe ducked a blow and slammed his left fist into Lazare, following with a right. He barreled into him, both going down and rolling. Rafe came out on top and hit him with a right jab and then a left, until Lazare threw him off.

Rafe kicked him in the middle; Lazare came back, walking into a punch, then catching Rafe and sending him toppling back against the bannister.

As they battled, the smoke and flames grew. Shouts came from outside, and firebells clanged. Rafe at last was venting all his rage at Lazare, raining blows down on him. Suddenly both of them stood to face each other. Rafe pulled back his fist and threw a punch with all his might. His knuckles cracked on Lazare's jaw, and Lazare's head jerked back.

Lazare lost his balance, falling backwards, his arms flailing as he fell through a wide window, glass shattering as he dropped into the flames outside.

Rafe gasped for breath, coughing, his lungs on fire. As heat enveloped him, a curl of flames set his sleeve on fire. He batted it out, looking around for an escape.

The door was in flames. Rafe picked up a chair and threw it through another window and ran, leaping over flames and hitting the ground rolling. He came to his feet and yanked the cravat from his face to inhale cool night air.

Men were throwing buckets of water at the fire, and firemen fought the blaze with a new-fangled pump and truck. The fire roared now, sending great columns of smoke spiraling into the night sky, and the acrid smell stung his lungs. He felt the heat come in waves against him, and as he watched the roof crashed in, sending sparks and flames shooting skyward.

Rafe picked out the forms of Caleb and Ormonde in the crowd of firefighters, bathed in an orange glow, and then saw Chantal standing with Amity and Darcy. Locks of her hair had come free to spill over her shoulder and curl near her waist. Her dress looked orange instead of white.

He crossed to her, and when she saw that he was alive she raced toward him. He scooped her into his arms and strode across the wharf to his ship. Cool night air and darkness enveloped him as he walked away from the burning warehouse.

"I'll take you to our cabin," he said, his voice raspy and his throat raw. "Then I have to go back to fight the fire."

"Rafferty, Lazare's dead. I saw them pull his body from the fire."

"Are you all right?"

"Yes," she cried, holding him tightly. "I was so frightened. I could see you fighting him, and see the fire growing."

"It's over." He strode up the gangplank of the deserted ship, and guessed the captain and crew were fighting the fire. He entered their cabin and set her on her feet, looking down into her eyes as she gasped. "Rafferty!" She touched his bruised cheek and cut mouth. "I hate him! I tried to kill him!"

"Your aim must be improving, because you shot his pistol," he said, touching her bruised cheek and feeling another flare of anger. "My Chantal, always, always in the middle of the fracas . . ."

"My eyes were closed when I fired. He's dead, and it's his doing. If the town burns, the Galliards will be hated."

"I've got to go back to help fight the fire." Rafe turned her face up to kiss her, tasting salty tears. "It's my warehouse and I belong there, but I won't be long."

Chapter 32

The cabin was spacious, with a bed built against the bulkhead that was the size of three of her beds. A wardrobe was built into the bulkhead, as well as a desk and a wide seat near portholes that were large enough to give a good view during daylight hours.

Chairs, a table, and a washstand were fastened to the deck. An alcove had been fitted with pipes and a tub, and she could run water into it by gravity flow from a container overhead.

She moved around a cabin that showed Rafferty's hand in everything and also his love—the luxurious furnishings clearly had been made for her.

Finally she began to unfasten the long row of buttons down the back of her wedding dress. Before she stepped out of it, holding it closed behind her, she gathered up the train and went out on deck to look at the warehouse. Fire still burned in Rafferty's warehouse and she could see that it was going to be a total loss, but they had contained it so that nothing else burned. After terrible fires that had wiped out the city in early years, citizens now poured out in droves when even the fire bells sounded, to help fight any fire.

Chantal returned to the cabin to get ready for her new husband. When she had dressed in her white silk nightgown from Paris and combed the yellow hair that cascaded down her back, she put down her hairbrush.

She gazed through a porthole at the last of the fire, now only smoldering ruins. She waited for what seemed like an eternity before she heard footsteps move purposefully toward the cabin. The door opened, and Rafferty stepped inside.

Two lanterns burned, giving a soft yellow glow to the cabin. His blue eyes met hers and then he looked at her slowly, his gaze lowering, drifting down over the thin gown.

With whispers of cool silk she moved toward him, wanting to run and fling herself into his arms but taken aback by his appearance. His lip was cut and swollen, his cheek cut and bruised. Dark smudges were on his temple and jaw. His shirt was ripped and burned.

"Oh, Rafferty, you're hurt!"

The corner of his mouth rose in a crooked grin as he looked down at her, and then his smile faded. He caught her hands and held them out. "Chantal, you're my wife. I've wanted to marry you since that night you were on the rooftops. I've been in love since the first moment I saw you."

Holding out her arms, he looked at her in a slow appraisal that drifted down over the clinging silk gown with its lace inserts. She felt her nipples tauten as he looked at her intently. She tingled in the wake of his perusal.

"Finally," he whispered, "you're mine. And you look beautiful."

He released her hands and tugged his shirt out of his trousers, pulling the ruffled shirt over his head to toss it down. A cut ran across his chest.

"Oh, Rafferty, you're cut and bruised!" She stepped forward to kiss his chest lightly and he inhaled, causing his chest to expand. With a low groan he wound his fingers in her hair, tilting her head back to look down into her eyes.

"I hope I can give you the world and make you happy."

"All I want is you," she whispered in return.

He unbuckled his belt and pulled it free, unbuttoning his trousers and shedding them and his boots. With his gaze locked on hers he reached out to slide his hands over her hips, catching the soft silk in his fists.

As he lifted the gown over her head, Chantal held her arms up, feeling the material slip over her body.

Then she was naked, her golden hair spilling over her shoulders.

He drew another deep breath and peeled away the rest of his clothes, as his gaze feasted on her and made her tingle in eagerness. He stepped forward, picking her up and carrying her to the bed, whose covers were turned back.

"Do you know this will be the first time I've had you in a bed?" he asked in his deep, resonant voice. "That first night in my small room, I wanted you in my bed."

She wound her fingers in his hair and sat up, pulling him to her, raising her mouth for his kiss. In minutes he turned his head to kiss her ear. "We have all night and all tomorrow and all week. And I'm going to explore every inch of you," he said, shifting to take her foot in his hand and kiss her slender ankle.

Later he caught her hands lightly and held them above her head against the bed, holding her easily with one hand.

"If you touch me now, I won't be able to hold back and love you the way I want to love you."

"I *have* to caress and kiss you," she whispered, her hands caressing his thighs.

His eyes darkened, and she gazed at him as he moved between her legs and lowered himself. His shaft was hard and hot and her hips rose to meet him. She gasped with pleasure, moving with him, feeling their hearts beat together.

"My love," he whispered, and then sound was lost as need enveloped her and she moved with him until release burst.

He held her close against his length, and Chantal clung to him. As her heartbeat slowed and her body cooled, he stroked and kissed her, murmuring endearments, and she was overwhelmed with a sense of fright for how close she had come to losing him, to marrying the wrong man. She wound her fingers in Rafferty's thick, soft hair.

"Thank heavens you're stubborn! If you hadn't persisted . . ."

He sat up to look at her, his black hair tumbling over his forehead. "You're my life, Chantal," he said solemnly.

Her heart beat with joy as she came up in his arms to kiss him, knowing that this was the man for her—forever.

Dear Reader:

Thank you for buying my book and thank you for your letters about my Western trilogy. On a research trip the uniqueness of New Orleans sparked my imagination. When I learned that in the mid-nineteenth century one in five New Orleanians was Irish, I wondered what it would be like for a penniless Irish immigrant to land at New Orleans. Romantic, steamy, beautiful New Orleans is a magic city of tantalizing gumbo and other delicacies, and elegant, ornate French and Spanish mansions with their fancy ironwork. Into this comes Rafferty O'Brien, and he is caught up in political riots and a code of honor under which disputes were still settled by duels.

Memphis, the next book in this saga, goes from the battle of Shiloh to the booming river city of Memphis after the Civil War. It is the story of two strong-willed people, Caleb O'Brien and beautiful Sophia Merrick. Sophia is the fiercely independent woman Caleb saves from arrest for sedition. While she fights falling in love with a man of opposite beliefs, Sophia is caught up in a fiery passion that places both their lives in danger when Caleb opens a railroad from Memphis to the West. I love to hear from my readers. If you would like a *New Orleans* O'Brien bookmark, please send an SASE to Sara Orwig, P.O. Box 780258, Oklahoma City, Oklahoma 73178. Best wishes until we meet in *Memphis!*